THE JUDAS GLASS

Also by Michael Cadnum

Skyscape
St. Peter's Wolf
Horses of the Night
Ghostwright

THE
JUDAS
GLASS

Michael
Cadnum

Carroll & Graf Publishers, Inc.
New York

Copyright © 1996 by Michael Cadnum

First edition March 1996

Carroll & Graf Publishers, Inc.
260 Fifth Avenue
New York, NY 10001

ISBN 0-7867-0239-7

Library of Congress Cataloging-in-Publication Data is available.

Manufactured in the United States of America.

98 97 96   5 4 3 2 1

for Sherina

> As West and East
> In all flatt maps. . . . are one,
> So death doth touch the Resurrection.

John Donne

> You see the lizard
> only
> when he sees you.

Joy Collier

Part One

1

I will never forget the sunset.

I was heading east, across the Bay Bridge, and my hands, the steering wheel, the cars all around me were touched with a platinum radiance.

No one was going forward. I had plenty of time to edge the car over to the far left lane and look back. No other driver appeared to notice anything unusual, everyone sitting behind steering wheels, eyes straight ahead. My view was blocked by a truck carrying a mountain of used tires.

"The water coming out of the tap was blue," I said into the car phone.

"We don't dispute that," said Stella. "There's no argument. Blue water came out of the faucet."

Traffic stuttered forward a little and I let my own car drift ahead. Before the mountain of tires could block my view again, I looked back once again.

I still couldn't see. When the traffic rolled ahead of me I stayed where I was until the mountain of tires honked. Then I accelerated briefly, and shot another look westward.

"Can you see that?" I breathed.

Something glorious had happened. A glowing scribble, a chalk flower in the sky.

"All I can see is the second floor of this parking lot," she said. Stella Cameron worked for huge clients. This time it was the water company. We tended to work like this, by telephone, never seeing each other.

"There's some kind of burst of light," I said. "Out beyond the Golden Gate."

"You're in love or something, right? It's not like you to sound like this."

I hated the way Stella guessed right so often. "It's really amazing!" I insisted.

"Maybe something blew up," she said. "I'll get the news on the radio."

I could turn on KGO myself, but the thought hadn't occurred to me. Stella was thinking of bodies strewn across the Pacific. She was thinking insurance, settlements. The East Bay Municipal Utility District was a lucrative client, but nothing compared with families of the bereaved.

"Imagine my clients," I said, trying to get back to the business at hand. "Hard-working people with four children. The husband's a carpenter, and the work is seasonal, at best. He raises zucchini and the wife bakes zucchini bread, sells it to the neighbors. The oldest son mows lawns. Likeable people, can't bring themselves to poison gophers. These people turn on the water to make orange juice one Monday morning, and the water that comes out is blue."

"At last I'm out of the parking lot." Her voice was crisper, the buzz of static gone. "Christ, I just about ran over the world's oldest man," she said. "How does someone like that manage to get himself dressed and walk around? I was twisting my head, trying to look for your catastrophe."

Traffic moved, stopped. I craned to look back again whenever it was safe. When cellular phones first came out, I hated guys who did this, talking while they changed lanes, checking out the view. We were all easing forward, and then we passed the cause of this delay, a sparkle of brake lights in the far left lane of the bridge, two cars, and a man and a woman looking bored and in control.

As a child I would not have understood their expressions, two adults indifferent to this drama—*how can they be so calm?* But now I understood how they felt—they knew what *could* have happened, how bad accidents can be.

We were off the bridge, picking up speed. "It's not only a matter of admitting liability," I said. The truck full of tires was beside me, all of us approaching the speed limit. The worn tires did not jiggle as the truck pounded over cracks in the freeway.

"It's just some funny-colored tap water, Richard. It's not such a big deal."

"It's a matter of fulfilling an implied covenant." The word was old-fashioned, but I saw things that way. Some things weren't supposed to happen. "Ordinary people should be sure their drinking water isn't going to make them sick—"

"Nobody knows why the water coming out of the taps was blue," said Stella. "Nobody will ever know."

I braked hard. A van full of what looked like test dummies was pulling out of the wasteland beside the freeway.

"The taxpayers shouldn't be forced to pay for a protracted legal battle," I said. I liked putting it that way, reminding her how the headline would look.

"There's a principle involved," said Stella. "Isn't that what you were just saying?"

The van was full of monks, Buddhists. I did not bother passing. It gave me time to look to my left, where the sun had set and the flower that hung in the sky had stopped expanding and had begun, subtly, to be erased. I thought: how high it must be. How cold it must be up there, the ice.

"When they raised the chlorine levels the water wasn't blue anymore," I said. I was winning my clients' case, but at the same time I was getting mad. Most of my clients were underprivileged in some way, single parents, elderly, the young, people just starting out. My cases were almost always against developers and utility companies, faceless organizations that hired gunslingers like Stella. I was good at what I did. I didn't make as much money as Stella Cameron, but if a retired couple woke to find the foundation of their new garage cracking down the middle, they called me.

"EBMUD is going to hate this," I said. *Eb-mud.* "They'll look negligent. They're responsible for the water toddlers are drinking, Stella. This isn't the first time this kind of thing has happened. The same blue water came out of kitchen faucets in Danville."

"I wish they hadn't settled that case. The company attorneys called me in on that, too. I had all these videotapes on the effects of solder on drinking water. You would have loved it."

"They had to settle. They were at fault," I said.

"Jesus, Richard, you are so *earnest*." She said this as though *earnest* was a synonym for *tedious*. "Wait, they're talking about your explosion." She turned up the radio in her car. I couldn't make out words, although the general tenor of the voices was bright and reassuring.

"A missile, right? They had to blow it up on purpose," I said. "It was off course or something."

"One of those missiles from Vandenburg Air Force Base," she said. "Unspecified military payload. I still can't see it."

I had expected something like this. Nonetheless, I felt a little disappointed. I think I had been hoping for something natural, a meteor, a supernova.

"Wait a minute," Stella said. "I finally got to a break in the buildings." She looked for a few seconds, her electronically amplified breath in my ear. "That? That little smudge in the sky! I thought you said it was amazing."

I was glad to get off the phone. The traffic was going faster than the speed limit now, trucks and sports cars almost bumper to bumper, banging over the cracked lanes of Interstate 80. It was one of those moments drivers experience when they allow themselves to realize *if someone sneezes we're all dead*. It was hard driving for a few seconds, all of us going too fast, just a few heartbeats of the normal, slapdash brutality, getting from place to place.

I had told Connie I would be running late, unpacking things in the new office. "Running late" usually meant I'd be home by nine, nine-thirty. I had plenty of time. I waited until I took the Ashby offramp, and, when I was going slow enough to do it safely, I called Rebecca. I told her I was on my way.

"You said we would have to rethink things," Rebecca said. There was pleasure in her voice, and perhaps a little amusement.

"I was crazy."

"You said your wife was getting suspicious."

I wanted to tell her Connie didn't get suspicious, she just tortured until everyone confessed. Besides, she had drained our marriage of affection over the last year or two, coming home late herself with the telltale clues even a workaholic husband like myself could see, the impression of unfamiliar phone numbers on the kitchen memo pad, matchbooks from restaurants in the South Bay, places I had never visited. Once, fishing in her purse for parking meter change, I had come across a necktie. It wasn't one of mine, but an expensive silk with bright yellow flowers, already out of style.

In love. I used to associate the phrase with Valentines, and the kind of old songs my parents had liked. Love had been something nice, a social amenity, like good food, shelter with a fruit tree in the garden. You could live without it. I had intended to be loyal to Connie, even though our marriage was by now little more than a domestic arrangement. She was my wife. I took contracts seriously, including my marriage vows. And perhaps I had, in some part of myself, given up on passion, believing that romance and all that it implied was for someone else.

That was before I met Rebecca.

The sprinkler was on. Snails escaped the wet lawn, surging across the stepping-stones. I couldn't really see their progress, only their urgency, necks glistening. The burst of color in the sky was almost gone, and I hurried up the wet lawn, rushing up the front steps to open the front door without knocking.

She touched my lips with her fingers, her knowing hands, and then touched the buttons of my shirt. What an encumbrance clothes are! I felt the foolishness of clothing around Rebecca, partly because they could not matter to her. Nothing about my appearance could matter.

But as always she surprised me. "These are new."

My own vanity was, at that moment, an embarrassment. How could I explain my folly to this woman? I was wearing a three-button ventless cashmere jacket and gray twill trousers, both fresh from my tailor on Bush Street. I had new shoes I wasn't sure about, black Italian slip-ons. I looked good, but there were no mirrors in Rebecca's house.

Besides, with Rebecca I wanted only to escape my clothes, to escape everything about my life, and I let her unbutton and unsnap. I had always felt my own nakedness as a simple matter, what I was reduced to when I bathed or visited Dr. Opal.

"Are you sure?" she asked, and perhaps for once Rebecca was uncharacteristically coy.

Was I sure? My body knew. She could feel it, too. I almost told her what I really felt. The reason I had tried to stay away from her for a few days was because she was *too* important to me, an obsession.

2

It was better not to break this silence.

We were naked in the darkness. I treasured this escape from my ordinary life, lying beside her. *In love*—in her room, surrounded by it.

She said, "Did you go to any parties?"

It was one of Rebecca's myths about me—that I was always going to political cocktail parties. It was true that I dropped in on a few such gatherings, but although I liked conversation, my personality was a strange mix of extroversion and shyness, and I usually left such parties early.

"One really splendid one put on by Great Western Savings, on a yacht in San Diego Harbor, right next to the USS *Abraham Lincoln*. I stood looking up at this gigantic warship while people around me complained about capital gains tax."

"I wish I went to parties like that," she said. "It sounds so glamorous."

"What I really like to do is talk. Basically, I'm all mouth."

"Is that a tongue in your pocket, or are you glad to see me?"

I laughed. Rebecca was a brilliant mimic. Besides, there was something sultry about her that Mae West would have never equalled. Where most people would have displayed photos of family, favorite artworks, Rebecca had shelves of CD's and cassette tapes, with twin Bose speakers in the corners of the ceiling.

"I brought you something," I said at last. I made my way naked to my jacket, folded over a trunk in the corner. The present was not gift-wrapped. I had chosen it because it felt so luxurious, because I knew she would love its touch.

She sat up, holding it to her lips, the fabric cascading down her breasts. In this muted light the midnight blue cloth looked black. "It's perfect," she whispered.

"I'm glad you like it," I said, my words so full of feeling that my voice was husky.

"You like giving things, don't you?" she said.

I let myself lie down again beside her. I wanted to tell her that I wasn't really a very generous man, that most of my present goodness she brought out of me. "To you," I said.

"Didn't you ever want children?" asked Rebecca.

I understood the innocent logic behind her question. I felt touched too deeply by her curiosity, especially since I had just used a birth control device, a condom, something I never had to use with Connie.

"No, I never did. I couldn't see myself as a father, responsible for shaping a tender psyche. Anyway, we couldn't."

"I'm sorry," said Rebecca.

"Connie has—a fertility difficulty." For some reason I didn't want to expose Connie's medical history. "She doesn't like to talk about it. Maybe I don't, either."

"You don't have to, Richard."

"She had an infection years ago, and now her fallopian tubes—I picture them as two little creeks that just empty out in the middle of the desert. We even visited a man in L.A. once, someone Dr. Opal recommended. He sat us down and gave us the news that some things are not meant to be."

"You still love her," said Rebecca.

I had a vivid impression of Connie, hunting down Rolaids, calling Matilda at home, fretting. It was after nine by now. "I should hate Connie for the way she's treated our marriage. But I don't."

"When you talk about her you have affection in your voice."

"That's one of those things women say hoping to hear it denied."

"Do you know so very much about women?"

"I'd be a fool to say I did."

She laughed very quietly. "How did your lecture go?"

"It wasn't much of a lecture. More of a harangue."

"Did they like it?"

"They didn't tar and feather me." Actually, there had been applause, and it had been genuine. It was one of my talents. I give a good speech, even when the effort is wasted.

"You never told me what it was about."

Connie never asked how anything went, not a hearing, not a lecture, not even an interview that would show up in the paper the next day. "I didn't want to bore you."

"Tell me now."

"I'm not that cruel."

"I'm waiting very patiently."

"I talked to the California Association of Realtors about the responsibility of realtors in preventing overdevelopment. It's not so much that we'll lose rare species of wildflowers and butterflies if we subdivide every hill in the state. I like animals, but I think people are more important. You develop a community too fast and you have overcrowded schools. You don't have enough parks. You have a sort of null prosperity. Everything is new, but it isn't a community."

I waited for her to agree that this was too boring, but Rebecca touched my face with her hand. "I bet you changed some minds—woke them up to some new ideas."

I had to laugh. "They invite me to their conventions so they can tell themselves how progressive they are. They can't be such bad people—they sat and listened to Richard Stirling for an hour."

"I bet some of them left impressed." She felt for something in the dark, her silver bracelet.

I ran my hand along her side, her hip, her thigh. "I don't think it works—arguing with people. Even when you prove them wrong, with charts showing how they've failed, they see you as a form of live entertainment."

" 'Ethical barbarians,' " she said.

When I didn't respond, she said, "I'm quoting you. I have your book on tape. That's what you said banks and developers amount to."

I was a little embarrassed that this lovely woman would waste her time listening to one of my fairy tales on how to make banks socially aware, how to encourage financial institutions to open more branches in the inner city, how to avoid excessive lawsuits by having contractors do the job right in the first place.

Our nakedness seemed vulnerable at that moment. The quilt over us was not a magnificent antique meant to last forever, the collection of one-sided records in the hall was not a storehouse of music that would survive for generations. It was all so easy to love, and easy to lose. I took her in my arms, and experienced the most pleasurable combination of protectiveness and lust.

Connie would have said, "Again? Already?" And laughed, not sure she wanted to continue, already having collected herself back into her normal state of mind. Rebecca did not know that this was unusual for me. To her I was a sexual creature, easily aroused, not a distracted man with a mind riddled with while-you-were-out memos.

Her body was made for mine. Her knees parted around me, her heels finding a place on the small of my back. But without a prophylactic this time, and neither of us noticed, neither of us gave it a thought. As though we already knew what was going to happen and celebrated in its shadow.

There was no hurry. It was late, approaching midnight, but I didn't want to leave.

I was dressed again, feeling both reassured and artificial, as I sometimes did when I followed my consultant's advice regarding what to wear for the cameras. Auburn jacket to go with your hair, blue ties to match your eyes.

Rebecca wore her kimino, her feet bare. She was on the dark front lawn, reaching for the faucet and finding it. The sprinkler's glittering spider of water shrank, hesitated, and vanished. The lawn was saturated, a sudden puddle of water appearing with each step.

"There aren't any snails, are there?" she asked.

I stooped to pluck one from the stone before her and toss it into the darkness. When she sat beside me on the front porch I soothed a grass clipping from her foot.

"I want you to do something for me," she said.

Anything, I wanted to say. Anything in the world. But I said nothing. We both knew that I had accepted limits on what I could do for Rebecca, the time I could spend with her, the love I could give her.

"I'm recording a few pieces," she said, in that off-hand way people sometimes use to share worrisome secrets.

"That's wonderful!" I put my hand around her wrist, around the silver bracelet I had given her, silver otters interlinked, chasing each other.

"It's terrifying. They want that Chopin thing everybody does, Fantasie-Impromptu. And the others I do."

Her talent awed me. I had taken a few piano lessons as an eight-year-old, when my father said a well-rounded person should be able to improve upon his parents. He meant this jokingly, believing himself to be superior to most of his fellow Homo sapiens, including, although he would not have put it bluntly, myself. He was so self-confident he could admit to being incomplete in trivial ways. However, several weeks of "In An Indian Wigwam" had everyone agreeing that perhaps riding lessons were a better idea.

"This was the kind of break you dreamed about," I said. "Why are you so nervous? I've never known you to be nervous." Despite my failure as a fledgling pianist, I had always hungered for music, high music, low music, everything from Bob Wills to Benjamin Britten. I think my lack of talent left a dry arroyo in me, a feeling of failure, a canyon I wished could sport poppies. I couldn't listen to a driving drummer, or a sizzling bassist, without finding my hands twitching, playing air guitar.

She made a gesture, annoyed humility, with just a hint of pride. "I'll also record a few things of my own. Just a studio on Arch Street, nothing major."

"It's fantastic!"

"I'd like you to be there."

Her success was mine. "I'd be delighted. Tell me when."

She hesitated. "You don't have to."

I was tugging the black leather calendar from my jacket pocket. "I'll have Matilda do major surgery on my schedule."

"You think about cutting a lot," she said. "Flaying, stabbing."

"Figures of speech," I said.

"You don't have to decide now," she said.

"I'll be there," I said, with some heat. "I want to be there. I feel honored—"

"We can go on like this for a while. But some day you'll have to choose."

There was never a time when I forgot that she was blind. Everything about her house, the way she listened, the way she made love, was colored by this presence of a way of life very different than mine.

From the first moment she asked if she could touch me I had never imagined her to be anything else. But I found myself looking into her eyes, wondering how long I could go on like this, impatient with my life. Rebecca was so unlike anything I knew that I was afraid of my love for her.

"You'll do wonderfully," I said. And yet I felt slightly strained, despite my sincere pleasure for her. I was a little bit jealous of the new possibilities that might open and distract her, take her away.

"You're going to stop seeing me," she said.

She said *seeing* this way, just as sighted people do. "I wanted some time," I said, forgetting the first thing you tell a witness— think before you answer.

"No, don't lie to me, Richard."

I actually put my hands to my lips. It was body English that any criminal lawyer would have recognized as a confession. I had been about to mislead the court. How could I tell her that I loved her so much I felt threatened? I was used to my life having structure, logic, love providing a pleasant hedge of greenery, nothing more.

"Thursday afternoon," she said, "two o' clock. Just be there. I need you."

Unlocking the car, I nearly turned and went back to her. I had forgotten to tell her about the explosion, the missile, the bright scrawl in the sky.

I drove the streets of Berkeley, taking Oxford Street after passing the stadium and the Greek Theater. As I drove, the phone trilled. I almost answered it, my hand falling to the receiver before I could stop myself.

I let it ring. I didn't feel like talking to Connie right now. But I didn't turn off the ringer, taking some masochistic pleasure in letting her nag me.

The phone stopped its bleating and then started right up again. This was pure Connie. She let it ring five times before she hung up and started again.

Some people expect an attorney to be able to pick up planet Earth and drop it on someone's head. I told new clients to make a list of what they want me to accomplish. I told them to sit down and put it in writing. But, I liked to add, don't leave the paper lying around. For some reason women appreciated this approach more than men, especially the part about folding the list and hiding it. For all the respect and even adoration I sometimes received from happy clients, I had never been unfaithful to Connie—until now.

The phone stopped. That only meant that Connie was calling the office again, maybe calling Matilda at home, being reassured by that wise woman that she hadn't heard of any accidents on the Bay Bridge.

So what was the problem? Why didn't I tell Connie to call Jessica Friedlander or Ben Sattler—both perfectly good divorce lawyers. Or Stella—Stella would nude-wrestle a crocodile for the right price.

Rebecca was exotic, a woman who lectured in musical theory, and played the piano well enough to have prizes, framed documents, hidden away in her closet. Even her handicap made her a creature from another world, and she was in every way too much my dream of what a special woman should be. She had been blind since the day after her tenth birthday, a brain lesion caused by a hit-and-run driver. She was beautiful, needful in a way that wasn't clinging. She said she had never played as well as she had since we became lovers.

And Connie? I tried to make a list of Connie's virtues but the phone started in again and I didn't bother. Besides, I was beginning to feel that flutter as I turned left onto Capistrano Street. I still took my marriage seriously in one part of my mind.

3

"I could fall over something," I said. A new rug was bunching up behind the door, one of those Zapotec rugs with animal patterns, bears or trunkless elephants.

She didn't say anything for a while, let me imagine what she might be about to say, put words in her mouth.

She spoke. "I've been sitting here looking forward to this. Wondering what you'd say."

As usual the living room was a new configuration of vague shapes and objects; a cello, it looked like, leaned against a wall, couches moved around, something that looked like an Easter Island profile over by the window.

She said, "You didn't answer your phone."

I had to watch where I was going. I flung my briefcase onto the sofa, turning on one of the table lamps. The little lamp was pretty, but didn't make much light. I didn't have to look to know where she was, red fingernail to her front teeth, tapping her bicuspids the way she always did, with one of her unhappy smiles.

I turned to look. Yes, there she was. In me Connie had seen status if not big money, life with a Name Lawyer. What, I asked myself, had I seen in Connie?

"I know who you've been with," she said.

I didn't like this, Connie referring to a woman she had never met, someone she could never imagine, let alone understand. I kept my temper. It was 12:13 A.M. and I felt fresh. If Connie wanted the truth she could have it. Here it was, the little chat that would blow up my marriage, one of those wobbly buildings too dangerous to leave standing.

One light wasn't enough. I steadied a pole lamp as I bumped into it. I struggled with the button until it came on.

Connie's laptop was folded shut. A box of paperclips had spilled, glittering metal clamps on the carpet. There were folders in a file at her feet, a white box with black wheels. I was always stumbling over rolling files in the bedroom, the library, white bookshelves of Etruscan matrons and Hopi fetishes.

"You turned off the light when you heard the car," I said.

"Did you see the light go out?"

I didn't answer, but she saw my eyes flicker to the invoice from Afri-art, *two fertility figurines, ebony.* She didn't sit here under blackout conditions writing checks.

"There're two kinds of people," said Connie, pretty in her dressing gown, something expensive, padded shoulders, lavender. She was wearing fresh makeup. "People who sit on the back porch looking in, and people who sit on the front porch, looking out."

Connie was making a mistake. If she wanted an honest talk she should stick to issues of truth. If she began to argue she would be playing a game I was good at, even though it was a talent I did not much appreciate. "Meaning what?" I asked pleasantly.

"You're one of those back porch people, Richard. You don't see the view." Her blond pageboy hair and bright lipstick made her look smart, and she gazed at me in a way that made me realize how important it is to be able to see, how if you couldn't use your eyes there was so much you would have to guess about the world.

But I could see Connie's uncertainty: she was caught up in her own rhetorical device. Even now she couldn't stay mad, not wanting to deceive herself but doing it anyway. She wasn't sure.

"You sat here in the dark," I said casually, "working up that figure of speech?"

"You're so dumb," she said. But the power was fading from her voice. She was slipping into the accent of her family, Arkansas poultry ranchers who moved to California. They had gambled their future on Swanson's pioneer frozen dinner, turkey with mashed potato. They were rich.

"Sometimes you look so wonderful, Connie. Cool, professional. Like you deserve all those cute little reviews you tape to the shop window. And other times you sound like the girl from Turlock, Turkey Capital of the World."

She shocked me. I should have expected it, but I didn't. "Please be nice enough to deceive me, Richard. Go ahead. That's what I want." She was in tears.

"Don't be upset," I said. I meant it. I couldn't talk to a crying woman.

"I *am* upset. I sit here in this house—in our house—and I know. I know you are fooling around out there, Richard!" This was said with tears, anguish, everything she could throw into it, her words bent out of shape into that hillbilly accent she was ashamed of and never used except when she was unthinkingly sincere.

She won. She didn't win the truth, but she beat me at whatever contest we were in. I stood there and my mind emptied. I told her I had been unpacking with Matilda, that the office was a mess, half the fluorescent tubes in the ceiling flashed like strobes, it almost gave me a petit mal just trying to set my California real estate code in the right order.

I should have confronted her about her unfaithfulness. I never had. She left evidence on her desk, notes in handwriting I didn't recognize and told myself not to read, masculine writing I registered subliminally, *Until Tuesday night. This is to replace the one I tore.* I could only guess what garment that referred to, what sex-pot scarlet panties, what see-through negligee. Different handwriting each time.

She had that way of fitting her thumbnail into the line where her front teeth met. It made her look both calculating and defenseless, and with tears on her cheeks I knew there was no way I could hurt her, not tonight.

"I couldn't get Matilda at home," she said. She sighed, not a conversational sigh, but a real one, painful to hear. "I'll pretend everything's all right," she said.

But she didn't pretend. She wept. I had never seen her like this. After four years of marriage you assume you know your spouse, but here she was, grieving over my unfaithfulness. I had that only partly unpleasant insight—she really loved me, after a fashion. She had trashed our marriage, left it out under the wind and rain for some two years, but now that it was over she did what was, for Connie, the logical thing. She wanted it back.

I shouldn't have mentioned Turlock. "We can't have a lamp like this in the house," I said, fingering a cloth wire that led from the greenish-brown base of the lamp to the wall socket. What looked like Bakelite, an early, virtually archaeological plastic, was crumbling around the two prongs. "It's dangerous."

"Solid brass," said Connie.

I worked the switch but the lamp would not turn off. I jumped back as a spark bit me and, at the same time, the room went black.

I didn't mind the dark if she didn't. I was suddenly very tired, and I had the bad feeling that Connie half-expected our discussion to be consummated in our marriage bed, the way so many of our fights had ended early in our relationship. I had the briefest image of Connie in her passion, and the image gave me neither pleasure nor hope. The only message I felt from my genitals was a mild, post-coital pain.

I worked the plug loose from the wall socket, and heard the whisper of her dressing gown as she approached me. When I stood she took me in her arms.

And she guessed my thoughts. "Richard," she said at last. I didn't like the way my name sounded, spoken with such feeling. "You mean so much to me."

Round One was over. I had not done well. I groped in the kitchen and found the circuit breakers, a metal door that opens to metal switches. I fumbled for the switch and when I found it light showed dimly from the living room. It's one of the modest but real pleasures of life, fixing a simple technical problem. I leaned against the sink, trying to tell my inner voice what I would tell Connie tomorrow, after I had given it some thought.

I gave a quick left jab to the inflated plastic figure on the breakfast counter. He reeled backward, and just as quickly came back to his upright position. Popeye. He was one of my favorite cultural icons, nostalgia blended with my own desire to have a secret weapon, a can of spinach somewhere on my person at all times. I had a shelf of Popeye videos, the great ones, the ones Max Fleisher produced. I had a rare almost-virgin celluloid of the fifteen-minute cartoon of Popeye as Sinbad the Sailor.

Larkin was in his exercise wheel, but ran across the cedar chips to climb into my hand. The white hamster looked up at me as though he knew exactly what was wrong with my life. A few good Vitapellets and maybe a piece of celery would fix me up. I had bought Larkin at a pet store the week before. His cage had sat next to an albino python, and it didn't take much imagination to see that Larkin should either change careers or write a will.

I took a quick shower, yucca blossom shampoo and a big, new loofah. I wiped the condensation off the mirror. I looked good, just a little sunburn. There was a faded scar on my forehead, a ghostly smile. You could only see it in very bright light. At the age of six, in my family's vacation cottage, I had run full speed into a wall mirror, shattering it.

There is a process to going to bed, to losing ourselves for the night. As much as we want sleep, it is a challenge, an emptiness. My habit was to finish with the fussy details, washing, flossing, and then wander down into the kitchen for a small drink of brandy. Sometimes the habit changed, almost without my willing it, and I switched to port, or stopped having even this small taste of alcohol and found myself preferring a glass of ice water.

Whatever the liquid, the act of drinking meant that I could let go of my world for another night, that today had sustained me and so would the coming morning.

On this night I went though my step-by-step preparation for bed knowing that an honest man would leave now, pack a bag and phone a hotel. Feeling bruised and dishonest, when I settled under the covers I hoped she was already asleep. Instead I heard her say, "I thought you said those reviews looked great."

The newspaper clippings she stuck in the window, she meant, turned into oversized reproductions by the photocopy shop down the street. What had been a few inches of type blared at passersby on Solano Avenue. *Sierra Imports—A Feats for the Eyes*. That typo was a particular standout. Many a pedestrian had tried to insert the *s* in the right place, but the reviews were on the inside of the glass. The volunteer copyeditors' corrections were washed away every two weeks by the window cleaning service.

To change the subject I said, "Do you realize what a burglar could do to this place? Even this room—look at all those glass lamps."

"I hide the most valuable stuff," she said.

"You mean that crawl space in the attic? That's the first place burglars look. They don't look for wall safes. They march right up into the attic, brush all the rock wool off the heirlooms and leave everything else. It's months before people know what's missing."

She said, "You know I would kill to keep you, Richard. If you needed a kidney or a lung out of my body, it would be yours. You know that."

This gave me no joy. She might give me a kidney, but I would pay an impossible price for it. Yet this was what I had loved about Connie, once. This liveliness, this shallow expectation that she could pretend the past had never happened, that the present wasn't the way it really was, had won me. She had a grip on life.

I tried to convince myself that what I felt was respect, companionship bordering on a fraternal regard. So it was a kind of love. But I didn't lie, and I didn't say anything further to cause her pain. I couldn't tell her that although I still felt a stony affection for her, now I knew what love was. Tomorrow morning I would tell her I was leaving her, and then I would make plans to move my things out. Maybe it would not be so difficult. Maybe I should tell her now.

But I felt sorry for her. Her breath was slow, even. She was asleep. There was a creaking, squeaking persistence from a distant corner of the house, Larkin in his exercise wheel. I could not interrupt her slumber. I couldn't shake her awake to tell her that I was going.

There were extra suitcases in the attic. I would pack those.

I told myself I couldn't sleep, but I did, skimming in and out of dreams, checking the digital clock on the nightstand as though it helped to know how much longer it would be until daylight. I lay on top of the blankets, sharing the bed with Connie out of habit, but not really *in* bed with her. We had slept like this many times before.

The light, when it came, was dull gray. I looked perky in the mirror, my appearance a lie. I have always been fascinated by mirrors. My first science project was on the history of the looking glass, polished tin Egyptian mirrors, all the way down to the refracting telescope on Mount Palomar. Family lore explained my collison with the mirror by emphasizing my fondness for looking at myself. *He thought it was a room with a cute little boy, and ran right into it.* The right hand that lifts the comb to the hair is the left hand of the Other. A book held up to a looking glass shows each letter reversed, the sequence of symbols from right to left, but the order of the lines, from top to bottom, is not changed. The world is answered with an image so faithful it is unintelligible.

I was putting on a new shirt with labels still attached, telling me that my garment was "born of unequalled quality." The label was wound around a button, and I had to use a pair of toenail scissors to cut the string. I tucked the shirttail into my trousers as the phone rang.

It was a whisper, one of those sounds that carry harder than screams.

4

"There's somebody here!" I could hear Rebecca turning to listen, her nightgown rustling, her breath a soft thunder into the receiver. "There's someone in the house!"

Call the police, I began to say. Why did you call me first, why didn't you punch 911? I didn't have to ask. I knew why—I knew in my heart how much I meant to her. But before I could tell her what to do the connection went dead.

"What is it?" asked Connie, rising on one elbow. "Is it Dad?"

"No, it's a client."

"It's not Dad?" she asked again, still half-asleep. Her father had suffered heart trouble a few years before, and a phone call at a strange hour made both of us fear bad news.

"Some kind of emergency," I said. I stabbed numbers into the phone, 911, that magic code. I got that one-two-three ascending tune the phone company plays when you have misdialed. I tried again and got it wrong once more, my fingers working so fast I pushed two numbers at once. "A client having trouble with a prowler."

"Which client?" Connie was asking. "Richard, tell me what's happening."

"Nobody you know," I said, steadying myself to try it again.

"It's too early for anything to go wrong," said Connie. She knew better. There were phone calls at odd hours. Once a landslide took a just-finished house halfway down a hill while my client rode the floor screaming, pulling on his pants. An attempted suicide in the midst of an eviction process, an ex-wife who wouldn't vacant the Stinson Beach weekend retreat—there were emergencies even in my prosaic practice.

I did it carefully this time, a stiff-fingered caricature of a man making sure he got it right. The phone company took its time.

And then there was that electronic staccato chime, the sound of a phone ringing. The phone was ringing beside a dispatcher's elbow, as though this was just an average call to see if the car was tuned yet or to see if someone's secretary could rearrange that meeting. The phone was ringing and I was standing there with my eyes shut tight.

But just as I sank into the chair in disbelief one of those efficient voices was there, one of those bored voices you know has answered thousands of emergencies. And I realized it was all in my mind, that the wait had not really been so long after all, the problem was being handled, there was a city out there, services.

I told him the address, cross street College Avenue, a big brown-shingle house. *With wisteria on a trellis.* I saw the house in my mind, green garden hose looping across the front lawn. The dispatcher said the incident had already been reported, making an effort to soften his voice, to sound reassuring.

"Who is it?" Connie was asking. "Richard, all you have to do is give me a name. If it's a client, the client has a name."

I scrambled down the stairs. "Richard, I don't like this," Connie was saying from the bedroom, and I could picture her staring straight ahead, listening to the front door as it shut.

The Mercedes wouldn't start. And when it did I couldn't see very well, the windshield covered with blisters of dew. The windshield wipers only made it worse. I was halfway down the street before I realized what I was doing to my life. I was deciding. There would be no returning to Connie.

Driving cleared the windshield. There was no doubt in my mind. Rebecca was caught up in one of those too-common felonies, breaking and entering, and I could not hide a thought from myself. Maybe assault. Maybe rape. I ran a red light on The Alameda. I ran another on Cedar, and almost hit a jogger in a baggy white sweatshirt plodding methodically up the middle of the street.

It was a blessing. I told myself how lucky I was. I could see how much Rebecca meant to me. The air was milky white, half smog, half spring haze. A man in a large brown overcoat rummaged through the trash at Shattuck and University, and litter had been strewn across the street, paper hamburger cartons and wads of pink and silver aluminum, the sort of colors I associate with Valentine's Day and New Year's Eve. Plywood had been nailed over one storefront, particle board over another. Two dogs frolicked past a mountain of sodden newspaper. The sidewalk glittered with broken glass, someone's recycling gone awry.

My tires squealed and I prayed as I sent mental messages. I'm coming, Rebecca, and everything will be different. It isn't just a man coming, another unfaithful husband, a man duplicitous by habit and profession. This was a new day on its way, a break with the past. Nothing would be the same.

I saw the smoke from two blocks away, billowing over the rooftops. The smoke shouldered upward and flattened in the morning light, plowed eastward by the breeze.

It has nothing to do with her. There was a time when smoke was the sign of village life, of industry. Only in the contemporary imagination is so much smoke necessarily sinister. I was scaring myself. Everything would be okay.

I nearly rear-ended an old Toyota, its red finish faded to pink, that made its way up Derby Street delivering newspapers. I laughed at myself, a soundless, stiff-lipped chuckle. I was never calm in a crisis. I didn't actually panic, I just quietly disintegrated. I leaned on my horn to clear a quartet of cyclists heading toward the smoke. One of them turned his head to look at me before giving way with a look of intelligent incredulity.

Lime green fire engines were parked with the authority of freight cars, blocking the street. I braked the car, and then was in the street, running toward her house. It was all changed, unfamiliar, the wisteria and its trellis gone, the roof alive. Water was spearing the flames as I arrived, and sirens were still approaching from the distance.

I was on the lawn when a bulky figure stepped in front of me, walking backward as fast as he could. He was a big man in a fireman's coat trimmed with strips of day-glo green. He said the yard was off-limits, and tried to straight-arm me. "You have to go back to the curb."

As I brushed past him, he tackled me, almost knocking me down. The fireman and I struggled, his sheer bulk and animal power bearing me to the wet grass.

He was strong, and he wrestled me into a gym-class hold, a position I remembered from a lecture in how arrest warrants were served. I suffered a few moments of pain compliance, and then the wind slackened and the smoke drifted our way.

The smoke tasted poisonous. A house does not burn with the thick, stifling purity of grass. It has a bitter stink, furniture and wiring and in this case something else, the metallic tang of gasoline.

"Mr. Stirling," gasped the fireman. I was a little surprised he knew my name, but my face was often in the news, defending tenants against landlords and speculators.

As soon as he said my name I had some power over him. Not much, but a little handhold, a tiny bit of leverage. "She's in there," I said.

Another man might have used the momentary lapse in his grip

to spring free. But I knew that my best plan was to talk, to explain that Rebecca had called me, that there had been a prowler, and that I believed she was still trapped. I kept talking as I got to my feet, and when I saw my chance I ran.

He had me again, but only for an instant. The big man called for help. I broke free, rolling, twisting. It was difficult, the stronger men clinging to me as I screamed her name.

The windows were darker recesses in the flame. The heat warped the air, sending me reeling involuntarily backward. I waded forward against the naked power of the heat.

5

I *would* breathe, I told myself, but just once. Just one deep breath.

That single breath filled my lungs with poison. I could not hold it. I coughed painfully, calling her name. I clawed the floor, digging forward on my elbows and knees. I groped and found the sofa. The coffee table was on its side, and I felt something plump and soft, a pillow.

There was a sizzling sound from the recesses of the house, her record collection, the shellac seventy-eights frying, the quilt smoke by now, the piano a flaming altar. I was breathing her possessions, inhaling and exhaling what was left of her. I gagged, bawling her name, and dragged myself forward.

The bedroom was gone, fire, terrible heat. I fought my way to the kitchen, the linoleum blistering. I thought I heard her voice. I couldn't be mistaken—it was her.

Finding the stove helped me—I knew where I was. I knocked something over, a clattering mop, and an electric cord caught me as I crawled. Something fell, a coffee maker, a blender.

I knew where I would find her, where she would go if she was hurt. And she was. She was sprawled on the bathroom floor. Blood splashed around me. The smoke was not as bad there, and she lay beside the bathtub, the water running, the slop of blood and luke-warm water pooling, the drain plugged by a washcloth.

She did not open her eyes. Her hands were ice. I could not stand to see what he had done to her. A human voice kept repeating the single word *No*.

I dragged her, the flames thundering, the low ceiling of smoke pressing me to the floor. *No*. My voice, the only word left to me. And the thought came to me, with the resonance of a tune I had finally recalled, something with the sweetness of a childhood memory. I might as well stay here.

I might as well die with her.

When help arrived, goggles and a gas mask bending over the two of us, it could have been a hallucination brought on by the venom in the air. It could have been an apparition boiled up from the rupture of my own synapses as I sprawled there. The smoke cleared with the blast from a fire extinguisher.

A cup was pressed over my mouth.

I shook my head, hard. But the hand pressed all the harder. "Breathe!" said a voice.

There was the bleary impression of daylight, emergency lights flashing, the engines of the firetrucks rumbling, people in the distance. I turned on the wet lawn and Rebecca was there, but I could only see one hand thrust out between the bodies that knelt over her.

I almost didn't recognize her nightgown, the flimsy cotton soaked with blood. I wanted to hide her near-nakedness from these earnest strangers as they strapped her into a stretcher. I wanted to shield her from the eyes of spectators, neighbors in clothes thrown on over pajamas, joggers, eyes hopeful and afraid, and fascinated.

I found myself standing, facing the growing crowd. I was soil, dirt, ash, and sweat, standing there in the morning sun. At my feet was the garden hose. The firefighters had trampled the lawn and pressed the green coil deep into the turf.

"You'll want to go with us to the hospital," said the fireman. He held no grudge against me for the struggle. His eyes were compassionate, and I was surprised again at how men and women used to calamity can still express kindness. This time he kept a good grip, arm around me.

She was already in the rear of the ambulance, the paramedics not bothering to turn back to check on my condition. But that arm around me led me to the ambulance, pushing me forward, not for my sake, but for hers.

Because we wanted to go fast. We wanted to hurry. Speed would do the job. That's all we needed. Haste, and all would be well.

The ambulance had to swing around a car parked in the street. My car, I thought dully. My own car is in the way.

The siren was on, although in the morning sun there was no sense of flashing lights, no sense that we were clearing the street ahead of us of traffic. I found the sound of the siren exciting and reassuring in a disconnected, boyish way.

I took her hand, outthrust again between the bodies of the people working over her. A syringe plunged into her chest. I held her hand and looked out at the receding image of parked cars, cars easing back into the flow of traffic.

6

The frenzied protocol of the Emergency Room left me thrust to one side with a yellow tank of oxygen. I kept a mask cupped to my face for a moment or two, the cool air flavored with rubber and something undefinable, like breeze off a snow bank. Then I let the mask fall away. What happened before me was in bright segments, inhuman technological events, injections, muttered commands.

This was how they save you, I told Rebecca in my mind. This is you, back from wherever you are hiding. See how many people want you to live. It was a mandate, a verdict. Everyone who thinks Rebecca should live raise your hand. So many hands, so much glistening scarlet.

When I was a boy my father had been cheerful about medical facts, sometimes inappropriately so. When a foundry exploded in Emeryville, my father removed sixty-four steel fragments from the abdominal cavity of the plant foreman. When I asked, my father made his wry smile and said that of course his patient lived. But the foreman died a few months later, in a car accident. This was life to my father, triumph and disaster decorated with the Christmas-tree ornaments of a surgeon's self-esteem.

When blood is exposed to air it changes into a gel. Calcium and blood proteins, aided by adrenalin, change from water to clay. Look at all those, my father would say, scooting off the metal chair, away from the microscope so I could see the metropolis of flying saucers, red blood cells.

"What we need are next of kin," said a voice, a cop, a man I knew.

He gave me a few seconds but I could not think.

"Parents, siblings," he prompted.

"Pennant," I said. I had never considered what a jaunty name it was. Her surname sounded disembodied, the entire conversation having the rude crispness of a search warrant, *the residence and curtilage of Rebecca Mary Pennant*, her womb, her flesh. Some of the semen was mine, I wanted to say. Some of it was my own act of love still living inside her.

Her brother looked nothing like her, short, slender, much younger. Her parents were compact, weathered people in well-pressed, simple clothes, graceful as she was—as she had been. They wore glasses. All three of them. I could not help noticing this, or noticing the way her brother did not meet my eyes while her mother took both my hands.

"Thank you so much for everything," said her mother. "She

used to say she had a new friend." I recognized the giddy emotional state, a woman not knowing how to behave now that so much of her life was gone.

"Don't go in," I said. I turned to her brother. "You should go in first." *Go in first and make sure they have covered her, make sure they have washed away some of the blood.* He wore glasses that were ardently unstylish, owlish, round.

"Yes, Simon, you go in," Rebecca's mother was saying.

Simon looked up at me and I could see how much he resembled her after all, the way he was considering before he said anything, the way he saw something in me I was not aware of myself, some reason to trust me.

Her father had a small gray mustache. "What do you know?" he asked. "Tell us."

I couldn't tell him.

"I want to hear what happened, Richard. I want an explanation." He had a slight Scottish accent, and seemed both brisk and badly shaken.

He was ready to blame me, if only because I was the messenger. Neither parent really understood. Her father was abruptly inquisitive, her mother sweetly vague. But neither of them could accept what was happening. And maybe they were right. Maybe the force of disbelief would work a miracle.

I turned to her brother and put a hand on his shoulder. "I'll go in with you," I said.

Afterward we came out into the corridor again. Simon put his arms around his mother, not saying anything. She whispered something and he nodded, and I could not bear to see the expression in her eyes. Her father stood apart, a wiry man leaning into a breeze, but there was no wind in the corridor, only what was happening.

"I'm all right," I said.

"But I still take you all the way down," the orderly said. He was a tall, stout man, shaved perfectly bald, his tobacco-brown skin glistening. At six feet and one-hundred and eighty plus I was hardly a weakling, but he looked down at me with an air of self-assurance.

"It's okay," I said.

He pointed at the wheelchair. This was not a casual contest of preferences. How many centuries of hospital lore had led up to this policy—they can fall and break their heads open in the parking lot, but not in here.

"If it makes you happy," I said.

"It fills me with pure delight," said the orderly.

It was a shock: it was not yet noon.

I was surprised to see Steve in the lobby, holding Connie's hand. Connie was staying quiet, sitting there, eyes on me.

"We didn't know what to expect. We thought you'd be in overnight," said Steve, stammering. Steve was my only client to have money in serious quantities, but we had never been especially close. I was touched that he had taken the trouble.

Then Connie was out of her chair, standing straight, jacket over one arm, a businesswoman with little time to spare. She was pale, her lipstick too dark, tiny fine lines of weariness around her eyes. How much had she been able to figure out, I wondered. Everything, judging from the stillness in her eyes, they way she held herself in. That was okay—I hoped that she knew. I couldn't bear telling her.

It was a surprise when Connie touched my face. She looked me in the eyes, and kept me there, like a woman trying to remember a secret.

"A terrible thing," said Steve. "Absolutely terrible."

"Sometimes we don't realize the kind of world we live in," said Connie. She said this without much feeling, and there was an unspoken communication between us: we were going to have a very important conversation soon, whenever we both felt I was strong enough to take it.

"Maybe we are better off not knowing," said Steve. When he closed his eyes as he spoke his stammer was not so bad.

"They towed your car," said Connie.

"Naturally," I said, intending irony. But as soon as I said it I didn't care. If they mashed the car into a glittering cube of scrap steel it would not matter. I had picked the car out of a brochure, *that one*, I said, and then worked the dealer down to such a low price he kept saying I was killing him, like it was a joke. Yes, I had agreed. I was killing him, and we had both laughed.

My car represented a problem I could relish, something to think about. Even in my reduced state I was still a proceduralist. There is a method, always. Someone has to be called, a fee has to be paid, a form signed. Besides, I knew people in the police department.

"It was a mistake," she said. "I told them so, and they agreed."

"They?" I said. It was hard to move, talk, think.

"Someone parked the car on College Avenue," said Steve, "A meter maid tagged it in a red zone. The car got towed, and then Connie—"

He had trouble saying her name, the hard C stopping him, a rock he kept trying to scramble over, slipping.

Tickets. Parking meters. It was all so fiercely ordinary. A skinny young man flew past on a skateboard. There was my car, at the curb. I was almost sorry to see it. I felt like a man about to give away all his possessions. I wouldn't need this Sahara-brown, option-loaded vehicle anymore. It was at that moment that I caught myself, like a man about to embezzle, his hand on the check, his pen poised to forge a signature. A crime—I was thinking of committing a crime, violating my moral duty. I had been thinking that it would be better to take my own life.

"She was raped," I said.

"Terrible," stammered Steve at last.

Even talking about it was brutal. Having begun, I plodded ahead. "And stabbed. Many times." *Eleven times.* I couldn't say it.

Steve Fayette couldn't get a word out, just shook his head. I had misjudged this man.

I continued, "And he's still out there, still at large." Never before had at large sounded so literal, the openness and vastness of the world. He could be anywhere.

"It was wonderful for you to sit with Connie," I said.

"Anything I can do," said Steve.

"I think I was a suspect for a few minutes," I said. "I sat there running through the very short list of criminal lawyers I can stand to be around."

"Are you sure you feel okay?" asked Connie.

"One of the detectives told me it was not that uncommon for a killer to set a fire. It destroys evidence." I swore to myself: he would pay for it.

"It's utterly senseless," said Steve, with a languid gesture, a man waving away a gnat.

"They'll catch him," said Connie dismissively. Rape, murder— Connie had more important things to think about.

"I don't suppose you want to drive," said Steve. He had a manner so gentle, so detached, that he seemed to drift through life.

I said, "I better call Matilda, see what she's had to do to my schedule." I wanted to say that I wanted to drive all the way down University Avenue, into the Marina, all the way out the Berkeley Pier, into the bay.

But instead I settled into the car, finding the *window down* button, hating the stuffy air. I had always disliked those cardboard windshield guards, but now I could see the point.

Connie got in beside me, shut the door, and without speaking fastened the seat belt.

I picked up the phone, and Connie's hand took the phone away, tenderly, putting it back into its cradle.

I don't know what I was going to say to Connie, but when I turned to her and began to speak I started to weep. It was the second time that day I had been another man, someone not myself. Once I had climbed into a fire to save a life. Now I grieved more fiercely than I could have imagined possible.

7

You can't drive, I told myself.

But I could, taking a brittle pleasure in the operation of the vehicle, avoiding collisions. Connie didn't say a thing, just sat there with her arms folded.

A eucalyptus had fallen across Capistrano Street, barely missing a blue Lexus parked at the curb. The owner of the car was turning off its car alarm, shrugging sheepishly at the scattered but grateful applause that came from front porches up and down the street. We couldn't drive straight down the street; I had to drive around the block to get home.

We had not spoken on the way from the hospital. Now we both strolled silently up the street to look at the fallen tree. We were grateful for the distraction. The roots had levered out of the ground, and the smell in the air was sundered earth and that cough-drop scent of eucalyptus.

When a man in a yellow hard hat failed to get his chain saw working it was a moment of mild drama. A dozen people were watching, and a companion in a white City of Berkeley pickup called out something with a laugh. The man with the chain saw took his time, going back to the truck to put on a pair of ear protectors, rubber earmuffs with a large cup that fit over each ear, as though lack of readiness on his own part had crippled the saw.

Maybe he was right. It started easily, the air discolored with exhaust from the motor. The saw bit into the tree and white sawdust flew. The blade sliced into the tree easily, seventy years cut through in less than a minute.

When the tree was cut in two, one side sprang upward, severed but connected to the roots. The top half fell hard to the street, the shaggy branches and leaves quaking, settling.

We could hear the chain saw even in our house, the door shut. I looked at myself in the bathroom mirror, and was surprised at how commonplace my appearance was. People in movies are stained by crisis, smudged, artfully bloodied. Only my shirt was stained, with Rebecca.

I took it off, and folded it carefully, and put on another shirt just like it, fresh from the cleaners. And then I realized that my dark trousers, olive cavalry twill, were also stained, and I put on a pair of chinos, a man at leisure, time on his hands. I washed my face and shaved, and gave myself the same look I shot myself between meetings, when I popped into the men's room to congratulate myself.

And then I stood with my hand on the the doorknob and could not move. Sorrow broke over me, leaving me helpless.

It was a form of comfort to dial my office when I was downstairs again. I gave Matilda an expurgated rundown of the day's events. "You should be in the hospital," she said.

"They told me I was okay."

"But your lungs might be damaged."

It was like her to think of my body like this. She was gifted when it came to dealing with computers and fax machines. I wondered if my lungs were a variety of office equipment to her. An emotional collapse would mean the same thing. If I couldn't breathe or think anymore she'd be out of a job. Besides, she had asthma. I could hear her wheeze as we talked about smoke inhalation.

"Tell Stella Cameron I can't make that phone conference today—"

Matilda took a deep, forced breath, using her inhalor. I waited for her to exhale. "She cancelled anyway," said Matilda. "She's having a baby."

I stared at my appointment book, my own printing dominated with names and numbers Matilda had added in her rounded handwriting.

Matilda read my silence correctly. "No, I don't mean she's having the baby today. I mean she's pregnant and she is having a checkup. Just routine, her doctor had to switch his appointments around."

Even in my emotionally ragged state I marveled that Stella Cameron had been impregnated. It wasn't that she was unattractive. She was very good-looking, the way a cruise missile is good-looking. Unless Stella had been artificially fertilized there was a man out there who deserved an award. And I had just spoken to her yesterday. People had so many secrets.

"I'll take care of everything," Matilda was saying, with that trace of accent that made her sound so intelligent. Perhaps it was the implication that because she was fluent in at least two languages, she was superior in other ways, too. Perhaps it was that Spanish grace in her voice, with its hint of Old World manners. I had the feeling that I could vanish from the planet and Matilda could keep my practice going for weeks—maybe months.

I hung up the phone and found Connie organizing her briefcase, finding a place for her laptop in among the catalogs.

"I think if I dropped dead Matilda would rearrange my appointments, turn off the lights, and go shopping," I said.

"She works for you," said Connie. "She doesn't necessarily love you, or even like you." She was pale, her face showing no feeling, her movements crisp and exact. "How's her asthma?"

"She's on a new aerosol, albuterol. It seems to work."

"I thought Matilda might be the one," said Connie. "So much of it is proximity, the women men spend time with."

That was one way to handle it, I thought, like a subject on a talk show. Intellectualize it, make it a subject, not a crisis.

"What do you think we should do?" I asked. It was a dangerous question, the kind I was trained to never ask.

"We won't have our big talk right now. I'm in the middle of figuring out new inventory software," she said. "And a couple from La Jolla is flying up just to look at that cork-pull, the one you made fun of."

"I didn't make fun of it, exactly. It looks like a water pump. Who would use that to open a bottle of wine?"

"Wine stewards," she said, putting a hand over her eyes for a moment. "People collect them. I have to be in the shop in half an hour. Go take a rest, and maybe have some of that rhubarb pie."

"I feel all right," I said.

"All right is what you are not, Richard," she said with the gentle condescension of a woman talking to a child or a very cantankerous old person. She was impatient, too. And angry. It would be awhile before she would let it show, but I could tell, the way she kept flicking her hair back, the way she sounded understanding.

I made coffee, poured whole beans into the electric grinder, set the coffee filter in place, the deliberate steps a boy would take when asked to make fresh coffee for his parents.

When I had a nice steaming cup of French roast I strode into the living room and said the words I had planned. They came out pretty well, without preamble. "I'll go stay in one of Steve's apartments."

She took her time turning to look at me. I could see her debating whether or not to have that important conversation now. "We'll have plenty of time to talk," she said. "I do have some regard for your feelings. You're upset."

The living room was not as cluttered as it had appeared last night. The cello-like shape against the wall was what it appeared to be, a stringed instrument, and the Easter-Island profile was a carved Polynesian idol, grimacing, showing its teeth made of cowries. Connie made money in her shop, but she spent the cash on new imports and paid a crushing insurance premium every six months. Every now and then our home became a temporary showroom, when her shop was crowded and someone had driven up from Carmel to pick up a five-thousand-year-old Cycladic figurine that would match their new sofa.

"I know it's a little like having a spat right after Pearl Harbor, but I feel like finishing everything." I sounded like a man who would torch his own home.

"Shut up, Richard. I want to have a nice long talk. We can both air out our feelings. This isn't the time."

"Ask me. Anything you want to know."

Connie looked away, gazing at the fierce mouth of the wooden idol.

I told her everything, with some soft-focus over the sex, the other, spoken intimacies. But I held nothing else back. Rebecca's music, her blindness, her fondness for scrambled egg sandwiches. It didn't even take very long. This secret love, this wonderful, departed woman, and I could summarize my love for her in the same amount of time it took a cup of coffee to go from hot to warm.

Connie straightened the wrinkles out of her skirt, smoothing them with one hand. "I know how much you need me," she said.

"Connie, you don't grasp this essential point. Give Stella a call. She's smart. She's fair. She wouldn't mind giving you a little legal advice. It's time we both woke up."

"You think it's that simple. We'll file some papers and end what we have together."

"It's already over."

"I won't forget how you treated me, Richard. You have torn something out of me." She was at the front door, years of television causing me to expect the parting zinger, the exit punchline. For the moment, she had power over me, and she knew it.

This was her chance, a crippling parting shot. She stood at the door, looked at me, and said, "Our marriage may be over. I'm not conceding that it is. But I'm going to see you through this crisis. Before I can help you, though, I do think I'll need some time to myself, to prioritize." *Prioritize* was one of Connie's pet words. She liked to make lists, what had to be done and when. My name would move to the top of her list.

Once again I felt sorry for Connie. I stood there watching her back down the driveway in her Volvo. She caught my eye from the driver's seat, just before she steered the car up the street.

Neither of us waved.

8

They were in the phone book, Mr. and Mrs. Thomas Pennant. I called them, and Simon answered. I asked how Rebecca's parents were bearing up, and I heard the young man take a shaky breath and let it out again before he answered. "Not so good," he said.

"Maybe if there was something I could say to them—"

"The minister is here," said Simon.

There was a voice in the background, Rebecca's father. I couldn't make out what he was saying. There was an additional masculine murmur, the voice of reason, compassion.

"If there's anything I can do, Simon," I said. "For you. For any of you. Please call me." I gave him my number, and I could hear the faint squeak of a felt-tipped pen on paper. "And please tell your parents I called."

Simon thanked me, and sounded like Rebecca, his voice warm, full of feeling, so that I did not want to hang up the phone, even while I watched my hand complete the act, settling the receiver into its cradle.

Connie was late. She was usually home by now. It was dusk, and she always called if she was running behind schedule.

I know a lot of people. Solitude had always been a style that looked better on other people. I enjoyed company, someone else watching the television in the shifting light. Surprised by grief, what was I to do but accept the condolences of my friends?

Dr. Opal called, asking how they had treated me at Alta Bates Hospital. "You deserve the best treatment there is," he said.

The sound of his voice brought back memories, good ones, a sense that the world was an ordered place, rational and loving. Dr. Opal had long been a father figure to me, warm-hearted during my teenage years, when my father was distracted and driven to lose his frustrations in a staggering work schedule. Since my father's death, Dr. Opal was a link with the sunnier aspects of my childhood. "Sometimes emergency rooms are a zoo," he said.

"You don't like zoos?" I said.

He chuckled. Dr. Opal had gone sailing with my father in the old days, when my father owned one of the first all-fiberglass hulls in San Francisco Bay. Dr. Opal rarely practiced hands-on medicine anymore, always flying off to sit on a commission or give a lecture. His manner, however, was healing, his voice, his touch, always reassuring. "If you need to talk about your loss, Richard, I want to help you," he said.

"Do you ever have the feeling that life isn't anything like what you thought it was?" I said.

"All too often," said Dr. Opal. He hesitated, perhaps not wanting to offer unwanted advice. "Drop by and see me. I still make that chili you used to like. Or stop by the office. It's been a thousand years since I played tennis. It would do me good." He was lonely after the death of his wife. I realized this as I stood there, hearing in his voice the rasp of incipient old age. Sometimes grief makes us more sensitive to the feelings of others, and makes us realize that we have, without meaning any harm, neglected someone close to us.

When the doorbell rang I was on the phone with Stella. I assumed it was a friend dropping by for a cup of coffee or a drink. But when I opened the door, telephone to my ear, no one was there.

There was the lawn, the street, the sycamores. Like many people who prefer the telephone and the computer to the concrete world, I felt myself once again baffled at how a house manages to exist, walls, floors, the door swinging on hinges that never squeak, despite the fact that I had never once oiled them.

I stepped out onto the porch, Stella talking all the while. "If this isn't the moment, Richard, I can call tomorrow." A large, flat package leaned beside my front doorframe.

"I can tell you have news for me," I said.

It was almost as tall as I was, wrapped in brown paper. Connie often had imported items delivered here, especially after hours or on weekends. I dragged the package into the room awkwardly with one hand, and leaned it against the wall beside the cello.

"EBMUD wants to be held blameless," Stella said. "No admission of liability. They don't know why the water was blue."

"They like unsolved mysteries?" I asked.

"Are you sure you want to talk about this? I don't want to bother you with stupid stuff like this—"

"I'm listening," I said.

"They don't admit it *was* anything but crystal H-two-oh." She said it like this, deliberately, distancing herself from what she was saying and, oddly, giving it more force. She made no further reference to the way I sounded, to the fire. But she had never mentioned her pregnancy either.

"I have Polaroids," I said. Matilda had them on file, three snapshots of water that looked like dark blue fountain pen ink.

"Truth issues aside," said Stella.

"I can certainly understand that." Even in sadness I could think like that, easy, minor concessions that were meaningless. "But isn't there a larger responsibility? How do they know it won't happen again?"

"I'll have a letter off to you in a couple of days, Richard. You might explain to your clients that time is of the essence in any proceeding. What's the use of big money ten years from now?"

"That's a very good point." Meaning: we win.

"And I think we'll be talking settlement a few days from now," said Stella.

"Matilda tells me you're—" Why is it difficult to say *pregnant?*

"Very. It's a girl. You never wanted to go into criminal law, did you?"

"I did practice criminal law once, actually. When I was an innocent lad. I had a client who had languished in Santa Rita, a man who met a twelve-year-old girl through a pen pal service for convicts. Got out of jail, met the girl in a motel on University Avenue. She told him she was seventeen. There was a healthy list of charges against him, every variety of rape, plus assault."

"Great moments in jurisprudence," said Stella.

"The story is short, and not one I'm happy to be telling. The girl vanished, the DA didn't have a real case without her testimony. My client walked. I disliked him so much I swore to myself I would never handle a case like it, ever again. And I haven't."

"I wondered why you paddle your canoe up and down such a backwater, real estate law. Aside from seeing yourself on television all the time. You going to run for senator or something?"

"Why not?" I meant it as a joke.

"We have to have a meeting on this other thing, that burglar alarm fiasco. I want to see you in person," she said. "Lunch."

I had taken the security alarm case on behalf of a retirement community, not one of the luxurious ones where retired surgeons drive golf carts down the middle of the street, but a simpler, plainer community in Daly City, elderly people with rooms too full of furniture. Stella was going to lose on that one, too. Maybe this was why she wanted to meet in person, put a little extra spin on the ball.

I carried the portable phone back to the package and examined the way the brown paper had been folded and sealed. To my surprise, the label was addressed to me. "Any time," I said.

"Tomorrow."

"What's the hurry?"

"Curiosity."

Jesus, Stella Cameron was flirting with me. It was like being courted by the SS. Besides, I wasn't in the mood for any of this.

She said, "What I mean is—how are you and Connie?"

"It's too complicated to explain right now," I said.

I opened the wrappings just a little, enough to be able to see. The brown paper tore easily enough, but it was sealed with the plastic, shiny, never-rip tape prized by delivery services.

"Remember when you thought we'd be partners?" she said.

What a mad thought *that* had been. "Years ago."

I picked at the tape. What had begun as curiosity was becoming a matter of stubbornness. I fetched a pen knife from a side table, a mother-of-pearl-handled tool about the size of a switchblade.

"I always wondered when you'd get tired of Connie," she said. "Or maybe vice versa." Hormones, I thought. High on pregnancy, and pissed off because her clients couldn't keep copper salts out of the plumbing.

I carefully cut away some of the tape. It was this quality of stubbornness that made Stella a successful attorney. She lost cases, she won cases. She came back, like the flu. She asked, "What are all those little noises?"

"I'm opening a package."

The paper peeled away, a wide corner of it. And there was my own, living image—hair uncombed, my chinos a little wrinkled, phone to my ear. My reflection stared back through a snowfall of black, unmoving flakes. I tore the paper all the way.

It was a mirror. The looking glass gave the room around me a yellowish tinge. I recognized this mirror.

Or perhaps I was mistaken. The frame was exceptionally hard wood, almost the tone and density of ivory, with worm holes here and there. A carved head surmounted the entire piece. A horse, I thought. Or, more accurately, a unicorn. Its horn had broken off, the break the same sienna hue as the rest of the frame.

I knew this mirror. I recognized it, but couldn't quite place it in my past. It had belonged somewhere in my earlier life, in a bedroom, or a rarely visted hallway. At some point it had vanished.

What made me do it? I saw it happen like a story in the slowly turning pages of a picture book. My hand stretched, it touched, it lingered.

Damn. I withdrew my hand. I had cut myself on a crescent along one edge of the mirror, where the glass had broken and did not meet the frame. It was not a bad cut, but it stung.

I have always found mirrors mesmerizing, the way the plane answers the world with an image that seems just behind the surface of the mirror itself. The sweater tossed down on the chair behind my image was as far within the mirror as its twin, one of the cashmere pullovers Connie had given me, was behind the living, actual man. Thinking about mirrors always gave me intellectual vertigo.

I knelt to find the label. It was typed, an old-fashioned, lick-and-stick patch of paper with *from* and *to* preprinted. The return address portion was left blank.

"Richard, are you still there?"

I told her I was.

"Smoke inhalation can be very dangerous," Stella said. "It can affect the way your brain works."

I was bleeding. I sucked my finger. Just having the mirror in the room made the house more spacious, the air like early morning.

I chopped bell pepper. I thawed hamburger in the microwave. I was making a casserole, something from my days at Boalt Law

School, a dish prized for bulk as well as flavor, something I thought would be soothing.

I called Connie's shop. I got her answering machine and hung up on it. I called my office and got my own machine, Matilda sounding a little seductive, as though leaving a message was a romantic moment in everyone's life. Maybe Connie had not been so foolish. Wrong, of course. But Matilda had a certain charm. I took the casserole out of the oven and let it cool. I flicked on the television, I turned it off. I turned on lights, I listened to music, Bach's organ fugues progressing like a convoy of battle cruisers.

When I turned off the classical music I heard the neighbor's guitar. He almost always kept the Gibson muted, in deference to the rest of us. But I liked the ragged, pensive chords. I once stopped by to pay him a compliment. He was a gangly nineteen-year-old, a computer trainee heading a group whose favorite number seemed to be something like "We Are the Blow Jobs." His parents were on sabbatical in Israel. I told him that he was pretty good, and pointed out that he used the same brand of guitar as Chuck Berry. He grinned and told me not to ask him to play "Johnny B. Goode." I grinned back and told him he could do worse; it was the quintessence of American rock & roll.

My young neighbor's music had taken a more and more tuneful turn, losing that ugly edge that made his former music so lively. But I was entranced by it, until the amplifier made a single electronic burp and the music stopped.

Now and then I passed before the mirror where it leaned against the living room wall. I could remember it now, or I thought I did. It looked much older, not only thirty years older, but a century old, as though the thing had been left out in weather, or buried.

I remember my parents referring to its absence. When it vanished from our lives one day my mother had said it was stolen. "Why they took it and nothing else is something we can marvel at and be thankful for," said my mother. It was typical of her spoken pronouncements. There had always been something eighteenth-century about her speech, parallel structure and balanced sentences predominating, especially when she was nervous and more careful of her phrasing. "No doubt it was far more valuable than any of us imagined," she had said.

It was very late before I realized that Connie was not coming home. I could take no further interest in the looking glass, despite my dull wonderment that an artifact from my early years could, on this wasteland of a day, suddenly reappear.

I didn't dream that night. I didn't sleep well, waking every half hour or so with a feeling of dread. When I would stir, even before I could remember the cause of my grief, I felt the loss, the weight of it.

When daylight came, yellowish light leaking through the curtains, my hand was numb. I had the impression that my right arm ended at the wrist. I blinked, wanting to lie there, wanting to get up, wanting oblivion.

It was warm near my body, but around the edges the fluid was already cold. Before I knew what it was I sat upright, and flung myself away from the bed, across the room.

On the bed was a pond of ink, pooling in the canyons and harbors of the sheet. As I stood there aghast, I couldn't help thinking how upset Connie would be. *My God, I'll have to order a new mattress.*

I opened the curtains, and the scarlet gleamed, so much blood.

9

"I don't want to give you advice," said Dr. Opal. "Friendship, affection, those I can give. But advice—" He gave a shrug.

"Go ahead," I said.

Dr. Opal took the white coat off its hook on the door but instead of putting it on, he draped it over the back of a chair. He had always done this, moved things around while he talked. It wasn't absentmindedness so much as a need to reassure himself: the world was real, so was he.

"You don't really like zoos," said Dr. Opal. He put on a pair of glasses with magnifying lenses attached, giving him a strangely multi-eyed appearance. "Do you?"

"Where else can you see a kiwi?" I said.

He smiled thoughtfully, as though he could hear my inner voice, what I really wanted to tell him. "I just got back from Sydney last week," he said. "My book on the valves of the heart, revised edition. I gave a lecture, signed a few copies. I still have a little jet lag. It's pleasant, like an out-of-body experience. Let's see the finger."

I sat where I was, my finger wrapped. "I bet you didn't see a kiwi," I said.

"I'm on the State Commission investigating cuts," joked Dr. Opal. He was a large elf with white hair. He resembled Jiminy Cricket in the way his features were both comical and handsome. His face creased into a smile. I had met Connie at one of his parties. *There's this special woman I want you to meet, from the middle of nowhere.* "Let's have a look."

I'd wrapped my right forefinger in tissue. I had always been a little squeamish about wounds. Dr. Opal looked over the top of his glasses. "Bashful? About an ouch on your finger?"

"I cut it opening a package," I said.

"One of those killer envelopes I keep hearing about."

"More people are injured by packaging than automobiles," I said. "I'm urging legislation, seat belts, and helmets for the office."

Dr. Opal smiled with just the slightest gleam of impatience. I unwrapped my finger. The cut bled. First scarlet pearls welled along the abrupt line of the narrow opening, like a paper cut, fine, clean. Then a trickle began to spend itself down my finger, coursing across my palm.

Dr. Opal had once insisted that I call him Sam. It was what everyone else called him, he had said. But it wasn't true. He was one of those doctors so beloved and so respected even old friends called him *Doctor*. Friends his own age might call him *Dr. Sam*.

But in a civilization where everything was on a first-name basis, Dr. Opal stood apart.

"The only kiwi I have ever seen," said Dr. Opal, "was in the London zoo, in the nocturnal section. Flying foxes, too. My mother used to say God had a sense of humor, look at all the funny creatures He made. She was right. The world is full of wonders. Tell me about this woman, Richard. This pianist who meant so much to you."

I couldn't say a word. I shook my head.

"You must have loved her," said Dr. Opal. "I certainly can't imagine your father charging into a burning building."

I sat there, on one of those examination tables covered with white paper, and gave him a brief, agonized explanation, truthful, fragmented.

He looked at me appraisingly. "You were in love," he said at last.

"You sound surprised."

"No, maybe just envious. I used to hope there was enough life in me to let me find a Rebecca or two before I go the way of the great auk." As he spoke his hands were on me, steadying me so he could look into my eyes. "You loved her that much."

"It frightened me, too. That much love for someone. Love in my view used to be like a low-grade fever, something you got over. Not—" I controlled myself with difficulty. "Not like this."

"Unbutton your shirt." He put the cold mouth of the stethoscope to my chest. "Take a deep breath."

Dr. Opal struck me as someone who had made the right sort of bargain with life. His teeth were even, his stride buoyant. He could be peppery, but people liked him all the more for it.

My father had dropped dead one Sunday at three o'clock in the afternoon at a tennis ranch near Phoenix. And he had always hated tennis, taking up the game to please his new girlfriend, a tanned, blue-eyed creature who wrote a sports column. I had often wondered how strong my own heart would prove as I got older.

"I'm so sorry, Richard," said Dr. Opal. He slipped the stethoscope from around his neck.

"You would have liked her."

"I like a lot of people." He gave me a smile that made him look just a little less avuncular and more like what he was—a man whose wife had died seven years ago, and who never expected to remarry. He was not resigned so much as realistic. I thought then that I must seem strangely passionate to him, angular, with much to learn.

He opened a glass jar of cotton swabs, long lengths of wood tipped with white turbans of cotton. "I thought when I reached my golden years I would understand people," he said. "Do you know that feeling, that expectation that when you get old you'll be wise?"

"I keep hoping."

He replaced the metal lid without withdrawing a swab. "It's happening. I think I'm beginning to get wise. I can feel it, falling over me like sunshine. Wisdom. Do you know what I've discovered about human beings, Richard?"

I gave him a look: tell me.

"They expect too much from life. They expect too much from themselves."

"You make wisdom sound depressing."

He laughed and gave a shrug. "Do you know why people don't live to be five hundred years old? Because we'd go crazy. One stupid century after another—we couldn't stand to look at it happen, over and over again."

"What's wrong with my finger?"

His look was quizzical.

"There was blood all over the sheets."

Dr. Opal considered this. "That's very unlikely, Richard. From a little cut like that. You're exaggerating."

"Look at it—it's still bleeding." But it wasn't. The blood on my hand was already drying to a brown, Turkish-coffee glue.

"All over the sheets," I repeated, without much conviction. How much *had* it bled?

He applied a bandage. His touch was gentle. In ancient times, when people knew little about medicine, Dr. Opal was the kind of individual who still would have cured the sick. His presence, the way he pressed the white tape over the cut, made me believe that healing had already begun. The adhesive strip on my finger was pristine, white and comforting. I crooked the finger, straightened it. It no longer hurt.

"What you want to remember is that time teaches us," said Dr. Opal. "I think it's the only thing that really does."

"What kind of advice is that?"

"And you also want to remember that Connie will try to keep you. Not because she bears tremendous affection for you."

"I thought you *liked* Connie."

"I do." He gave an apologetic smile, as though to say, *It's just my insight acting up again.* "Take care of yourself. Come over for dinner sometime. It's only a mile or so away, but we only see each other around Christmas, maybe run into each other at Park & Shop." He moved a chair squarely in front of me, and sat down. "Do you know how few people write a personal letter to me—actually put a letter in an envelope and lick a stamp? Or pick up the phone and give me a call to see how I'm doing?"

I wanted to tell him, just then, how I had really cut my finger. Not just a vague story of a package—tell him what had arrived, unexpectedly, after so many years. But for some reason I didn't.

I kept it secret.

10

Half the house was still there.

The brown-shingled walls were charred, the shiny black of graphite. The brick chimney towered out of sodden wreckage. But some of the upper windows remained unbroken, and wisteria clung to some of the unburned portions of the house. A cushion leaned on the front step, the remains of the sofa. A rain gutter dangled.

Yellow police tape spun and straightened slowly in the light breeze. An official notice had been stapled to the charred front door, declaring the dwelling sealed. The lawn was flattened, trodden.

I didn't hear a step until someone was beside me, and when I was aware of him he had already spoken.

Simon gave me a sad smile. "The chief of police was here about twenty minutes ago. Getting his picture taken."

His round spectacles reflected the morning light. He wore a v-necked gray sweater, and carried a large manila envelope.

"Chief Timm thinks he's running for mayor or state senator or maybe Secretary of Defense next year," I said. "On the Public Hanging ticket. I like Joe, but he thinks every homeowner should have a neutron bomb."

"He gave me these." They were mug shots, serial killers, police composites, a coloring book of police failure. There are good reasons why I'm not a criminal lawyer. I didn't even want to take these pictures from Simon's hands, but I did.

"They have no idea, do they?" I said.

"They say it was probably someone she knew," said Simon.

"Let me guess—male, furtive, a red can with *inflammable* in yellow lettering."

"They say it could possibly be one of these people."

He selected a large glossy from the array in my hands, a man with a narrow face and thick eyebrows, a child's memory of how almost all adult males look.

"He wanted to know if Mom or Dad or I had seen one of these men, hanging around, stalking her."

"These must be people who specialize in burning after they kill," I suggested. I thought: people like this look human, but they aren't.

Simon could not speak. His shoulders were trembling.

"They'll find out who did it," I said. "They start with no idea, and then little by little they put together a case."

"They don't care, really. It's just another dead body to them."

"The police hate this sort of thing as much as we do," I said. It was true, but it sounded false. Why was I defending the cops?

"That makes it even worse, doesn't it?" Simon said. "That they care and still can't stop him."

"If anything *can* make it worse."

He dropped all the pictures onto the lawn, the top photo edging out so the top of the man's head was visible, dark hair combed back, a 1940's movie idol. Simon was up the steps, into the ruined house.

I called after him, but he was moving too fast.

I caught up with him just as he was removing a strip of *Police Line—Do not Cross* tape that had wrapped across his chest.

He did not say a word. He was far into the house, and I heard something break, wood, part of the floorboards. It smelled dank, evil, and something inside me could not stand to hear the soft, steady tune of water trickling in the darkness. There were splashing sounds, his footsteps.

"Simon, it's not safe," I called. The sound of my voice unsettled something. There was a tinkle, a vague thud. Something broke under my shoe, a white porcelain knob.

"I'm looking for something," he called.

"This is a bad idea," I said, feeling logic go stupid in me. Why was it a bad idea? If the police showed up, I would deal with them. There was a crash, wood splintering. It was dangerous—that made it a bad idea. I didn't move another step. The ceiling was a wasteland, black, peeling.

All of this could come down. The floor sagged under my feet, something in the timbers giving way. But I felt that I was in collusion with Simon now, trespassing for some important reason.

It didn't take long before a flashlight probed the dark, illuminating puddles, twists of naked wire, nailheads in the walls studs. I was standing out of the splash of morning sunlight, and I stepped carefully to where I could be seen. "I'm Richard Stirling," I said. "I'm the attorney of the deceased."

Why did I say that? Why didn't I say *I'm the lover of the deceased?*

"This is all off-limits, Mr. Stirling," said the broad-shouldered silhouette. The cop relaxed a little, leather creaking.

"I know that," I said. *Dazzling rebuttal.* "We thought we smelled fire," I said.

Actually, agreeing with your opponent is a good idea. But before the cop could reflect that no police procedure in the books required him to argue with a trespasser, Simon was there with me. The cop studied both of us. "Step out here," he said, uninvitingly.

The police can be nice at times like this. They were more than nice—they were apologetic. They would have to take us into custody. I was apologetic, too. I kept my tone light, and my message clear.

More police came, an audience, and I was in my element. A few neighbors dropped by, and I was recognized, the lawyer, the would-be hero. I could see why they might mistake their duty, I told them. I gave them my best smile.

After a few minutes of that the cops were relieved to ask us to leave, please, and not come back. They didn't want us to hurt ourselves.

As I walked Simon to his Honda Civic he slipped something into my hand. "I found what I was looking for," he said.

I kept my hand closed. I looked away, unable to respond.

"She liked it very much," he said. "She could feel them with her fingertips, the sea otters. It was the only jewelry she ever wore."

It was a nugget of silver. Unrecognizable. My gift to Rebecca was distorted, destroyed. But at the same time it still existed, was still what it always had been. Only the craftsmanship, the hand-worked echo of nature, was gone.

"I want you to keep it," I said.

I wondered if this was something he would understand. Some people would be greedy for a lump of precious silver, others indifferent to it.

"She was nervous about the recording studio," he said at last. "She said she had a friend who would be there to give her confidence." He opened the car door, and got in. He put the gnarl of silver on the passenger seat beside him.

The Berkeley Police Department is housed in what looks like a prefabricated office building with dozens of windows. You can look in and see nothing of interest, and the cops can look out and see the busy traffic of Martin Luther King Junior Way. In the park across the street there were so many drug arrests the police had almost surrendered, turning to handing out leaflets warning about the dangers of dirty needles.

Chief of Police Joe Timm was coming down the stairs, laughing. When he saw me he walked toward me, his arms spread. He hugged me, hard. The man had been a quarterback for Cal, and had played twelve years for Saskatchewan in the CFL. He squeezed most of the breath from my body.

"Thank God you're all right," said Joe.

"Tell me everything you can about the Pennant case," I said, aware that I sounded like someone in a detective movie. *Just the facts.*

"We'll find him. And I'm sorry about your personal bad news. I was reading her obituary—"

"He'll do it again," I said.

He crinkled his nose dismissively. "We think he was probably someone she knew—"

"Maybe her brother. Maybe her father. Maybe I'm still a suspect."

Joe shook his head. "Someone from her past," he said.

"It's not a matter of building more gas chambers, Joe. And it's not a matter of making sure everyone has an AK-47 under their bed, either."

He turned to gesture to his two companions: this would only take a minute. Then he turned to me, and his full attention was a little fearsome. "What do you suggest, Counselor?"

"Tell me what I can do," I said.

He spoke without any conviction. "You can sit down with a detective and tell us everything you know about her past. Old boyfriends, maybe even an ex-husband."

There was so much I didn't know about Rebecca, and would never know. "This is just going be another open case, until nobody cares about it any more."

"What are you going to do, Richard?" he asked gently. "Find this guy all by yourself?"

"Absolutely."

We both laughed, without any humor. Timm had a Ph.D. in Criminology, and as a former athlete had an undeniable macho edge over me. "Was that why you were tampering with the site of the crime?"

"How is that patio of yours?" I asked. There is nothing quite so effective as an oblique response.

He leaned against the banister. "Cracked."

"Of course it's cracked. Why do you think most people put in redwood decks? You put in concrete slab patio and the earth's movement jams the patio against the foundation. You get cracks, you get spalling. You still have a lawsuit, Joe. The contractor should have known all the real estate in the hills is slowly moving northwest, maybe an inch every three years. That patio is just a big unreinforced pudding. You were what we call in legal terms *cheated*."

"Maybe, but what are they going to do, tear up all that cement?"

Why not, I nearly said, but then I thought about it. I imagined jackhammers in the Chief's Japanese garden, boots and hard-hats among his bonsai maples. "If that's what you want."

"My wife wears a defibrillator," said Chief Timm.

I told him I was sorry to hear that, but that it was wonderful what doctors could do.

"Yeah, doctors," he said, meaning: not lawyers, not cops.

It was almost noon, and I had that harried, all-too familiar feeling of running late. It was almost a relief, work as painkiller.

But I *did* believe in justice. A bridge is a symbol of faith, and a concrete manifestation of human will, and so is the body of law we have inherited, as alive as any other legacy. I half forgot this, but I was always rediscovering what I really felt, like a man surprised into tears or laughter in a movie theater. It happened to me more and more frequently, a feeling of outrage.

As I drove across the Bay Bridge toward San Francisco my finger was numb, my entire hand losing feeling. When I rested it on my pantleg I could feel it through the wool fabric, cold and lifeless.

11

My parking place had my name on it, black on a white background. The space was clean, with freshly painted lines, bright yellow. There was a new security setup, little video cameras replacing the old ones which had done so little good.

San Franciso could be like this, warm sun appearing suddenly, barely smoggy blue overhead. I welcomed the sunshine, taking my time, knowing I was going to be late for lunch with Stella. A man was breaking down cardboard boxes, flattening them. A woman laughed, and someone somewhere above me in a building was whistling a tune.

My entire arm was without feeling, and I would have sought medical advice except for the attitude Dr. Opal had encouraged me to adopt, that the cut beneath the white bandage was, after all, only a nick. Blood always looks vivid against a white sheet, I found myself thinking. Surely it was not as bad as it looked. I swung my arm, flexing my fingers. The muscles worked, the thumb wiggled back and forth.

There was a step beside me, and I turned.

"I thought I'd come see your new office," said Connie.

She was dressed in clothes I had never seen before, battleship blue skirt, matching jacket. She was wearing more makeup than usual, a new shade of lipstick. She had put effort into her starring role here on the sidewalk.

"Are you all right?" I asked.

"How do I look?"

She looked great, but I had no desire to pay her a compliment. I took a certain satisfaction in the thought of her sitting in the car, wondering if I would ever show up. "I always wondered what it would be like to separate from you. How ugly it would be. How hard we would be on each other."

She said nothing, looking serene.

Without being aware of it, I had anticipated talking to her, and been a little anxious about it. It was a relief to have our first words spoken, behind us, the conversation underway. I found myself asking where she had spent the night.

"A hotel," she said.

I also deserved a vague answer. "I was a little worried."

"You must be joking."

The elevator was unoccupied except for the two of us, the doors quietly sliding shut. I pushed the button for the nineteenth floor. The elevator was fast, making me feel a little light-headed.

"I popped by the house," she said. "I thought you might still be there. Who did you murder? The bed is a mess."

I held up my forefinger, and made it take a bow, like a fingerpuppet.

"What did you do, cut it off?"

The elevator slowed and stopped, and there was that briefest moment that so often occurs in elevators. I thought: the elevator door won't open, and we'll be trapped. It takes place on a preconscious level, but you know in one part of your mind that what closes might stay shut.

The door opened to busy people hurrying back and forth in the halls. Handsome people, suits, briefcases were reflected in the floor. Their feet made sounds I had never registered before, squeaks and patters along the waxed surface. We approached the door to my office. I pushed the buttons of the security code with my bandaged finger and nothing happened.

"That's very impressive," said Connie.

"The office is totally impervious to any intruder, even me."

"Completely safe, I can see that."

I stepped to one of the red phones next to the fire alarm box and asked if someone from security would be so kind.

"Don't be embarrassed, Richard," said Connie.

"I'm not embarrassed."

"You bring me here to see your new office, and then you can't remember your code. What was it? Your junior high locker combination?"

Connie had a way of holding out one hand as she talked and not quite looking me in the eye. It meant she could say almost anything and you were to take it as a joke.

The security man was quick as a track star, a young man with a steel tooth. "Good morning, Mr. Stirling."

"I punched in the right numbers," I said. But I felt the potential chagrin—maybe I'd made a mistake.

"Computer's out all of a sudden. It's a new system they put in after the man with the gun. But right now no one can get in if they aren't already in. I've been running." He said *running* with a long upward lilt, so you had to imagine it in italics. "It's got a manual override." The tooth was bright.

"I know the feeling," said Connie.

Inside, she made a show of touring the place, running a finger over Matilda's desk like someone inspecting for dust. I led her into my office and showed her the view, Bay Bridge, bay, buildings.

"I don't see any bullet holes," she said.

I didn't want to talk about bullets. "Steve Fayette gave me a call and said it was the chance of a lifetime to get a place like this. I got a break on the lease because of—what happened. I don't feel happy about it."

She put a hand to one hip. "You said you could see the bullet holes." You could hear the country girl in her voice, someone who had been raised shooting ground squirrels.

"If you stand here," I said, "and tilt your head like this you can see where they spackled them in. See? Maybe fifty holes."

"I don't see them."

"Feel."

I ran her fingers over the spot where a hole had been patched. She withdrew her hand quickly.

"He killed nine people," I said. "Three right here. People sitting at desks, paralegals." It proved, I thought, that rooms are not haunted. Imagine the terror—and all of it here, where I was standing now, an ordinary office. I tried to put the images out of my mind.

Connie was silent, looking down at the new carpet, Viking gray, one-hundred percent wool. "You ought to put up some pictures."

"I'll get around to it."

"Tell me where it came from. That mirror."

I turned to look at her. "I thought you would know."

With Connie I often felt myself slowing down, laying down the retort carefully so she could serve it back over the net. I had almost wanted her to criticize the new office, just so I could show her the built-in safe, and the new oak filing cabinets. I didn't want to discuss the mirror.

"It's big," I said, "It has a handsome frame. It's old, a little damaged. In myths, the unicorn could be captured only by a virgin holding a mirror. The animal fell in love with its own reflection."

"It's priceless. There was one like it in the Christie's catalog last September—"

"So it can't literally be priceless."

"We can't even afford to keep it," she said. "The insurance will kill me."

"You better update your alarm system." I made a point of saying *your*, not *our*. I pulled open one of the new oak drawers. It was empty except for a trace of sawdust.

"You have no idea where it came from?"

"It showed up," I said. "All kinds of things show up. Maybe it was stolen from a museum."

"Three months ago," said Connie, to change the subject, gazing at a shiny spot in the plaster, a row of spots. "I imagine they couldn't get the blood out of the carpets."

"It's a major misreading of the Constitution, letting people walk around with weapons like that." I was about to say more when I reached deep into the manila folders and started. "Jesus!" I stood straight, kicking at the desk and missing.

"Paper cut?" she asked.

"All the feeling just came back into my arm. God, it hurts."

"Poor baby," she said.

I had always wondered what sort of ex-wife Connie would make. Would she be hateful, vindictive? Or would we be able to have conversations, like this. "Office work can be rough," I said.

"Brave boy," she said.

"I'm going to get a sofa," I heard myself say.

"That'll be convenient," she said.

I did not bother responding.

"There's something sexy about wool carpet," she said. "It's rough and soft at the same time."

I answered after a long moment. Connie was good at being suggestive, but her effort was wasted on me. "Matilda's picking up a new prescription," I said. "She'll be back any minute."

"But she won't be able to work the combination," she said. "The computer's dead. She probably spends all her time talking to her boyfriend even when she's here."

"She's married. Three kids. You know what's weird—my arm is numb again, just like that. It flashed on, like a neon sign, and then —I saw Dr. Opal this morning and he practically laughed me out of his office."

"What are we going to do, Richard?"

She meant right now. I could see it, the way she pouted, looking me up and down. There was something special about me today, something she liked.

She tilted her head, letting her hair fall to one side. She seemed to be remembering something about me she had recently forgotten.

"Connie, I didn't know you were here," said Matilda, bustling into the inner office.

"I was enjoying the view," she said.

Matilda Duron was plump, dark-eyed, one of those people you like because they're smart, efficient. But right now she looked lovely, nubile, wearing a new shade of lipstick and just a little more eyeliner than usual. Her black hair was held back behind her neck with a gold clasp, and gathered up. As Matilda turned to look back at me, I realized that if she brushed her hair out, it would be luxuriant.

"We have the X-rays on that building in San Mateo," said Matilda. "The stairwell has the steel supports but the parking lot doesn't."

"That's great," I said. "That means any earthquake over 5.1 and the parking lot turns to granola."

I shut the door so Connie and I were secluded once again, and Connie pushed at her hair, gazing at herself in a hand-held mirror, tempting her hair back into place.

"The vast majority of cases against builders are settled in favor of the buyer," I said, trying to sound like a lawyer again. "My client with the parking lot X-ray has a great case against the builder."

My trousers were stained with dark discolorations like ink-blots from the burned house. I took a suit out of the closet. It was a ventless single-breasted suit, navy with chalk stripe, and I put it on over a white cotton shirt with a soft point collar. I found myself wishing I had some way of seeing myself. I was going to have a full-length mirror installed on the back of the door; Matilda had called twice asking when it would be delivered.

Connie held out her compact. It trembled with the slight unsteadiness of Connie's hand. I had to take a half-step to one side and crouch a little to use it. The looking glass threw a silvery light into the room, echoing the hazy sunlight from the window.

I wasn't sure I liked my tie, a medallion pattern, port-dark behind gold print. "You look great," she said, as though complaining. She snapped the mirror shut, and found a place for it in her handbag. "The obituary said she was planning a tour of the East Coast. The article quoted Van Cliburn as saying she had the best touch of any of the younger pianists. There was a picture of her. She was lovely. Private services, donations to the Center for Independent Living."

I hadn't known about the tour of the East Coast. More secrets. Unless the *Chronicle* got it wrong, as it sometimes did.

She had that serene expression again, and I knew her well enough to ask, "Have you been seeing a doctor?"

She did not deny it.

"You're not—" I didn't know how to ask. "You're not sick—"

She gave me a secretive smile.

"What was it this time," I said, "a new fertility drug, a new surgical procedure you read about?"

"You know I've never given up hope," she said.

"Maybe it's better to be realistic."

"Laser surgery," she said. "It's only scar tissue."

"You're just torturing yourself."

"I scheduled it. The procedure. They'll do it at Stanford, next week. I won't even have to stay overnight."

"If that's what you want," I said.

"I'm not doing it to punish you, Richard."

And I saw that maybe she was, putting herself through further pointless hope, even surgery, to give me something I didn't want.

"Because I want a future, too," she said.

But not with me, I wanted to tell her. I still felt a threadbare affection for Connie. I couldn't help it—she lived for the moment, like a ferret.

Tonight, I thought, we will have that long talk.

12

I took a moment outside the restaurant, raising my arm and letting it fall a few times. I gazed into my reflection in the glass door.

Angina. I was raised in a household where medical magazines sat on the side table with the junk mail. But this was my right arm, not my left, and this wasn't straightforward pain. A former decathalon champion had suffered a stroke just a few weeks before; I had read about it over my bran muffin and decided to skip my usual second cup of coffee. I felt clammy, and told myself I was going to give myself a panic attack unless I calmed down.

The numbness, the iciness, crept inward, across my chest. But I looked all right, judging from my reflection in the glass door of the restaurant, my image alongside the credit card decals.

In fact, I looked great. For the moment I trusted that half-truth we all take to heart: looks are everything. I squared my shoulders, and my hand reached toward its reflection in the door.

Stella was late, too, so I sat alone wondering why I had gotten out of the habit of having a drink before lunch. Just one would help. I was in pretty good shape in terms of weight, a jolt of naked calories wouldn't hurt.

I ordered a scotch and soda. The man at the table next to me was signing a credit card slip, the entire skeleton of a fish on his plate.

Poison. I had picked up some poison through the cut, maybe touched a rose leaf recently powdered with whatever chemical paralyzed aphids. I remembered my father sprinkling chlordane on ant holes, a vaguely green powder now long since proscribed. Maybe I had inhaled something in the smoke, burning polystyrene, old wiring.

I had expected it, but was still surprised: a new version of Stella Cameron made her way through the crowded restaurant. She had been a well-tailored, carefully manicured woman, one of those people who prefer salad and always skip dessert. Now she was glowing, rotund—pregnant.

In my view, heavily pregnant women had always seemed non-sexual, having slipped into the ranks of the purely maternal. I had, without thinking about it, seen pregnancy as a sign of promise, that life was going on, but in a way that was slightly unsettling.

I took her hand with my left, and felt the pulse in it. She was replete with life, pink and wide-eyed, out of breath with the effort of walking.

"I couldn't stand to breathe that stuff outside," she said. "Do you have any idea how many parts per million there have to be before they call the air unhealthy?" She narrowed her eyes at me. "You hurt your arm?"

"Threw my arm out. I was playing touch football. Rotator cuff, putting a little extra spiral on the ball."

"Football," she said, not believing it.

"Sure. I'm pretty good at it."

"Who do you play with?"

"Some guys."

"You know that missile that blew up?" she said. "It was the first time Vandenburg Air Force Base has launched anything in years. Their big chance comes along—*kablooey*. Almost as frustrating as practicing law."

"You don't find law frustrating," I said. "You love it." My drink arrived, and I took a taste. I blinked and put the drink down, stung by the carbonation of the soda and the tarry undertaste of the scotch. Had it always tasted like this? The stuff was undrinkable.

"Yeah, but sometimes a client blows up." Stella seemed to find it hard to take her eyes off me, too, and I couldn't help glancing in my spoon at the distorted, cartoony image of myself. I still had doubts about my tie, the gold medallions. I took a long drink of water, crunched a piece of ice and swallowed it.

As soon as I left here I would call Dr. Opal's office and insist that I needed blood work. The phrase offered so much hope. I had heard my father say the words on the phone so many times. I think it was the *work* part of the phrase that I liked, ambitious capability, like *road work*. I was going to be okay.

We ordered, both of us deciding to have squid. "Do you look more like your mother or your father?" she asked when the waiter was gone.

I was aware that genetics might be of more than passing interest to her. "I'm a morphed-out version of both," I said. "All mixed together."

"I think all my mother's genetic material hit the beach and died. I'm more like my dad."

When had I last seen Stella? I didn't know how to ask if there was a husband, a manly, non-spouse daddy striding proudly somewhere. I wanted to ask her who *she* played with.

"Who gives a shit about automatic security systems?" Stella was saying. "You can't protect people forever. I have this theory that we're all the result of some violent thing that happened a long time ago, an emotional Big Bang."

"I think it's called the Fall. Adam and Eve," I said, half-joking. "The Garden of Eden."

She shook her head smartly. Theology didn't go with lunch. "My client knew when he sold the condo development that he was misrepresenting the medical alert system. The buyers of the individual units were assuming the debt. The homeowners had to pay off the alert system, but they thought the system was included in the price of their unit. It was a surprise. We concede that."

Maybe the mirror held some sort of antique poison. Arsenic. Curare. The restaurant was crowded, a woman smiling, a thread of meat between her teeth.

Strong scotch, I told myself. One taste and I'm blotto. "Notice," I said, sounding calm and clear-headed, "that when we say something was a surprise we mean that it was bad. There are good surprises, you know."

She chewed some bread, swallowed some ice water. "So what you want to know is: is my client going to reimburse yours for the system out of his own pocket, and then dig deeper to pay damages, too." Her client was not a person. It was a developer based in Maryland. "And my response would be that—"

"It's paid for by now," I said. "The homeowners voted in a special assessment and paid it off. Each retired couple had to cough up four thousand dollars. These are elderly people, Stella. They need walkers, hearing aids. They weren't prepared for the extra expense. These people are victims."

"I dropped by Greenwood Meadows," she said. "These are tennis-playing, tanned business people. It's all this early retirement. People who run marathons are pulling down these incredible pensions."

She looked down at the table and picked up a fork. "One of them made a pass at me."

"I said they were old. I didn't say they were dead."

"One of these dashing guys, a silver fox. Put his hand right here, like this. And said he loved a good mai tai. And I go, 'Oh, is that what you call it?' "

"One of the plaintiffs had a heart spasm last week," I said. "He pulled out the little plug in his den, the little thingy with the red cross on it. Paramedics were there in two and a half minutes. He had total coronary occlusion. The Medisafe computer to the rescue."

She gestured with her fork, a shrug. "It works."

"It works! Because the property owners raped and pillaged their children's inheritance to pay for a system they thought they already owned."

"The Medisafe people sold this system at a loss to begin with. It was their first big project, and they were proud to be able to put little thingies on bathroom walls and kitchens so people could have total coronary occlusions and live. It's not like calling 911, Richard. With this you get a document, a phone bill, except a computer recognizes what apartment is involved, preexisting medical conditions, what medical response team is notified, what medications are recommended—"

I hadn't realized how passionate I had become. "These are retired teachers, Stella. Retired social workers. Even their dogs are old and frail. You can't cheat people and then act like you deserve some sort of applause."

Stella sighed. She straightened in her chair, easing her back. "She kicks."

I must have looked stupid, sitting there with a piece of bread in my hand, not quite following her.

She patted her abdomen. "Both feet."

"That's not fair."

"I'm supposed to tell her to stop wiggling?"

"Changing the subject by referring to your condition. How can I match that?"

"Are you wearing contacts?"

I said I wasn't.

"Your eyes look a different color or something. I get so bored with all this. You know, I'm starting to think maybe capital punishment's not such a bad thing."

"You're baffling me today, Stella. Leaping from subject to subject."

"You know, if I didn't know better, I'd say you weren't you. When I saw you my first thought was: he's a new man."

I was rolling a fragment of bread into a ball, hard. If I fainted would I pitch forward, my face in the tablecloth? "You can never get a squid when you need one."

"You look like you could be your own brother. Like those twins that impersonated each other, those gynecologists. You know how twins are. Little differences. The baby's father works for American."

I stared at her, her words almost making sense.

"The airline," she said. "He does something in security."

"Keeps airplanes from blowing up," I said.

"We may get married," she said. "And on the other hand . . ."

Stella and I had once nearly spent a night together, after a party in Sausalito, supporting each other tipsily up a steep, narrow street.

I had kissed her. And she had been willing, her arms around me as I suggested we could come back for her car in the morning.

But then her keys had dropped, all the way into the creek beside the road, and by the time I had fished out the Great Western Savings key ring we both were willing to pretend it had been one of those non-events, something we both would laugh about.

"What happened to your criminal case," she was asking, "the guy with the twelve-year-old pen pal?"

"That was years ago." I didn't like talking about it. It brought to mind the man who killed Rebecca. "He was stabbed. In Folsom. Turned up dead for the morning count." She waited for more, one of those lawyers who find perpetrators fascinating. "By that time he had graduated to other crimes, other attorneys. He was convicted of felony murder, ran over a newsvendor after his partner tried to rob an ATM with a sledgehammer. God, I'm glad I don't deal with people like that."

"What happened to the twelve-year-old girl?"

I could hear my eyeballs swivel in their sockets, wet, rubbery friction. "They never found her." I ran through a list of pharmacological items they were likely to have in a restaurant: aspirin, Alka-Seltzer, vodka.

"You like the way I look," Stella said.

"Full of life," I said.

"I look really good with my clothes off," she said. I didn't like her smile. I didn't want to touch the scotch, and my water glass was empty. My legs were going numb. This was it—I had to leave. But I couldn't. I just sat there.

"You can feel her," she said, sitting sideways, the navy blue maternity dress stretched over her round belly. "She's doing a scissor kick with one leg."

"Stella, please excuse me." I was on my feet, my napkin tumbling to the floor. "I'll be back in just a second."

She gave me a look of real concern. Maybe I could just go out for a a little fresh air, I thought. Maybe I could just go out and walk around the block. Or call an ambulance. I leaned on my chair. I wouldn't be able to make it out the door.

Every plate was a display of minor carnage, broccoli florets, mustard sauce, cutlet bones chewed down to a few whiskers of meat. And squid, doubloons of breaded tentacles, fried tarantulas.

"Can I help you, Mr. Stirling?" The woman in the black jacket was not worried that I was running out on the check, and yet in the time-honored tradition of restaurant management there was always that hint of civilized paranoia, too many butter knives had vanished over the centuries. Not to mention diners choking on chicken bones, pearls, succumbing to ptomaine. How sick did I look? How likely to sue did I appear, walking as briskly as I could through the busy crowd.

"I left something in the car," I mouthed, or maybe I said it aloud.

I brushed past a woman taking her time, sorting through her purse, and I apologized, as I hurried onward, wrinkles in the carpet. There were more than wrinkles. There were waves, combers, the floor rippling, the gray mat just inside the door crooked, backing up, fighting underfoot as I performed the public courtesy of straightening out this oversized welcome mat, kicking it back into place.

But I was in too great a hurry to do the job right. I stumbled. The glass door broke around me, over me, and I was outside.

13

Broken glass.

There were big sections of it, all over the sidewalk, all the way to the curb.

The day was bright, dazzling. Sunlight glittered on the chain of a terrier being led around the corner. Sunlight sizzled off the door handle of a sports car as it passed. I had to figure out what had happened, reassure myself that I wasn't hurt. I leaned against a parking meter, holding myself upright, wanting to laugh— chagrined.

I felt shock, embarrassment, and also relief to be outside. But my emotions soon drained to a peculiar, vacant residue. This was not related to the numbness that had claimed my arm. The numbness was gone. My right arm, my left arm—I could swing them both, wiggle my fingers.

I was basically fine, I convinced myself. I was experiencing a fairly understandable physiological state.—I had plunged my head into the glass and through it, my entire body following. The transparent barrier had been sturdy. Give the designers of the glass credit. It was strong.

I turned to tell people that I was not usually so clumsy. And then I began to think a little more analytically. A door that could give way like that should be labeled more clearly, *exit* or *entrance only*. The restaurant was guilty of serious negligence. The public had been at risk. I had been at risk. Me. This human being.

I wasn't embarrassed anymore. I was ready to take some legal steps, do the right thing for myself and for the people who were gathering, open-mouthed, giving me troubled looks, some of them stepping forward, involuntarily, instinctively helpful, some of them taking a step back.

The woman in the black jacket stepped carefully through the door, where shards still shark-toothed all the way around the frame. There was a pink carnation on her lapel, fastened there with a tiny brass safety pin.

"Don't move," she said.

The sphinx speaks! The secret is revealed! I could laugh! Human speech is uttered after an age of silence, and she talks like a movieland bad gal, an archetypal tough babe with everything but a gun.

Don't move! Of course I would move. I'd move all around, arms, legs.

"We just called 911," she said.

I made a little exhalation of breath, my lips puffing out, a dismissive moue. Who needed 911? Besides, the emergency service was overrated. I could cite case history. But it was nice of her. She was a civilized woman, a professional restaurateur. Her hair was tinted, too yellow. But a man could fall in love with a woman like this, her eyes so full of feeling.

People were gathering on the sidewalk, proverbial travelers, shocked at what they saw on the wayside. No, I wasn't drunk. No, I had not been set upon by thieves. No, nothing in the kitchen had caused any of this.

Stella appeared, not nearly so pregnant-looking now that she was outside in the sunlight. She took slow steps. All that broken glass around her, she didn't want to slip. "Be careful!" I said.

Or tried to. I could not utter a sound. I could only whisper. I tried again, and this time I sounded good. Maybe a little shaken, but audible. "Be careful, Stella."

"Don't just stand around like this," said Stella to the group of ashen onlookers. She grabbed at a man's trousers and I laughed, a gasping sound. What was she doing?

There may have been a siren, approaching from far off. Stella had a belt, tugging it through the loops, the owner of the belt helping her, releasing his length of black leather. Stella stooped, breathing hard. She worked the belt around my thigh and wound the leather around itself, tugging, twisting.

My suit was ruined. There was a gash in my trouser leg, and another on the other leg. And blood, blood all the way down inside my shoes, my sock sodden, blood squishing out every time I shifted my weight. And spurting, an art-school-pretty gout of it, syncopated, the sidewalk vermilion, glass and fluid so much slush underfoot.

I sat. The parking meter dug into my spine. It was uncomfortable, having nowhere to lie down. That was what I wanted suddenly. I needed rest.

"It'll be alright, Richard," Stella was saying, with something like anger. "Do you hear me? It'll be alright."

The pond expanded. Dust scummed the surface. It was what had been mine, and kept me alive, unthanked, unconsidered. So much scarlet.

My father did not come to see my mother die. He was in London, lingering there on purpose, afraid. I had slept in a chair in her room, the staff of Herrick allowing flowers, although the rules were against it. And it was like watching a person go to sleep, but a bad sleep, nothing pretty. Drowned-looking, at one point during the vigil she spoke. She looked up at me, possibly recognizing me, and asked, "Is it Easter?"

She was puzzled, I suppose, by all the flowers, the colors she could make out without her glasses on. And later I would tempt myself with the consolation that it was for her, the one, main holiday, the open door, the easement, the way out. From that moment I never respected my father as much as I had before.

Glass crunched under Stella's feet. This was something I could not change, a page I could not turn. The people around me could not see what I did, looking up now at the sky. This pregnant woman I did not really know very well, despite our years of association, was calling to me to hang on, hauling at my jacket, trying to awaken me from what I knew was a kind of justice. Not punishment, but right.

"Be careful," I said again.

I was echoing the last coherent words I had spoken, and having found them plausible enough when I could still think, I uttered them when I barely could open my eyes to look.

I would describe a last insight, a prayer, a loving memory. But there was in me an empty certitude. Everything solemn, everything profane, was gone. If there was a thought at all it was of Rebecca, not as a person—I could not form a clear memory any longer. Not even as a creature with a name.

But as a conviction—that she had gone ahead of me. Into this.

� Part Two ✻

Part Two

14

I could move my tongue.

Just a little, pressing it against the ridges of my palate. My tongue had a life of its own, an inquisitive gastropod.

I was somewhere safe. Very safe. And very quiet. Every thought was heavy, and I let myself drift, encouraged that people would take care of me now.

I tried to remember the ambulance. I tried to invent the memory of a surgeon, intelligent, helpful men and women. This taste in my mouth must be anesthesia. *I'll open my eyes in just a few seconds. Just a few more—I'm gathering my strength.*

I let myself drowse.

The first time I looked through a microscope was on a summer afternoon, using the big olive-green Bausch & Lomb scope my father kept under a cloth on his desk. My father had been a distant man, but kind, in an impersonal way, as though trusting that something in my chromosomes would guide me where I had to go. He was, however, visibly pleased that hot day when I asked him to show me something under the microscope, and he came back into the study smelling like someone who had been making sandwiches—there was a smell of onions about him, which was explained when I saw the membrane of onion skin on the microscope slide.

He touched the transparent skin with iodine, and the entire membrane was transfused. He rotated the lenses to get the power he wanted, and then turned to me and said, "There you go."

It took a moment to see into the tube, and not at its side, or at the obscuring filter of my own eyelashes. At last the disk of light was clear, and even more distinctively patterned when I touched the focus dial.

I saw a city. The buildings, seen from above, were rectangles, worn, or crafted, into modestly irregular patterns, like pueblos, or drawings of biblical towns. There was no single identical geometry to the long, corral-like shapes of this village, and yet there was a general similarity, so that after even a moment or two one could sketch a typical structure, locate its purple-stained center, and describe the thickness of the walls.

We were made of these little prisons, flush to each other, wall to wall. Life consisted of confines. It was constructed of prisons, tiny castles. What could not define itself was so much fluid. To live was to be a fortress.

I felt my teeth with my tongue.

It had its own life, this searching morsel, probing. Soon I would open my eyes. Soon I would make a sound.

15

It was better not to wake. Waking was a room just to my left, beyond, and I knew as soon as I was aware of waking, saw it as a threshold I could cross, that it was too late. I could not go back.

I wanted to stay as I was—as I had been. There was, however, no slipping back into full unconsciousness. There was a sensation that time had passed. There was no particular event, or series of changes, that made me believe this, and I was aware that this sensation impressed me as unlikely. But even doubt is an event, an experience.

There was an interlude, a long period of almost sinking back again. I was aware, but did not attach myself to this awareness, out of focus, dazed into a near-slumber that I knew I had just ascended from.

Something was wrong. Something in me would not be still. This urging was a cricket, ceaseless. I could not silence this nagging, bright inner-voice.

Not yet, I longed to convince myself. I could wait a little while longer. But I was forced to begin to wonder how badly I was hurt. It was not that I remembered an injury, no accident, no fall, no stunning impact. But I knew that I had been unconscious, and some instinct made me try out the word *hurt*.

I slept again, but it did not last.

My awareness returned. I was hurt. I was hurt badly. There was no pain, but there was a sensation of water in my lungs, of cold and a heavy weight on me, in me. I tried to breathe, and I could not. I could not take a breath.

And then I was afraid. I could not block the fear: I was in pieces, dismembered, scattered. There was no reason for this fear except that I knew, deep beyond hope, that I was mortally injured.

I tried to call out, and I made no sound. I could not so much as whisper. I had felt cold before this moment, but now I felt the chill throughout my body, and I tried to move.

I tried to move.

There was no life in my arms and in my legs, no power in me to twitch a finger, stretch the tendons of my legs. I knew I must be paralyzed, willing to address the horror intellectually, in a fragmented way, to fend off the full realization of my condition. I opened my eyes.

It was not a darkness like any I had ever seen. I thought my eyes were gone, the nerves surgically severed. I thought some sickening dislocation had ruptured my body, an explosion or the impact of a car.

I wondered, with an odd lucidity, whether I would die soon, if this shard of consciousness was what my nervous system seized on, a benign separation from the trauma, the sort of addled bliss one hears that people enduring great cold experience.

I had to do something to break my silence. I needed help. I tried to calm myself, but it was futile. I tried again to breathe and the full horror of what was happening pressed down on me. I had not been dying. The dying was before me, yet to take place, and it was going to be agony. It was beginning now.

At that moment, I could move.

One hand, my right, shifted upward though the dark. I felt a tingling numbness, as though the circulation in the limb was poor. I drew my hand up my chest, a cuff whispering over a shirt front. The fingers continued over a cold surface, buttons, a jacket's lapel. I touched my face, and there was no feeling.

And then there began to be feeling, in my fingertips, in my lips. It was the inactivity, I thought, the disuse of my nervous system that made me so numb. The engine of my body was just beginning to turn.

My eyes hurt. My fingers found my eyelids. There was a hard plastic lens on each eye. I pried each seal free and blinked. The plastic disks shifted, falling away on either side of my face.

Now I could see. But there was nothing. Only dark.

Okay, I told myself. I'm blind. That was bad. That was very bad, but not the worst thing that could happen. I stretched my hand out and up. It did not travel far. At first it was a welcome sensation. I was feeling something with my outstretched hand.

I pressed my hand flat against the fabric surface that was not far from my face. For a moment it was a relief to be able to feel something so exterior to myself, and a source of hope that I was at last able to use my senses. I patted the satiny surface, trying to imagine its nature, and guessing. And rejecting the guess as impossible.

I began to cry out, virtually soundless screams, breathy, empty cries. I couldn't open my jaw. I pounded on the soft cloth surface with my fist. I hammered against a surface that made almost no sound, my blows muffled by the fabric and the feeling of a great weight beyond the barrier of wood and cloth.

I rolled myself to one side, and then to another, shifting my weight, pushing against the side of what I sensed to be an adult-sized crib, trying to reassure myself that surely I was in some ambulance, or in a medical facility where the attendants had momentarily left me in a chamber used for CAT scans, or perhaps I was in one of those grim fixtures, an iron lung.

I knew I wasn't blind. I was seeing what was really here. There was no light, an absence of even the hint of variation in the flat perfect darkness. Above the top of my head, below my feet, around me in all directions, was a box, a padded container.

I squirmed, then bunched my body, spasming, every muscle straining. I tried to call out, feeling my way around this prison. My nose was clogged with wadding. I dug the cotton free with my fingers. I forced my jaw apart, struggling, pulling out what felt like thread. With a strange absence of pain I pulled a needle from my gums, and another.

I tried to sit up and struck my forehead. I kicked, ripping at the cloth above me, clawing at the hard, slick-varnished surface before my face, suffocating as I fought the dark.

And then, at last, my lungs dragged in a breath of air. The right lung filled slowly, and I could feel the spongy airsack inflate and falter, sodden and disused. I coughed. I took in another breath and both lungs unfolded, breath growling in and out as I coughed, hacking, spitting, and half-swallowing cold sputum.

I gasped, my mind swimming, as I wondered if I had been stricken with pneumonia. But I was breathing. I cried out. My voice was a churn of phlegm and air, an animal bawl more than a yell. I took in another breath. I released it in a cry so loud it hurt my vocal chords and made my ears ring. Again and again I called, until my voice was ripped, strained soundless.

But they had heard me. They were hurrying to where I lay, reassuring smiles on their lips. Here they were, surely, the sounds of my fellows.

It was going to be all right. People are kind to the injured, and make provisions for them. I was misunderstanding the nature of my confinement. Light would break into my world, light and a caring face. I readied something to whisper, a message of gratitude that I could express with what was left of my voice.

I would apologize. How silly of me. What a mistake I had made. I would have to put it into words for them. I would laugh as I said it, laugh until my guardians were laughing too, at the outrageousness of it, the mad, hilarious blunder I had made.

I would tell them what I had thought had happened to me, and I would hear them repeat it to each other, to the others who ran up to help, to see what had happened, to join in my reunion with reassurance.

But there was no light. There were no voices, no smiles. What had sounded like hurrying steps was only the sound of my own heart, startled into contraction, stumbling into a pace that matched my feelings. The air tasted mineral and dank, and it was scented, too, with the essence of the box that held me, cabinet-maker's wood stain and furniture wax flavoring each breath.

16

The cloth ripped, and my fingernails tore at the surface of the wood, dug into it, my blows and kicks altering the pressure of the air.

The shallow walls of the place were ruffled, a quality of wedding gown finery about the drapery around me and the pillow beneath my skull. I felt my hands grow powdery with residue, damp dusting my flesh. I lay still.

There was a stony quality to the damp that held me, a smell of wet earth. That was exactly what it was, I told myself. I was buried in the ground. I had a sketchy but emotionally vivid sense of what such internment entailed. There was, of course, a wooden box and its contents. Then I imagined a concrete vault, a box of man-made rock. And then I imagined the proverbial six feet of earth, clay, sand, roots, sod, and living grass all topped off with a headstone.

I tried to imagine that I was having one of those nightmares that involve a dream of waking. You dream that you are awake, but the nightmare has merely reached a new chapter. Dreams end eventually. Actual consciousness would break, and I would be in a bed, among the living.

I tried to deceive myself, but it did not work. I argued with myself, picking apart my despair. I could not remember my life very clearly. If I could reason, then, I could think of a way out. Panic would confuse me further, and might use up the oxygen in the small space.

I recalled funerals I had attended, sunlight, date palms and a gray hearse rolling slowly ahead of black limos. I recalled Easter Sunday afternoons, florist's paper crackling around wet stems. I recalled bank upon bank of marble plates, with names chiseled into the stone.

As a child I had wandered through the place, looking upward at stained-glass windows and feeling the sense of awe one might discover in a vast library, but this was not a library. I tried to take some solace in the belief that I must be close to the remains of my father, my mother, but the thought gave me no comfort.

When I cried out there was only a loud whisper, a sound like someone learning to whistle. Beating against the lid of the casket was futile. I was too close to the lid to be able to strike a resounding blow. All I could do was squirm and kick. It was more satisfying to kick against the foot of the casket. I could hunch myself, like a woman in labor, and then kick hard with my heels at the butt of the coffin. That made noise, a thudding, cloth-muffled bumping.

I had an urgent, nearly surreal fantasy of what I hoped would happen. A caretaker or a family of mourners would pass by and hear what had to be the sounds of someone trapped. An ear would be pressed, and others called to listen to the commotion behind this brand-new marble plaque. I imagined the disagreement, the disbelief, the scurrying to get help, the consternation.

I stopped and listened. I stilled my breath, and discounted the rubber ball of my own heart, and listened to everything around me. I strained to hear distressed whispers, weeping silenced, ordinary conversation hushed. I pictured a boy, a youth awkward in his dark suit, leaning, sure he was right, afraid he was, certain no one would believe him, gesturing to an older sister. Two or three more people would be here now, listening to the two half-grown children explain that they heard something, and no they weren't joking.

Why hadn't I learned Morse code, I asked myself, kicking with both feet. Was SOS two long, two short, and two long? Or should I give in to all-out panic, make a noise that could not possibly be misunderstood by mourners with, understandably, some reluctance to realize that what could be lost in such circumstances might insist on being found.

I tried to calculate how long it would take for an assistant manager to be summoned, someone with a fist full of keys and a brisk sense of what to do in cases like this. Surely this happened sometimes. There must be procedures to be followed, workers skilled at levering open what they had a few days before sealed shut.

I braced myself, and kicked, repeatedly, furiously. I stopped and listened to the quiet. There was no one coming.

I wanted to sleep but knew I would wake only to sleep again, and if I woke after that I would only repeat the page after page of waking and slumbering until it was all over. I could feel it already, the long weariness I would never shake. The exhaustion was more than a condition of my body. It was a fact of nature, like gravity, and it had me.

I kicked again, driving downward with both feet. I was not dying yet. I was ready to return to whatever mistakes I had made, and do it all over again but right, this time, bringing justice and humor where before I must have hurried past on my way to—what?

This time when I kicked there was a difference. I heard a change in the note my heels struck against the heavy wood. I kicked again, and heard a high, fine tune, the sound of a seam in the wood parting.

I hunched, seized whatever I could find to steady myself, and kicked again, and kept driving my feet downward until the cracking sound could not be mistaken. I had hoped that as the casket weakened I would see light, but there was only further darkness. In a panic, I kicked harder than before, and the wood shattered, and something else gave way, too.

I scrambled halfway down the broken coffin, and kicked against a concrete seal. This time I did not stop to listen. I knew strength, something in me that would not weaken. The concrete slab was shifting, a low, deep note, nearly bell-like, solemn, a door of stone working outward.

It must have taken a long time. Perhaps I stopped and drifted into sleep, to wake and work again. That would explain why I was not aware of how long it took. At times it seemed that the stone trap fought against me willfully, sealing itself tighter than ever. One moment there was dark. And then it all changed.

One edge of the concrete seal was gilded with light. The light widened into a wedge, a painful spear of illumination. And then as I kicked once more it fell away.

The sound was so loud, and the light so bright, I cringed involuntarily for an instant. And then, to my frustration, I could not easily snake my way down and out. I was held by the white satin fabric, gripped by the narrow box. I wrestled, straining slowly, out and into light so complete it was nearly blinding.

I fell. My perch was higher than I expected, and the fall much farther.

I spilled out onto a floor, and lay there and told myself that I didn't have to move, ever. I could stay right where I was. They would find me. I had done enough. My joy was so thorough that I barely noticed the pain, the weight of so much light making me sit up, blinking, covering my eyes.

I was nailed into place, pinned by the light. It cascaded from above, and I crouched on a flat, polished surface trying to recover my vision. There was no moment in which I mistook this illumination for the sun. It was unmistakably artificial, tight, tiny coils of filament radiating this flavorless light.

I could not wait. I had to hurry. I was in a hall, in a building with a high ceiling. I was reminded of a post office, one of those mornings as a child when I had gone with an adult and seen the wonder of the post office boxes, the rolled sheafs of mail behind the small windows, eash message yet to be discovered, the whole veiled secret of one's business and personal life.

My knees were weak. I took a step, and felt them buckle, one foot out, the other dragging. I fell.

I wanted to laugh. The clown returns from the lost! I stood again, and kept myself upright only by leaning heavily on the gleaming surface of the wall. As the wall supported me, I could feel the imprint of letters, words pressed against my skin through my clothes. A name was cut into the face of the marble, and a date of birth and a date of death. A tarnished metal vase held dying flowers.

The fragments of casket, the chunks of concrete and marble, lay behind me in a glaze of fresh dust. The concrete grit whispered beneath my shoes. What a mess, I chided myself, trying to make a joke of it. A hiker in the wilderness is supposed to pack out what he packs in.

I sensed the discarded husks, the earth-cold members of this assembly, all around me. There was an odor, concrete and spent flower petals underscored by the refrigerator-aura of old flesh.

Was there a moment just then when I was aware of being watched? I crouched. I was aware of an intruder. Or perhaps it was help, happening upon the scene at last. I tried to call out, attempting to call hello, like someone arriving home after a vacation to find the apartment not quite right.

I could barely raise a whisper. There was no sound, no movement. I ran, and fell. My body slid, carried by momentum, and then I worked myself slowly upright. My need to flee this place insisted, and I felt my way along the empty vases, the impervious names and dates, sometimes disturbing with my passage a withered rose.

I saw the darkness of night, outside, beyond a hall. There was a desk, a large, empty executive-style block of furniture, and beside it a metal folding chair, left partly hitched-up, as though someone had started to fold it up and heard a phone ring.

A cord ran across the oak floor, into a desk drawer. I hooked my finger around the door handle, and pulled. There was a white, compact telephone, tucked away so the bereaved would not be troubled by the sight of such an ordinary object.

I suddenly saw what a piece of stage craft this mausoleum was. What a story I would tell. What a mistake you made, I would tell my—

My what? My family, my wife, my children, my friends? I was a man who had just that moment forgotten the right word.

Then I began to feel anger. This couldn't be blamed on one physician, or on a mortician. The whole array of medical professionals and undertakers, everyone involved, had made a huge blunder.

I recalled my wife, but I had trouble actually seeing her in my mind. Her name was Constance. Connie. She had been deceived by people she trusted, medical authorities. It must have been terrible for her. My career, my associates—it was dim, but I was beginning to see it all now.

But there was another, more important woman. Rebecca—I wanted to call her, to tell her I was back again, it was all a mistake. I lifted the receiver to my ear. The dial tone was hideously loud, and I held the instrument away from my head. I tried to remember my own phone number. I struggled to remember Rebecca's. I tried to make the numbers on the telephone make sense. I had trouble recognizing the characters as meaningful symbols.

I pushed the O. Something would happen. Some voice would respond. It was then, as I depressed the one button I was able to recognize, that I saw my hand.

My skin was mottled with discoloration, the way the mattress of a chaise longue dapples, when it is left out for too many rainy nights. I was mildewed.

I could not answer the steely muttering of the telephone. My voice was too soft, too broken. And besides, I was paralyzed by a question I had to ask myself, one little point of order before we resumed after this recess.

How long had I been asleep?

I slipped the phone back into its cradle, and shut the drawer, carefully, quietly. I was eager to cross the floor, eager to be outside, and so I hurried unsteadily.

I reached for the frame of the glass door, and when I had a decent grip, I pushed. Nothing happened. I pushed again, my weight behind the effort, and the door was solid. I turned my head, listening.

Surely there was movement, back there, behind me. Someone used this desk, a caretaker. He heard me. Sounds echoed in this place, and I had not even tried to keep quiet. There were footsteps.

I turned to listen, and then with desperation, and revulsion, I pushed again, and this time I felt something surrendering inside the lock, a catch showing its age. I leaned heavily, something snapped, and I was out.

17

There was a troubling, purring, breathy sound from the expanse of neighborhoods, and it took me a moment to realize that this was the normal sound of streets, freeway, railway, late night traffic, all the way down to the bay. The night was starless, furred with cloud.

The cemetery sloped downhill. I followed the road past yews, eucalyptus, and pepper trees dwarfed by excessive trimming. The smokestack of the crematorium was sheltered behind a peaked roof, and water flowed into a pool beside the empty parking lot.

How could I be sure this was really happening?

I ran my fingers through the wet grass. I gripped the metal gate that blocked the parking lot. I believed it. It was real.

I laughed windily, and shook the post of a stop sign, hanging on to it for support, feeling like a drunk in a cartoon. The vacant asphalt was a plain of rich smells, oil, the flat scent of sand and the perfume of wet earth and weeds, sour grass and dandelions. Poppies were trembling along the sidewalk, the blossoms closed tightly. An empty carton of food lay, half unfolded on the curb, letting off a smell of corruption, beef and vinegary ketchup.

It was useless to look for a telephone with my voice the way it was, so I made my way up Colusa, away from the lights advertising a dry cleaner and a florist.

Crumpled foil reflected the night sky, the wrinkles limned by the residual neon that reached even this far from the florist's shop. The streets were relatively quiet here, only an occasional car turning a corner in the distance, turning into a far-off driveway. A few people were still coming home. It might be approaching midnight, I thought, or a little after. I had another, more troubling question.

I tried to put the question out of my mind. Shut up, I told myself. Don't think. Just keep walking.

I had assumed that my coma had lasted a matter of days. How long could a body linger, dehydrated, unnourished? I could not calculate my survival beyond a week or so.

But the scene around me was one of late winter, or early spring, the soft rainy season of the Bay Area evident in the moist manure spread among the naked stalks of roses, in the drying tendrils of twigs and trash in the grill over a gutter drain. A cherry tree was in full blossom, the invisible blush of fragrance all over the neighborhood.

My memory stopped on a day I could remember with some difficulty, like someone sitting down to a game after a long break, wiping dust off the checkerboard.

The evidence was there, in the birch trees' still-naked branches, in the puddle that ran along a seam in the street. I told myself not to think about it. I would have time to ask, time to fill in the calendar. I reasoned that I might have been hospitalized for several weeks, months, or even years, before I had been interred.

I had to stop and lean against a stone wall.

I held on to the wall for a moment, block upon block of cement chunks piled on top of each other. Were the cars around me the models I remembered, or had years of new design made them all strange?

I trudged on, trying to reassure myself. I passed a Honda, a Chevy pickup, a motorcycle on a driveway under a plastic tarp, the tarp held shut by a clothespin. This was the world I had left. Here was a cardboard box, sodden, and run over so many times the pulp was streaked up and down the street.

If a police car had passed I would have flagged it down, but as it was I had a long walk before I found my way home. I ran when I could, but my stride was strange, drunken, my ankles turning and nearly causing me to stumble.

I tried to believe that I grew stronger as I walked, more sure of my stride. As I hurried I tried to think of ways to tell my wife that I was here again, that I was alive, and that everything was going to be fine. I also had time to explore how I felt about Connie. I wanted to give her the good news, and see my house, familiar furniture, friendly walls.

Farther away, across town was the house where Rebecca lived. She was the sole human being I really needed to see. But first I would go home. I needed clothes, and I needed to orient myself just a little more firmly in place and time. I knew that Connie was not the person I most wanted to see, but I accepted her as a part of a homing instinct that led me forward.

I remembered the route as I traveled it. I had a wonderful secret, but I also realized that the shock would be great—maybe too much. I tried one fantasy after another, the rung doorbell, the whispered announcement of who I was as Rebecca unfastened the chain. But it wouldn't be Rebecca, it would be Connie. I didn't want to hurt Connie. I considered a trip to a police station so I could scrawl a note and have them make a call first, before I drove up in the backseat, grinning officers slapping my back all the way up the front steps.

I stood on the front lawn of my house.

The walk that ascended to the front steps was cracked, and in the cracks were the spurts of new grass. The grass here, and the lawn on all sides, had been mowed recently, within the last day or so.

I climbed the front steps, and then I hesitated. I was so close, but I could not bring myself to press the doorbell. There was a new anxiety.

What if Connie had moved? What if this house was inhabited by strangers? The new inhabitants would waken, someone fumbling down the stairs. The porch light would flood the steps, and a stranger would stand there, blinking, suspicious, telling his dog to stop barking.

I tried to prepare some remarks that would explain my presence, like a fatigued salesman pulling together his spiel. It was amusing, in a way, but I could think of nothing that I could deliver that would do anything but cause confusion, or even alarm.

I was wearing black shoes, and a black suit I did not recognize.

My tie was probably silk, a solid color, black or navy blue—I didn't recognize it, either, and I found myself wondering who had picked it out.

There would be time for doctors to marvel at my recovery. I could visualize the photocopied documents, surprise tempered with explanation. I would enjoy that, reading how they would attempt to explain away the most egregious medical blunder of their careers.

I found my way to the back fence, and the gate creaked, dragging slightly as I opened it, scraping over a length of garden hose. I closed the gate behind me, and stepped over a large plastic bag of Vitagrow mulch, unopened. A rake lay beside it, tines turned upward. It wasn't safe to leave a garden implement like that.

I leaned the rake against the wall. How foreign such things can look—a pair of gardening gloves on a back step, a steel claw, used for scratching weeds, a box of snail poison, with a drawing of a snail, horned and muscular, printed on the side.

The back door was locked. I should have expected this. I twisted the knob, and my hand slipped off. I had trouble getting a grip. I jiggled the door, considered knocking, and told myself that this was an even worse plan than ringing the front doorbell.

I was glancing around, telling myself not to make noise, telling myself not to lose my temper, telling myself that this was only a minor setback, when I gave the knob another determined turn, and the door popped open.

It hadn't been locked after all, only warped in its frame. This could mean that the house was abandoned, neglected for months, the doorjambs swelling with the wet weather.

I called her name, a scratchy whisper. The kitchen was warm, a compost of coffee grounds and lettuce leaves somewhere under the sink. There was a cup in the dish rack, and a kitchen towel neatly folded. I searched eagerly.

Here was her leather appointment diary. Here was her address book, her favorite gold ball-point pen, with a matching refillable gold pencil she never used. Here was the mail, the bills to be paid in the pigeonhole of the downstairs desk.

There was a set of handle bars, a large front wheel, a wrench gleaming on the carpet. She had been setting up an exercise bike.

And here on the coffee table was a plate of smoked almonds, with a space in the salted nuts where someone had pawed a handful. There was a paper napkin, folded once.

The magazines were on the side table, photos of smiling, evidently newsworthy faces I didn't take the time to recognize. I was trailing one hand along the banister, making my way up the stairs. Her name was on my lips, my tongue, my vocal chords ready to call, as best I could, in whatever stage whisper I could manage, when I stopped outside the bathroom.

And for the first time I began to be afraid of myself. Not of any situation I found myself in, not of any lingering health problem I might suffer. I loathed myself for hesitating. I meant that one part of my mind admitted the irrational possibility.

I didn't need to drop by the bathroom, with its sink and its tub and its toilet. I found myself reasoning, like a traveler in an airport, asking himself if he should empty his bladder now or wait until later, on the plane. I was stalling, afraid of waking Connie.

I needed time, I told myself. I was blundering ahead, sure that I just needed a few minutes to understand what was happening to me.

I was afraid to go into the bathroom. I was afraid of something very specific, something that waited alongside toothpaste and deodorant soap.

But as soon as I let myself realize how frightened I was, I knew how badly I needed to talk with someone. I strode down the hall, put my hand on the bedroom door, and let the door swing inward.

I couldn't even see the bed for a moment. The headboard belonged over against the north wall, and here it was, in a completely different part of the room. And it wasn't the same bed. Our bed had been simple, maple, box springs, a mattress: a place to sleep and make love.

This bed was grand, with bedposts and a carved fleur-de-lis in the headboard, dark wood, and old. The bed was empty. I found myself gazing down at the hotel-room neat sheets and pillows. There was no one in the house.

I remembered now what had happened. It was one of those moments when the speaker loses his place, the speech vanishes.

He looks down at his notes, mentally groping. And it all comes back.

I knew it all, every wrought-iron detail. My marriage with Connie was finished. Rebecca was gone. I would never see her again.

This nightstand was new, but the dresser was one she had brought from her family home when we were first married. Here was a burn along the front edge from one of her father's menthol cigarettes, from the days before his heart trouble. A hand mirror, face up, reflected the vague light. Another, full-length mirror, hung on the back of the door, angling from where I stood.

I turned on a switch with some difficulty. It was one of those mock-antique kerosene lamps, the switch a knob made to look like it had something to do with advancing the wick. I closed my eyes against the sudden light. I was sickened. Usually when a light passes though our eyelids we see a shade of red, small blood vessels, skin. The light through my eyelids was gray. I fumbled, and snapped off the light.

It took awhile for my eyes to adjust. She had added to her collection of hurricane lamps, the genuine article, pale wicks curling in vinegar-yellow kerosene. A row of them gleamed on a high shelf.

I didn't recognize any of her clothes in the closet. Some of the dresses were gradually familiar as I hunted, sweeping them aside, the metal hooks scraping along the rod. But she had new clothes, dozens of suits and skirts I did not recognize.

None of my clothes remained. Not one hiking boot, not one necktie. Nothing.

A rush of light swept the room, and tires crackled in the street, a car turning, tires squealing against the curb. I recognized the way she drove, a deft u-turn the street almost could not accommodate, and the way she parked abruptly, the car always either too far out, or jammed against the curb.

When I imagined what I had to ask her I could not picture the conversation. There was too many questions, one on top of the other, and too many answers I did not really want to hear.

Footsteps on the front steps. A lurch as she tugged the front door, worked the key again, and got it open. She was in the house.

She snapped on lights downstairs. She kicked off her shoes, one of them skidding, thudding against a wall.

While she was in the downstairs bathroom I crept down the stairway, and out the front door, feeling myself abandon every false hope. And what did that leave? I asked myself.

What friend did I have?

18

Walking uphill was difficult.

The winding streets and the steep sidewalks presented a challenge. I was in the Berkeley Hills, quiet residences and a drowsy sense of up-market college town security making me feel naked, out of place. I had the sense that if I thought too intently on what I was doing, or where I was going, I would rupture something in myself, or in my consciousness, my sense of reality. It was best to keep walking.

The brick wall was covered with ivy, a mature plant, not yet in leaf, the muscular vine spread wide. Cracks marred the wall, the breaks following the outline of the bricks, zigzagging downward. I climbed the ivy. My awkwardness surprised me, my body almost refusing to cooperate. I swung myself over the fence.

I landed hard, but on my feet. A small field stretched before me, recently plowed. Some of the clods curled, slightly gleaming, while other were round and full-bodied, and crushed gently under my steps. At the edge of the plowed land a small army of saplings crowded together, an orchard in the making, due to be planted in a day or two, I guessed, each tree's roots wrapped in a cloth ball like a boxing glove.

I made my way across the grounds of a rambling house, the main building far ahead, the lights on upstairs. As I approached the house I crossed a well-established garden. Rose bushes sprouted new, dark-red growth, and the pungent, creosote-scent of basil surrounded me, a row of young herbs.

A sound reached me from inside the house, music, a symphony, I supposed, the music unreal and distorted in my ears. A few dandelions punctuated a lawn, a garden hose wound up into a tight spiral, the brass nozzle drooling water on a sidewalk. I nearly tripped over a wooden spindle and wire hoops stuck into the grass, the relics of a game I recognized with only a little difficulty, croquet. This was a grand building. I had explored it as a child, from the tidy guest bedrooms, to the rough-finished cellar, the furnace huffing on with the authority of a generalissimo.

I opened a sliding glass door and stepped inside. I was eager, now, feeling that this night's journey was about to end. I knew this place. I had sat in this chair as a boy, my feet unable to reach the floor, and as a young man, watching the Superbowl.

A step creaked the floorboards, and a chair scraped the floor, muted by carpeting. A faint rustling followed, paper, I thought, a book or a magazine.

A bony thing, a mallet with a long handle clattered as I tread upon it. A wooden ball fled my foot, and as it rolled it began to gain momentum. The sound of its orbit across the hardwood floors echoed, until at last it reached a carpet. Its career across the floor halted, then continued across the rug, but quieter, now, almost silent.

The only light reached me from upstairs, and from the peculiar silence I could tell that the rolling wooden ball had made too much noise. The sound of the orchestra died. I could hear what happened next, a long moment of suspense, as though human attention itself was a presence in the room. He was listening.

The dim light delineated drinking glasses, the too-sweet perfume of liquor in the air. I held a wineglass by the stem, and tapped it with my finger. He heard me, there could be no question. I wanted him to know there was someone in the house—I did not want to startle him more than I had to.

I settled some drinking glasses into a tray, gathering them from the comfortable clutter of magazines and newspapers. I did not bother to keep the glasses from tinkling, hoping he would come down to see what guest had returned to help clean up.

"Who is it?" It was so good to hear him speak! But I did not like the quaver in his voice, the uncertain quality that made him sound vulnerable.

I took a wheezy breath to answer him. I spoke. But I could make no sound, only a wet rasp. "Don't be afraid," I repeated, still making no sound a human ear would recognize.

I coughed, gagged briefly, and tried again.

"Who's there?" asked Dr. Opal, this time coming halfway down the stairs. I could see him! He hunched sideways, peering. "Susan?" Then, in an altogether different tone, the tone of someone sure that he is not alone. "Susan, if it's you, say something."

I was embarrassed, aware that I was trespassing on his private sense of security. I had no idea who Susan was. I had no right to intrude on him. The tone of his voice was no longer simply questioning. He was concerned, growing frightened, turning to go upstairs again, and I called out as loudly as I could, "Wait! Don't be afraid. It's only—"

But I could not project a sound, my whisper shrieking in the room, as he hurried back up the stairs, across an upstairs room and snatched up a telephone.

He identified himself to someone on the phone. Taking action was something that steadied him. Emergency room crises over the years must have accustomed him to assuming control. "I think I have an intruder," said Dr. Opal.

I did not know how I was able to fling myself upstairs so quickly. I was in the room with him. His back was to me, and he was repeating his address, the cross street, Grizzly Peak Boulevard. I did not recall Dr. Opal's hair being so white. I hesitated, shrinking back to the doorway.

It was an amiably cluttered room, piles of manuscripts and quarterlies, computer software and bills. I recognized two of the faces on the wall, black-and-white snapshots enlarged so the casual smiles and wind-mussed hair were imposing and slightly out of focus. My father, in a white, short-sleeved shirt, a blurry hint of masts and sails behind him. My mother in a dark dress and her favorite pearls, inappropriately dressed for what she was doing, brandishing a badminton racket. The shadowy grid fell upon her cheek, her eyes, as she held the racquet to ward off the photographer's attention.

The sight of the filing cabinets, the coffee mug on the desk beside the old IBM Selectric, made me feel welcome. I had enjoyed this room as a boy, my father and Dr. Opal leaning back in their chairs to swap medical tall-tales. A sink sparkled in the corner, the porcelain chipped, a black half-moon along one edge. Perhaps the more youthful Dr. Opal had considered seeing patients here, or perhaps professional habit made him uncomfortable in a room where he could not scrub his hands with Betadyne.

He hung up the phone, and turned. I could tell by the way he moved, one hand out to the chair for support, that he knew at that instant he was not alone.

I said, "Dr. Opal, I need your help."

This time my voice was a healthy stage whisper. Dr. Opal froze, moving only his hand, which kept searching for support, fumbling beside the box of paper clips and the half-lens reading glasses.

Then he seized the desk chair. He rocked back, leaning against the big metal desk, and held the oak captain's chair between us. His white hair was uncombed, and his bathrobe was hanging open, the cloth belt dangling. It was an expensive-looking robe, blue with gold piping, and his pajamas were silk, dark blue to match the robe.

"What is this?" he said, planting his feet, ready to defend himself with the heavy oak chair. It was the tone of outraged authority, a medical professor discovering an unemptied bed pan. I had never seen this side of Dr. Opal. He looked older, drawn, but at the same time stronger than I would have expected, an adrenaline boost making his voice that of Hercules. "What do you want?"

I would have chuckled, and congratulated him for his spirit, except for my concern for him. Only one light illuminated the room, a crook-neck desk lamp. The lamp did a good job on the array of papers on the desk, but I stood just out of its range. As I drew closer, putting out my hand to reassure Dr. Opal, the sight of my own fingers, the back of my hand, made me thrust my hand into my jacket pocket.

"I'm sorry," I coughed. The words were impossible to distinguish, but my voice was stronger. "Please don't be afraid," I urged. This time I sounded human, almost like my usual self, except for a syrupy rattle in my voice. I could be a man recovering from a bad chest cold, nothing worse.

He let the chair fall with a crash, and I was at his side as he collapsed, easing his fall, so that he would not hurt himself. At once he tried to scramble to his feet, grasping at the leg of his desk.

Don't be afraid. I touched his cheek, his skin hot. *Be still. Please help me.*

For some reason I expected my thoughts to cause some change in him. "What is this?" he gasped.

It was just like Dr. Opal, I thought, to speak in questions that demanded answers. And yet his heart was pounding. I felt remorseful. I should have thought of a better way to step into his life. "There was a mistake," I said.

For a long moment he fought nausea, and struggled to keep from fainting, staring at me, blinking.

"I need you to step back," he said at last.

"I know how hard this is for you," I said, wanting to add more, to tell him everything.

"Step back," he said. "So I can get up."

I did as he asked, all the way to the wall. When he was on his feet he wrenched the desk lamp so its blinding vector of light was directed at me. I could not see anything but the bright knob of the bulb. I cringed, but stayed as I was for a long moment of his ragged breathing.

"Tell me who you are," he said. But he knew. Already he could tell.

A knock. At the front door downstairs. Dr. Opal did not move. When I tried to say another word I coughed, and I spat into the sink. I was unable to suppress the thought: *necrotic.* I got the faucet to work and rinsed it down.

A police radio squawked somewhere outside, a stutter of static making a noise like a footstep in gravel. A hushed rumble reached us, the sliding glass door. One of the croquet balls rolled again, this time all the way down a hall until it met a wall with a pleasing *pock*, like the distant kiss of baseball against bat.

"It's Richard," I said. "Richard Stirling. Please help me."

19

Please help me.

Downstairs a male voice was muttering. It was easy to imagine the police speaking into their transmitters, telling the dispatcher that there was no one here, or that they had arrived too late, the owner was not responding to their arrival, send more units.

I'm really here.

Dr. Opal took one step, and then another, approaching me. There was a long, indecisive moment. He put his hand on my sleeve, feeling my arm through the damp cloth. "Tell me your mother's maiden name."

He said this evenly, steadier now that the police would be in this room in seconds if he raised his voice. His manner told me that he expected, or hoped, that I would be stymied by this question.

"Reed," I said. "Her maiden name was Reed. She loved pink marshmallows. She died of a burst appendix." *No one else can help me.*

He did not examine me closely as he passed me, heading out into the dark stairwell. He had a determined quality to his stride, a man braced to get something done. A flashlight beam caught him.

"Gentlemen," he said. "I'm Dr. Opal. I'm sorry I troubled you. I thought there was an intruder, but I was mistaken."

He gave this brief speech from the top of the stairs, resembling an admiral addressing his staff as he leaned on the rail. He gathered his robe around him. If you didn't know him well you would not detect that falseness in his tone. He sounded cheerful, a man apologizing with grace. "It was a cat, knocking over some of the dinner glasses." He gave a forced laugh. "I can't tell you how embarrassed I am."

It sounded completely fake to me. I could hear that tone under-scoring each word, the barely suppressed desire to flee from the house.

The cops didn't believe it either, even though Dr. Opal went downstairs and turned on the lights, complaining with phony heartiness about a neighbor's tom cat, "The boldest animal I've ever seen. And so smart."

There was something wrong, and the police knew it. Dr. Opal expanded on the subject of cats, their mischief, and the neighbor-hood crime you heard about, burglars and worse. I had trouble making out what he said as he led the officers into the front yard, thanking them, apologizing for the state of his nerves.

An office is a pleasing hideaway, both apart from the world and linked to it by telephone, computer, correspondence. One of the photographs on the wall was a young boy holding a cowboy hat the way an adult would hold a birthday cake. The boy was smiling, but it was the way children often smile for cameras, dutifully, not really very happy.

A small mirror hung on the wall beside the door. It had not been cleaned recently, and was dotted with flecks of lint. Go ahead, I urged myself. Take a look.

Dr. Opal was still somewhere outside, making conversation, stalling, I supposed, not wanting to come back into his house. He was the sort of person people enjoyed talking to, and I could pic-ture the police relaxing, happy to delay their own return to duty, while Dr. Opal disguised his own panic.

Take a peek in the mirror, I told myself. Don't you want to know how you look?

The glass answered the room with a second world, a twin room, but reversed, papers, reading glasses, a stapler on the edge of the desk.

Nausea. I picked up the chair, set it down on its four legs, and sat.

When Dr. Opal stood in the doorway. I had to ask, "What happened to me?"

Did I catch a whiff of liquor, a quick stiffener before he faced me again? "A better question would be—what happened to *me?*" Dr.

Opal shook some small yellow pills from a vial. "Why did I do what I just did?"

"That little boy in the picture," I said. "With the cowboy hat. It's me."

He returned the vial to his shirt pocket and took the pills without bothering to get a glass of water, popped them into his mouth and swallowed.

"Yes," he said, after a long silence. "It's you."

"Are you all right?" I asked.

"I'm terrific. Just wonderful. I just take pills for recreational purposes. And to make sure I don't have a cerebral hemmorhage."

"How long ago did it happen?"

It.

When he did not answer, I said, "How long have I been gone?"

"You collapsed," he said, haltingly, "outside the restaurant about nine months ago."

A digital clock on a bookshelf displayed the time, but I had trouble making sense of the numbers. *Nine months.* "I didn't know who else to turn to."

He reached for my hand, felt for my pulse. His touch was warm, his fingers gentle. There was the slightest hesitation, a suppressed shudder, as he felt my throat, searching for evidence of heartbeat there. He fumbled briefly in his desk drawer and found a penlight. He held his breath as he leaned close to me, shining the light in first one eye, and then the other. The light pained me, searching, probing, but I steeled myself until he was done.

He dropped the penlight into the drawer, and leaned against the desk. At last he said, his voice hoarse, "You have a pulse."

Of course I do, I wanted to tell him. How could I walk around without a pulse?

"Barely. Enough to keep you in a coma. Do you know what I was feeling down there," he said, "talking to those cops?"

I waited.

"When I was done making sure I wasn't going to hyperventilate, I was getting angry."

"Angry?"

"I thought for some mad reason you faked your death. I thought you decided to hide out somewhere, playing dead while we had a funeral, prayed over you, mourned. Richard, we grieved for you." He was angry now, full of feeling, tears in his eyes.

"You were the only person—"

"You did the right thing," he said. "Who else could you turn to but me. I understand. That's about all I *do* understand." He kept talking. It seemed to help him maintain his composure. "I was working late, expecting to be up most of the night working on an article on the thickening of the pericardium. The lining of the heart."

I knew what the pericardium was. "You had a party."

"A young doctor who rented an office in my building. He's starting up a practice in Seattle."

The artery in my leg was leaking. I held up my hand in an apologetic gesture, an indisposed house guest. The fluid on my hand glistened like water, but it had a strong chemical smell. It was flowing from my body, but it was not blood. The odor brought back memories—biology class dissecting bull frogs, my father using pinchers to fish the strangely elephantine lump of a human heart from a jar.

He shook his head. "You have a pulse, Richard, but that's all you have. I know what that liquid dripping onto the carpet is, and so do you." He didn't want to say, pausing like a man on the high dive platform, fidgeting, not wanting to take that final step. "It's formaldehyde. Embalming fluid. You seem to be breathing, but I can't believe any dynamic exchange of gasses is taking place."

"But I'm here, talking," I said.

Perhaps the pills he had taken, and the bourbon he had swallowed, were taking effect. I could feel some of the fear go out of him, leaving him rational, clear-headed but unnaturally calm. "Your pupils are fixed and dilated. Your skin displays a definite pallor. The blood vessels of your eyes show an absence of circulatory activity. I'm glad to be talking to you, Richard. I knew I had lost you. It was the death of a son." He did not have to add: *but this is not what I prayed for.*

I was thirsty, parched, dry inside. I couldn't see very well, my eyes filming, my eyelids slow to respond, each blink an effort. "Don't take me to the hospital."

He didn't seem to hear me. "There was an autopsy. The medical examiner had a stroke two months ago, but the findings were very clear. You bled to death."

"Connie has a good case against the restaurant. I have one, I mean. I walked right through that glass door. Let me stay here. I trust you." And I sent him the thought with my mind, begging him, from my soul to his. *Hide me.*

There was something about my plea that surprised me. It was not like me to make such a request, not so insistently. I should have placed myself in Dr. Opal's hands, and relied on his good judgment.

"You must be tired," said Dr. Opal at last, the solicitous host.

"Very. But I'm afraid to go to sleep."

He considered this.

"It looks like you're planting some fruit trees," I said. "Out in back."

"An orchard," he said. "Plums."

We both heard it, a new voice downstairs, a lovely female sing-song. "Dr. Sam?"

"Good Lord," said Dr. Opal. "It's Susan."

"Samuel?" sang the voice.

"Who is Susan?" I asked. Nobody had ever called him Samuel, except for his late wife.

"A friend. A good friend."

"You weren't staying up all night, not to finish an article. You expected her. You have—" I had to think of the right phrase, but my brain, my nervous system, was beginning to fail. "You have a woman friend."

He was pale. "I had a feeling Susan would come back."

"I don't want anyone to see me," I said.

20

He shut the door of the office, and told me to lock it from the inside. Locking the door became the focus of all the mental and physical effort I could muster. There was a click. I tested the door, and I was safe.

Safe, but much weaker, now. I was depleted, every object in the room drained of color, all of it turning into a black-and-white photograph.

"Did you hear that?" said Susan, somewhere downstairs.

"No one ate the macadamia nuts," said Dr. Opal.

"I thought I heard a door," she said.

"They ate all of your vegetable pâté," he said. "Look—there's nothing left but this smidgen."

"You don't have to sound so puzzled," she said with a laugh. "Didn't you like it?"

Perhaps I was a little miffed at Dr. Opal for being involved with such a bustling person. The late Mrs. Opal had been a quiet woman with a kind smile, someone who never did anything like cook or wash dishes. She had been regal and charming, and—it was a handicap that gave her special weight in my childish view— color blind. It would have been a shock to see her peeling a potato.

Now here was a potential new Mrs. Opal, downstairs hustling party remains into the dishwasher, speaking in a loud voice over the sound of running water. Her voice's carrying power made it easy for me to hear every word she said.

Everyone else in the East Bay seemed to be asleep by now, and here was this jovial temptress beguiling Dr. Opal with stories of how the poor dear she had driven home couldn't even put her house key in the right little slot. She had no idea a pineapple juice and something, vodka or rum, would do so much damage.

"Good thing you offered to drive," said Dr. Opal.

"You look so tired, Samuel," said Susan, her line of chatter pausing. "I'm sorry. I should be going home. Do you realize what time it is?"

"No, I'm glad you're here," said Dr. Opal. He meant: and I'll be glad to see you some other night, too. He was about to add that he could finish washing the cheese tray or whatever it was himself—I could feel his impatience.

But Dr. Opal's characteristic niceness was proving to be a handicap. "I told you I would take care of all the little chores," she said, and Dr. Opal must have given her some sign, weariness, dismay, some expression she misunderstood.

"And you're so exhausted," she said. Cupboards opened and shut. "I'm tired, too," she added, her words full of meaning.

Then I realized that Dr. Opal wanted this woman to stay. He enjoyed her company, and he did not want to be left alone in the house with me.

"Why don't you let me make you a hot toddy?" said Susan.

I couldn't hear Dr. Opal's reply.

"It's no trouble. Go on upstairs and go to bed. I'll bring it up in a minute."

Dr. Opal said he really had to be alone tonight to finish an article he was writing. It was a shame, he said. He would love one of her good lemon toddies.

"Some other time," said Susan, giving the words a forlorn twist.

"I hope so," said Dr. Opal said, with a fervor she could only partly understand.

The mirror insisted. It had the same leaden commanding quality a sign has, far from any human agency, police or security guards, to enforce it, *No Trespassing* or *No Smoking*, words so black and so peremptory that most people feel compelled to obey.

Come look the mirror said.

I felt the mirror's continuing pull. Surely I had been mistaken. Surely I could stand before that glass and *see*. The Latin *mirari* means to look at with wonder. The wonder of proving to myself that I was outrageously mistaken. Imagine my mistake, I would say, years from now.

Some say Narcissus sinned, falling in love with his own reflection. Others say the reflection sinned, hungering for its image in the twin mirrors of Narcissus' eyes. The invention that gave birth to our world was not the hearth or the wheel. It was the looking glass, like this rectangle, this window on the wall. I knew why Narcissus kept looking into his reflection in the quiet water of the stream.

Pounding.

He was outside the office, pounding, saying what people say when the knob won't turn. "Richard, let me in—are you all right?"

Had I fallen? Or had I lain myself down to sleep, without really wanting to. I don't need rest, I told myself. But what I meant was: I didn't want to lose consciousness.

A rattle, and a period of intense quiet. At last Dr. Opal was in the room, the lock picked. Or maybe there was a spare key somewhere, a bottom drawer, a shoe box full of keys and foreign coins. But each old key clearly labeled—his life was intelligently cluttered, not chaotic, everything in its place.

He bent over me. "She's gone," he was saying. "I practically had to drag her out of here. I thought she was going to move in this very night."

When I didn't answer he felt for my pulse.

"I'm going to go out for half an hour or so," he said. "I'm coming back. I don't want you to worry." His reassurance made me worry all the more. I knew he had mixed feelings about returning.

He saw the fear in my eyes. *Don't leave me.*

"I promise," he said, "I'll be right back."

Didn't he know anything? Didn't he know that a living person can make no such promise? Every sort of harm could happen to him out there, in the night streets. I tried to warn him, to ask him to stay here, but I felt absurdly wasted, withered and boneless, and I could make only a senile *ah*, the sort of noise proverbial doctors are always wanting you to make as they depress your tongue.

It even sounded as though I agreed. Uh-huh, yes, go. Instead I was trying to say *No*.

Fish are like this, pancaked on the bed of ice, eyes like the elevator buttons you push and feel the finger sink in and change begin to happen, levels descending, the floor rising. Fish have that tragic-comic gape, the comedy mask and the tragedy mask interbred to produce this, the never-closing expressionless gawp.

I couldn't move. When I was aware of anything, I could see the photos of my family, my father's hairless arms, the gray net over half my mother's face, like a mermaid who will escape the fisherman this time, but not for long.

It was hard for him to move me. He had been trying, panting, the carpet bunching up under me. Now that I was awake he was trying to encourage my cooperation. He gave up and unzipped a black leather bag.

"It took me a lot longer than I expected," he said.

I was against the wall in the next instant, sitting, trying to make sense of what was before me, the plastic bag of solid dark color, black, or near-black, an alloy of beet juice and mother earth.

Dr. Opal was wide-eyed. I tried to encourage him, to tell him to hurry, but instead I could only open my mouth in what must have been an unsettling smile.

A stainless-steel rack glinted in the light. Plastic tubing snaked in the light from the desk lamp, and my skin was numbed with alcohol. No, Doctor, I wanted to tell him. No need to worry about infection in my case.

A needle slipped into a vein in my arm. The substance flowed, the loops of plastic tubing turning red, pretty as a Valentine's Day streamer, the red defining its way downward.

Into my flesh, this scarlet skywriting, this course of port wine up my vein. I could see it happen, all the way along my forearm, a serpent that gave pleasure as it pierced—pleasure and pain as the collapsed tunnels and cavities of my body inflated, tingling. Until even the black-and-white photos on the wall were rich with hue.

"Thank you, Dr. Opal," I said, the pole wobbling, the plastic bag of blood swaying. *How did you know?* I wanted to ask. *How did you know exactly what I needed?*

My voice was strong. I could inhale deeply. My lungs were clear. I told him what to do next, and he followed my request, looking ashen, thin-lipped. When he was back in the room he carried a pan, something to do with stir-frying, I thought. A little nick in another plastic bag of blood and the fluid pattered musically, the notes growing more and more alto, until at last they were too low for human hearing, the bag empty, the final drops shaken out.

I lifted the pan with its wobbly burden. I put my lip over the edge of the pan, tilting it like a punch bowl, a partygoer dispensing with glass cups and ladles, tilting the entire fragrant brew and drinking. I drank it all.

When the pan was empty I set it down and slipped the needle from my vein. Dr. Opal was not quick enough to help me. A drop of blood glittered there, and then my body drew it in, the entire pearl disappearing into the tiny puncture.

I sensed the neighborhood around me, the lives.

He helped me into a spare bedroom, the one he saved for medical celebrities. "I painted the watercolor next to the closet," he said.

I let myself pretend to be weaker than I felt, while he showed me the amenities of this large guest bedroom, switching lights off and on, demonstrating the cord that opened the curtains, with all the brisk apathy of a bellhop. But I knew why he chose this room.

He shut the door and left me alone, only to return with a piece of furniture. I listened as he slid it along the carpet, a stout oak chair, one from the dining room, I guessed. He propped it under the doorknob outside. This room had a particularly strong door, a barrier designed to protect the rest of the house from the snores and love-moans of visiting guests.

The windows were double glazed, and had the gelatinous quality of bullet-proof glass. At some point in the past security precautions had been taken. A visiting Russian physicist could rest his sleepy head without the least apprehension. I was trapped.

It was a pleasant room—floral print drapes, a gray carpet. A slapdash, colorful watercolor decorated one side of the room, a sailboat in a sunset—or sunrise. With difficulty I managed to make out the signature, SO, like a mild challenge.

An Eisenstaedt portrait of Robert Frost commanded one wall, with that airless, preserved quality of certain photographs, the living moment turned to silver. Directly across from Frost hung a wood-framed, full-length mirror.

I could not help looking, once more. Perhaps, I told myself, this mirror will be different. Surely it would. All I had to do was take one more look.

I could see the entire room, if I shifted from angle to angle. But I could not see myself.

21

Was Dr. Opal on the telephone? Was he faxing word about me to people I did not know and could not trust? I crept to the door, but all I could hear was Dr. Opal's restless quiet, the slap of his slippers as he tossed them on the floor, the tinkle of liquor into a glass.

Dr. Opal stopped pacing his bedroom. He was listening. *Don't worry. It's nothing. Only the house settling. Or that neighbor's tom cat again, such a devilish creature.*

I turned the doorknob and pushed. The chair creaked, the joints straining. I visualized the chair, the glue, the legs, all of it fighting my weight. A chair leg snapped.

I was in the hall. Time was not fluid. It jumped, like a badly mended movie. One instant I stood on the stairs. And then I was outside, just beyond the sliding glass door.

Upstairs I could hear Dr. Opal wandering again, opening drawers and shutting them, unable to lie down and unable to sit still, taking reassurance by moving things from place to place. Springs whispered. I could almost see him, lying down, hands over his eyes, not sleeping so much as waiting for day.

I would go for a walk.

The sight of my own footsteps stirred something in me. I was here. I was real. On my way to the house, what seemed like hours ago, I had left footprints in the field.

Suddenly I was sprawled beneath a tree.

I rolled onto my back and gazed upward at the towering eucalyptus, scales of bark dangling from its branches. Bits of twigs and tangles of leaves rained after me, and gradually slackened, until a last leaf spun down and brushed my cheek.

I blinked, and my vision remained clear. I will get up, I told myself, and everything will make sense. I could breathe freely, and I filled my lungs and exhaled several times, the air cool and flavored with eucalyptus and wet earth. A wadded corn chips bag lay nearby.

I had the impression that I had just fallen, hard, from a great height. I couldn't recall in any detail the events leading up to this moment. *Don't think about it. Don't ask yourself how you got here.*

I listened hard to the noises of a less sedate, more work-worn part of town. I pulled myself to my feet. As I had walked to Dr. Opal's house my joints had creaked and strained, but now they were supple. I flexed the long tendons of my legs, stretched my arms. Each step crushed the bell-shaped eucalyptus seeds, and I groped my way through fallen twigs, down a slope, toward a creek. Flattened cardboard boxes had been used as sleds on the bare dirt, tearing paths in the weeds.

A drainpipe emptied into the creek, horsetail reeds growing around the steady trickle. The vague, reflected light off the clouds swam in the current at my feet. A metal shopping cart leaned in the current, bearded with scum.

Children murmured in their sleep. A car gleamed faintly in the creek bed, windows smashed, the doors missing. The seats were gone, the hulk abandoned, blistered with rust. I sat behind the steering wheel, my weight on the bare, crumbling springs. The chassis settled, groaning. This was where I could spend the rest of the night, I told myself, like a boy in his dad's car.

I had never felt so free of care. The weariness and the chill were gone from my body. The stream flowed into the car, eddying, and my feet splashed as I pretended to drive, stepping on the accelerator, a metal knob. To my surprise, when I turned the steering wheel the front end shifted, the bare wheel grinding on the stones.

I *was* a boy. I had that feeling I'd had when reading alone, finding an amusing passage, laughing out loud, and feeling the rightness, solitude blessed. I felt a thrill. I was a child again, but with a man's knowledge. I had mourned, I had worked hard, I had seen thirty-eight summers fade. And now this legacy was mine. I had the powerful feeling that, if I willed it, the car would lurch out of the creek bed, and hurtle through the air, wherever I willed it to go.

The flow of the creek was strong, parting around me as I left the car and waded upward, passing willows trees and mossy rocks. I dug my fingers into the bank and hauled myself up. I swung over a fence. A house ahead of me was pink halfway up, where the paint must have run out. The rest of the stucco was weathered and gray, iron grillwork over the windows. A clothesline dangled a few bone-white clothespins, and a bicycle frozen with corrosion lay abandoned behind an assembly of scrap wood, two-by-fours and warped plywood.

I treasured each detail, the two ancient tennis shoes left on the back step. On the other side of the fence, a dog put its snout to a knot hole, sniffed, and stole away into the dark, whining.

I passed through a gate and stood in the middle of a street, beside a manhole cover. There was a billboard ahead, huge, colorful, laughing people. I took a deep breath. The air tasted of mildewed porch sofas, dry rot in floorboards, new green, sour grass, rye. And dogs—there were dogs everywhere, unable to bark, nosing the air, skulking at their chains.

A bird woke and scratched for a firmer grip on its perch in an eave. All of it asleep, but a sleep so restless, so close to waking. I could hear the whispered questions, men and women talking in their sleep, a jet aircraft far above, the freight of so many lives. All of it so rich to me that I could name each man, each woman, know the nightmare as it stirred, and stretch a hand to still it. I hushed the unseen children, the infants around me. Could I really do this? Calm the psychic seas for many city blocks around me, with a raised hand, without a word. With a thought?

There was bass-note snap under my feet, in the earth. Creatures stirred at my passing, gophers beneath all of this, the ivy, the early spring blackberries, living barbed wire.

People. I wanted to see people, to hear them talk, to show myself to them. I knew it was reckless, but I couldn't keep myself from brimming over with the news.

Besides, I wanted to know the answer to a few riddles, just one or two, like a man needing a dictionary even as he speaks, with delightful fluency, a new and very foreign tongue.

In what seemed like a matter of moments I was in another part of town, among expensive houses again, sports cars in driveways under tight-fitting canvas covers.

Sensations, not thoughts. I laughed, my head thrown back. I could sense people around me awaken at the sound. Traffic grumbled down in the flat of the city. Perhaps there was more freeway noise than there had been earlier. There was so much restlessness, activity mistaken for power.

How many hours had I wasted, sitting in the law library, driving alone across the Bay Bridge? I had not enjoyed the fellowship of people nearly as much as I could now. I saw how important it was, that warm country, friendship. I had wasted so much time!

I had overlooked so much during my years as a waking, working human being. If a garden hose is left long enough on the grass, it leaves a yellow shadow, a photograph of itself. The newspaper tossed on the crabgrass, the empty, scummy wading pool among the succulents—they all leave an image of themselves when we move them at last, a place where the sun has failed.

I let myself into Steve Fayette's front garden, the black iron gate closing quietly. The house had a porch light styled after an antique lantern, and a big red front door. I turned the doorknob, pushed, and the chain broke.

I remembered where he kept the key to his burglar alarm, under the asparagus fern. I had thirty seconds before the police were automatically alerted. I turned off the blinking red light. Steve had been pensive about his money, not always sure what to do with it. A gigantic television screen graced one wall, and a telescope, the lens carefully capped, aimed at a corner of the ceiling. Everything was custom designed, the fat leather furniture, the huge glass coffee table.

A sculpture hulked like a meteorite beside one of the bookshelves. Few books occupied the space. Instead there were photographs, graduation pictures, wedding portraits, nieces and nephews. And a photo of Steve beside one of his race horses, the thoroughbred turning one dark eye toward the camera.

A bowl of fruit was star of the show on the big, shiny dining room table, bananas still green at the tips, a decorator's idea of how fruit should look, crown jewels. The house was earthquakeproof, according to the designer, and that meant that the floors were thin, and trembled with the slam of a door, expensive paintings hanging crooked on the walls.

I slipped into the master bedroom, and I was not surprised to see her there, my wife—my widow. So this was the next chapter in her life.

I understood. Steve was pleasant company, and nothing solves cash-flow problems quite like cash. Steve did not look healthy in his sleep, shadows in his cheeks, his jaw slack. But Connie slept with an ironically virginal air. She looked not quite innocent, but vacant.

To look at them like this was pleasure. Poised over them, I was capable of the common misdemeanors of an ordinary man, burglary, voyeurism. But this was all I wanted, I told myself. Just a look, just a sip of their presence.

And then I stopped myself. I wanted to be a secret, it was true, but didn't I want something more? What was I, a salesman, pressing a pamphlet under the doormat? And not even a calling card—I would leave soon and they would never know I'd been here. I wanted them to know. I wanted them to ask each other if they had heard something in the night.

I had never noticed it before, how the pulse thrums in the tissues of the neck. And in the blue veins of the temple, and in the sheath of bone and fibers, the wrist. If the blood Dr. Opal had given me, lifeless, refrigerated broth, had given me such vigor, imagine, I thought. Imagine what *this* could do, this oxygen that was even now nourishing the dreams, supplying memory with its color.

I heard something.

It was a sound that chilled me. A sound that Connie heard, too, throwing her arm out and lifting her head from a pillow, only to let it fall back. She said something, a sleepy, non-word. It was in answer to this metallic, wheedling noise outside, beyond the walls. This agonized, insistent declamation, full-stereo, now, everywhere.

Birds. That's all it was. Finches, sparrows, robins, juncos, to-whees—ordinary birds. That was all.

I was out of the house. I could not run in a straight line. I staggered. I was weak again. Dr. Opal's house was not far away, not far at all. But where?

It was going to be too far for me, as the coast is too far for that passenger who cannot swim when he struggles, the luxury liner so many pinholes of light.

I was running like the last, bedraggled participant in a marathon, a man so late the spectators and the judges have long since gone, nothing remaining but the route, the route that is always there, whether the race is run or not, the sidewalk with a yellow plastic tricycle left out overnight, the glowing blush of a windshield in the coming dawn.

22

I fell into a field, clods and furrows. An armored beast, many-legged and encased in a segmented shell, tumbled onto my thumb as my fingers dug into the earth. It worried at the knuckle before it, uncuriously wondering if it should continue its march.

Thoughtless, it was living enough to roll into a ball as I nudged it gently with my other hand. I pulled myself to my feet, one foot dragging. I flailed my way ahead, hating my body, a stunt-clown, corporeal joke.

At the last moment I tripped on a hoop of wire on the lawn. I tumbled, and rolled onto my back. I would get up soon. Very soon. As soon as I could move again.

A face. It was the face of a referee, peering down, inquisitive, urgent, even a little annoyed.

"Richard—where did you go?"

I tried to tell him to get me out of the sunlight, and all I could do was hang on to him, dragging at his bathrobe, that luxurious robe, a gift, I was sure, from Susan. Susan, who must have admired these pajamas. *Oh, wear the nice shiny blue ones, Samuel.* Or perhaps the pajamas, too, were a gift. I had slept through a Christmas, and a New Year's Day. And who knows what wars and what discoveries, strikes, political pronouncements, distant coups, civil wars.

"Richard, where were you?"

"Help me," I heard myself croak.

I was desperate in my idiocy, a man rising at life's banquet needing the Heimlich maneuver, demanding CPR, no one understanding.

So if this is how I die again, I thought, I will have this absurd last moment, one foot stuck though the loop of a croquet game, and the other digging spasmodically, excavating a divot.

Until I climbed to my feet again. With Dr. Opal kneeling on the lawn calling after me, I ran toward the house, hard, straight for the wall, the solid stone and mortar. But I knew where I was going. I saw the pane of glass behind the pruned stalks of poinsettia.

I dived through a window. I scrambled down inside the cellar, into the odor of damp and mildew aged to a kind of soil. The hot water heater, the shiny Sherman tank of the furnace, all of it in darkness. I tore at the old asphalt tiles, pea green floor covering, the ancient tar brittle, the flooring peeling away.

I dug with my hands, a diver desperate for air. But I was not climbing upward. What I wanted was not oxygen.

It was this hiding place, among the roots of the foundation, among the gravel and the dirt, and deeper, as far as I could go.

23

An engine puttered somewhere at the edge of the world. People spoke, their voices strained by the stone and clay. It was all so far away, and I was so deeply asleep. Iron drilled the earth. Roots were thrust into place, tamped down with boots. What we mean when we say we had a dream is: something real that didn't happen. If this was a dream, then it was one that had a life of its own. When I half-woke it continued, an interruption of the silence.

I tried to roll over, to cry out, and I was made of dirt.

The water heater whispered, a ring of blue flame illuminating the cellar. I was standing unsteadily. I didn't go anywhere, looking down at my shoes, dark, dress oxfords.

How many times had I hiked a hill, and found a hole, dirt flung wide, and wondered what creature had excavated such a hiding place, and how it knew, in the busy hive of its genes, how to mine such a sanctuary.

A phone rang. I put my hands to my ears. I was in a hallway, in a familiar house.

When I put one hand out to support myself I left a dirty hand-print. Someone answered the phone. It was Dr. Opal's voice. I could not make out the words. I was leaving footprints, faint, dark tracks across the brightly lit kitchen, into a room lined with book-shelves.

Dr. Opal's library was crowded with volumes, hundreds of books. I bumped into a dictionary stand and the thing fell over, the un-abridged dictionary landing heavily.

"Let me call you back," said Dr. Opal, somewhere in another part of the house.

I righted the lectern, and put the book back where it belonged, having a little trouble with it, the book falling open, almost too heavy for me. Beyond the curtained windows it was evening.

"I was worried," said Dr. Opal from the doorway. "I spent the whole day convinced that you'd never wake again."

I wondered if this was something Dr. Opal wished for, in one corner of his mind. I found a box of tissues and tugged until one tore free from the box. It startled me, the way another sheet sprang halfway from the slot, like an eager thing. I blew my nose, and was troubled by what I saw in the tissue.

He asked, "How are you feeling?"

This was not simple social courtesy. The question had profound medical implications. I dropped into a leather chair, a soft trap I would have trouble escaping. Dr. Opal turned on a lamp beside me, lifted one of my eyelids. I stuck my tongue out as a dim joke, the eager, cooperative patient. But he examined my tongue briefly, smelling of liquor and looking defeated.

"I want to know how this happened," he said.

Yes, I thought—so would I.

One of his shirt cuffs was unbuttoned, and it flapped as he ran his hand over his hair. "Don't you wonder how you happen to be here?"

He seemed to want me to say something. I did not feel quite able to respond.

He took a swallow from a brandy snifter. "Where did you go last night?"

It was time to talk again. I coughed, took a breath, gave it a try. "I went for a walk," I said. I sounded pretty good, a man needing that first cup of coffee.

He sat down across from me, sinking into an overstuffed chair of his own, the leather old and wrinkled, flakes of it peeling at the seams. "Where did you go?"

"Not far." I didn't like lying to him. "How far do you think I could go, in my condition?"

He gave a skeptical smile. "I have some . . . sustenance for you. I think you need it."

"I can wait." My voice sounded flat, my tone too even, the voice of a man weary or depressed to the core.

"I'm surprised you aren't asking more questions. Of course, that was always my own personal game. I saw life as a list of questions in one column, followed by spaces in which we are supposed to pencil in the answers. You must be curious. You must want to know the etiology of this—"

The legal phrase was *proximate cause*. "I never knew you drank heavily," I said.

"I don't." He lifted his hand, the sleeve flowing around his gesture: usually.

"I know this is a terrible strain. And an interruption."

As though I had just given him permission he drained the rest of his brandy. "I have a series of lectures starting this week at Stanford. 'The Function of Intuition in Diagnosis.' I cancelled my first lecture. I said I had the flu."

"Please don't do that sort of thing. Come and go as you normally would."

"You are already in the news," he said.

I gave him a questioning glance.

"There was a tiny little article among the washing machine ads. Something about vandalism in Fairmount Cemetery. One or two markers defaced, and a body possibly stolen. Possibly. They are investigating. The article makes it sound like a juvenile prank. Doesn't mention you by name."

"So much else happens in the world."

"Exactly."

"I want you to find the location of something important," I said. "Will you be able to remember what I'm telling you?"

"You don't suppose I have practiced medicine for so many years without developing a certain talent?"

"You've had quite a bit to drink. You really ought to take care of yourself."

"I feel pretty good, but entirely too sober."

"I want you to find a mirror."

"I have mirrors, Richard. Although to be honest, I am a little surprised you would find them useful."

"Do you remember that cut in my finger?"

"I remember."

I examined what remained of it, a fine line in my finger, like the mouth of a lizard. "I want you to find the location of the mirror that arrived the day before my accident at the restaurant." I could see him weighing the word. *Accident.* The unexplainable—birth defects, plane crashes, my presence there in his study.

"Connie knows where it is," I said. "Ask her."

"You think she'll tell me, without wondering?"

"Tell her you want to buy it."

"Maybe she's forgotten about it," he said. "Months have gone by—"

"She doesn't forget that sort of thing. Also, I want to know what is happening in the investigation. Rebecca's murder."

"Actually, I think I've heard about the investigation recently. The police haven't forgotten about it, far from it. Rebecca Pennant, wasn't that her name?"

I must have nodded.

"She was one of those people who matter to a community, especially when they are gone. There was a scholarship set up in her name by her parents."

My memories of Rebecca kept me silent.

"What else do you need?" he asked gently.

I needed more than I could say, and we both knew it. "Clothes."

"Of course."

"George Good's on Bancroft Avenue carries my size, jacket size forty-three; my waist is thirty-four, inseam thirty."

"Very good, sir," said Dr. Opal, doing a very decent English valet, Jeeves on too many tranquilizers.

"I think I owe you something," I said. "For all your help."

"You don't owe me anything."

"I feel deeply indebted to you."

"You would do the same for me. If I—"

"Somehow it's hard to imagine you . . . doing what I did. Coming back."

He gave a short laugh. He was coherent, but much more intoxicated than I had thought. "You think I lack the persistence."

"No, it seems characteristic of me, somehow. The kind of thing that was always going to happen."

I meant this as little more than an unfunny joke, but Dr. Opal looked thoughtful. He said, "You have a theory."

"Theory is too elaborate a word. I want to understand what happened."

"So do I. And you think it had to do with the mirror?"

"I'd rather not speculate," I said.

"Secrets within secrets." He smiled sadly. "Do you know who really grieved for you, Richard? Connie was very badly shaken, of course. We all were. But the woman I thought would have to be sedated was the attorney, the pretty one—"

"Stella Cameron."

"She was stricken."

"I need a good attorney. We have a lawsuit against the mortuary. We have a suit against the restaurant. And I want to know what happened to my estate."

"You left a will?"

"I never got around to writing a will. Committing one to paper, I mean."

Dr. Opal cocked his head. "You should have seen a lawyer."

"I want to know if Connie is going to sell the house. She has her sights on better places. And we had some investments. Not as many as people might think. Connie's porfolio was all in Polynesian war clubs, and I tended to have clients who weren't exactly rich."

"What bothers me, Richard. . . ." He paused. "Is that you're envisioning returning to a normal life."

"If the Farmer's Life Insurance policy paid off I suppose I owe them a lot of money. Or Connie does. That brings me to the subject of divorce. I owe Connie at least some sort of reasonable settlement."

"Richard, I think you misunderstand your situation."

"I'm just reviewing some areas of concern."

"I don't think it's going to be that easy," said Dr. Opal.

"I'm alive."

"You are plausibly alive, yes. As a legal entity you may be more alive than you are from a medical standpoint. On the other hand, there was a death certificate issued."

"I have legal rights, Dr. Opal. You'll certify that I'm alive, and then the death certificate will be rescinded—"

He was shaking his head. "And you want to stay secret. One word of this. To anyone. Anybody at all. We'll have television helicopters overhead, crashing into each other, in less than five minutes."

"I shouldn't have put so much pressure on you."

"You know what you owe me? Fairness. Honesty. To me, and to yourself. You won't be able to sell a house, you won't be able to open a bank account, you won't be able to get a library card." He lifted a hand. "Well, maybe a library card. But you get my point."

I did get his point, but I didn't like it. He was right, of course, and I had known this instinctively. But I didn't want to accept what he was saying just now.

"I was there," he said. "I helped pick out the casket. I helped Connie pick out that tie. Connie insisted on a new suit, don't ask me why. I planned the service with Connie. We included that passage I thought you always liked, the poem by George Herbert. I got up and I had to read it. I don't know how I managed without breaking down. It was that kind of memorial service, people sharing what they remembered about you—"

"Thank you for being such a help," I said.

I thought for a moment he was going to break into some powerful emotion, anger or sorrow.

"You're thinking of getting married," I said.

"Susan's a lovely woman."

"You're very lucky."

I parted my damp, three-button jacket, summer-weight wool. It was not a bad choice. What sort of conversation had passed between them? *No, not the pinstripe, not navy blue. Too bad he doesn't have a nice, dead black three-piece.*

"Please don't go anywhere tonight," he said. "I have all those cartoons you used to like, Road Runner, and Bluto getting beat up. They're up in the game room."

I couldn't help feeling pity for Dr. Opal. He actually thought I could spend the night watching classic cartoons. I couldn't keep the affection from my voice. "Maybe I'll take a look at them."

"Rest awhile. That's the best thing a doctor can tell a patient."

I waited until he was asleep, and covered him with a blanket, tucking it carefully around him.

Then I opened the sliding glass door and gazed at the field. It was not a flat plain of clods, anymore. The young orchard was in place, rows of trees. A small tractor was parked near the lawn. The sounds I had heard during the day, the voices, the sound of the iron drill—this was the result.

From far away, beyond the garden, down the street somewhere, there were voices, laughter—people.

I left to join them.

24

My body was dry inside, my organs working against each other, dust against dust. I folded myself into a crouch beside a barbecue, old ash in a brick fireplace.

On the other side of the wall were the sounds of laughter, a woman's voice. It was not a laugh of mirth as much as a social sound, flirtatious. A glass chimed, champagne. It was good wine, judging from the fine fizz of the bubbles.

I was over the wall effortlessly, with a thought. Beyond the lawn a house was brightly lit. The windows threw light on the stepping-stones. A man in a dark suit was putting out glasses, dozens of them. Someone carried an ice bucket. A woman was bent over a table, arranging napkins, and as I looked on there were sounds of voices lifted in greeting, people arriving.

I watched for what might have been a long while, too rapt to attempt much, fascinated by the theater beyond the dark. People were gathering. People were accepting drinks. People were eating little finger-sized sandwiches. I felt like a child at the head of a stairway, looking down at a party and thinking: the adult world.

I could not resist the desire to enter the party. More people had arrived, and I wanted to be among them. I belonged there, among the attractive women, their necks and jewelry and slender wrists.

There were sordid implications in what I was experiencing, but I did not allow myself to consider them. I persisted in the fantasy, clear as a scripted scenario in my hands, that I could walk into the party, introduce myself, and be welcomed, a man with a really interesting story to tell.

I strolled over to the potted daphnes. They were flowering, the perfume of the tiny lavender-white trumpets so strong it was almost unpleasant. I felt loose-limbed and ready for whatever might happen.

I did not have to wait long. A woman detached herself from the growing crowd, stepped to the sliding door, and, finding it slightly open, did not have to do more than slip out. She found her way across the stepping-stones.

She was sporting narrow heels, and her step was mincing as she made her way out of the glare of the electric lights and opened her handbag. The clasp released, and she selected a cigarette with care, as though each one was significantly different from the others. When the cigarette was between her lips, she snapped a lighter and took a moment to touch the tip to the flame.

She wore a black dress with black lace sleeves, her satin handbag glittering, accented with what I took to be rhinestones. I fit into a shadow cast by a wall, and then quietly matched the shape of a shadow thrown by a giant urn, a red clay container of earth. I moved on, fitting almost exactly within the shadow of a birch tree, the spindly twigs still bare.

"Aren't you cold out here?" said a voice. A male figure tiptoed around a snail on one of the stepping-stones.

"It's nice," she said.

"They ought to put some kind of poison out," he said.

She didn't understand, or care.

"Doesn't it sort of drive you crazy to step on them?"

A show of indifference.

He said, "What really disgusts me is that pause before the crunch," he said.

She smoked.

He said, "You're just pissed off."

She dropped her cigarette, squashing it.

"It's a chance of a lifetime," he said. "So I commute. We'll be okay."

Her act of extinguishing the largely unconsumed cigarette had meant something, but he did not seem to notice.

"Or maybe we won't be," she said.

He shrugged. Like many people, he liked to maneuver in the small harbor of limited emotions. If love was difficult, he would survive without it. "Maybe we won't."

I had the almost pleasurable sensation, as I watched these two strangers, of feeling that I knew them, that what they said was known to me before they said it, that I could read their feelings.

She was not as hurt as she pretended to be. They were new to each other, still demonstrating how free they were to leave each other behind. I wanted to tell them to seize each other, forget everything, and find a place here on the soft grass and make love, now, without another word. But they insisted on talking.

Now the glass door was open and other partygoers wandered outside. One of the men pointed to a place in the garden and said that he was thinking of a new room, a new wing, maybe enclosing the garden with dwelling space, a villa in the Roman style. The party was a housewarming, I gathered, the new owners expansive in their enjoyment of their new home.

The couple strolled further into the garden, near the birch trees. He spoke about a salary, about how good the benefits were, and she responded with a feigned boredom, all of it like a rehearsal not going at all well, the wrong actors, the wrong lines.

They walked a little farther, beyond easy view of the other celebrants, but it was not lust that kept them there. They were talking about where they would eat when they left. They were talking about wine lists. They were talking about a restaurant that had closed, how much better it was than any of the remaining places to eat. They could talk about anything, and they kept to this tired, shallow subject, what to do next.

I enjoyed it, though. It was as though these two prime creatures were deliberately feigning stupidity, each mocking the other with more and more vapid remarks, waiting for a laugh so they could both break down and take each other in their arms, and admit it was all a joke—no one could stand here on a night like this and talk about which restaurant had the best chocolate truffles.

I laughed.

They stopped talking. The man looked my way, scratching his cheek. The young woman lifted one foot to adjust her shoe, working her finger under a patent leather strap. The sound of my laugh had disturbed her. She looked around, straightening her lace sleeves.

"Champagne gives me an instant headache," the young woman said, still looking in my direction. I felt a thrill—she could see me, but didn't realize what she was looking at. "I think it's the carbon dioxide," the young woman was saying. "Or the sugar. I get so pissed off that people just expect you to stand around and get a migraine. They all know that I can't drink."

The other party guests had paused, glanced absently in this direction, but they were turning now to examine the arthritic knobs of rose bushes, the new red leaves sprouting from the stumps.

"Go in and get me some Diet Pepsi," she said. But at the same time I could sense her shadow-thought. *Don't leave me alone.*

"We don't have to hang around," he said. "I'll just tell them we have to go."

"Don't put any ice in it," she said. "Or better yet, see if they have any coffee."

They didn't see what was happening as I left my place, and skimmed the grass, quickly, silently. But she heard something, putting out her hand to one of the trees.

"Or aspirin," she said. "That would be heaven."

The man made his way back toward the light, and stopped at a stepping-stone. He very deliberately put his weight on one foot, flattening a snail.

The young woman turned back toward the house, looking toward the playhouse of colored lights, the sound of laughter. She didn't want to stay here, so far from all of that. But she waited anyway, wanting him to get her what she needed from the house. She was a tapestry, hours of watching television, days of boredom, mistaking it for life, school, cars, her first sex in a hotel room with CNN on, statesmen, mouths talking. She reached for the remote with one hand while a climax pulled itself closer and closer.

Surely this was not what I wanted. I was stepping very slowly toward her, drawing near. Until I was there with her, beside her.

But I did not touch her. The actual scent of her body was disguised with counter-smells, crushed flower petals, alcohol. The tobacco smell surrounded her, slow to dissipate. Standing so close to her I was enveloped in an aura of smells, and, I saw, an actual aura, colors, the heat of her. She lived by getting people to do things for her. She ruled by suffering. Petulant, quick, she changed homes, and controlled men, by finding a new source of minor pain.

But it was real, this anguish. She did not know how to take pleasure in a night like this. She was restless, demanding a plan, a schedule of events. She was smarter than most people, and thought she deserved to be somewhere better. She rubbed her arms with her hands.

Shhhh.

Just that, a non-word. *Hush. Be still.*

I was the one who made this sound, I was the one who knew so much. She turned and saw me.

"Who is it?" she asked, as though she almost recognized me, almost knew who I was.

"Come away," I whispered.

How did I know exactly the words that would draw her after me? I had her by the hand, pulling her back into the mossy area near the wall, dark green.

"Wait," she said. Not waiting, following. I knew how I must look to her.

A garden hose had been wound tightly and tucked away behind a stand of papyrus. The tall, pom-pom head stalks nodded, stirring, and one of her feet caught one of the outer loops of the hose. The hose sprang free, without a sound, the head of the hose a brass pistol-like device that fell outward, shifting across the lawn as the hose unwound, releasing all the tension the gardener had wound into it, forcing it into a spiral.

Her eyes made me hesitate. There was an inner argument, a part of me telling myself that this was an outrage.

It gushed as fast as I could swallow, and I closed my eyes. Her breath caught. She was choking, and I stroked her with one hand, soothing her, and I could feel her breath grow steady again, a long, slow exhalation, a long, peaceful intake of air as I lowered her to the ground. Her arms fell to either side, and her scarlet nail polish grew steadily blacker against the pallor of her skin.

When I was finished, I gazed up at the gallery of lights, each smiling face a source of illumination. One man broke away from the group, saying he would be right back. He carried a cup and saucer, and approached us, calling her name.

25

As I drew closer to the party I entered the light that fell from the windows. I had never felt so sure I knew so many people. It was like one of those dreams, a homecoming, grandparents and uncles, a longed-for Thanksgiving.

I was a sailor home from a war, a man after years of wandering. I had been away too long. This place belonged to me, this house, these people. I was dazzled by an insight I knew was an illusion, like a man boosted by cocaine into a clarity and optimism he had never experienced before.

I looked down at my clothes, my hands, and I was amazed at the transformation. The patina of mildew on my jacket sleeves, that foxing on my skin, was gone. I knew the danger, but I could not stay away a moment longer.

I entered the house.

They'll know at once, I warned myself. It will only take one look.

As I passed people they fell silent, and turned my way. People followed me with their eyes. This was the worst place I could be. This was madness. But I could not separate myself from all these human beings. I wanted to be close to this crowd of faces, feel the heat of their bodies. Surely someone would recognize me. Surely one of them would turn out to be a landlord or a county supervisor, someone I had dismantled in court. Surely someone will look at me and know where I had been for so many months.

"I'm so glad you could come," said a voice.

He took my hand. He was a tall man who had lost weight recently, the flesh on him loose, his smile bright but something unsteady in him. He wore a suit that was new, and tailored, I guessed, to fit his new, gaunt frame. I knew what he had been through. I could see it in his eyes, breathe it, his memories suddenly my own, the severed ribs, the weakness, the welcome visits of friends to his hospital bed.

"How could I possibly stay away?" I heard myself ask.

"You look terrific," said my host, shaking my hand, not wanting to release me.

"I have a cut," I said. "I hope I didn't get blood on your new suit."

The cut in my finger was bleeding, slightly, and he looked at it with the wonder of a worshiper touching the tears of a marble statue.

"No problem," he said with a laugh. My touch, perhaps even something about that tiny kiss of blood on his wrist, seemed to give him strength. "No problem at all. I'm really embarrassed. I know we've met, but I can't place you."

"I just had to drop by," I said.

"I'm so glad you did," he said. He leaned into me, one hand on my shoulder. "You know, I wasn't sure I should even have a party."

"They can be a strain, meeting so many wonderful people at once."

"Well, it wasn't just that. So soon after my operation, I wasn't sure I was up to it."

"Your heart."

"Do you know how many people are walking around with pig valves? But when it happens to you, well, I keep thinking I shouldn't be alive." He held a nearly full glass of sparkling wine, but it was not alcohol that brought out this desire to confide. It was something about me.

"It's a miracle," my host was saying. "But you know there's a dark side to it." He paused, perhaps surprised at his sudden desire to be frank, to hunt for words to describe feelings he would ordinarily never admit. "There is a problem with depression after an operation like that."

"It's more of a struggle than people realize," I said.

He squeezed my shoulder, delighted to find someone who understood him. "Something's been altered inside," he said, taking his large hand away from my shoulder and placing his fist over the place where his heart was beating, that other fist, inside, kneading life. "And your body knows it."

"Of course it does," I said, dazzled by the power I had over this man.

"You know, I really am surprised that you could make it—" This was the place in the conversation when I would supply my name, or give him some idea where we had met.

The young man from outside joined us. He was breathing hard. "I can't find Maura."

"Forget Maura," said the host with a cheerful dismissiveness.

"I got her some Excedrin," said the young man. He held them in his hand, two white pills. "And some coffee."

"She probably went out to look at the stars," said our host. "You can see them if you get far enough away from the houses, away from all this light."

"I can't see Maura actually going out to look at the stars," said the young man.

"I wouldn't worry," I said.

The young man toyed with the pills in the palm of his hand, slightly annoyed by them, as though they might dissolve. He slipped them into his pocket, meeting my eyes. He smiled cautiously. "I'm anxious about everything. I haven't been able to sleep very well. I'm starting a new job." Then his eyes narrowed, as though he recognized me. Or as though he mistrusted something about me, something about my appearance, my voice.

"I'm surprised she could stand to leave such a wonderful gathering," I said.

Relax. Everything is fine. Like a county-fair charlatan, a stage hypnotist, I worked at his doubt, steaming it away. He was more vigorous physically, and less clouded by inner fears than my convalescent host. He gave me a slight frown, and I could see him wondering at what he saw, like a man looking at a wax dummy, or a work of art that wasn't quite right.

Then he gave the smile of a sufferer when the painkiller takes effect. "She likes being unhappy."

"She wants too much," I said.

"I want to introduce you to each other, and here I am—" My host was making an effort to catch my name once again. *Both of you will stay happy. You will not worry, and you will not wonder who I am.*

The young man turned to the host. "We should all play some sort of game. Or—do something instead of stand around like this. Look at all of us. You'd think we were all—sick. Or old. People just stand around drinking and what we should be doing is—" But I could sense his vocabulary, and his range of ideas, falter. Raised on television, maintained by financial reports and computer screens, he could not describe the sort of Saturnalia his spirit required.

I left them. I moved through the room like a politician working a crowd, a successful leader, a statesman, one people have been longing to meet.

"There comes a time," a man was saying.

"But the poor thing," said the woman.

I joined the man and woman, standing over a cat half asleep on the apron of the fireplace. The white cat was emaciated, the fur around its mouth dirty. The cat stirred, purring at my touch. I could feel her ribs, the sharp point of her haunch.

I let the cat nose my cut, and lick the blood, the teasing rasp of her tongue delightful on my finger.

"You want nature to take its course," said the man. "You don't want to have to put an animal to sleep."

"It's such a euphemism," said the woman. "Such a way of not saying what it really is."

"I suppose you could call it putting her down," said her companion. "Or destroying her."

I sensed that it was my presence that made them glow and kept their conversation circling around the subject of mortality. "What do you think?" said the woman, clinging to me, hanging on to me, giving me a look I could not mistake.

"Isn't it a kind of sleep, after all?" I said.

"Yes, of course it is," said the woman.

Just then there was a cry from out in the darkness, out beyond the edge of the property, beyond the place where any of the party-goers had any business wandering. A cry. And not a cry of delight. And not of pain, either. It was a phrase, repeated.

Someone had found one of Maura's shoes. There was laughter, out by the mossy reaches of the garden. And another shoe. Someone was calling, "I bet she's running around naked out there." The party was flowing outside, now, into the garden, despite the chilly evening. Who could stay indoors on a night like this?

"Need some help?"

I ignored the querying voice. I held a car key in my hand. The streetlight shined off the row of cars. The emblem on the key ring was hard for me to make out, but I reassured myself that it was just a matter of trying a few locks.

"Sir, can I help you?" The parking attendant, rented for the occasion, wore a blue jacket with the parking company's logo on the pocket. Something about my manner bothered him. I was not hurrying to a car for cigarettes, and I wasn't getting into a car and driving away.

This was one of those pricey, hilly neighborhoods. Cars were parked everywhere, barely leaving room between them for the car that might want to leave. A pinecone lay in the middle of the street. I used to pretend these were hand grenades as a boy. I stooped, bounced the pinecone in my hand once or twice, and then threw it hard, high into the air.

He sounded apologetic now. "Sir, let me get your car."

I never heard the pinecone hit the ground. Something brushed my pantleg, stroking my ankle. It was the white cat.

The same white cat that had been so emaciated was beautiful, sleek and purring. Wanting to lean against me, wanting to close her eyes and possess me, in that affectionate claim of ownership cats make, insisting that she had found what she wanted, and would keep it. One taste of my blood. Just one taste.

I could imagine what Rebecca would say about all this. *What do you think you're doing, Richard?* I found a car door that the key fit, and opened it.

How long will it be before they find her body?

I had a memory that didn't make perfect sense—the young woman flung high into the sky, cartwheeling, into the trees. I couldn't do that, I told myself with a laugh.

It was impossible.

And what, Rebecca would ask, are you doing now?

26

The steering wheel was very slightly smudged with finger oils. The vinyl seat covering sighed and squeaked under my weight. The glove compartment was crammed with maps of L.A., the Southwest, and assorted gas station receipts. The seat was just about the right distance from the steering wheel, but I made a minor adjustment to convince myself that I knew how to do this.

It took me a long moment to find the ignition. The engine caught, and failed, and caught again. Even then I felt the awkwardness, gear into neutral, parking brake sticking. I fumbled at the dash until the headlights blazed, too bright. I gripped the gear shift. The engine made a chorus of low, vibrant sounds. Some mechanism in the car released. The car charged forward. My feet fumbled. I stood on the brake.

There was a small shelf in the dash, a plastic packet of facial tissues and an oversized plastic paper clip around neatly folded currency. A pair of sunglasses peeked from a flap in the sunvisor. I had an instant of insight into the owner of the car, his name on a parking place. He wanted a boat, a new house, children. He liked to drive. He was good at numbers, hated cats, a natural second-in-command. I had taken the keys from someone at the party, not even deceiving him. He watched me do it, and I told him not to worry, I'd be back in a minute.

I squeezed past the parked cars, clipping a fender on the right, a bumper on the left. I swung from one side of the street to the other. I overcorrected, steered too hard, scraped another parked car, chrome squealing.

Something broke off a sports car and fell, glittering in the rearview. I picked up a little speed. A mailbox sprang up ahead of me, and I careened over it, the post snapping and scraping the bottom of the car. I was grinding across someone's front garden, a bed of daisies ahead.

They floundered, a small hill of flowers going under, the car rocking gently. Weeds leaped ahead of me, green oats, foxtails. I steered down a vacant lot, plowing through the tall grass of a hillside. I felt a sense of dislocation rather than panic. The vehicle rocked, suspended. The car teetered off an embankment, a small avalanche cascading.

The four wheels landed heavily. The car swung, and came to a stop. Gently, the car began to roll forward again. I steered the car down the correct side of the street, a boy taking a driving test and failing it. This was an orchestration of heavy steel, and the tires turned with a dozen concurrent whispers over the reflectors on the roadway and the fine, random spots of oil.

I should be perspiring, I thought, that cold, novice-driver's sweat. But I wasn't. The palms of my hands were dry, my heartbeat steady. I didn't feel anything like normal anxiety.

But I wasn't exactly pleased. The freeway was a mistake. As soon as I took the onramp I wanted to slam on the brakes. Lights flared everywhere, and the car made insane noises. Every car was a box and in the box was a human head, or maybe two, faces staring straight ahead, lips moving.

The toll plaza. The Bay Bridge. I tried to remember what to do next, but the car would not obey. Someone leaned on their horn, a brassy noise that made me cringe. I killed the engine, and restarted laboriously. I slipped a bill from the money clip.

A toll taker's hand accepted it, a new bill, barely creased, but already scented with finger oils. I did not make contact with his hand, but I could sense it, calloused, hot. I didn't know if he would offer me change. I left the toll gate before I could find out.

The bridge traffic was aglow, brake lights seeming to pull me unward, entranced. I still had trouble reading words. The markings on the green-and-white traffic signs looked only vaguely like language, and the words on the various dashboard instruments, which I knew told me how to turn on the heater or squirt the windshield, were meaningless hieroglyphics.

The weight of the car was disturbing, directing a chassis of so much mass by turning a wheel. Aiming the car down the stuttering stripes of traffic lanes was enough to make me hang on to the steering mechanism with desperation, gripping it with both hands, like an overcareful drunk, steadying himself to a constant speed, weaving all the while.

Each car in the rearview mirror skulked behind me like a Highway Patrol unit. I was like someone performing a familiar task backward. When I followed the traffic into the tunnel through Treasure Island I was sure I would never reach the end of the light, the shaft of echoes.

I approached each stop sign with painstaking respect. I braked, came to a complete stop, and then gradually depressed the accelerator. I parked badly, tires squealing against the curb.

I got out of the car, locked it, and pocketed the keys. I kept everything step by step, a driver's education manual. The air tasted salty, with an undertone of moist earth, mulch, and lawn clippings.

There was a moss-furred quality to the seams in the curb. The world was green, potted plants waiting to be put into the ground. Each knot of leaves had a plastic stick bearing the name of its variety and a few words, how to keep the plant alive.

I had expected it to be difficult. It was not. I was up the trellis, and on the roof of Stella Cameron's house, aware of every sound in the neighborhood.

Stella would be startled, but I would calm her. After all, we had legal business to discuss. How much did the water district offer, I would ask her. And don't tell me Steve Fayette decided to put you on retainer. I wanted to ask if she would help me sort out the insurance, and have a nice, discreet chat about Connie.

I knelt beside the chimney. The warmth within the dwelling rose up, invisibly, through the roof. I moved silently. I had never been acrobatic, but I found it easy to hang before one window, and then another, listening, my head upside down, ear pressed to the glass. The shingles were redwood, fine splinters breaking off as I shifted.

Someone was awake in the house, a soft tread and a creak as a door opened. I listened as the steps returned to another part of the house, and a body let itself fall into a chair. Tiny, persistent, a new continuous sound broke the silence—a television, volume turned down.

Did I hear a quiet, animal gurgle somewhere near me? I did not move, listening. Then I dug my fingers into the sill, working my fingernails into the window frame.

I was close to falling headfirst from the roof, and even when I began to slip I did not release my grip, digging my fingers harder into the frame, through the widening gap between frame and sill. The catch broke, and the window opened easily, all the way.

I was quiet, tumbling gracefully to the hardwood floor. How was it possible that I could be so skilled at this? There was a smell in the air, talcum, plastic, and warm flesh.

I crept to the crib, and leaned over the slumbering infant, the warmth from the baby's body rising up from where it lay, a palpable glow. A cloth frog, a beanbag, stood guard in one corner of the crib.

The infant made an almost inaudible sucking sound, the lips pursed to draw milk, dreaming that primal reverie, the dream of nourishment.

The infant's pulse was not located merely in its neck and its wrists. This small human's heartbeat was visible throughout its body, in the dome of its skull, in the wrinkles of its eyelids.

I wanted to kiss the infant. That was all I wanted to do. I was awed by its perfect, undefended sleep, and I wanted to express my love for it, my love for each child, my affection for the living. I reached down, and the heat made me flinch.

I straightened for a moment, and then resolved to try again, and this time I gathered the infant in my hands. The baby arched its back. Its feet kicked within the bed clothes, a sleeping bag with legs. The baby opened its mouth, a gray crescent of gums. It made one, single bleat. I cupped my hand over its skull.

The hair was fine, thick. I brushed the baby's forehead with my lips. Surely the baby must have a fever, I thought. It was so warm! It was why I was here. I had brought it a gift, not of gold or frankincense. A gift of myself, my smile, my tongue.

The baby took a breath. It boxed the air with its fists. *Hush* I commanded, sending the message with my touch. Be still. There is nothing wrong. I lifted the infant to my lips.

And paused. Downstairs a door opened. She was listening. She was listening, and she could hear me. I don't know how, but she knew her baby was not alone.

She ran up the stairs, and I barely made it to the window before she burst into the room, turning on the light.

27

The sky was beginning to color to the east.

This had happened rarely in my life—staying up all night, long enough to see dawn. And it had sometimes given me a sense of wonder, and of personal accomplishment—I had been enjoying myself so much that I had forgotten the time. It had also given me the sense of certainty that jet travel can sometimes give, the ability to acknowledge by my own experience that the earth turns.

This growing light gave me no joy. I parked not far from where I had taken the car. I left the key in the ignition, feeling a mix of regret and insouciance. There were no police cars, no emergency vehicles. The street was empty now, the party long over. I hurried through the silent streets, and ran easily through the young orchard, leaves stirring as I passed.

I wiped my shoes carefully, and tiptoed into the house. The sight of my footprints on the kitchen floor startled me, and I squeezed out a sponge from under the sink, wiped the floor, and cleaned my handprint from the wall.

I called his name and heard no answer, and I felt a stab of anxiety. His chair in the library was empty, the old leather impressed with the shape of his head, the weight of his body.

The white plastic cap to a vial of medicine lay like a poker chip on the carpet. A book on blood chemistry, complete with diagrammatic depiction of molecules, hexagons linked to hexagons, was open on the desk. The crust of a sandwich oozed jelly beside an empty coffee cup.

I could create a narrative from what I saw, an order of events. I saw him waking, making himself a sandwich, coffee. I saw him reading, studying, intent. I saw him going down to the cellar, making sure I was still there. I saw him leaving the house in a panic.

He was talking to someone. I was no longer a secret.

I found myself in the cellar. It was no surprise when I found the spade lying on the asphalt tiles. He had prodded my burrow, done a little digging, and discovered my absence.

He had swept the floor at some point, scraps of tile and fragments of broken glass in a neat pile. The glass was reflecting the hint of sunlight, each transparent fragment. I had to leave this place. I couldn't stay here.

But I had no time.

"I was about to call the police," said Dr. Opal, startling me. His eyes were bloodshot. He walked slowly down the cellar stairs and leaned against the washing machine in the cellar, his arms folded, a man waiting, in no particular hurry. "When I realized you were gone."

I didn't have time to talk.

"I'm not going to be able to keep you here," he said.

I gazed upward at the underbelly of the house, the flooring overhead, the bedrock outcropping at one end of the basement, supporting the weight of the house. I asked, "Where were you?"

"Your tone of voice could use some improvement, Richard. I've never been a big proponent of manners. I'm not that much of a hypocrite. But every now and then I could use a little in the way of courtesy, just a little effort to be civil."

I wanted to tell him what I had done, and at the same time I knew I never would. *But I didn't hurt Stella's baby. I never wanted to.*

There was so much I could have said. But I had to turn away. I could only shoulder my way into my burrow under the floor. Even here I could feel morning in the timbers of the house. The sun pressed down over the peaks of the roof, a weight, a heavy blanket, and every nail bit a little more deeply into the studs and floorboards, bearing the burden.

Words are only breath when you speak them. They only do harm, bless, question, when they are made of air. When they are kept within they are made of blood, and dark, holding up their many branches like woods of quiet trees.

All that day of darkness I was filled with things to say I knew I would never utter. I curled in the smell of wet bedrock, and waited.

I woke. It was not like the waking of a normal man, that first stirring, drowsiness, perhaps a return to dreams, perhaps a mandatory rising, yawning from the bed.

I was glad to retreat from sleep's hole.

I stumbled upstairs, across the kitchen, into the broad dining room. It was evening. Dr. Opal leaned on his elbows, his eyes bright, a bowl of something at his elbow, soup, the liquid drained, vegetables stuck to the sides of the bowl.

I sat at the other end of the table. I did not lean forward. I did not want to be reminded of my absence in its polished surface.

"I have some clothes for you," he said, indicating a dark jacket hanging from a door doob, pant legs trailing on the floor. "Although you look like you don't really need them."

"You visited Susan last night," I said.

His tone was not apologetic. "I needed company."

"You didn't mention anything to Susan, did you?"

He put his hand on his soup spoon. "Of course not."

"She didn't wonder," I said, "what you were doing climbing into her bed for comfort at what—midnight? Three in the morning?"

"Even if I mentioned to Susan that I had an old friend visiting me, a nephew, say, getting over a terrible experience, she would not pry."

"But that's not what you told her, is it? You didn't say anything."

"I asked her for some Benadryl and some codeine, and I went to sleep." He let me think about this, and then he said, "I don't like being treated with suspicion, Richard."

I was right to be suspicious. "I'm sorry."

He acknowledged my apology with a nod.

"Did you talk to Connie today?"

"She remembered the mirror after a little prodding. She's had a lot on her mind. She says the mirror was a gift from Rebecca's brother Simon. After your death Simon called, and with some embarrassment asked to have the mirror back again. He took it with him when he moved to Crescent City, on the coast up near the Oregon border."

"I know where Crescent City is," I said. "We all went steelhead fishing there once. You and my father. And me."

Dr. Opal's eyes looked bloodshot, but his gaze was steady and he looked like a man who had spent the day making up his mind. "Salmon of *some* kind," said Dr. Opal. "Maybe sockeye."

"It was steelhead. That means the mirror somehow fell into the hands of Rebecca's family at some point over the years. I wonder how that happened?"

"I wonder why you take such an interest in it," he said.

I should have paid more attention to this remark, but when I offered no reply, he added, "Connie is pregnant. The laser surgery worked."

"I'm so happy for her," I said. It was an automatic pleasantry. I was happy at the news. Surprised, too. Not at Connie, with her intrepid march toward anything she wanted. I was surprised at science, at medicine—that a doctor at Stanford could succeed after all else had failed. I felt a flash of cold envy, too. Toward Connie. Toward Dr. Opal, with his new love, the woman with the ample medicine cabinet and apparently no hesitation in helping him take care of either a party mess or a hangover.

Dr. Opal was watching my reaction carefully. "Steve Fayette is the father."

I had to laugh. "Steve always had luck." What I meant was: life had come easily to him.

Something about my response satisfied him. "And the investigation of Rebecca's death goes forward. They have some leads. I like talking like that—*leads*. It's all lab work, you know. Doctors, cops. We all wait around for a lab technician to get off his lunch break."

"You spoke to Joe Timm?" I asked impatiently.

"After a day of trying and failing. It turns out an old friend of mine was the heart specialist who did Mrs. Timm. Strings were pulled, hints dropped. Timm called me, and told me, just between the two of us, that the San Francisco cops are staking out a duplex in the Sunset District, on Noriega. It's rented by someone who studied music in Salzburg at the same time Rebecca was there."

"A musician?"

"A man named Eric Something." He gave the last word the authority of a surname, so that I misunderstood for a moment.

"You have been busy," I said, with my old manner, the way I used to speak to him.

"So have you," he said. His face was alight with suspicion.

"You loved my mother," I said.

He did not speak for a moment. "Your father was one of those people who are so self-centered they are geniuses of egomania. He could have sold self-esteem, bottled it."

"He was a good doctor."

"He had a phenomenal memory."

"What would my mother want you to do now?"

"Universities have kept secrets before. The University of California and Stanford have both used a degree of tact when it came to nuclear matters. I think I could organize a very fine team of scientists who could help you and at the same time keep you invisible."

There was the woman at the party, Maura. But I didn't hurt Stella's baby. Why would I harm an infant? "All I want is a little more time."

"Why? What's going to change?"

"Am I asking for so much?" *You know you can trust me.*

He closed his eyes. He opened them, blinking. "You'll stay with me tonight," he said. "You won't go out. We'll play chess."

I had a shadowy memory, rainy days, various companions getting out the chess pieces, rooting around in the game drawer for a pawn, telling me what a great game it was.

I felt a little sorry for Dr. Opal. I wouldn't need the clothes he had bought. I wouldn't need his help, his advice. His love for me was misplaced, so much wasted effort, but I couldn't tell him this.

"There was always something special about you," said Dr. Opal.

I stepped to his side, the smell of his soup nauseating me, chicken broth and peas, a strip of egg noodle like adhesive tape on the pale blue bowl. I put my arm around him and I could feel the bones of his shoulders, the thinness of his upper arms though his shirt. How much longer did he have, this wonderful doctor, this man who was out of his depth, now, lying to himself, pretending to be reassured. Did he have ten years of health left? Not even that many, I told myself.

With a chill, I realized what I was thinking.

Lie down, I told him. *Lie down and rest.*

Emergency vehicles clustered around the house where the party had been held the night before. Uniformed figures stood around, conferring, waiting for technicians. A flash ripped the dark, someone taking photographs of an object caught in the branches of a tree, one arm thrust up from the bundle like a fencer's lunge.

At first I walked. Taking my time. What did I expect? What was done was done. I liked the sound of that, adolescent finality. I could pretend for an instant that I was free of all responsibility. Then I began to run.

28

I wandered far. That now-familiar feeling was returning, that feeling of being mummified inside. The street was wide and lined with squat buildings, car stereo shops, pottery seconds, fire insurance offices.

I was in a time that belonged only to myself. Cars, when they passed, were quaint, like the vehicles in historic sepia prints, relics. The profiles of the drivers looked out of date, a species all but extinct.

In these mottled shadows from shop windows and streetlights I passed few pedestrians, men striding swiftly, others huddling on benches, on curbs. It could not be late at night, but aside from a few furtive figures and the occasional car, the avenue was empty.

I smelled it before I saw it—lighter fluid, an odor I remembered from picnics at the beach, my father trying to fire up a hibachi so we could grill the hot dogs, the charcoal refusing to burn. It was a smell reminiscent of Frisbees and sunlight.

Sounds came from a short alley between two one-story buildings. Three young people were laughing. They were dressed identically in black leather, the kind motorcyclists wear, zippers gleaming. The lighter fluid squirted from a can, saturating some clothing and a sleeping bag piled in a shopping cart.

Another person stood to one side, one hand out, beseeching them. The laughter continued. A match sputtered, refused to light. The owner of the shopping cart was saying something. He was a bald man with a shaggy beard clad in a thick sweater and baggy, loose-fitting pants. He looked like a someone from another era, a serf from a land of famine, a day laborer who followed the muddy highway.

"Come *on*," said one of the young people, a stocky youth with blond hair. I had the general impression of physical power, the young people built to be pioneers or soldiers.

Another match caught fire, a red jewel that swung upward, through the air, touching the sodden fabric of the sleeping bag and fizzling out. For a long moment the bearded man examined the things he owned, patting them, reassuring himself that they were intact.

The fire started without a sound, spreading quietly in a quicksilver web over the mound of possessions, and then the skeleton of the shopping cart filled with light.

The bearded man beat against the flames with his hands, gingerly picking through the burning objects, cursing the pain. He was stubborn. The other three looked on with interest, applauding with something like genuine appreciation. The bearded man found what he sought. He tossed a smoldering object into a puddle, a small radio, and another object joined it, a box of what looked like fishing tackle, monofilament and a few brightly colored lures.

The three young people were etched by the firelight, observing the bearded man. One of the figures shook the can. Lighter fluid squirted again, this time splashing the clothing of the man with the beard. He did not notice, and even when he felt the fluid seep through his clothing he did not appear to connect the sensation with any personal danger. His manner seemed to indicate that he had weathered indignities before, and that he knew that this, too, would pass.

I could not move quickly enough. When I cried out they did not hear me. Another match refused to light. Fingers persisted, fumbling. This time the entire matchbook was set alight, a tiny, burning pamphlet of fire.

The burning booklet leaped through the air. Flames fingered upward along the bearded man's pantleg, and he sat down, rolling, smothering the fire.

A hand shook the can. There was plenty left. One of the young men saw me as I approached. "What are you looking at?" he said.

The blond one said it, too. "What are you looking at?" It was a challenge, an invitation. One of the young people wore lipstick, and had a full figure. She laughed, and there was a steady, arrogant quality to her. This victim didn't really matter. The bearded man was comic. Perhaps their encounter even held a kind of justice. They were young and strong, and he was not.

It was the sight of his possessions still burning, everything he owned, that angered me most. I seized the arm of one of the young men, the one trying to get a cigarette lighter to spark. I took his arm, like an importunate usher.

"Get your hands off me," he said in a tone of outrage.

I did what he asked. I held up both my hands, palms out. Everything would be fine. It was closing time, and we could all go home.

He worked his lips together, puckered, and was about to spit into my face, when something about me dried the spit in his mouth.

"I won't hurt you," I said.

He kicked me. His heavy black book struck my knee, right on the cap. It was a good place to kick an opponent. The blow paralyzed my right leg. He was good at what he was doing, kicking me again in the other knee as I stood rooted, not falling, but not quick enough to defend myself. He took a swing, an awkward right cross, and I was slow to react. One side of my face lost all feeling.

I drew him toward me with the dash of a man demonstrating the tango in slow motion. I spun him around, whirling him by one arm. I drove his head into the wall.

It was not a very thick wall, stucco, cheap construction. The blond one was upon me, a clumsy tackle. I did not go down. He punched me, digging an elbow into my ribs, gouging my face. His thumb dug into one eyeball, my vision lost in a burst of flashing color.

I picked him up and held him high over my head. The young woman joined the struggle, kicking me hard in the groin. I turned away and slammed my burden against the stucco, so hard the wall came away in chunks, chicken wire and tar paper.

I blinked, clearing my vision. The young woman was on my back and she had something around my neck, a length of rope or a bicycle chain, an impromptu garrote. While she clung to my back, I seized the blond young man, slamming his skull against the ground until his hair was gray and scarlet. Then, before I knew what I was doing, I sank my teeth into his neck.

Not for long—for only a few heartbeats. The young woman sprang from me and vanished. I pulled myself to my feet, panting. The remaining leather-jacketed figure jerked its head out of the crumbling wall. His face was shiny, a mask of strawberry jam.

I took hold of an arm and slammed him into the ground. His head broke, and then his neck. Several times I drove him into the ground. As he broke apart, he snapped sloppily, noisily, piece by piece.

When I was done I was alone. The bearded man had abandoned his smouldering possessions, and the young woman was running.

The sound of her steps was very clear, and the wheeze of her lungs, cigarette phlegm.

She was far off by now, and I stood in what looked like a small lake, body parts and wrecked clothing at my feet, a stew of ordure and nourishment.

I was faster than I expected to be. I caught her from behind, picked her up, and carried her. I kicked open a gate of chainlink.

"Please don't hurt me," she said when she could talk, breathing hard.

"Hurt you!" I said. I could not keep a tone of amazement from my voice.

"Please."

But her *please* meant something different now.

I wouldn't dream of hurting you. I fell to my knees. She put her hand to my eyebrows, touched my lips with her fingers. "I think," she said. "I think I know you."

"Be still," I said.

"Do I?" she asked.

As I drank she continued to ask, as though she could almost remember and needed only a hint, just one hint, which day it had been, which moment we had shared, this woman I had never seen before.

I found my way west, under the freeway. The overpass thumped and hissed with traffic. Railroad tracks gleamed. I knew where I was going, and what was about to happen, without being able to name it.

Reeds snapped underfoot. A killdeer broke away with a cry of alarm. I waded into the bay, in the quiet surf that barely stirred the driftwood, the styrofoam and plastic trash. I waded all the way out, my body so filled with heat that it streamed from the cut in my finger, hot, salty.

I put my head back and drank in the sky. I didn't simply look. I looked and I owned. It was absurd—I knew this. But I felt that I was right to sense something of myself among the stars, and I laughed.

I swam. What was swimming, I wondered, but a way of not sinking? Of finding the body continually supported by the next stroke, and the following, until the horizon is touched, that edge of everything.

I cried out. My hand stung. My fingers stretched. Both hands were breaking, the knuckles dislocated, my thumbs agonizing. I could not take another stroke. I slipped under the water.

But I kept swimming. I glided, the stones and sea plants of the bay grazing my belly. I tried to work myself to my feet, but this landscape was unfamiliar to me. When I lifted my head I could not reach the surface of the water.

With one kick I was free of the water, in the air. I breathed, and it took me upward. My hands reached, and my body followed.

I fell upward, unfolding, my cranium changing shape, and when I could not keep silent any longer my voice was a high, tin wire. But I could still hear it, my hearing transforming, too, the impossibly high grace note the only sound I could utter.

A treasure trove opened before me in the darkness. Wealth glittered. This was mine, as much of it as I could take, all this topaz, these rubies, this crush of light.

It was the light of cars and buildings below me, slipping farther downward as I climbed, the necklace of the Bay Bridge reflected on the water, the spires and citadels of the city across the bay drifting closer as I breathed air into these foreign lungs.

The wind caught me. I spread my hands outward, the leather spans lifting. I was terrified. Surely this would all end in an instant. I would wake, or my bones would snap, and I would plummet.

I claimed something as I tumbled, caught myself, climbed higher. I knew this was what I would never turn back from, this unsteady mastery. The city streets teemed with traffic, the antigens and corpuscles of light, and the Golden Gate Bridge held itself against gravity as I did. The pilons and the cables suspended the earth's pull gracefully.

Graceful as the wing is, hovering, describing the wind as it ascends, nightbirds far below, spidering across the surface of the bay.

�֍

Part Three

�֍

29

When I was eight years old my mother told me a family secret.

I remember the afternoon perfectly, because my mother had taken the unusual step of spreading a picnic near the arbor. Both my parents thought the property to be larger than it really was, and they had constructed a trellis and a woven-stake arbor, only to finally celebrate sunny afternoons in a garden where there really wasn't room to do very much.

My mother shook an afghan out on one of the well-manicured rectangles of lawn, and we sat there, the two of us. She said that she would tell me something very serious, a secret, and that after she was done telling me I could ask any question and she would answer me. Having said that, she left me with a plate of tomato and cheddar sandwiches, a family favorite, and went inside for lemonade. I had time to wonder what was coming.

We lived only a few blocks from the house I later shared with Connie, years of my life in the same neighborhood of stately, college-town homes, live oak trees and occasional outcroppings of native stone. The large boulders butted from certain gardens like the heads and shoulders of giant champions, and I think I had felt a little let down by the fact that my boyhood home had not possessed an up-thrust boulder of its own, only a garden of gladiolas and a lawn of bermuda hybrid with a sprinkler system.

The sprinkler was on a timer. Throughout my childhood, my young adulthood, my university years, except in the heart of the rainy season, every predawn at four o'clock the sprinkler came on. It was a satisfying, lulling music, the deep calm one always gets from water flowing just beyond one's sanctuary, a feeling of cozy security.

I recall this long moment, waiting for my mother to return, as the peak of my childhood, an afternoon I look back on with nostalgia, but with no desire to relive the events again. I do relive it by seeing it so clearly in my mind, and given the opportunity to reinhabit the past I would decline. I am no longer that boy, finding a lawn moth, cupping it, letting it go. I squinted at my mother as she approached with a pitcher of something pink, not lemonade at all. I was glad; it was raspberry Kool-aid, which I actually preferred, at that age, to real juice.

She told me this: before I was born my mother and my father had wanted a baby. They had a baby, a little boy. But this little boy had not been strong, and he had needed help my mother and my father could not give. The child lived now in a hospital near Santa Rosa. I recall finding the word "hospital" strikingly out of context. A growing boy, older than myself, would not like a hospital. My father had shown me around Herrick and Alta Bates many times and I associated such institutions with brisk people carrying clipboards, slowly efficient people pushing gurneys of dirty laundry. And people too weak to crawl out of bed, watching television, expressionless, arms dangling.

It was important for me to know this, my mother said, because my brother had finally gone to sleep. It was hard for my mother to tell me this, and even harder for me, in my pained confusion, to shape what I imagined to be an entire range of sensible questions an older child or an adult would ask. Instead, the only question I could think of was, "What was his name?"

In my present state of experience, I know that an adult would be only a little better equipped to comprehend the hardship and loss my mother's story involved. And that a name, Andrew Morris Stirling, is as much as many of us ever have of each other.

And so I entered the prime years of my pre-adolescence with the opportunity to mourn a brother, to resent my parents for keeping him secret, to wonder at the nature of a handicap so severe the love of a younger brother, and two parents, would be meaningless.

It was a wisdom I would carry into my adulthood, and it colored my decision to study law. Love cannot struggle far up the steep foothills. Understanding, hope, delight—they all grow weary. Something about life baffles each of us, and only under the protection of experts with hands and habits like gardeners can some of us survive.

I believe that I fell at the end. It was a graceful fall, and I did not hurt myself.

When I outwardly resembled a human being again I was on the ground, on a walkway of crushed gravel. It took me some time, but the effort was a pleasure, recalling fragment by fragment the recent joy. A fountain trickled, and I recognized the neighborhood, one of the more exclusive neighborhoods of San Francisco, upper Broadway, housekeepers and security guards.

I gathered myself from the fine, hard points of stones, calculating my fingers, my teeth, assessing myself as a new creature, one that was like a man only in the most superficial way.

Someone beyond a hedge was walking slowly, a flashlight beam breaking through the wall of green. I tried to estimate the hour, but all I could tell was that there were still stars above, and that only toward the east did any of them seem to be growing dim.

The flashlight swept the gravel walkway. I had many miles to go before I could join Dr. Opal. I would not be able to make that journey tonight—or any other night. Now that I understood my own nature I could not stay with my old friend. I could not play out my nights in a mock-human existence, passing the nocturnal hours in the same routine thoughtlessness with which human beings spend their days.

I knew now what I was able to do, and I would not turn from this new course, this new responsibility I had undertaken in my heart.

In the growing dawn I found a swimming pool under a blue plastic cover. The cover was littered with pine needles. The needles rolled gently as I stirred them, slipping into the dark water.

Sleep. My mother said my brother was asleep, and I knew what she meant without question. It didn't even strike me as euphemism, merely an alternate way of saying what we knew to be true. That death was a kind of sleep, and that oblivion could be cruel, but was by no means the greatest evil.

My body drifted downward, and I stretched out on the bottom of the pool.

And slept.

30

For a moment I didn't know where I was. And I was happy.

I used to keep a journal. I knew the pointlessness of it, writing words no one would ever read. The writing itself became the point, covering the pages, what I had for lunch, what movies I stood in line to see, who sent me a letter after such a long wait. All through my college years I kept a variety of notebooks, spiral notebooks from the campus bookstore, handbound books from England.

In recent years I had dug them out of the box in the bedroom closet. It wasn't by accident, one of those rainy afternoons, cleaning out the closets, absorbed suddenly in old photos, old letters, and the engaging embarrassment of one's own old philosophical inquiries. I had sought them out deliberately when I knew that Connie was being unfaithful to me.

I had known it was only a beginning. Connie was a force of nature that could be observed, monitored, and perhaps ignored—but never stopped. I had read through my notes of nearly twenty years before, surprised at how only two decades had already yellowed the margins and faded some of the ink. To my relief the diaries were not embarrassing so much as a reminder of how much I had forgotten. I had noted with enthusiasm a new album by B.B. King, a production of *Twelfth Night* by the Berkeley Shakespeare Theater, and in almost every instance the party I described or the exam I had taken was an event I had completely forgotten.

Water gurgled. The sound kept me awake, listening to the slop of water in and out of the filter valves of the swimming pool.

The sheet, plastic and vast, lifted and fell with the very slight current, a current so slow in was almost nonexistent. If I could stay here, I knew, it would be like happiness. Water supported me, my body drifting with the slack current. It tasted of stale bleach, human body salt, and algae, a mixture of chlorophyll and mucilage. I opened my eyes.

I could not go back. I could not wake up in a bedroom with a woman, my closet filled with my clothes, my memories. It was not simply that Connie had thrown the box and its contents away by now, along with everything else that had been mine. I was never going to be able to engage in even a fitful, sporadic coupling with a woman I called my wife, or get up in the morning to sit in commuter traffic on the Bay Bridge.

The plastic tarp clung to me, stuck to my wet clothes. I was wrinkled, my fingers white and creased as the underside of a mushroom. I left sloppy wet footprints on the poolside concrete, and my trail reflected the stars.

A siren rolled along the edge of my hearing. Something else heard it, too. From beside the hedge came a diminutive howl. I was taking one slow breath after another, my heartbeat sluggish, heavy in my ears. The creature scrambled across the gravel, paws in the sharp stones. At the sight of me the beast froze. The animal would not take a further step, but stood trembling. The tiny haystack of hair showed teeth, giving a faint growl.

I smiled, stretching forth my hand. "Come here," I breathed.

A back door opened, and a man's figure in silhouette called, "Harold?"

The man could not see us; we were sheltered behind a juniper, a great, sprawling shrub. The wire-haired terrier looked back toward the house, briefly.

I felt a tender contempt for the man at his doorway, calling for his pet. How little the man knew about the hunter who ate dog biscuits from his hand. I laughed soundlessly, and the man put his hand to his throat.

He wavered in the doorway, thinking he should venture forth, prefering to stay where he was. I ran my tongue over my lips, over my teeth.

I sent a blessing, a farewell. I surprised myself—compassion swept me. For this man, tired, frightened of something he had sensed, for this dog, oblivious to everything but my hand.

I walked the streets, aware of my skeleton, soap-pale within my muscles, a glow-in-the-dark pirouette, a railway of calcium, linking tunnel to spire. Maybe, I thought, I will get by tonight without touching anyone, without doing any harm.

Each passing human was a village of smells, eddies, warm currents. When I found myself on Geary I turned west, and passed restaurants and bars, the traffic a stunning cascade of headlights and brakelights. Sometimes someone exiting a restaurant or a video store would catch my eye as I passed, I could sense her turn to gaze after me.

I could only guess how I must look, soaked through, my withered skin the color of the fat people cut from beef before they roast it. But people responded to me as they would the most handsome individual, the way people respond to the sight of a race horse in its prime. Surely tonight, I tried to convince myself, I would be able to find what I wanted without harming a living thing.

But as Golden Gate Park closed around me, the trees singing with the breeze, I grew weary. A whisper high up stopped me. Twin talons released a branch. The bird saw everything in its world. It saw me, the buttons on my shirt, the way each button reflected the lick of a passing searchlight in the clouds, a celebration somewhere. The owl took it all in, the field, the city. Held it all in its vision.

The raptor circled, abruptly. Was I mistaken, or did it make a sound just then, an inward cry? The bird plummeted straight down. And had something. Something alive, something warm in the hook of its beak. Something that would not die, its heart beating, all the way back.

The streets were laid out in a grid, running east and west, the ocean not far away, shuffling and dragging, Ocean Beach. Small houses adjoined each other, and all I had to do was find the people who were watching, sense their alertness. Noriega Street was not far from here. I could almost sense their vigil, the intensity of their boredom, their worship of routine. For the police the pursuit of a killer was a matter of putting in the hours, filing the reports. They would be paid even if they caught no one.

I had a purpose now. I knew what I had to do. But I would need more strength than I had. *Need.* What a simple word, the sound of something common, sweet. I admitted myself into an apartment building, the door opening at a touch.

For Rebecca, I told myself.

I was doing this for her.

I stepped into an elevator. I felt unsure what to do next. I pushed one button, and it lit up, and another, and it lit up, too. What a mistake it had been, I scolded myself, getting into this box. What would happen if some nice matron or some young wife with a load of groceries, or a whole family, stepped into the elevator at the next floor? What would I say? My clothes were still wet enough to drip water onto the floor. When the cell began to move it was slow, the walls and the floor vibrating.

The cable suspending the cage groaned, over my head. The machinery that lifted me was hidden, whirring somewhere in the shaft. The elevator was slowing down. It stopped. The door wasn't opening.

When the elevator door opened I was happy to abandon the cell. The hall carpet muted my steps. I climbed out a window, onto the steel bones of the fire escape.

The young woman stood before a mirror. If she had been less absorbed in the sight of her own nakedness she would have heard me. Even when she felt the chill of me she was reassured by the mirror: she was the only person in the room.

But it was the reflection that made me hesitate. A tiny patch of sticker blemished the glass, the remains of a price tag. She stood close to the glass, her breath flickering on the surface, stroking her eyelashes with a fingertip. Like a parakeet who surrenders to its double, and courts it, plastering the image with disgorged seed, the woman freed a dark crumb of makeup from her lashes. She held a sweater of red cashmere before her, studying it in the mirror. She let it fall.

She touched one breast, one nipple. I had the impression of her depth, her sensations, the way she colored with laughter, with pleasure. Her blond hair was cut short, a scratch on her forearm, a cat or a thorn. Or a lover—she did not share the apartment with a cat, and the only garden was four stories below.

She turned and fell back against the mirror, crossing her arms over her breasts. An observor might have misunderstood our tableau and seen two people startled by an explosion, or a shout in the street.

A metallic rumble. Somewhere in the house. In the kitchen—a garbage disposal.

The mirror. Only after awhile does it occur to us again, the emptiness of the reflected world, its sterility. I reached past her to touch the glass, and to my surprise left a fingerprint.

Not a whole print, a smudge shape like an exclamation mark. I ran my fingers through her hair, soothing the line of her jaw. The garbage disposal was silent. Footsteps approached, and veered off into an adjoining room.

It is rich with proteins, serum albumin with the bland flavor of eggwhite, serum globulin, the taste of whey, and fibrogin, tasting like flesh, like meat. Antibodies, calcium, magnesium, sulfates, phosphates—blood knows nothing, loves nothing, never dreamed or grieved. It is a mix of urea and fatty acids, and more. Something I drank along with the flavor of an inland sea.

The mirror made a constant hum, a radio tuned to an empty wavelength. I had not been able to hear it before now. I could see every nuance of color in the light reflected by her lips, her teeth, her open eyes.

The door opened after a perfunctory knock. It was a snapshot, a woman shocked, unable to move. She was almost identical to the woman before me on the floor, but dressed in a white T-shirt and denims, her feet in fuzzy blue slippers. A long second. Nothing happened, and then the door shut, hard.

Leave now, I prompted myself. Go on—right out the window.

But I didn't leave. Like an ordinary felon I wiped the mirror with my sleeve, removing the fingerprint. I made my way into the hall, listening. Why wasn't the woman in the T-shirt on the phone? Why wasn't she calling the police? Instead there was a scrabbling sound, heavy objects muffled by cloth, by cardboard boxes.

Run now, I told myself.

But she has seen me, I cautioned myself. She knows what I look like. I hesitated, telling myself that it didn't matter. No one would believe her. *Of course they will—there's a dead woman in the bedroom.*

What kept me, engaged in this mental debate, was pleasure. Deep pleasure in every breath I could hear from the room beyond this doorway, her frenzied breathing, the gasps of effort as she hurried across the room and into the hall, her eyes wide, her mouth twisted with some passion I could almost name. She was beautiful.

It was loud. The noise cancelled every other sound. The hallway was milky with a sudden pollution, and the Chinese New Year flavor of gunpowder. A spent shell spun on the floor at her feet.

No feeling. No pain.

She shot me again. This time my hand was on the gun, and the flash seared my flesh, my rib cage resounding with the shock, my feet almost knocked out from under me. I snatched the weapon from her hand and tore at it with my fingers, wrenching it, bending it, the firearm making tin-woodsman creaks as I twisted it in my hands. I let it fall.

You will remember nothing. None of this.

My thoughts hammered her. They stunned her. I never touched her, but she fell back, as though struck. Her eyes went blank.

I nearly made it to the fire escape before I slipped on the blood streaming down from inside my jacket, down my pantleg. I collapsed again on the steel steps, tumbled, caught myself. I could feel them now, the two bullets inside me, dragging me down.

I closed my eyes and cried out, the sound of my voice an outspreading ripple, a flame touched to a clear plastic sheet. With my eyes tightly shut I could still see, as with a ghostly sonar, a street, the cars, the trees.

I released my grip from the fire escape but did not fall. My sense of purpose stayed with me, as I rolled to avoid a high-tension wire, and looped high over a rooftop. My wings rustled, a riffling, gentle repetition, the sound of someone doing card tricks in the dark.

31

When I found them I was not surprised. There was only one car, a pair of watchers, one youthful, the remnant of a pimple on his chin, the other using the time to fill in reports, pressing hard with a ballpoint pen.

They were bored, but remained vigilant in a careless way. The focus of their desultory attention was a pink stucco duplex, two twin houses adjoined, the floorplans mirroring each other.

I used a certain caution as I closed in. Some instinct guided me back into human form, and as I groped, staggering, surprised to be so suddenly a man-like being again, one of the policemen saw me.

The car door opened. The young cop hiked at his pants, made sure his weapon was in place at his hip. But then I could feel his conviction fade. I was only a shadow, a blowing, dark rag, shapeless.

I pressed against a wall, and knocked over a plastic baseball bat left leaning against a drainpipe. The comically oversized Whiffle bat rolled, all the way out to the driveway, and down, following the slope out to the gutter, where it stopped.

Both cops were watching now. Their alertness awakened, I could feel their suspicion, worrying at me, prodding. *What was that?* The older cop buttoned his jacket, both of them in plain clothes, dark jackets, light brown pants.

It was hard for me to breathe. There was a throb deep inside my abdomen, and my shirt front was wet again.

Alongside the house ran a sidewalk, redwood chips crowding in over the concrete, all the way to the back garden. I had expected weathered squalor, piles of discarded newspapers gone soggy, an old lounge chair. Instead there was a quality of tidiness, clay pots with aloes and pear cacti, and a newly painted picnic table.

A small green bottle of ant poison lay on its side, beside a yellow-sponge squeeze mop. The back porch was slightly warped, steps weathered, but the impression was of domestic order, plain, nondescript, but homey. The back door window shivered as I gripped the doorknob, twisted it, and the lock gave way, the door splitting, glass breaking.

Pain prevented me from entering the place. Sharp pain. I sat on the back steps, retching. I coughed. An ugly joke was being played on me. I could survive two gunshot wounds only as a winged creature. As soon as I was human again the two projectiles were right where they had been, and they hurt.

I could use the telephone inside, I thought. I would call Dr. Opal. I would have to act quickly. But I couldn't move. I sat where I was, breathing hard.

I coughed again, a juicy, broken wheeze. The pain was changing, my innards shifting. I tried to stand up. A stone worked its way up my throat as I gagged. I spat.

Darkly glistening, a bullet lay in my hand. Coughing again, my body laboring, I produced another slug. I threw them both hard, into a recess of the yard, and took a moment to steady myself.

"I heard it," said the older cop, much older, retirement perhaps months away. I could hear the resignation, the feeling that it would be much easier and more pleasant if nothing happened. They stood in front of the house, on the sidewalk from the sound of it.

"Somebody getting sick," said the younger cop.

"Kids," suggested the older man.

The cupboard doors had been removed—the scars where the hinges had been were painted over with the same off-white enamel that coated the rest of the kitchen. Coffee mugs were lined up neatly, five of them, each one a souvenir from somewhere, the Santa Cruz Boardwalk, I thought, Solvang—I had trouble reading the words. A single water glass glittered upside down in the draining rack.

I could hear Rebecca ask *why*.

Justice, I would have told her.

No, she would have whispered. Not justice.

There was the scent of something rich, the essence of something tropical, and I found the source in a straw wastepaper basket, an empty Hershey wrapper. The living room was spare, a sofa, an armchair, a pole lamp with a brass-colored lampshade. Each room had the painfully ordinary air of prefurnished living arrangements, carpet clean but worn where the television cable ran from the wall to the brand-new Sony.

Not justice, Rebecca would have said—something else.

I had to see and touch what had belonged to him. Two blue Hathaway dress shirts were folded in the dresser, still in their laundry wrappers, next to a pile of JC Penneys v-necked T-shirts. I found a scrap of what looked like a nonnegotiable paycheck stub, witholding tax and a gross pay amount, but I still had great difficulty making sense out of numbers and letters.

Not justice—revenge.

The closet was underpopulated with clothing, a Harris tweed sportscoat hanging beside a Van Heusen aviator shirt. There were shoes, Rockport dress shoes, well-worn, and a pair of Fila running shoes with a hole in the left sole. There was a laptop computer, a Toshiba, in a leather carrying case, a Rolodex pocket planner in one of the zipper flaps, and even so, among the neat row of pencils and colored pens, I felt that much was missing, that the police had been here and taken whatever they needed.

There were weights in the closet, a barbell and an assortment of black iron plates in various sizes. They were the only items in the place that looked disordered, left casually as though their owner did not intend to leave them unused for long.

He was a man of such simple tastes that I could only conclude that he either had not lived here long, or he was one of those people who neither drink nor read, and have the habit of falling asleep in front of late-night talk shows. A computer consultant, I thought—a programmer, a troubleshooter. Someone who could leave in a hurry and replace everything.

Except that in the wastepaper basket cellophane glittered, the sort of wrapping that seals compact discs. And here in the night-stand drawer was a pair of earphones, the earpads worn, faded.

I found a wadded-up sock. It smelled very faintly of human presence, bacteria, someone by no means habitually dirty. There was a scent of aftershave or cologne as well as the natural, low-tide perfume of sweat.

I breathed the scent of this cast-off stocking, and let it fall. I stood, scenting the air around me, and seeing. Not seeing these walls, and not this place, but Rebecca's house, the fire, the carpet bunched and smouldering, the taste in the air, on her, of more than smoke.

My hand took it down from a shelf before I had time to consider it: a miniature bust, a composer. I turned the key on the base, and the inner workings spun. The thing chimed in my hand. In my present state of mind the notes jangled tunelessly.

There were voices in back of the house, now, a whispered, "Listen."

"I don't hear anything."

"It's a music box." The younger man's whisper could not disguise a note of tense hilarity. "Someone is playing a music box."

I wanted to tell them that the man who lived here was not coming back. I could feel him out there, the v-necked T-shirt, his new athletic shoes, his raincoat. I knew how his mind worked. He thought in flat, simple symbols, like the icons for files on a computer screen. Like the notes on a page of music. My mind pieced together the tune the music box had played, Chopin, the Minute Waltz.

Enjoy your new life, Rebecca would say. She would press her fingers over my lips when I began to argue.

Enjoy your powers, she would say.

Leave this man alone.

"Look at this," said the younger cop. "Busted. The back door is totally busted." He said this in an outraged whisper.

But I knew what they were thinking—breaking and entering.

Wait for backup. The command was never given. I met them at the back door like a landlord welcoming the police he had requested a half an hour ago, and both cops were open-mouthed, one of them producing a small flashlight, the other one, the younger cop, reaching for me, catching me, pulling my arm around behind my back in a maneuver I recognized from playground scuffles and courtroom testimony of arresting officers.

Before they could get a good look at me the flashlight bounced off the ground. The older cop threw himself into the struggle, but both of them stiffened, sensing something, beginning to lose enthusiasm for embracing me. As I spun away, the older one put out his hand.

He grabbed the shoulder of the younger cop, but the younger man would not listen. "No, don't go after him," said the man who knew better, the man who would survive the last months of his career and retire in peace.

The younger man, responding to the same impulse, could not stand to see me escape. He tore himself free from his partner, digging into his clothing, pulling out his gun.

32

In the infinite theater of the outdoors the young cop's pistol did not make much noise. The tiny pops I left behind sounded like the beginning of a labored celebration, firecrackers whether anyone wanted them or not.

Even when a bullet whipped through the air to my left no urgency was attached to it. The *smack* it made as it struck a newly shingled roof was the random flaw in a sound track, old and badly used, the single skip in an old record. But he persisted. Long after my fleeing form had begun to skim along the ground, far beyond what he could see with any accuracy, he ran after me, shaking spent shells from his revolver.

A black rope lashed me, a powerline. I clung to the coarse cable with my feet. I snapped at the air, trying to work my small bones into a position of comfort. The powerline crackled. My breathing was fast. My heart was a tiny drum roll. I was both webbed and furred, swinging upside down.

Below me the cop ran, slowed, stopped, looking up the street, walking out to the middle of it. The scent of his perspiration was in the air. A car slowed, sounding its horn, then sped away. The weapon in the man's hand became not a symbol of authority but proof that he was desperate, a frightened figure, necktie over his shoulder.

With my eyes closed I perceived a distorted photocopy of a bus as it approached. The dark was rich with thousands of tiny wings, moths, fine details, the Jerusalem cricket laboring like an astronaut in the dark lawn.

I let go, fluttering downward. With an effort not unlike a push-up I arrested the fall, rolled, kneaded the wind, fingering my way upward. The young cop did not even see me, regaining his composure, tucking his gun back inside his clothes.

And if he had seen me his mind would have taken in nothing— only the night, and something night-colored and quick. Nothing, something that did not matter, outside the human vocabulary.

My hunt began.

Even in flight I was methodical, seeking to master my experience. Skin extended between the elongated finger bones. The leather membrane attached to the sides on my body, and to the crooked remnants of my legs. The tips of my wings moved the greatest distance, generating thrust. The inner wing, closer to the wet fur of my flanks, created lift.

Mist captured me, then broke up, and I was above the choppy, gauzy alps of the clouds. A scratch of moon illuminated the cloud, the white wrinkles of the surf far below.

There was a rumble to the south. The jet powered upward, far off. But it was not long before the air around me churned with the punishment of the engines.

I screamed, and the diameter of sound flashed outward. I fought upward through the cloud again. The bay was black, marked by tiny crawling lights where traffic crossed a bridge. A boat or a buoy, a single lint of light, floated unmoving in the emptiness. Far across the bay, to the northeast, was Rebecca's grave.

Sometimes I would slip, like a person drowsing and startled awake by the act of sleep. I would jolt to my human senses and panic, and begin to plummet, forgetting I could climb upward again only by remaining wordless, disregarding everything I had ever known.

I coasted, fluttering, gliding, breathing the potpourri of human odors from below. There were too many people here—the search would be endless. But my new incarnation endowed me with an inhuman single-mindedness.

A mirror experiences no fatigue. When the room is empty the glass stands sentinel, reflecting the unstirring room, the drift of dust motes in the sunlight from the window, the blouses, the scarves, abandoned on the bed. It echoes the light without weariness. Locked in a cell, a closet, sealed in a carrying case of pine, the mirror answers the dark with dark.

A computer searching for a name in a long scroll of text could not match my patience. Besides, I knew something about my quarry, what he preferred, where he would choose to disguise his life, the plain habits, the simplicity.

I knew his thoughts, the cheap transistor radio of his psyche. I knew his smell.

I called Dr. Opal, once, from a pay phone beside an apartment building. I asked the operator to make the connection, and Dr. Opal's voice was in my ear before I expected it, eager, full of hope.

"Where are you?" he asked before I could speak more than a few words.

"You can tell them," I said. "They won't be able to catch me." This wasn't what I had intended to say. I simply wanted to be sure that Dr. Opal was not distraught, and I was curious—how much did the police know?

"Tell who?" He searched for words. "Without you here as proof I would sound crazy."

And I realized that he really didn't know. The death of the woman at the party, the news reports that must have circulated by now—he had not heard them, or he would not let himself connect them with me. He was deceiving himself. He would not let himself understand how dangerous I was.

The finest mirrors of the early Renaissance were created in Venice. The guildsmen there knew the craft of sealing an amalgam, silver or mercury, onto a sheet of glass. One night, the story goes, one of these master artisans fled Venice. He rode west to sell this trade secret to another principality. The man was stabbed to death on the road to Bergamo, the single plunge of a stilleto through the heart. His throat was cut to finish the job, and he was left beside the road for the magpies.

Except for one hand. This hand was carried back to the Doge's palace in a blue silk sack. The noblemen of Venice knew how imperfectly a report reflects the truth, even the testimony of a trusted assassin. They needed proof.

33

Broken sleep met me as I skimmed porches and fire escapes. Lovers lost all passion, dreamers all sequence, as I fingered past each human form, sorting, glancing, tasting the air. My search was a kind of sleep. He was the dream. I hunted the bungalows and apartments of the Richmond District, of the Sunset, the lawns and window boxes of Parkside.

Nothing escaped me. The spaghetti of streets, the warehouses, the television antennas commanding Twin Peaks, the Mission District, garages, empty playgrounds.

I searched for two nights.

On waking each twilight I was weaker, and when I fed I became more alive, more tireless, more determined. I could feed on the wing, hovering above a sleeping man or a woman, piercing and lapping with my tongue, the tongue itself a coiling, demanding organ, nursing the blood from the vein. Only what I needed, I promised.

All for Rebecca.

When I tried to remember my life as a man, the memories were beyond reach. It was a mild surprise that when I recalled anything about my life, I remembered houses, steps, doors. Human dwellings, decals worn thin by sun and wind. I could not remember faces, laughter, affection. Sex was impossible to imagine, a fleshy knot.

But I did have one or two vivid memories. Of being with my father in a lab, beside glass boxes. Wood shavings curling around sleeping white mice. *What experiment are they for?* I asked. Or maybe I didn't have to ask. "Little animals like that die so people can live," my father said.

The statement baffled me. My father laughed gently, maybe embarrassed at his own didactic blather. "They can see if a new medicine will kill people by using it on rats and mice."

I knew that already. But what I had not known was how like someone I had known a mouse looked, gazing up at my shadow with his blood-dark eyes. I had not known how unfeeling my father was, opening his appointment book, ignoring the living creatures all around us. The rats dragged skin tumors the size of oranges through the curls of wood.

When my mother died I called my father in London. He was staying at the Savoy, and I hoped he wasn't in his room, calculating the time difference. He was eating breakfast, I told myself. He was taking a walk by the river. But he answered just as I was about to hang up, just as I was feeling thankful that I had bought a little more time.

"But that's not possible!" he'd said.

I let him try to convince himself.

"I don't believe it," he said, stern, in command.

I experienced a weird pleasure, feeling superior, because I had already seen the truth and accepted it, having no choice. Having held her hand, feeling how heavy it was, how empty of love.

My days were spent under houses, under the roots of trees.

On the third night my hunt seemed about to end.

I could scent him in the wind, and I could guess at his dreams, the badly sorted deck of cards, the half-waking fever. He was sick, and he was always afraid.

South of Pacifica a neighborhood stretched away from the ocean, following a creekbed up into the hills. It was a populated woodland, firewood on back porches, tin-roofed cabins next to three-story houses, pickups parked beside Porsches.

I could smell him, with the disgust I had previously reserved for things decayed, fly-worried fish in an alley. I descended. My wings brushed the arching branches of the redwoods. I felt gravity press my body into the mulch.

I scuttled awkwardly over the roots, decayed wood on my leather wings. I panicked. There was a pair of eyes across the creek, an animal snouting the air. I dragged over a rock, tumbling down the bank.

Stand. I craved my old body, wanting to climb to my feet and take a human breath. But I was helpless, splashing into the water, swirling, struggling to get airborne.

Stand up. The bones of my legs unfolded. Flesh cascaded down and around me, molding itself, joints, organs. My skull ballooned to its usual, human capacity. My vision faded, flattened, lost detail. My finger bones ached, metacarpals throbbing.

I opened my mouth, blinked. I took a breath, and let the air out, feeling my chest lift and fall. The pair of eyes in the brush watched me. Whatever sort of creature it was, it would not turn, would not run, backing slowly away.

I was clothed as I had been, jacket, shoes, the clothes oddly unstained. My shoes filled with stream water, the cuffs of my trousers getting wet. I bent low and lapped the water. I spat it out. To a living man perhaps this creek would have tasted refreshing, but to me it was a dilution of the roots and road cuts the water had traveled, the larvae already teeming somewhere in the canyons.

My quarry was nearby. He was in one of the cabins behind the trees, but I could not be certain which one. A radio alarm came on, mid-song, country and western music. The bronze tang of coffee drifted in the air.

I told myself to find him now, finish it.

I flexed my hands. A large bird swept all the way from the upper branches of a tree and perched on a stone across from me. The black beak parted. The bird spoke, a brief, ugly noise.

The crow was not hostile, but suspicious, curious. I made a noise, too, echoing his, but with an added twist: I belong.

The crow cocked his head. Perhaps he saw me as potential food, sensing in me something of the gibbet, a man left unburied as a warning. The large bird spread his wings and without seeming to make an effort glided all the way across the stream to my bank. His flight was lovely, the product of more efficient engineering. He dipped his head, fluttered his plumage, black feathers already blue with early day. He made no further sound. When he left me I felt the hardness of my solitude, how even the uncaring fellowship of a bird was welcome.

Hurry, I urged myself. There isn't time.

A jay laughed, coasting upward. Its feathers were blue, shocking blue—like something broken open, a gemstone, an exotic fruit. It was almost day. I held my breath, trying to sense him, where he lay sweating.

No time. I had no time—all day I would be helpless. I splashed across the stream, and climbed carefully over a fence, to find myself on a large pile of chopped cordwood. The splinters were white, the sap glittered.

This was where he lived, that chain saw, that ax. This was all his. He was waking. He was lying in that room beneath a wool blanket. I knew how languor kept him there, a drowsy erection, sleep in his eyes.

His part of the house was on stilts, a wing added on to the main body of the house. I could hear movement, floorboards, clothing. Urine plunged into the water of the toilet, a loud, animal gush. I couldn't stop myself from giving a low laugh.

I crept beneath the porch, pinecones, dog turds aged white. The floor creaked. A child's voice rose, bickering, whining. *No.* A woman's voice. A child cried. Something didn't make sense. This wasn't right, not the right people, not the right place.

A pinecone gleamed, casting a squat shadow. Pine needles caught the light, a thousand pinpricks, dazzling. Too late. The sunlight had arrived, and I was in pain.

He was waiting for the tap water to run hot. A silhouette rippled in the pebbled window, a profile. He was studying his face in the mirror.

34

The chalk of the bones begins to ache, the salts of the blood solidifying, silt in a river. The stone of the body wakes first, the minerals and fats that, in a living man, are the least alive.

It was very early evening. Sunlight faded from the ground above me. The earth was decomposed wood mingled with sand. The vegetable matter fermented, a warm musk, like maturing tobacco.

And then I remembered what a special night this was, with a child's joy at remembering that this is no ordinary morning— presents are waiting.

My skin was seething with life. My eyeballs, my tongue. Tiny legs searched me, an army under my clothes, up my nostrils.

I shrugged out of the earth, climbing through the shell of a decayed log. I strode, a living map, lips and fingertips busy with the city of ants, all the way to the creek. With a sigh like an apology I knelt in the current, and lay down flat on my belly on the rocky bed.

The water was flowing more quietly than the night before. The current did not entirely cover me. I had to roll on my back and look up at the trees while the stream washed me clean.

It didn't work. Hundreds still clung to me. Button by button I labored to remove my clothing. Undershirt, Jockey shorts, shoes, black stretch socks. Until I was naked.

The gunshot wounds had healed, the scar tissue gray. One of the bullets had entered between my ribs. A gunshot rips the body. I have always been conservative about certain personal articles. I would wear a favorite undershirt until it was thin as gauze. I used to keep Levis until holes appeared at the knees.

This was my body. My bones, my skin. I felt a worried compassion for all that was left of me. My penis was shriveled, my skin blue in the poor light. Until then I had tolerated the ants, finding their attentions drily amusing. Now I shuddered. I rinsed my clothes carefully in the stream.

I tied my shoes with fingers that slipped, bent clumsily. There was a struggling ant on my sleeve. A sense of fellowship made me hesitate. I blew on him gently until he vanished.

A trail broke the shrubbery beside the stream, the lights of houses in all directions, muted by branches. Someone was dribbling a basketball, steadily, followed by the silence and the metallic *chonk* of the hoop. Meat was frying, blood and fire.

On wings, I ascended the hill. A deer lurched out of the underbrush. She was riveted, staring downslope, looking at the place where I had been an instant before.

My wings embraced her. She shied, kicking. My fangs broke the fine, dry grassland of her hide. A tick scurried away, a trickle of mercury. I supped as she ran, and when she faltered, crashing heavily through a crown of ferns, I clung harder. Her blood tasted of new leaves, of the young green of the oak trees, the early irises, fiber and membrane. I had an emotional rush of images—smells, sounds, sunlight through tender grass.

Her hooves clattered. She dashed across a street, catching the attention of a woman gathering groceries from the trunk of a car. The deer sprang and stumbled, forelegs crashing into a compost heap. I loosened the trap of my fangs and let her go. She tossed her head, cantering sideways, until she found the ancient trail again and kept to it, hard, all the way up the hill.

I studied the rambling house from outside. Smoke drifted feebly from the chimney. A swing had fallen from a tree, a tire under a long tangle of rope. A tiny green figure stood attention on a stepping stone, a plastic soldier.

The killer's smell was all over the ax, the chain saw, the battered steel wedge. I crouched under the kitchen window, pine needles crisp underfoot, envisioning what was happening inside.

They had eaten tuna and macaroni. The empty tuna cans were secured in this metal garbage can, the lid weighed down with two large rocks. A discarded microwave oven leaned against a stump, its glass window shattered. I heard laughter from inside, two children playing with a squeaky toy.

Rebecca would plead again: leave him alone.

I made my way up the back steps. The back door was unlocked. Perhaps some of the powers of the doe were present in my caution, alert to the sound of a newspaper page turning, children giggling in a distant room, water squirting. A new microwave oven sat on the sink, next to a cookbook open to a photograph of a casserole. I was able to make out a word: *French.*

Tuna and French Onion. I could read! At the same time my resolve began to shrink. A can opener, a jar of instant coffee—perhaps I had made a mistake.

I spoke where I was, staring at a kitchen cupboard. "Tell me about Rebecca."

But I spoke before I was prepared to, startling myself. A red kettle on the stove vibrated with the sound. A wooden salad bowl crammed with seed packets, recipes, letters spilled over onto the table. An oven glove, red plaid, hung on the wall.

You heard me, don't sit there reading the newspaper pretending, praying.

There was no answer. I had the sickening feeling that my voice no longer reached human ears. I could hear myself, but no one else would ever understand me.

Gentle, civil. "I need to talk to you."

In response there was a long silence. I trembled. *I had no voice.* Joy, doubt, hope. As a living man my emotions had never surged through me with such strength.

"Who's there?" he demanded.

Perhaps doubt exists as a whetstone, to give a sharp edge to the will. It was like a chance to meet a long-lost brother, a meeting dreamed for years. The voice was not welcoming. It was taut, comically suspicious. I entered the living room.

He didn't know how to build a fire. A few flames shivered around a largely uncharred log. I found myself in a spacious, wood-paneled room with a shaggy carpet, various shades of brown, the sort of carpet design to not show wear. The easy chair was still warm. It moved, barely rocking.

A woman put her hands on her hips in the doorway. She was looking back, away from me, into the bathroom. "I'm not happy about what I'm seeing," she said. "This room is a complete disaster."

A can of beer was open on the sidetable, yeast and malt sugars. A newspaper was spread across the floor, a trail of printed pages marking his retreat.

I picked up a metal bowl, puzzled by what I saw, dessicated crumbs. It took me a heartbeat to realize that she had spoken. "What do you want?" The woman held the front of her blouse, squeezing the cloth, one hand on the doorframe.

I lifted a hand, reassuringly, but not giving her my full attention. I couldn't shake the feeling that I had followed the wrong man, and, what was worse, I couldn't make sense out of anything. It had taken me half a minute to identify a few crumbs of potato chips.

Get out of here! She could not say this, the words choking.

Her eyes were blue. I admired her blowzy, blond attractiveness, her show of courage falling apart now that she had a better look at me. I gestured apologetically with the bowl.

One of the children was calling her, that urgent syllable, *Mom*. In my mind I could see it all—the warm bath, the talcum powder, the clean towels. I had lived like this! I could not quite believe it, but I knew it to be true. I had lived a childhood of comfort, an adulthood of ease.

If only I could set eyes on the children's faces, see them, pink and wet from bathing. If only I could approach them, lay a hand on their heads, feel their hair, their wet arms, help dry them off, kiss them where the skin was so suffused with rose the pressure of my lips would force a white shadow.

I put the bowl down carefully, on the coffee table next to a nutcracker. The bathtub drain opened, and water begain to ebb into the plumbing, gurgling, the flow down and under my feet.

She wanted to scream. Her words were there on her lips, but I silenced her, touching her hair, combing my fingers through it, unfastening the clasp that held it into a bun, letting the long blond hair fall free.

I had failed Rebecca.

It was something this woman would understand. I could tell her my story, the long search, my instincts faltering. What woman could listen to a story like this unmoved? The children could listen to my tale, too. I thought I had run my quarry to the ground, but instead I found a man at peace, at home, reading.

Red splashed her, covered her.

Something hit me. I did not understand, but more importantly I could not lift either arm. I could not take a step. I could not turn my body, or cry out.

Scarlet gushed, her hair dark with it. I couldn't speak. I could not breathe. Something had my throat. One knee buckled. I could not stand upright. There was a dark, iron taste at the base of my throat. I staggered.

My head rolled, forced to one side by a heavy, unyielding wedge. I gripped something, a span of wood. It was slippery. I could not lift my head, and I could not turn it. I could not move my tongue and my windpipe sucked air.

The head of a weapon was buried in my neck. The woman screamed as I slammed into a wall, a shelf of porcelain animals crashing. I got a grip on the shaft of the tool. I sawed it back and forth, levering it, my blood spattering the carpet. I pried the ax free, and turned to find the man who had done this.

The force of the turn flung my head from my shoulders. My vision yawed, my head connected by a slim sinew. The ceiling swung upward. My severed neck tendons spasmed, writhing far into the stub of my neck. Until this moment there had been no pain.

The ax fell to the sodden carpet. I put my hands to my head and put it back where it belonged. The pressure of spouting blood nearly forced my head off again, and my legs were unsteady as I tried to turn from one direction to another without unseating my skull.

A new pair of earphones lay beneath a lamp. A magazine was folded open to a photograph of a concert hall, a conductor, a grand piano. When I saw my assailant at last he was picking the ax out of the widening flood in the carpet.

All I had to do was fit the carotid arteries back together. My heart pumped the hot fluid into my arms through the great brachial highways, down my legs through the femoral aqueduct. Only in the one crucial point of severance was there serious injury, but it was grievous. I tried to grip the rubbery worm of a neck artery in my fingers.

I saw how this woman had been taken in, how little she knew about him, how much he had lied to her. I could taste his envy of Rebecca, his failure, his refusal to play the paino because he could never equal Rebecca. And because he could never court her successfully, never seduce, never win, he had killed her. I perceived all this as he lost his footing, stumbling into the easy chair, the newspapers splashed with red.

"Don't!" he cried. A tall man, stout, blond hair, big, square hands.

The woman had grabbed the telephone off a pile of magazines. She was hyperventilating, and when she had someone on the line she couldn't say anything. Her breath was loud, each exhalation a scream.

"Don't," he said, more calmly, taking the phone away from her, hanging it up. The hair on his arms was blistered with my blood. She clutched at him, at the phone.

I felt tipsily peaceful. I was struck by a memory so vivid I wanted to share it with both of them, interrupting their frenzied argument. Once, in my childhood home, the fish pond had to be drained. It had never been a success, back beyond the arbor, a concrete pond of black moss and two albino carp. Mosquitos festered in late summer, and frogs discovered them, and at last my parents decided to drain the pond and start over.

The gardeners used a small, one-cylinder pump, the water saturating the lawn, and I helped rake the black grass, scrubbing the pond with bleach. When it was all done, I was disappointed. Standing beside a plastic bucket of slow, stubbornly twisting fish, I looked down into the bare cement bowl and realized that I had expected a surprise, a treasure, a golden secret.

And all I had was this. This emptiness, this numb, pleasant sensation in my arms and legs.

35

He slapped her. Then he hit her, not as hard as he could, but enough to make her hair fly out from her head. "Stop making all that noise," he said. She had her fists up, covering her ears. The children were in the bathroom, bawling.

At first I was sure I would be able to climb to my feet at any moment. I lay on my side, my ear on a heating grille in the floor. A strange inner pain awoke in me, a desert spreading, dehydration, hard drought. The children were crying so hard their noise echoed in the heating ducts.

He put his arms around her, neither of them able to speak, rocking, dappled with blood. I could not move. I was certain I did not have a heartbeat. Then it pumped, once. Blood squirted briefly from my neck.

"You don't know anything about me," he said, his voice broken. "All you know is—why don't we call the police."

"You killed him!"

"I hope so."

"Tell me—" She had to stop to take a breath. "Tell me why."

He sounded almost patient when he said, "Please shut up."

"He wasn't doing anything, Eric." She wanted to stop talking, but she couldn't, now that she had her breath. "We get people like this in the woods. Mental hospitals let them go."

Eric. I had always admired the name—it smacked of Norsemen, exploration of the high seas.

He said, "Go shut the children up."

She didn't argue but stood where she was. Her hair was stringy, clotted.

My heart kept squeezing, at about the same rate as a crocodile's on a winter day. I felt systole, and blood gushed a little more feebly than before. My heart seemed permanently contracted. At last the muscle relaxed, and the valves in my chest fell silent for another age. So it was a sort of pulse, I consoled myself. There was so little fluid in my body that my eyelids dragged over my eyeballs, and stuck.

I managed to open one eye, barely. Eric wiped his hands and forearms on sheets of paper towel. The crumpled, sodden paper littered the floor. His voice was almost kind as he insisted, "Would you go tell the kids to shut up?"

The kids had fallen quiet. It was a shaky quiet, though, and what he meant was: go find out what they're doing.

When she was back in the room, he continued, "I'm going to cut this carpet out, the whole thing. It's cheap stuff, tell the landlord Randy puked on it. Go get me all the knives you have." He was keeping his voice steady, but it was a pitch higher than it should have been.

She hurried from the room. A drawer opened, shut. Soon, I promised myself, I would move one of my hands. She pulled a new-looking Bowie knife from its sheath, the light from the steel reflecting on the ceiling.

"They don't make this kind of knife to cut up carpet. I told you to go get every kitchen knife in the house, all those fancy knives, every one of them."

"They don't make those to cut up carpet, either."

His voice was very quiet. "Go get the kitchen knives, Helen."

He stood over me. He began to bend over to take my pulse but couldn't bring himself to touch me. He looked at me, then looked at the mess on the carpet. There was a dimple in his chin. He massaged one of his arms, kneading the muscle. I could read the look in his eyes: maybe he should get the ax again.

She came back with a handful of blades, dropping one on the floor. I could contract my right hand, make a fist, release it. He selected a long butcher knife with a wooden handle. It was the wrong knife for the job, and his hands kept slipping off the hilt. He made a grunt of effort, stabbing the carpet. He worked on his knees, cutting, sawing. "Move that chair out of the way."

"Let me do it," she said.

"I have to use your car. Go out to mine and get the gas can from the trunk. Put it in the backseat of the Chevy."

She was gone a long time, and twice he rose to his knees and listened. There was the sound of a trunk opening, the slosh of fuel in a can. By now I could wiggle all my fingers. My severed tendons shuddered. Soon, I promise myself, I would try to shift my head.

She entered the room again, flushed, panting. He knelt to his work, slicing the carpet, tearing it. "What are the kids doing?" he asked.

"I told them to dry off and get into their jammies."

There was silence from the bathroom, the tub empty. It seemed his attack had never happened, except as a forgotten, faded prologue to the sound of carpet tearing. "You better use *this* knife," she said.

He accepted it from her. The work went more quickly. There was a thought-out non-logic to everything they did; as long as they had some sort of plan he wouldn't hit her again. "You told me I could stay here, and you promised you wouldn't ask a zillion questions. You liked it, didn't you. A man with secrets."

Her voice hard, she said, "He's still alive."

"He can't be."

She said, "Look at his eyes."

He glanced at me, made himself give me a long look. She was on her hands and knees, gathering fragments of a porcelain dog.

"You can clean that up later. Tell the kids to hurry up and get into bed. I'm going to take a shower, change my clothes. I'm going for a drive. I want you to promise me something."

She didn't respond.

He held the knife, pressing the ball of his thumb against the blade. The flesh of his thumb was indented in a fine line where the steel pressed it. "I'm sorry I hit you," he said. "I need you to promise me something."

She said, "I think his foot moved."

"Can you promise me, Helen?"

"I don't know what I'm going to tell the kids happened out here." She sounded firm, but not as sure of herself as she wanted to be, an elementary school teacher refusing to panic. "Randy already asked and I told him to mind his own business. I believe in being frank with children."

He fell into the easy chair. He shook his head, meaning: let me rest a minute. He grunted and, without getting up, drew the handle of the ax toward the chair.

Once during a tour of the Natural History Museum in San Diego, my father and I were shown into a library by a smiling, white-haired woman. The woman made me feel terribly shy. At the time I had no idea why, in that lack of self-knowledge peculiar to children. I realized later when I saw her photograph in a magazine that she was beautiful, refined. She and my father made what I ignored as medical chit-chat. So when a certain drawer was pulled out I was unprepared. I should have been warned, but both adults had ignored me, joking about money and politics, the dead language of adulthood.

A strange map spread before us on the blue felt. Ivory-yellow, a fine net stretched outward, a web of highways, a ghostly city in the the shape of a human body. "A nervous system," said my father. "Belonged to a cleaning woman. She left it to the museum." The nerves of the dead woman were busy around the empty hole of her mouth.

It was appropriate that my most stark confrontation with the architecture of the body and my first insight into the power of a bequest should occur at the same moment. In the boiler plate and codicils of a will, the dead stand witness among us. In the macrame of the nervous system something of the cleaning woman remained faithful.

"I'm worried," Helen said, tugging paper towels from the roll. "About the psychological damage to Diane, especially. I have that plastic liner on the mattress from her bedwetting—"

"And milk gives Randy a rash," said Eric.

She let the roll of paper towels fall. The cylinder of paper touched the swamp of blood and pink began to spread across the green-and-white floral print. I felt her anxiety. It passed through me like pain: *He's going to use the ax. He's going to hurt her.* She said, "I promise."

He heard it—wet fabric whispering. One hand felt for the ax handle. His fingers made sticky, kissing sounds on the wooden shaft.

She said, "He's moving."

After this was over, I promised myself, I would give my body to medical science. The graduate students would file in not ready to believe, every one of them doubting. Even as I stepped to the lectern and opened my notes they would not know what they were looking at. And I could tell them that memory is the cruelest faculty, the first, most lasting form of torture.

I was so careful to deceive myself.

36

A house plant gleamed in a clay pot. The dark green foliage, the glaze of salts on the pot, the farmland scent of the potting soil—it was all so out of place where it was, beside a tattered pack of playing cards on a table. The ceiling was sheet rock—a plant has such power that it will ascend even toward a sky of stone.

There was blood on the ceiling. I rose from the rug slowly, section by section, with the movements of an elderly dandy, straightening the crease in my damp trousers, adjusting my cuffs, steadying my head with the gesture of a man with one hand on his hat.

Helen looked on with something like rapture. If I was alive, she knew, then the future held all manner of stunning possibilities. My presence worked in her like oxygen. She wanted to touch me. But at the same time she recognized that there was something grotesque about me, something terrible.

Eric was sweating. He stood with the ax in one fist like a berserker about to jump from a great height. My neck muscles cramped, veins fitfully reasserting themselves. I wavered dizzily, so feeble that my movements were the slow, languid gestures of someone swimming through zero gravity.

When he hefted the ax again, it took me a long time to lift my arm, the deltoid muscles of my shoulders weak, my forearm strengthless. I slipped the blow, and he staggered into it, landing on all fours. The house plant in the corner shook, stem and leaf.

He flung the ax away and scrambled. He snatched something bright off the drenched carpet. The nap of the rug squeaked and squelched under our feet. He passed at my belly with the hunting knife. I saw how he must have borne down on Rebecca, how little she could have guessed about him, how helpless she had felt.

I took him into my arms as the knife slashed me, tearing my shirt, my skin, the muscles of my belly. "Get the ax," he cried, yelling, full-throated.

He stabbed me, working hard, plunging the knife, ripping my jacket, tangling the blade in the cloth, fumbling, losing it as it tumbled to the floor. He told her to pick the ax off the floor. "Use the ax."

I laughed, a little sadly. I had wanted an adversary.

"His legs," he was gasping. "Hit him in the legs."

We rocked in a silent waltz. He had been young once. Music had meant so much to him. But he had always been coarsened by ambition, stubborn in ways that made him tireless when he should have rested, industrious when he should have walked beside the river, watching the leaves turn from green to scarlet with something almost audible, that sound like held breath.

He knew this now: he had hurried to the bulletin board, across the plaza with its red and white umbrellas, the pigeons, the white crumbs of bread. He wanted to see the scores, to see where his name appeared on the roster of the gifted.

He was not the first human being to want too much. He fought me, fists, kicks, with all the loud bravado of a theatrical double, a man pretending to be in danger, miming a death-struggle, his voice draining to a shrill, piping *No*.

He was senseless when I killed him, unpacking his body of its organs with the careful concentration I would have used on a trunk full of curiosities, heart, lungs, the pipes and ducts of food and air, until there was so little left of the living man, so little structure, that I had to stop my dismantling and attend to her.

She was crouched at the door of the bathroom, and continued to scream when I touched her cheek soothingly. What she had just seen had broken through her joy at my presence.

There was nothing I could do to quiet her, so I pressed my fingers over her eyes and told her to sleep. I draped her over the quilt on her bed, a sailboat pattern, an heirloom, beautiful, stitch by stitch.

The children hid in the bathtub. They wore pink pajama bottoms, and each wore a T-shirt representing a superhero.

Sleep. I did them no harm. Their bodies were warm in my arms as I carried them one by one to the bedroom, toys all over the floor and a few ants around the sticky half circle left by a can of cola.

And now, Rebecca would say, you are going to turn yourself in. Now you will call Dr. Opal.

Because it was over. I had accomplished everything I had set out to do.

I wiped blood off the phone with a paper towel and told the operator I wanted to speak with Berkeley Chief of Police Joe Timm. Instead I was connected to the Berkeley Police Department, a woman's voice.

It was only after persisting and getting the answering machine in Joe Timm's private office that I remembered a fragment of a phone number. I tried various combinations of digits, and when I heard Joe Timm's voice at last I felt a flicker of satisfaction.

This was miles from Joe's jurisdiction, but he would know what to do. "I found Eric," I said.

"Eric," he said, almost guessing what I was talking about, almost recognizing my voice. "Who is this?"

"He killed Rebecca," I said.

"Where are you?" said Joe, mystified, but thinking fast.

Joe was asking questions as I put the receiver down beside an ashtray, a bowl of blue glass. The sound of his tiny, electrified voice followed me until I was outside. I washed myself with a garden hose, but the effort wasn't really necessary. Even my appearance seemed to regenerate, my clothing healing as inexorably as my flesh.

As I turned off the water, twisting the handle of the garden faucet, a woman stepped out of the shadows, a man behind her. "We heard noises," said the woman. "We almost called the police."

"Yes, it was a little noisy in there, wasn't it?" I said. The melancholy I should have expected was setting in. I could stop now— stop everything, and step off this one-man merry-go-round. I had done everything I wanted. I could wait here for the call to be traced, for the police to roll up and take me in.

Neither of the neighbors were afraid. They were dazzled by my smile, trusting me to join them, go with them back into their bungalow. "We just wondered if everything was alright," said the woman, softening her voice seductively. Her accent reminded me of Connie's, a country twang modified by years of watching television.

"Everything *is* all right," I said.

I liked these people, the man in a baseball cap and jeans, the shapely woman in a plaid blouse. I could go back and play Scrabble. They would have been delighted to let me win, letting me make up words, all x's and q's, and for a while I even walked back with them the woman taking my arm, leaning close to me, the man trailing, honored by my attraction for his wife, willing to participate in a night of voluntary cuckoldry, watching George Raft talk tough while I took my pleasure in the bedroom. And I nearly walked up the steps with them, almost closed the door behind me.

But I knew what Rebecca would tell me. I knew I had lied to myself. I was not going to let the authorities take me in. There would be no audiences, no foreign experts. No release from my condition. I no longer wanted answers. This was what I loved—

this minute linked to minute, this power to endure. I wanted more of this, night after night just like this one, two people standing close to me, offering me their lives.

37

I climbed high into the hills. Motorcycles had cut scars in the landscape. Rusting equipment loomed, chains and iron wheels scattered behind barbed wire. I plucked at the barbed coils, slipping through.

I felt my way downward, across a cliff face of glossy, green serpentine, into an old quarry. Rail tracks led upward to the base of a cliff, and then stopped, and the man-made canyon had that profound quiet of industry left to decay.

I was hoping for a mine shaft, and had entertained the thought of finding a cave. But as dawn approached I had to be satisfied with one of the fissures in the cliff, cracks that stretched deep into the stone. I crept into the dark, not certain what form my body would take as I hid farther into the hill, whether human, or winged, or some new disguise I did not want to name.

When I woke I fed again.

This time I found a community of new houses, sod still rolled up like carpets, bare ground and huge boxes at the curb for recycling, the flattened cardboard that had contained refrigerators, stoves.

I embraced a woman sitting on a brand-new patio set, blue canvas directors chairs, an iron table. She was half-turned to look inside, a stereo rumbling, a song I would have known in my other, human life. She was smoking a cigarette, the heat of her spiced with nicotine, the last words she spoke a laughing, "Stop it. I told you stop it," trying to guess. Trying to name which friend I was, until she was silent.

In my man-like guise I threaded a path through a bank of iceplants, the succulents in flower, a carpet of blossoms. Highway One was crowded with traffic, headlights, brakelights. It was still early evening, two men entering a bar, another man trying to use a pay phone, his fingers drink-clumsy, having trouble with the coins.

Justice, revenge, I could hear Rebecca say. *I had what I wanted.*

The beach was empty, except for a couple huddled near a huge gnarl of driftwood. The log smouldered, the wind kicking the smoke into flame. A face turned away from the firelight, and I heard a voice ask, "Spare some money for food?"

So often in the past I had received such a request with little interest, although I had sometimes dropped a few quarters into an outstretched hand. But now when I could not, I ached to do something human, commit a simple act of generosity.

I jogged south, away from the restaurant and the parking lot, across the sandstone rubble along the face of the cliffs, until I was was well away from sight or sound of human beings.

The salt foam was cold, but to me it felt tropical. I climbed along the limpet-spiked stones. I considered trying to die again, wading into the water, drowning. With amused bitterness I realized that I could probably inhale and exhale saltwater like so much thick air. It could not take my life. But what I felt was not like true despair. I was finished with my inner sunlessness. Something new was beginning.

A dark heap of animal life stirred. A snout lifted. A dark eye reflected the dim light. Two of the creatures were small, shielded by the adults. The sea lions observed my approach, one of them pushing himself up and out of the pile, wrestling toward me.

Just as a page of writing reflects an author's state of mind, and just as the concentration of a reader echoes in turn that mental landscape, so I was one of life's seconds, not life, but free, as poetry is, or the image in a mirror.

I cast no reflection in a glass because I *was* a reflection, broken out of the frame and glass.

The sea lion dug his fins into the stoney beach, but with each movement he swung his body to one side. He could not approach me directly, because one of his fins could not bear his weight.

He rushed me, a growl, a lunge. I hushed him with a whisper, and knelt beside him. The animal gazed into my eyes, and I had an instant comprehension of what he saw in me. I had begun the evening with a sense of self-loathing, but he saw me as a fellow mammal, possibly a curiosity, but nothing worse.

The fishing line around his forelimb had dug into the flesh. I untangled the knot, and gently pulled the filament free. I tried to open the cut in my fingers, but it was healed. I punctured my hand with my teeth and let a little of my blood trickle onto his whiskery snout. He opened his mouth, like a hound eager for a treat, lapping the blood as it fell.

The world was fertile. These sea lions, Connie, Stella—each thistle on the cliff above stretched its brambles into a future. And I fathered nothing.

There must be some reason we love the end of the land, the emptiness of all that is left. We have to be in love to look at the turbulent void and feel that it belongs to us.

Perhaps it was at that moment that I decided what I would do, but my future was predicated in my growing recognition of my powers, and in my constant love for Rebecca. What had been an obsession for a living man had flowered into faith.

There was no reason for me to hope, and I had nothing like human expectation in the future as I circled, high over the surf.

The flight was long, or it was swift. I could not tell. I did not experience the journey as an event that took place within the fabric of time.

When I arrived at the parkland of sepulchers and tombs I did not search—I only found, without hesitation.

I was there, at the grave of the woman I loved.

38

I ran my hand over the dewy grass.

Her name was in bronze, a plaque bordered by neatly trimmed grass. A metal vase sunk into the earth held three red carnations. They were not wilted, not even slightly. The grass had grown over the grave itself, although a careful eye could detect the border of the more recent sod from the rest of the lawn. Deer scat darkened the bare ground under the trees.

The mausoleum where I had rested was up the hill. I gazed at it with no pleasure. A police car was parked at the entrance to the building. A policeman descended the steps, spoke to his partner without getting into the car, gesturing with a flashlight, the beam lancing the dark.

The flashlight beam silvered the blades of grass, the trees, and almost reached me where I stood. After further discussion, the car door slammed. The police unit rolled slowly, headlights sweeping the trees and grave stones, brakelights all the way down the hill, where they vanished.

Whenever I attempted to think like a man, to read, to plan, I felt myself become uncertain. It was a simple matter, discovering the gardner's equipment, the small green tractor, the tarps, the red-and-yellow cans of fertilizer. But then I was lost in an inventory of possibilities.

Tall rubber boots waited like prosthetic limbs beside huge bags of grass seed. There were so many tools to chose from, pitchforks, hoes, power saws, edgers with plastic containers of fuel riding piggy-back on the shaft of the tool, and all of it speckled with bits of grass and earth, plantlife long dried to yellow cellulose and dust.

But I could not find what I wanted, not until I kicked open a wooden shed. Hoes and rakes tangled with each other, the sort of tools medieval peasants would have seized if called to battle, axes and hammers—and spades.

Spades with sharp edges and long, grip-smoothed handles. I selected one, and felt the joy I had never appreciated in my years, the simple balance of a shovel.

I withdrew the red carnations gently, and laid them on a nearby grave. I took a moment to wonder at what I was about to do.

The first shovelful of sod was tough, the roots wire, the dirt gritty. I flung soil off the blade, the steel ringing musically at the instant the mulch and pebbles sailed into the dark. Again, my sense of purpose faltered.

And I thought as a person would, in the middle of the night, picking with futility at the hard earth. And worse— I felt the normal horror of such an act, the disturbance of bodies which had been committed to the ground.

But even as these thoughts troubled me, I continued to scoop the moist soil, digging deeper. The upper level of the ground was vegetative, roots and plant stuff, but there was no true topsoil. The sod had been rolled out like a living carpet, and beneath that layer the earth was an assortment of gravel and yellow clay.

As I dug I smelled the earth and breathed it, mud on my shoes. This work was not labor at all, any more than the stroke of a swimmer is labor. This soil was the source of my strength.

No other doubt touched me. There was no sense of an hour passing, or two, or much of the night. All I knew was that there had been a grassy patch of land, a prison. And now there was a vault, the earth thrown into a peak at the base of a tree.

Sometimes I thought I heard a sound, a voice, a footstep. and I would stop for a moment, and then start in again with renewed strength. At last the shovel rang. There was a concrete box, the blade scraping it, the last dirt dug away to expose the slab.

Kneeling, I broke a hole with my fist. I tore off chunks, letting the fragments sail high, out of the grave. When I had ripped away a large portion of the concrete, I gazed down at the glossy surface of the casket.

Gently, I tapped at the wood. There was the lightest film of mildew on the polished surface, and my touch left bold finger-prints. The casket reminded me of nothing so much as the hard finish of a grand piano. But a piano reverberates when it is struck —it echoes. This box was silent. I smoothed away the layer of mildew and the dark surface reflected the dim starlight.

The casket splintered with one last blow. The shattered wood caved inward, and I cracked open as much of the lid as I could easily reach. Don't think, I warned myself. Don't ask yourself what you're doing.

Rebecca.

I had to close my eyes and turn away.

The gray thing within was littered with splinters, and I told myself again not to think. *Don't think, and don't feel.*

Act. Quickly.

I broke the skin of my wrist with my sharp teeth. I found a vein, and plucked it. I bit again, and at last the blood was hot on my tongue.

When there was a stream of blood I lowered my arm to the parched thing beneath me, parting the cold lips, letting the life into her.

There was no sound but the trickle of fluid, a pretty sound, like ground water in the heartrock of a hill.

But it was nothing more. It was only a musical splashing that would make nothing happen.

I knew now, as I had not during my life, why animals awe us. They have no hope. No faith sustains them. They have power, and fear, but no past, and no future. The moment is their planet, their sky. But I was still human enough to desire, and seek. This new grief was hard.

Without reasoning, without understanding, I had believed I knew my own powers. The earthen body of Rebecca received my gift without sound, without movement, the blood emptying into her.

I heard them long before they reached me. The police radios crackled and jabbered. Doors slammed. Footsteps whispered across the grass, coming my way. A flashlight jittered over the upper edge of the grave.

I nearly gathered the cold remnant into my arms, and fled with that bundle to console me. But I saw how wrong I had been. I saw how I had violated her rest. I left her there.

I swung myself out of the hole. Figures crouched, beams of light catching me. There were three flashlights, four. The men circled, keeping well away from me. The flashlights trembled. Not one of them wanted to step any closer.

Something about me must have stirred compassion as well as fear. No weapon was drawn. There was a fragmentary truce, a radio lifted, a command given to other police in the distance. Stay away, I wanted to tell them. *Don't come near me.* Not for my sake. For their own.

"Richard?" It was Joe Timm's voice. He sounded shaken, his voice breathy. "We want to help you," he called, without any conviction.

When I fled now it was without hope. There would be no desire in me for anything but oblivion. Each breath was purposeless, each heartbeat the echo of a real heart, a real life.

I was far from the grave, running through the broad, raspy leaves uphill, land that had not been needed yet for the dead. I hurried higher up the slope. The eucalyptus trees stood tall here, and they had dropped such a multitude of branches and seeds that no grass could grow, only a few outcroppings of leathery weeds.

When the voice reached me I was lost to any thought, escaping through the trees, about to take wing. I half-fell, and turned, looking back, hating myself.

No, I told myself. I wouldn't let this happen to me. I wouldn't let my desires lie to me like this.

Richard!

It was not a voice. It was not a sound at all. It was my imagination, or what passed for it in a creature like myself. I supported myself against a tree, the blood flowing slowly down my hand.

I turned to flee again when my imagination stopped me once more. There was a cry. It came from below, somewhere beyond the trees. It came from, among the police, among the graves.

I knew that I was torturing myself. And yet I allowed myself to utter her name, a whisper. Three syllables.

Again the voice touched me: "Richard!"

I took a step down the hill, my foot half-slipping on the bell-like seeds of the eucalyptus.

"Richard, help me!"

It was Rebecca.

❄

Part Four

❄

39

Men climbed toward me, up the hill. Flashlight beams danced. There was a labored hunch to the way most of them ran, cradling shotguns. They made no effort to be quiet, fallen branches snapping underfoot.

It was wonderful to see him: Joe Timm was in the lead, out of breath. He nearly stumbled on the roots of a tree, keeping himself upright by seizing a branch. He turned to direct his men to fan out. I saw as never before how determined Joe Timm was. It was not bluff. It was a quality he had, like acute hearing: fear meant little to him.

But a few of my pursuers had heard her, too. They slowed, stopped, confused. You could see them eager to stay where they were, safe among the trees, and not return to the graveside, not hurry onward after me.

I won't hurt you, Joe.

I sent this thought without intending to. Joe stopped running, twitching the flashlight beam into the branches above, and back to the pebbles at his feet.

"Richard?" he rasped.

I intended to be reassuring. *I will do you no harm.*

He put his hand to his hat, tugging the brim. He let the beam of light play slowly, like a man watering a lawn. Had he heard her, too? Was this why he insisted on marching up the hill—so he could pretend reality was not unravelling?

No harm.

He took another step, straining forward, trying to see where I was. His shaft of light nearly found me. I was about to speak to him, to use my voice.

"Richard, it's wrong!" he called. "What you're doing is wrong!" His light lost itself overhead, in the trees.

I felt a twinge of fellowship. I wanted to ask him how his bonsais were, his dwarf maples and pines. I wanted to ask how his wife was doing, her heart. Already I was streaking across the hillside, dodging trees. I could not stay here a moment longer.

"It's not going to be as easy as you think!" Joe Timm called. "We're going to run you to the ground!"

This last rhetorical flourish was for the benefit of his men. There was something artificial about Joe Timm's behavior. Joe Timm alone would be a more quietly stubborn adversary. As long as he led other men he would feel the need to call out, to be seen.

It was easy to elude Joe and his police academy graduates. The most perceptive of them were baffled, heads together, uncertain. The more dogged, and less alert, were already thrashing the weeds in the undeveloped land. A bird startled by their passage broke from branch to branch, high in the trees.

I slipped into a dry stream bed, and followed the fold in the hillside down, in the opposite direction, back to the asphalt road. Two uniformed officers stood beside a car, and they did not see me as I sailed past. Was I a winged creature, or did I run on two legs, or four? I could not tell, and it no longer mattered.

There, you see, I mocked myself. My mind was teasing me, my hope coining counterfeits. I knelt at the grave. How many times have we heard someone call our name and looked back, only to see a stranger beckoning to another stranger, arms out to him, an embrace. It was one form of wisdom almost every human attains— to expect disappointment, to tolerate it, to sail forth on diminished expectations.

The casket was broken. I began to *see*, not to anticipate. I began to perceive what was before my eyes. The satin of the interior was pale, freckled with mildew and clots of earth. The grave was empty.

She called me again.

Her voice came from far away. I ran hard down the hill, then stretched into wing, soaring over statuary, gravestones and crosses. She was nowhere. There was only the still magic of the dark.

When I saw her at last she was a small white puppet curled into a hollow. I hovered over her, and knelt. I was afraid to look at her.

I reached forth my hand, tentative, disbelieving. She was warm. I touched my lips to hers and she was breathing. I gathered her into my arms.

I soothed back her hair and gazed at her. Already there was color and movement, her lips, her fingers. Gradually I let myself feel the first happiness. The police were lost, thrashing through poison oak, far up the hillside. The whisper of her gown was the only sound, that and my footsteps as I strode through a bed of nasturtiums, the green vines snaking across a sidewalk.

Her voice was a whisper. "Richard!"

"I'm here," I said. I wanted to add, *Everything's all right* but emotion made it impossible.

Her calls to me had ruined her voice and she could only whisper, "Richard, where are you?" She clung to me, hard.

I wanted to tell her I was holding her. I wanted to tell her we were together again. But I had to hurry. There was that familiar stirring in the air. A window across the street was suddenly a source of light, and a man parted the curtains. The sky was no longer simple dark. A cloud was taking on an outline, rose, egg-yellow, chalk blue.

I tilted a manhole cover, and dragged the big steel dish into the street. I lowered her into the round hole, and climbed down after her. I pulled the lid carefully back into place.

"Where is he?" she said, flinging one arm out into the darkness. She struggled.

I tried to tell her that we were safe.

"The house is burning!" she said.

"No one can hurt us here," I said.

"Richard, there's a fire," she said, controlling her fear.

"No," I said soothingly. "We're in no danger—"

"Save yourself!" she cried.

"The fire is out, Rebecca," I said. I laughed tenderly. "It's been out for a long time. The man who wanted to hurt you is dead."

I almost said: *the man who killed you.*

She touched my face. She touched my tears. She tried to kiss them away, but I turned my head. She was innocent of everything I had done. As joyous as I was, I knew the truth.

"Richard," she whispered. "I thought I would never see you again."

She wore a long, flowing gown, the fabric stiff with moisture, foxing. It was the sort of dress she would have worn for a recital, and even stained and soiled it was elegant. She became strengthless in my arms again, and I kissed her eyelids, hoping she could not sense my doubt.

I recognized the sleep that claimed her, the solemn torpor. "My God," I breathed, the words sing-song in my wonderment, my happiness, my fear. "What have I done?"

But she was here with me, now, and I would not lose her again. I carried her gently. The drain was corrugated metal, and I eased her along through the tunnel until we reached another chamber, this one smaller and crowded with pipejoints and metal housing for what I guessed was electronic equipment.

We slept there, among the rust and slowly dripping water. Sometimes a *clang* would reach my consciousness, a car running over the manhole cover. In my haste, I had replaced the cover imperfectly. It was loose, and every time a car ran over it the iron disk rang, an ugly, sour bell.

At some point during the day the manhole cover was pried free. Steps descended the ladder, splashed in the trickle of water. Voices echoed. I had the vague sense that a beam of light was stretching out along the drainpipe, the beam weak by the time it reached our hiding place.

I heard it, a voice in a dream. Joe Timm's voice, exhausted. "They could be anywhere."

40

She was still asleep, but I could feel her slow breathing.

I tried to sense what was taking place above us, in the world of streets and houses. So much of our lives is like this: trying to be where we are not, imagining what others are doing. Occasionally a car passed on the street above, but there was no hint of any danger.

It was painful to leave her, but I had to hurry. I lifted the manhole cover gently, slid it, letting it settle as soundlessly as possible. Two figures stood at the end of the street. A streetlight gleamed off the plastic visor of a helmet.

Joy made the porchlights, the parked cars, full of promise. I swept through the early evening. I had a new purpose, a new courage. I took only what life I needed, from a man working on a brilliant red sports car, from a woman bathing, from another woman pacing, peering out from between curtains until I took her in my arms.

How many times had I paused before a painting in an art book and thought: I'll have to sit down and take a long look at this some day. How many times had I heard a favorite piece of music on the radio and thought: some day I'll have to really listen to that. I had always been called away, frog-marched from insight and pleasure by my own hectic nature.

Once again I let the blood spill from my veins into Rebecca. I had the chilling suspicion that this time it would not work. I kissed her, and she stirred, but did not wake.

I told her I loved her. I said it like a man saying his last words, in a rush, just before vanishing from the earth. It was not even my own voice speaking, but something deeper, the humanity that remained in me.

�֍

At last she woke. Her fingers searched my eyebrows, my lips. "He was someone I knew," she said, her voice broken. "Someone who loved me, a long time ago."

"Eric," I said. "Don't worry about him."

If she was surprised that I knew his name she made no sign. "Where are we?" she asked at last.

The damp dripped. There was a far-off splashing, four legs breaking the water. I said, "We're in a special place," happiness in my voice.

She smiled. Her hand found the wall, the pocked concrete, a seam glued with algae. She recoiled slightly, and I could see her curiosity shift into concern. She turned her head to listen to the pattering of a small animal in the distance.

"No one can harm us here," I said.

She touched my lips with her fingers. "Your voice sounds so strange."

I laughed quietly.

She said, "There's something wrong."

"Rebecca, you'll have to be very patient."

"Tell me where we are."

"You'll only want to know how we got here," I said.

"It's a secret," she said with a tentative smile.

"You could say that." It hurt me. She could not begin to understand.

She thought I was being playful, coy. She felt the hard concrete wall again, the joint of pipes above her head. She said, "If you give me enough time I can figure it out."

"Try to stand up," I said.

She stayed where she was. "What am I wearing?"

"It's very pretty."

"What is it? Something my mother picked out. She always wanted me to look like the woman on a wedding cake. Did the studio call?"

Conversation like this was so sweet and so foreign to me that I had trouble following her meaning.

She sensed my confusion. "The Arch Street studio. I can hardly move my fingers! I won't be able to play like this."

I helped her to her feet. "You'll be able to do anything you want."

"They'll reschedule me," she said, as though it was a simple fact. She moved her arms, a mannequin come to life.

"Of course they will. If that's what you want."

"What color is it?" She pulled at the gown, trying to make sense of the way it felt, falling in hard folds.

"Sky blue, I think. Azure. Can you walk?"

"This place smells so damp." Her voice was soft, but it echoed. "We're undergound!" she said. "But— where are the doctors?"

"Try not to be so loud," I said, making it sound like a game we were playing.

"Richard—are you in trouble?"

I wrenched open a car door and stretched her on the backseat. Before now I had the impression that I could start a vehicle by my will alone, empower it with a thought. Now was the time to find out. I sat behind the steering wheel, slipped the transmission from *park* to *neutral.*

Ripe, generous—that's how cars had so often impressed me, pages of glossy magazines with a woman leaning against a fender. This vehicle was a thing of cold iron, grease and slag. I knew this hulk, down to the rust already beginning on the underside of the hood. *Fire.* It was stone that fire had melted, and now it needed fire again.

A spark. A cylinder jerked upward, and there was the pungent perfume, gasoline. The engine twitched again, a grinding, whining, choking sound, the starter failing.

The engine caught.

"I have a terrible feeling," she said from where she lay in the backseat. I steered clumsily, as before, almost clipping a parked car.

"I have a very bad feeling that you did something wrong," she said.

What is it that makes some cats feel they can do anything they want? I almost hit one that darted across the street, not even in a great hurry, running stiff-legged, its paws a blur.

"Tell me you didn't do it, Richard."

"Do what?" I tried to sound lighthearted, but I was having a surprising amount of trouble driving. My skill with automobiles was as bad as before, or worse. I searched for the brake with my foot and found it.

Rebecca sat up. She touched my hair, ran her fingers along the back of my neck.

"Richard, promise you'll tell me the truth."

"I'll try."

She didn't want to ask. But at last the question came. "Did you do something you shouldn't do?"

I gave a forced laugh. "Like what—murder Connie?"

"You're acting so strange, Richard. I can tell you're some sort of fugitive."

She said this without irony or exaggeration, offering the statement without a trace of self-consciousness. This had always amazed me about her, her grasp on the essentials that I had always been happy to overlook.

"What would we be running from?" I asked.

"You tell me." She sank back. "What kind of car is this?"

"I don't know. Something Detroit decided America needed to drive." I didn't want to tell her that I had picked it among the others parked along the street because it didn't have an alarm.

"It's not yours?"

"I stole it." This happens to me. I try to make a joke, and end up telling the truth.

"Richard, I'm afraid."

"Don't let a little grand theft bother you," I said.

"It's not that. If you feel you have to steal cars, steal cars. That's not what bothers me. I can tell something terrible has happened."

"Like what?" I steered, braked, lurching from lane to lane. The glow of freeway lights was ahead, an ugly destination I could not avoid.

Her gown rustled. "I don't feel right."

"I told you you would have to be patient," I said. "I won't keep any secrets from you. But you have to wait."

"Are my parents hurt? Is Simon okay?"

"Your family is fine, as far as I know."

"Richard, there's something wrong with my body." There was an uneasy shiver to her voice. "I feel stitches—some sort of plastic thread is holding me together." I could sense her wanting to say this with something like humor, trying to exact an explanation.

A stoplight changed. Traffic moved. The onramp lifted us onto the freeway, although I found the car mounting the shoulder, weeds and trash clawing the underside of the car. I wrestled it back into the slow lane.

"I was in a coma," she said at last.

If sleep reflects death, resembling it, then I could answer truthfully. "That's true."

"Why do you say it like that. *That's true.*"

This brief imitation of my own voice made me laugh. "I'm sorry," I gasped at last. "I can't help it."

She had not joined in my laughter. If anything, she seemed disturbed by it. There was an experiment I had been afraid of making. I made it now. I glanced into the rearview mirror.

There was no sight of her.

The mirror was empty, except for the headlights of the cars behind us on the freeway. Mirrors have always called to us, always wanted us to leave. Now this empty glass invited me, this stream of lights, the place we were fleeing.

The engine surged and faltered. The steering wheel would not respond to my grip, as though the power steering fluid was running out. When I changed lanes to pass a slow truck the car swung too far, nearly sideswiping a yellow van in the far lane.

"How long was I unconscious?" asked Rebecca.

I took an offramp, and stopped at a red light in a neighborhood of small shops, car stereos, custom kitchens. I had thought I could drive north, like any man beginning a vacation.

"I'll tell you everything you want to know. Right now there's something wrong with this car," I said.

"The car?" she said, not believing it. She was drowsy. "I can tell. There's something wrong with both of us."

I could sense her reluctance to fall asleep. Weariness claimed her as I drove.

"No, there's nothing wrong," I said, when I knew she could not hear me lie.

41

She woke once, calling my name.

I said that I was here, there was nothing to worry about.

"We have to go back!" she said.

The car lurched as I aimed and re-aimed, never getting it right, always overcompensating, the gravel of the shoulder crackling under the tires. "Back where?" I asked, trying to sound jaunty, Dad out for a Sunday spin.

She didn't speak for a moment. "It was a dream," she said.

Sometimes the accelerator stuck, or the fuel line clogged. The car lost power, only to roar ahead arbitrarily.

"It was one of those nightmares," Rebecca was saying, "where I had a recital in ten minutes, and I had to hurry, but I hadn't practiced the piece. Had never heard of it." She tried to laugh. "I had to go back for something. Something that would save me."

"You had to go back and practice," I suggested.

"No, it was something else. I had to be quick or something terrible would happen."

A bridge, girders and brakelights, hulked ahead. I patted my clothing. I needed money, and all I could find in the glove compartment was a map of Yosemite and every gas station receipt the car owner had ever collected. The brakes made an asthmatic exhalation every time I slowed the car. I knew I would not be able to steer the car past the tollbooth of the Richmond/San Rafael Bridge. I would scrape something off, a doorknob, a toll taker.

The wrinkled palm thrust itself out, a young woman in a knit cap, chewing a fresh stick of gum. The smell hit me, artificial mint, with a drugstore waft of lipstick and cologne. The woman did not look at me, and then, when her hand continued to be untouched by money, she looked into the car, into my eyes.

We aren't here.

There was a Highway Patrol car parked to one side. I accelerated as smoothly as I could.

"I can hardly wait to play the piano again," she said. She stretched out on the backseat. Her gown rustled, her hands, I sensed, searching her body. "The fire didn't burn me," she said, her voice nearly fading.

San Quentin was to our left, the famous prison a fortress, tiny windows. "I got there in time," I said. I hated how I sounded, cheerful, upbeat, the officer in a war movie who goes around reassuring the GI's. *Everything'll be fine, men. After all, we're already dead.*

She said, "But I have all these wounds."

I didn't want to say it. *He cut you so many times.*

At last I was able to escape the freeway, and drove with fanatical care past pasture with its scent of manure and pond-mud, ducks lined up along the mire. A mailbox leaped out of the darkness, and a fence post and a tangle of barbed wires barely avoided the right fender.

The Pacific. I could smell it. I rolled down the window and drank in the delicious promise. The car slowed stubbornly, iron wanting to turn back into stone, into earth. I let the vehicle glide to a dead stop.

We left the car at the edge of a salt marsh. A stilt or sandpiper broke out of the brush, its cry piercing the dark. The tide was in, the water shimmering around black reeds. Translucent plates of living matter caught starlight and glowed, jellyfish abandoned by the tide. A great bird, a heron, parted his wings but did not take the air, observing us warily.

I carried her. The wooden pier creaked under my feet, the dark water glittering through knotholes and the cracks between the boards.

"I have a better plan," I said, carrying her down wooden steps to the wharf.

"I think you were right," she said. "There was something wrong with the car."

My father owned a sailboat when I was young, a fiberglass vessel I recalled as remarkable for its whiteness. The hull was bright white, and the sails were so dazzling that one of the first times I ever wore sunglasses was on San Francisco Bay the day after Christmas. I had learned to tie a knot called a fisherman's bend, and I could read a compass. But now I untangled two faded lifejackets and wished I had some of my father's sailing skill.

The craft I chose was a cutter, with a single, bare mast. The hull was a flaking powder-blue, weather and sun having bleached what had been a darker shade. The small cabin was secured in a very unseamanlike way with a locked bicycle chain. The decking was weathered and peeling, and the quantity of rope coiled in the well was kinked and stiff with salt.

It was an old-fashioned craft, a bit of history, with a box of tholepins in the stern for no reason that I could detect, along with a toolchest of old hammers and nails, dusted with rust. Whoever owned this craft would not immediately notice its loss, while the other, racier vessels along the wharf smelled of brass polish and Valvoline.

I broke the chain. The interior of the cabin was tidy. A bunk, a shelf, a small radio. I made sure Rebecca was secure on the bunk, a folded wool blanket for a pillow. I kept my head down so I wouldn't hit it on anything.

The boat had a donkey engine, good for escaping the barnacle-crusted piers of the wharf, but little else. The engine coughed at my touch, and churned forth smelly exhaust. The propeller kicked up the dark water of the marina, foam and a floating napkin, a jellyfish.

The tide and the churning propeller compelled the vessel outward, the low hills embracing Tamales Bay on either side of the black. A light at the end of a distant wharf did not appear to move. After what seemed like half the night, at last it took up a new position behind us.

Points of light crept by. The keel sliced water, the fresh air soiled by the smell of engine exhaust and the sulphuric fume of the marsh on either side of the bay. The tide was falling, exposing wrinkled littoral. And if we were going to run aground this was where it would happen, where the current had silted the mouth of the bay, water swirling around limpet-spiked rocks.

Seabirds sprinkled the water, asleep or hypnotized by the rising swells, puffins, surf scoters. The bluffs where the land ended were pale, the surf busy, erupting and spilling along the beach. I guided the boat toward the northwest, with a light breeze on the starboard quarter.

But the weather was changing. As the keel cut the water I found the craft battling, swinging wide with the rising seas. I worked the bow up into the wind. Moderate waves, with rolling, breaking crests, tackled us, driving us south and, at the same time, gradually farther from land. Far to the southwest glided the lights of a great ship, a tanker approaching the Golden Gate.

When day simmered to the east I lashed the tiller and killed the engine. I did not question myself. I could only proceed, discovering what I knew only after I had acted. I nearly grieved when I wrapped Rebecca with rope, making an impromptu body sling out of this weathered cordage.

I fastened two large iron hammers into her bodice, lashed there by the ropes that cocooned her. She woke as I tied the last knot. "Tell me when we're there," she said.

How could I even talk to her? *Where*, I wanted to ask her. Where do you think we are going, so trusting?

"I will," I said.

"Are you cold?" she asked.

"No," I answered truthfully. I felt no cold, only an intensity of feeling.

"You sound cold, or scared. I dreamed," she said. "There were flowers, all different colors."

What couldn't I make myself sound jaunty now? Where was my spirit, now that I needed it most? "That sounds beautiful," I said.

"And a piano. A beautiful piano, and I could smell the gardenias."

Daylight seeped into the gray east. The sea was even heavier now, rolling, breaking crests. Foam broke from the crest of a wave and spun through the weakening dark. "I wish I had dreams like that," I said.

"Is it morning?"

"Not yet."

"We're in a boat," she said.

"It's a kind of yacht," I said. "A small yacht." I wanted to tell her there were people on the boat, cabins with bright lamps and crystal vases.

"You *are* cold," she said. Then, "I can't move my arms."

I put my hands over her eyes. I kissed her. *Sleep, Rebecca. All will be well.*

I carried her to the stern and held her, not wanting to release her. I tested the knot around the rail with one hand. It was my best knot, one I had learned to tie in my boyhood.

The air was seething, and a gull lowered itself over the boat, its wings alive to the strata of the breeze. It was able to hover, resting on the wind like a swimmer too lazy to kick, carried by the current.

Dawn was only moments away. The gull cocked his head, and I knew he was searching the boat for fish, for carrion. I seized one of the tholepins and threw it. To my surprise, I hit the bird, sending it tumbling, recovering, swinging far out above the boat.

I tried to lower Rebecca carefully, but at the last instant she slipped from my hands and was gone. The swell winked and shrank around the rope where it entered the water. I had a confused but vivid fantasy—barracuda, sharks.

Don't think.

I filled every pocket with nails, old iron spikes so rusty they were turning to stone, bristling handfuls of encrusted metal. I worked a hammer into my belt, a great iron battle weapon, and with my stiff fingers I fastened my rope beside Rebecca's, a stopper knot around the taffrail.

The water felt warm, bathwater rising up around me as I sank. I knew it was only the relative chill of my own body that made it feel so pleasant, but I welcomed the illusion. I sank downward, and found her, already unconscious, lost to the world the way the living rarely are. Her heartbeat was stopped. Then, after a long minute it pulsed, once, and fell still for another age.

I clung to her there, where sun was something out of a storybook, a tale that was not true.

42

Only once did I sense a living thing.

A warm wall glided past, sensate and superior. Lichen bloomed along this expanse, moss and the small plants that mistake any surface for soil.

But before I was fully aware of the whale, we were alone again.

Not to wake, I told myself. Not to know—that will be peace. But it was too late. My body swung, a pendulum. A tug from above and it swung again, and I clung to Rebecca to keep her near.

We were in a world made of glass, fine bubbles slowly ascending. The sky above was in fragments, torn scraps. And yet I felt the sure, certain knowledge that my companion was Rebecca.

But then, just as surely, the doubt began again, and a deep sense of wrong. I had deceived her. The keel of the boat was coarse with barnacles, and the rudder tugged back and forth with the current.

I hauled my body to the surface. The dark was blustery, the sea bounding and collapsing, waves clawed by wind. I pulled the rope hand over hand until Rebecca was on the deck beside me.

I freed her from the rope. She was gray, her hair plastered dark around her face. I did not allow myself to experience normal anguish at the sight. We were far at sea, the spindrift flying, the mast humming in a gale. But there was an odd island of tranquility about our boat, except when it staggered upward onto the crest of a wave.

She had my hand in hers. She was trying to speak.

"Heavy weather," I said, with what sounded to my ears like maniacal cheer.

She turned her head and coughed, emitting a trickle of seawater. "Tell me what's wrong," she said when she could manage to make a sound.

I will.

One hand crept out onto the weather-blistered deck. "Where did we spend the night?"

Where did we spend the *day*, I longed to say.

"Something wonderful has happened," she said. "Hasn't it?"

"Something wonderful," I echoed. I took her in my arms, kissing her, water seeping from her gown, her hair streaming. I had been selfish to bring her back to this.

"I dreamed we were living at the bottom of the ocean," she said. "It was just like land, hills and rocks. But there were only the two of us."

"And we couldn't drown," I said. "We breathed the water in and out, like air."

"That was the dream," she said. She touched my face, tracing my nose, my mouth. "I think I know what's wrong," she said. "I think I can tell what's changed."

"Don't try to think, Rebecca. Don't worry—"

"We're in the middle of a storm," she said, sounding unconcerned.

"In the middle of a storm, in the middle of the ocean," I said. I tried to argue myself out of a respect for what attorneys call truth issues. Did I really know my own nature, and what my nature was likely to become?

"I don't know anything about boats," Rebecca was saying. I could hear her unasked question: just how small is this yacht?

There was a simple pleasure in making conversation. It was constructed, tongue and groove, out of what we needed to say, and avoid saying. "You can call almost any pleasure vessel a 'yacht'," I said.

"We're alone?"

"Entirely alone."

She put out her hand and found mine. "Don't joke about this, Richard." But she had a strange smile, an odd certainty in her voice.

"There are worse things than solitude," I said.

"You're afraid to tell me," she said.

"Do you remember how much you disliked stepping on snails," I said. "They crawled out onto the stones—and you asked me to rescue them before you would go outside."

"What kind of an operation did I have," she asked, not a question so much as a gentle challenge.

A *postmortem*, I wanted to say. They stitched you up every which way because they knew it didn't matter.

But she was drowsing again, rocked gently by the shifting of the boat. I carried her into the cabin, and the water soaked from her gown into the mattress of the bunk.

Swinging on a bent nail was a weather radio, tuned to 162.55 megaherz, the National Weather Service. The batteries were al- most spent, the broadcast a whisper. But I could hear clearly enough the storm warning, *from the Channel Islands north, with gusts up to sixty knots.*

A storm was coming. A big storm, almost a hurricane.

I knew what to do without really knowing anything, flying with- out intention, soaring high above our craft. The sight of it far below would have troubled me if I had let it, such a tiny nutshell.

The wind twisted my wings, straining them. I blew like a hat in a cartoon. Weightless at times, I tried to fight the updraft that swept me into the clouds.

When a tanker loomed out of the storm, I labored toward it through the blowing salt spray. I missed the deck entirely, flattened against the side of the ship by the wind. I crawled upward, my leathery appendages slipping along the steel without a sound.

I rolled onto the deck and felt my body fall open like a book, losing itself to my man-like shape again.

The engine thrummed, and the big ship took the swells, settling just slightly to port and then correcting itself. It would be easy to forget the ocean entirely in a floating building like this.

The ship was a plateau of steel, as characterless and unlovely as a refinery. Rustproof paint, clay-red and sea-gray. The working and living quarters were units in a city, a place of duty and desultory recreation, paperbacks, videotapes. I had expected sailors, technicians, but I saw no one.

I paused beside a fire extinguisher and put my ear to the bulkhead. The grind of the engine was a rumor. There was a smell in the air I could recognize.

Two men sat at a table, eating from plates with sections, one compartment for string beans, another for Salisbury steak. It had been a long time since I had paid any notice to the eating habits of ordinary people, and the smell stopped me, microwaved flesh and canned vegetables. Surely that wasn't what food smelled like, I thought. I remembered eating with gusto.

Now I looked on with something like horror as one of the men tried to cut a string bean with his fork, a pale gray seed squeezing out from the ruptured pod. "You never see a flat," one of the men was saying, muscular, with hairy blond arms. "Not anymore."

They chewed.

The one with hairy arms continued, "The tires are too good."

"What are those guys doing?" said the other one, younger, with an accent I could not place, Scandinavian. "Along the freeways— you see them."

The hairy-armed one gave a nod and a smile, still chewing. "When I say *never* I mean same-as-never," he said. And for a moment I could not bring myself to interrupt them.

They did not speak again. They worked the half-chewed food around in their mouths. They both saw me at the same time, and they acted in a way that could have been mistaken as courtesy, napkins to lips, chairs forced back, both men standing.

This time I climbed straight into the sky. It was going to be hard, fighting the wind, and I wanted to gain as much altitude as I could.

I pulled upward into the rain, until the updraft of a cloud swept me higher. I panicked, until the ice begin to bristle my hair and I fell again, the grizzle melting as I tumbled.

I couldn't find our boat.

There was a hard logic to it. It was more than logic—justice. Its time past, the old vessel had vanished. Who was I to expect this miracle to spin itself out forever? I had lost her.

I screamed her name, my cry out of the range of sound. And I began the search, swell, valley, sudden mountain, beckoning plain, all of it below me, a world new every moment.

We all have the dream. We are called to take an examination, or show up to fill out a long, impossibly difficult questionnaire. Without passing this test, without filling out this form in the time allotted, everything we have accomplished will be lost.

The dream was true. It recurred because I had never seen that it was not a dream. It was the way I had lived my life, my existence a test.

I found it.

The mast stabbed the wind at crazy angles, and I fell toward the vessel certain that I would miss it and plunge into the waves.

I collapsed on the deck. I found my human shape, ulna, radius, the highways of bone reasserting themselves. I flung myself toward the cabin. Surely the iron melodrama behind such nightmares would continue to play itself out. I knew what would happen next —the cabin would be empty.

She was still there.

This time I opened several vessels in my wrist, subcutaneous and interior, veins and at least one artery. This time as she drank she lifted her head and drew strength from me with growing color, her eyes fluttering, her head falling back to the bed at last.

Blood pattered onto the floor, and I tasted the flow, drinking from my own wrist. Wrong, I told myself. I am using her, seducing her into this.

She sat up, steadying herself against the rocking of the boat.

"It's time to wake up," I said, sitting beside her, putting my arm around her. Blood snaked into my palm, already congealing, the skin healing.

"You don't have to tell me," she said in a rush. "I know."

"Let's not stay in here," I said.

It was better outside the cabin, in the wind. She said, "There was an autopsy."

This was my last, best opportunity to lie. Leave her one or two illusions, I urged myself. Since when is brutal honesty the wisest, kindest course of action?

It was over. She knew.

She continued, "I was dead. The coroner did an autopsy."

Medical examiner, I mentally corrected her. Postmortem.

"I know what you've done," she said.

I shivered. It was the strangest feeling—I could not meet her eyes. I said, "I am not proud of anything." It wasn't entirely true. There was some small pride I took in the way I had learned so much, in the way I had survived. "I didn't think I had any choice."

And shame. I felt shame, too.

The storm was dying. The quiet was what carried us, lifting and holding us. "We can't live like people," I said.

She laughed. I was astounded. Her laugh was tender, but it was mocking, too. I had expected shock and sorrow, dismay, the sort of self-loathing I had begun to expect in myself. "Richard, I have something to tell you."

"Forgive me," I said. "If you can."

"My gown is blue. Like the sky at noon. You're taller than I expected, and so pale, Richard. But beautiful—Richard, you're so wonderful!"

I looked into her eyes.

She spoke calmly, as though measuring her words, preparing me for them. "There are many things we have to learn," she said.

The boat slipped to one side, shifted, and rose again on the next swell.

Touching my lips with hers, she said, "I can see."

43

She still wanted to touch things, run her hands along the rails, the foot of the mast. She was fascinated by the lifejacket—*look at this color, Richard!*—but comprehended its purpose only when she looked away from it and her hands could search its straps.

She said she had trouble determining what things were. She knew all about clouds, and the ocean, and how clothing rumpled in wind, dimpling and smoothing.

Colors fascinated her, the weed-yellow ash of the mast, the green corrosion of brass fittings. I wanted to show her everything, trees, houses, faces, far-off cities, and all that offered itself to the eye was this lost storm, frittering itself away.

But it was more than enough, a few stars in the sky. She loved the way the weathered cordage twisted in her grasp when she tried to wind it into a loop. Whether by my will, or by an accident of the gale, the boat swung around and nosed south, and I stood at the helm pretending I had some choice in the matter. She crouched on the cabin's roof, hanging on to the mast, and kept looking back. When I waved I was stunned when she lifted her arm and waved in return.

"It's beautiful!" she cried.

Yes, I must have called. Beautiful as I rarely saw it, all the way to the horizon.

I was a part of her visible world. I felt how meager my appearance must be, how she deserved to see men and women in finery. When a gull adventured through the night she whooped, and the bird heard her, shying upward, spinning away.

"A bird," she cried.

The hours I had spent in recent nights all fitted together, and I wanted nothing but this, the boat racing ahead of the wind as I decided where I wanted to go, a new course, a new future. A puzzle is like that, one day fitting together into something like the scene on the lid of the box, the picture some rule-bound member of the household has put away so no one can cheat. The summer cottage of my boyhood often sported a card table with a jigsaw puzzle, a Monet garden or a Buddhist temple beyond a half-circle bridge.

When a whale broke water in the distance I scrambled to her side. The tail lifted drowsily, delicate at this distance.

Sometimes I manned the helm, but the boat generally drifted on its own, like a dray horse guiding itself homeward. I had not felt this way since I was a child—playing at some game, pretending to be pirates, knowing that soon some voice from the adult world would break the spell.

"We're dressed like we're going to a wedding," she said, running her fingers along the lapel of my jacket.

"I think we should compliment the limousine service, don't you?"

"What color are my eyes?" she asked.

"Ocean blue. Mine are almost the same color, sort of. More filing cabinet gray," I said.

"Agate blue," she corrected me.

"It's too dark to really tell." Our eyes were actually almost the same slate gray, but there was life in her eyes, nuance, humor.

"I'll see even better when the sun comes up," she said.

"I felt the whales when we were sleeping," I said, to avoid the subject of morning. "They were so close they nearly brushed us."

"I thought your hair was black," she said.

"I think it says *brown* on my driver's license."

"It's a reddish color. And your eyebrows have a hint of gold—I can hardly wait for better light."

"They migrate this time of year," I persisted.

"Your eyebrows?"

We both laughed. She ran fingers through her hair. "God—I wonder if there's a mirror in the cabin. Not that I'm eager. I'd rather put off my first look."

Tell her now.

"I'm afraid," she said. "Isn't that silly? I'm afraid to look into a mirror. The last time I saw myself I was ten years old."

I looked down over the stern, and even in the bad light I could tell. There was no silhouette in the shifting water, no sign that I was there.

I wanted her to see something spectacular, knowing that the ordinary glory of sunrise was forbidden. I knew she understood imperfectly what had happened to us. Morning could not be far off. She would discover what light and hunger changed in her.

The night turned warm, and stars broke through the clouds. No sign of daylight, only stars, the Milky Way, and man-made satellites ticking slowly eastward.

"I thought you would have a frown wrinkle, right here," she said, touching the space between my eyebrows. "From thinking so much."

I didn't want her examining me too closely. I let a little silence pass, water hissing as it rolled past the hull. "An airplane," I said, nodding upward, an aircraft high above the clouds.

"Tell me everything you know about this."

"Can't we just enjoy the view?" I said. I wanted to sound debonair, but my voice was ragged.

"If I knew all your secrets I would be miserable—is that what you mean?"

"There's Orion," I said, looking up again. "Taurus must be up there, too, behind the cloud."

"You're afraid!" she breathed, putting her arms around me. "Don't be, Richard. I'm so happy."

Perhaps it was her happiness that was beginning to trouble me.

"Eric Sunderland. Studious, insecure. Poor Eric," she said, when I had filled in the last details of my recent days. "He hated me because he thought it was easy for me. I got the scholarships, the prizes. He actually had talent for a certain type of music. Music with splash. Mussorgsky, Rachmaninoff. He could play that full-spectrum piano music much better than I could."

"He envied you," I said.

"Music was food for me. The struggle wasn't finding time to practice the piano. It was tearing myself away when it was time to do something else, like eat."

"He didn't have your talent."

"He did have a gift. His talent was different, but it was very much alive."

She had her arm around me, her eyes closed, as though the familiar world of touch was, for the moment, less overwhelming. We stood in the stern of the boat, where I would have held the tiller if the engine were chugging, if there were sail.

She continued wistfully, "Eric knew at some point he would never really go far in music. He had trouble keeping teaching jobs. He thought people were narrow-minded, put off by him because he had a bad temper."

I didn't want to think about Eric. I pictured him in his last moments despite myself, and I turned to look at the glassy wake of the boat. "You don't think I should have taken his life," I said. Why, I wondered, did I avoid saying *killing him*.

She put her hand on mine. "You shouldn't have killed Eric. It wasn't necessary. It was wrong. Look at us—this is all we need, isn't it?

"Eric doesn't make sense," I said. "Nothing about him does. You don't murder a woman because you envy her."

"But you might," she said, "kill a woman because you loved her."

I showed her the place on my finger, the cut. It was invisible now.

"You were going to sail up the coast to Crescent City to see my brother," she said. "To find out where the mirror came from. To fathom its secrets."

I felt miffed by her tone. "It was a plan."

"It was a good plan, Richard."

"Except for one thing," I said, prompting her.

"Connie lied to you," Rebecca said. "The mirror was never in my family. My family prides itself on plain wooden furniture, craftsman bungalows, pruning the roses the day after New Year's.

My father teaches engineering. My mother teaches remedial reading. They both believe in straight lines, neat handwriting, and balancing the checkbook."

I'd lost the argument, but persisted a little longer. "Maybe it was something you never noticed."

"Because I was blind I didn't realize we had an ornate treasure hanging in the living room?"

"You should have been an attorney."

She laughed. "And if Simon ever got his hands on something like that, I can't imagine him sending it to you as a gift. Simon would keep it and try to write his master's thesis on it. Simon conserves. Reads military history, loves the French Revolution. Giving you the melted bracelet was an act of real generosity on his part."

"I'm surprised I could be taken in so easily."

"I don't think she sold it, either. I think Connie fell in love with the mirror, and doesn't want you to have it."

I *will* have it, I thought.

"You certainly aren't going to break the mirror into a thousand pieces, Richard. I know you. You won't be able to."

"It's a dangerous thing," I said.

"Do you really think the mirror caused you to evolve into— whatever you are."

"Whatever *we* are."

"No, Richard—you brought me back into the world. Whatever happened between you and the mirror had to do with something in your nature, not in mine."

She was mistaken, I thought, but I let it pass. "There is some kind of poison. Something in the silvering, in the frame. Something toxic. The way mercury seeps into your body from dental fillings."

"I think Connie gave it to you," said Rebecca. "As an experiment, to see how you would react. Or out of vindictiveness, wanting to remind you of something."

"Then she must have known something about the mirror's history—"

"Something about its power," she said, just a trace of teasing in her voice.

"Knowing something about me," I said. "How I had always been fascinated by mirrors."

The sea was wrinkled, the swells constantly shifting the horizon. The sudden etching of shadows on the surface told me everything I had to know about why the gulls were pink, why the sea birds to the east were suddenly visible in such detail, in such numbers.

"Dental fillings don't do that, do they?" she was asking. "You just heard that somewhere. It isn't true."

I didn't answer. Dawn was nearly here.

After I cut my forehead on the mirror, my mother drove into Stinson Beach so a tanned, jolly, half-retired surgeon could chill my skin with a local anesthetic and take what he called a painless tuck, three stitches. I rode home in the front seat, marveling at all the blood on my T-shirt.

Rebecca was right. I didn't want to find the mirror. I wanted to stay like this, and some part of me sensed that, once I rediscovered the mirror, all of this would end.

44

As a child I loved rainy nights. I listened to the drift of the rain over the shingled roof and felt protected. As I grew older, and sued builders for roofs that could not withstand fallen branches, foundations built in dry creeks that flooded every January, I learned that no refuge is what it seems to be.

And yet, under the sea those long hours, I again felt protected. The waves were a quaking roof, the walls made of water.

So when I woke, the last light of sunset dimming from the water, it was a shock to find myself alone. I spun in the water, kicking hard in the direction Rebecca had been asleep during those hours of daylight. Her rope coiled and twisted high above, drifting. She was gone.

I scrambled to the surface. The ocean was calm, but a calm that breathed, alive. I called her name. The radio dangled from its bent nail, and the mattress on the bunk was just as we had left it, a wool blanket folded neatly at the foot. But the mattress was damp, and there were drops of water gleamed on the planks of the floor.

The Radio Shack receiver had been left switched on, faded now to an even more ghostly whisper, *three to five knots out of the north-west*, an innaccurate report. Still, I understood the instinct that had driven Rebecca to hear a human voice. I switched it off. There was a footprint, a parenthesis of water. She had sat here, on the bunk.

I could detect no wind, and the swells were glassy. I leaned against the stern calling, rushed to the bow, continuing to sound the three syllables of her name.

A gray whale lifted above the surface, breath fuming. It lifted a forked tail, lazily, and dropped it, a loud clap that reached me after a few seconds.

There were two layers of weatherproofing on the deck. The layer that was peeling, the outermost coat, was plastic, verathane. Then there was a yellow varnish, a coloring that did not peel away but wore through. Beneath it all was the decking itself, teak, fine-grained.

I had worn through to an inner core of myself. This was a substance that endured, my fiber. I climbed to the top of the cabin, crooked my arm around the mast, and called her name. In the early evening there were two tight clusters of lights, small craft making way to the north, toward the Golden Gate or Monterey Bay; I wasn't sure how far south we had drifted. For a moment the sight of these fishing boats or pleasure craft made me feel thin comfort.

But another sort of vessel, still far to the north, was heading this way.

The prow of this fast boat was cutting the seas. The waves parted neatly, twin leaves of water catching the starlight. The vessel sported a tall tower of radar equipment and broadcasting gear. A wide cylinder of light winked on, and its beam swept the water.

Surf worked the dark rocks to the east, cliffs and evergreens. The seas around the hull roiled, and something tangled and dark clung to the keel, slowing the boat. Some merchant marine or fisherman had spotted our boat, perhaps thinking we were in danger. But it was more complicated than that: we had left behind an abandoned car, not to mention an aggrieved boat owner. Perhaps all the deaths had been pieced together by now.

This new craft kept coming. I balanced briefly on the rail. Then I dived deep, slipping through the pods and stalks of a grove of kelp. A bank of fish broke around me, perch, shivering with the tide that swept through their fins, their gills.

My arms warped, my legs deformed, muscling into a shape that powered through the water. I had no clear concept of my body's configuration, only the awareness that I hunted and found nothing. Two otters tumbled through the water, awakened by me. They avoided me, and then tailed after me, urgent, curious.

A sea forest surrounded me. The vegetation was gigantic, hollow tubes connected to the sandy bottom with yellow roots. Mats of tangled plant stuff floated on the surface, kept bouyant with hollow knobs speckled with limpets. The stalks of the trees were bronze-brown, and they clung to my limbs, slowing my progress as I writhed and twisted.

The otters attracted my eye. They circled, and something about their curiosity guided me, as they began to wend onward ahead of me, as though they knew something.

What had I become now, I found myself wondering, a sea lion, that man-seal of legend, the Great Selkie? I floundered through the waves, and there on the beach was a scattering of logs, piled haphazardly together. But the logs were creatures, nosing the air as I dragged my body through the water. What I expected to be an arm was a broad, wet paddle, cutting the sand, and when I tried to lift my head I couldn't, my huge body clumsy and heavy.

At the very last a surge of foam caught me and carried me high onto the beach. The dry sand crusted on my flanks, loose sand in my nose. I sneezed. This was not a sneeze like any I had experienced before, the convulsion of a strange body. I was helpless afterward, flailing. My body wrenched, bones reknitting, my skull swelling again into a human form. It was painful, but sudden, and when it was finished I clutched at the wet sand.

I approached the sea lions with a thought that quieted them. At sea, the Coast Guard cutter bore down on our boat. Our bare-masted vessel was caught in the kelp, kept by the island of plant life from running aground. The Coast Guard beam illuminated the heaving sea weed, and the mast of our boat was a bright needle. Then the light dismissed our boat, and searched the beach.

Perhaps my presence would have made the beasts more restless, except for the distraction of the boat's searchlight. The seals were ruddy in this bright beam, auburn, brunette, their fur knicked and scarred. A loudspeaker sounded, words I could not make out.

I felt that some inner tongue, a power articulate in my psyche, could ask these animals where she was, and they would tell me. But it wasn't necessary. The way they had shifted along the beach, the sand scraped and molded, showed me where to look.

I found her human form on the beach, beside a huge mass of kelp. Her body left an imprint in the wet sand as I scooped her up and held her in my arms. I carried her through ferns, into the woods, to the side of a stream.

Human flesh itself was clothing for something effervescent, but I could not awaken her. She lay still, one hand open in the current of the stream, water streaming through her fingers.

A fox hesitated, one paw raised, ears cocked.

The air whispered above him. Wind, or a night bird. He couldn't tell. His dark eyes took in the sky, the leaves, everything that moved. But I did not move. I clung to the branch of a tree.

He lowered his head and lifted it again without touching the water. He heard it, too. The far-off rattle of an outboard motor above the rustle of the surf.

He sniffed the wind. Noise, and the scent of cold things, steel and rubber, and fuel. Silence was life. He lowered his nose and drank from the stream.

I did not want to take this quickness, this color. I found myself in a tree, hanging upside down, my body enfolding itself. The sound of his tongue on the water was not comforting, as the lapping of a family dog can be. It was a furtive sound, paws pressed into the mud of the stream.

I captured him. In an instant I knew what he knew, the field. And his prey, the sudden rush, the feathers, the warm heart, the quarry with its tiny bones, its stuttering blood.

She opened her eyes. As always, she touched my face, still trusting her fingers more than her sight. Then she looked up beyond me in wonder, and a little fear.

"Redwoods," I said.

Her lips shaped the question.

"Somewhere south of Point Lobos."

"A forest," she said at last. "How did we get here?"

I counted off her actions on my fingers. "You untied the rope. You swam up into the boat. You got tired of waiting for me—"

"Don't tease me, Richard."

"You tell me—what happened when you dived into the water?"

"I don't know." She meant: she didn't want to remember.

"I was very proud of that knot," I said. "Was it difficult?"

She gazed at her hands, her fingers, her nails. "No."

"So you do remember that much."

She sat up. Her fingers searched her surroundings, moss, wild iris, its blossoms folded, sorrel, like oversized shamrocks. She seemed to glow. "We need a doctor."

"That's a brilliant idea. We'll just drop in, sit in a waiting room, and then what? The doctor will ask us how we're feeling, and what will we tell him?"

She had already adopted the mannerisms of someone who could see, and expected to be seen in return.

"We have so much to do," I said.

She stood slowly, shaking out the folds of her gown. "I am starting to believe it all." She reached out to touch a sapling that was growing straight upward out of a fallen log. "I won't be able to see Simon again, or my parents. I won't be able to play the piano."

I had hoped to protect her. "You won't be able to see the sunlight," I said.

"You make it sound like good news."

"You flew," I said.

She was examining a redwood branch, the evergreen needles, the way leaf connected to twig, to frond, to the trunk, the tree sweeping upward. "I don't believe we can do that, Richard."

"Then how did you get here?"

"You brought me."

I smiled, shook my head.

She said, "I swam."

"I think the first thing you wanted to do when you woke up was take wing, like a gull."

"And I couldn't."

Another motor brayed beyond the surf. I parted the shrubbery and gazed out across the beach. Our boat was brightly lit. Yellow rubber rafts were tied to it, and men climbed the cabin, leaned over the stern. It was hard to make out what they were doing at this distance, but it was easy to imagine the radios sputtering.

She said, "They're going to find us."

45

We knelt beside the pawprints left by the fox. The stream spilled between two rocks, minnows asleep, each one flickering to stay in place.

A drop of blood gleamed on the stones. She could not stop herself from touching her forefinger to the blood and tasting it.

"Where is the fox?" she asked.

"He ran off, back to his foxy life," I said, trying to make light of his shocked agony, the way he had stayed still for a moment when I released him. The way he leaped at last, parting the grass. There was a path, still, where he had escaped. "I didn't kill him."

She put her fingers into a pawprint, lightly, and I could see her wondering about such prints, what it would be like to trot on four legs. She looked up and it took her a moment to find me because I had moved away from the stream, not wanting to see its pools empty of my reflection.

"But we do kill, don't we?" she asked.

As she bent over the stream I wanted to warn her. I couldn't keep the tension from my voice. "Carnivores take lives. Normal people eat meat."

She asked the question with a tone of deliberate innocence. "Is that what we are—carnivores?"

Even here the sound of outboard motors reached us, and the demand of an amplified voice, too far off to be understood.

"The fox must be very weak," she said. "If you took enough for both of us." She fingered a pebble, balanced it in her hand. "I forgot how many different colors rocks can be. All these shades of red and—look at this!"

The fox was very weak, but I did not tell her that. It had fallen twice, grass whispering, before it crossed the meadow.

She reached into the stream, the water reflecting starlight. "I was listening to a baseball game in the front seat when we had the accident," she said. "It was the last thing I remember seeing—the dials of the radio, my father's hands on the steering wheel. I don't think he really understood baseball. He wanted to, but it never made sense to him. I don't think he ever listened to another game after that."

She plucked a flat green stone from the stream bed, and even in the dark of night it was easy to perceive the warm green, the way the rock was almost translucent, veined with dark.

"I think it was harder on my parents than it was on me. Because they had so much faith in life, expecting so much for their children. Especially my father—he's so self-willed. One cup of coffee in the morning, one glass of whiskey on New Year's Eve."

I could hear it in her voice, how much she wanted to see them. "My mother had a cross made of stone like this," she continued, "on a gold chain. It was the only jewelry she ever wore." There was growing eagerness in her voice. "It's jade. And look at this—" She looked up at me with a smile, as though she had just proved something. "Agate—the color of your eyes."

She was going to perceive what was missing soon, unless I drew her attention from the water. But she had turned back to it, searching it for stones.

"This is why composers write symphonies," I said, trying to distract her with conversation. "Isn't this what music wants us to experience? This kind of life?"

"You mean, why play the piano when you can have a forest?"

"I didn't mean anything quite so extravagant. Besides, you'll have the piano, too."

"I don't see how, Richard." She leaped to her feet and took my hand, her fingers wet. " 'You'll have the piano, too,' " she said, a perfect imitation of my manner, the way I spoke, saving up my words and delivering them in a burst. "How can I tell my parents I'm alive—"

I tried to draw her away from the stream. "They'll be happy to hear from you."

"If I *am* alive."

I felt an urgent need to deny what she was saying. "You're as alive as you feel," I said, responding to her probing with greeting-card wit.

"Can I call them on a telephone?"

"We can do everything we want to do." *Come away*, I wanted to add. Come away and don't notice what is missing in the stream.

She grew pensive. "What's wrong, Richard?"

My laugh sounded forced.

But it communicated something to her. She turned from me, gazing back at the trickling water, and before I could stop her she broke away. She waded into the water, dropping to her knees. She crouched there, the water breaking and re-forming around her, gazing into the glittering stream.

❋

Long afterward she did not speak. She would turn sometimes, and study her own footprints, how water flowed into them, how they filled with light from the sky.

"Tell me how I look," she said at last.

With our mouths we swear to tell the truth, and with our mouths we lie. But when I kissed her now, feeling the fox-warmth that flushed her body, I no longer felt that I was touching Rebecca, the person I had once known. I was touching something more, something that I could name only with a shop-worn word, her spirit, her soul.

"Don't be afraid," I whispered.

She shook her head and smiled, bemused, not understanding why I was so happy. "When you look at me," she insisted, "what do you see?"

"Those hands I will always imagine on the keyboard. Or on me, on parts of my body. These." I kissed her fingers, one by one. They call it *power of speech* because it *is* a power. For the moment it failed me.

"If we don't cast a reflection in water—" she began.

"Don't think about it."

"—then we aren't real."

"There's so much else we can do." Meaning: if we can walk and talk we have to exist. It made sense, but I wasn't that happy with the argument.

She put her hand on my chest, a gesture she had always made during conversation, feeling my voice in my chest. This time it was to silence me. "Haven't you asked yourself why?"

"I ask myself every moment," I said. "Why I inhale and exhale, why my heart beats. Feel it. Is it pumping blood, or is it just acting like a living heart, the way the image on a movie screen acts like a person?"

Of course I knew what we were. I would not let her questioning look break my feeling of resolve, of exhilaration. To prove something to her, to dismiss her inquiries, I vanished.

I folded my arms and when I spread them I was winged. She

took a step back. Her eyes were alight with fear, her hair blown by the stroke of my wings. From far above the treetops I looked down, all I could see of her was a face and her pale hands; all I could hear was her voice calling my name.

When something makes no sense we assume we have misunder-stood. When reality stumbles we blame ourselves for inattentive-ness, for a false assumption. She abandoned her sight, eyes, and trusted only her other senses, reaching out for a fern, for the trunk of a tree.

Sometimes we expect to much of the ones we love. They can only think of what has been, not what we have become. The greeting, the plea, fail. From this height the Coast Guard cutter was made of light, whiteness shivering around it, the yellow rubber rafts glowing. Men cast lines to others on what had been our boat, the ropes invisible from here suddenly clear as a great beam of light from the bow of the Coast Guard cutter drenched the scene.

How long would we have, I wondered as I glided, settling down through the wet branches, the scent of earth rising up to me, the fragrance of the redwood bark and the centuries of redwood needles.

"Where did you go?" she asked in a whisper. I gestured upward, indicating the sky, but her eyes followed my hand, puzzled.

"Richard, don't do that again. Don't leave me."

They searched that morning, a small army of dogs and men. They gave directions through transmitters, shifted the gears of off-road vehicles, flattened ferns, tread moss, muddied streams. Their hunt was a dream that pricked me during my hours of torpor, images of men pouring coffee from thermoses, taking binoculars from cases, focusing on the distance.

We had climbed a tree from inside. The trunk was charred, the broken vault of the redwood more than enough room for two crea-tures. The day passed as nights pass. Rebecca was nearby, and that was all that mattered.

It was late in the day when a dog found us. His tags tinkling, his panting echoing dully in the chamber of the tree, the big hound whined, yelped, standing on his hind legs to get closer to our hiding place.

His barking stirred me. The dog lunged, struggling upward, climbing. The dog was clawing upward, charcoal raining down the shaft of the tree. He fell, hard.

But he started in again. He barked, a peculiar, falsetto shrill. "He treed something," said a voice.

"Idiot," said another voice, as though the word were a sign of affection.

The dog made a strangling sound when they dragged him away, snorting, panting. Was it another dream that brought the dog back? No other dog was so persistent, no other dog so eager. He yelped. He pawed the charred inside of the tree. Surely, I thought dimly. Surely this wasn't happening.

It was almost sunset when a metallic sputtering broke into my trance. It was loud. It was close. A motor was kicking, failing.

There was nothing I could do. My arms, my legs, were lifeless. I could only listen, unable to shake myself awake. The engine rattled powerlessly, and then it caught, full-throated power.

I could not stir against this paralysis, this drowse that shackled me. The entire tree resounded. The air screamed.

A chain saw.

46

Men shouted to make themselves heard above the shriek of the power saw. The saw lowered in pitch, sputtering, almost stalling. It cut into the tree.

The cathedral trembled. I opened my eyes slowly. Any last hope that this was a dream died. I found myself standing, my arms crossed over my chest, on a gnarled shelf high in the interior of the wooden shaft. Below me was an oblong of light, an opening too narrow for most humans. The illumination that spilled into the tree was the color of sunset.

The saw stopped. Men cursed, a dog barked, not barking so much as a hysterical canine tirade—*There they are*. The saw puttered like a motorcycle, gained strength, and sliced into the wood.

There they are! Motor exhaust drifted upward. I would be able to shift my arm soon. The men worked feverishly, trying to race the setting sun. The bulk of the big tree trembled, echoing with a series of methodical blows. An ax. The sawdust smelled like cinnamon.

It didn't surprise me, I told myself. None of this surprised me. *Now*, I urged myself. Move your hand. Turn your head. Rebecca must have taken refuge higher in the tree. She must be hiding up near the tapering chimney open to the sky. Black dust sifted down from the interior. The scream of the saw shifted to a new position, and another saw stuttered and started up, the men working fast, sundown nearly here.

With copious effort I discovered movement in my right forefinger. And then, like someone doing complicated mental calculations, I moved the forefinger of my left hand.

I had experienced dreams like this, my closing arguments, the jury's impassive faces, my best three button suit, and my tongue

would not work. My voice dead, my mind blank, my notes gib-
berish.

Hands tore the bark and light broke into the base of the tree.
The dog leaped into the opening, and clawed, trying to climb the
interior, barking crazily, his handler calling to him, the dog furious
that he couldn't get at me. *Let me go. Let me sink my teeth into him.*
He could taste me in his mind. How sluggish we seemed to this
dog, how obstinate and stupid. *I've got him!*

One of my hands reached upward and dug deep into the char
opposite me. My other hand joined it, and I hung there, gradually
climbing the shaft of the tree, toward the fading splash of sky.
Rebecca was not here.

They dragged the dog out of the tree, the beast yammering,
tearing at the soil. The ax blows resounded, and now there was a
new pitch to each blow, splintering wood. Far below, at the base of
the interior, a hand reached and missed, and tried again. The hand
found a grip and with a great heave a section of the tree broke free.

I dug my fingers into the ancient charcoal, and thrust my head
and shoulders through the top of the tree. The redwood was still
alive, despite its hollow core. They were killing it, and I knew as I
teetered there that Rebecca was in trouble. I couldn't see her, but I
could tell.

Richard—help me.

Joe Timm's face was gaunt, his eyes searching the ground with
nothing of his old self-assurance. Two hundred miles out of his
jurisdiction, he was not in charge of these people, but stood among
them with natural authority as lights were switched on so the saws
could finish their work.

Joe was unshaven. He wore a hunting jacket that hung loosely.
He touched his mouth and rubbed his bristled chin, a habitual
gesture, nervous. He put one hand on his hip, where a handgun, or
a flask, offered him some security.

How is your wife?

Joe did not look up, but he took his hand away from his hip and
stood like a man looking off the edge of a cliff. He bunched his
fists. And then, only after a long moment, gathering strength, did
he look up again.

The others saw me at the same time he did. The saw fell silent raggedly, sputtering, stalling. The dog saw me, too, and cringed, whining, circling, his handler struggling.

Joe Timm gazed up at me, and a sad smile creased his face. He shook his head. Compassion for Joe stilled me, so I was unprepared for the blast of the shotgun. Buckshot ripped past me. Joe spun to seize the barrel of the gun. The dog sniffed frantically, searching the ground, looking up, demanding. When he saw me the dog leaped in my direction, his chain a taut, straight line.

Then I saw her.

She was in the branches of a nearby tree, human, clinging. The branches shook. She hung on tightly, her face pale with the effort.

"Come away," I whispered.

She shook her head.

I stretched my arms, reached my hands, letting my fingers regain that scope they had come to know, and I toppled forward. The air supported me, and I rocked to avoid a branch. My lips could not form a word. I swam upward, glided, then scrambled, fighting, winning the treetops.

Follow me I called.

To the west a great wave broke, silent at this distance. To the east Highway One meandered, a string of emergency vehicles, police units, and what I guessed to be a forestry service bus. My inhuman eyes registered this, and I made sense of it only as I circled, my flight always half-broken, one wingbeat away from plummeting.

Below, branches crackled. Heavy feet broke brush. More people were hurrying toward the site. Could she hear me calling her name? Could she guess what had become of me, where I had escaped? I sailed wide over the place I had last seen her.

Treetops are a supple green, bright, half-air. In this night sky I saw what I wanted to see, as though my eyes were the source of illumination. There was no further sign of Rebecca.

What was it I dreamed of being as a boy? Did I want to be a racecar driver, a fireman, a soldier? Surely, all of that. The policeman, the Marine. I was no different than any other boy. And if I dreamed of flying, it was with a cape, or with the wings of a hawk, not like this, a winking, leather span.

But more than anything, I had dreamed of being a hero. In my childhood I had only the slimmest sense of what this amounted to, but I saw now that my adult experience had not made me wiser. All I craved now was to love, and to keep my love from harm.

There was still no sign of her. I hovered in place like a falcon, beating my wings. The bones of my wings ached with the effort. I hated bodies, not this mutant shape, and not the human body, but bodies in general, all bodies. Each one was a trap.

We don't have much time.

But the flight that would imitate mine did not take place. Something in Rebecca's character would not let this happen. I nearly fell, and fought hard to stay where I was. I had seen this, too. I had seen this, and known it was coming. I whirled, a brown leaf.

I heard her. Rustling, fluttering.

Branches swayed below, parted. Something struggled upward. A treetop shook, needles raining. A pair of wings escaped the trees.

47

We found ourselves on a cliff overlooking Highway One. There was a sheen on the two-lane road below, drizzle, heavy dew. Sky glowed in the distance, redwoods backlit by spotlights. Was it a helicopter or a low-flying aircraft, those lights circling, that engine sawing back and forth to the north?

Our perch was a log so old the bark was loose, shaggy with moss. Foliage sheltered us, young trees. Redwoods can reproduce like this, new trees towering from the fallen parent. Water dripped from a stream on a rock behind us, roots as fine as eyelashes.

She was aglow. She kissed me, and I could feel her heart. *No, it's not a dream.*

"They're right," she said.

Don't question yourself too closely, I wanted to say. I wanted to tell her to enjoy this, and not be too curious.

She studied her hand, ran a finger along her palm, her lifeline, the ball of her thumb. She looked at me. "I don't blame them."

Her acceptance of our condition surprised me as much as her compassion for our pursuers. But before I could respond she put a finger to my lips and said "Look!"

There was a row of them far below. A car approached along the highway and scarlet came to life, the outlines of the barrier picked out in jewels.

"Reflectors," I said.

"They keep cars from driving off the cliff?"

"That's the general idea," I said.

In an instant she was no longer beside me. I slid, somersaulted, and flew briefly, a drifting stocking. I joined her on the shoulder of the highway.

A pale orange sign leaned beside the road. There was a black puncture in it, a bullet hole. The black arrow on the sign did a swivel-hipped dance. Rebecca put her hand on the metal sign, feeling the hard edge. *Danger*, I knew the sign meant. *Curve*. The aluminum began to glow again as another car approached.

"They'll see us," I said.

It was too late. Like a figure frozen by a flashbulb, Rebecca stood, her fingers splayed across the gleaming goldenrod surface of the sign. The skirt of her gown fluttered as the car gusted past. And the sign was all but colorless again.

The brakelights brightened. The driver's hesitation was plain by the way the car slowed, almost pulled over. *Did you see that?* The car was around the curve, the sound of tires receding. A woman, the driver was wondering. Or something else?

Eddies of air carried us. The black chocolate of the forest, the wrinkled whey of the Pacific—it was all below us as we plummeted into the sky.

All day there was wind in the trees. All night there was stillness. Usually we explored second-growth, new trees half a century old growing out of the blackened, forested stumps. Sometimes a dirt road slashed the woods, until the ferns closed in around it and the road ended at a shed of tools, or a shed of nothing, empty, with bare, rusting coat hooks. When it was not yet night I would stir and smell the woods, the remains of redwood generations.

She wanted me to climb, swim, following her lead, and I did. Bright orange slugs, a variety of gastropod, escaped their hiding places each night, and this lowly animal was a prize, a creature like a human organ blessed with ugly immortality.

Such tentative eyes they had, these slugs, on stalks that shrank from touch, from breath. Rebecca loved these night creatures. She cupped moths in her hands, the tremulous, chalky wings that broke into flight at our approach. Mushrooms elbowed from the sides of trees.

One night a bat riffled through the air, making both of us stop involuntarily before we caught ourselves and laughed.

His squashed, delicate face seemed to drift above us with more than casual curiosity. His voice painted us, gilding our outlines. A particle of lint wafted upward and in an instant the bat shoplifted it from the air, before our eyes could recognize the prey, a minute moth.

When we shrugged upward, winged, we were not met with any ultrasonic cry of fellowship. His voice fell silent. The flutter of our wings was met with a scrambling, scratching tumult in the interior of a tree.

They spilled from a hollow branch with a noise like rustling silk. There were no more than a dozen. They eddied around us, pages blown from a desk, drifting, and our attemps to find a place in their circle was met with mild confusion. Our wingbeats rocked them, and they spun away. We settled on a branch, wings folded around us, and hung upside down, calling.

There was no answer. An odor stayed about the tree, a rodent-pungent lair that smacked of instinct and dumb trust in darkness.

There was a source of hot water somewhere in the mountains, and verdure marked the passage of the warm water below the ground, a belt of green. The warmth welled into the pool. We stripped off our clothes and bathed, the chime of the water as it spilled slowly through stones tranquilizing, hypnotic.

The next night we stood at the bat tree, calling playfully with our ordinary, human voices, paying them a visit, a page from a children's book, *The Solicitor Visits Mr. and Mrs. Bat.* But nothing stirred in the tree.

They were gone.

Late one night I heard her calling my name and I hurried to see her crouching on a path. A crumpled wad of silver, the size of a coin, lay in the dirt. "I know what this is!" she said.

"Buried teasure," I said.

"A gum wrapper," she said.

It was paper with a silver backing that could be, with care, peeled off into a sheet of fine foil. I had not paid attention to gum wrappers in years, although there had been a time in fourth grade when I specialized in making hard metallic pellets out of such stuff and throwing them across the classroom. I sat with Rebecca while we carefully separated the airy, silver-bright membrane, and then buried it like the first coin of what we knew would be a hoard.

People—we were more fascinated by human beings, even by fragments of their litter, than by all the grandeur of nature. I knew what this implied—but for some time Rebecca did not.

She was intrigued by water, the dripping sphagnum of the spring, the creekbed with its spent logs and rounded boulders, the stream ladling from shelf to shelf, step to step. And I knew, even if she did not, what attracted her to this flowing water, these standing pools of fingerlings, fins and slender bodies combed in one direction by the creek.

We can imagine the pond, the mirror, empty after we step away. But it *has* to be imagined. Living people never actually see an empty mirror when they stand before it. When she crouched and shivered the surface with a hand she was reawakened to herself, her own nature, and mine.

We bled deer for nourishment spiced with chlorophyll, letting the deer free when we had taken what we needed. We hid in the trees, and with the arrival of each night we found our way higher in the mountains. And I knew that it could not go on for much longer. I could feel the colors fade in my vision, my strength dim.

Mice awoke when we did, the forest taking on a new range of sounds, a hush that was only superficial. Every night was vibrant, and we did not feel banished to darkness. We were liberated into it, and relished every hour.

But as Rebecca came to know her own power, and came to understand what she could do, I found her talking more and more of the people she had known, her parents, her brother, even Eric. And I knew why.

She spoke of her favorite music, how easy the best pieces were to play, the sonata, the etude, how six-year-olds could master Mozart. And how difficult they were, how false this simplicity turned out to be. "Not what it seems," she said. "Simple like living," she said.

How many nights did we have, four or five, or more? There was no seam between them. The segments, night and day, were not barriers. Each night we came to life higher up in the mountains, deeper in the woods. We could imagine ourselves to be the beginning of creation, not fugitives from one.

"I think Mother came to accept my blindness," said Rebecca one night. "She said I would be a proof of God's love, and inspire people to, as she put it, 'carry their own crosses.' My parents believe. They have faith."

"Don't you?" I asked.

"A simple faith, like a whisper," she said.

Your faith will become even more simple, I thought.

On waking one evening we could hear them. Quiet voices, a crackle of paper, the sound of a zipper being tugged, snagging. It was across the forest, at the edge of audibility, but at times like this there was no sense of distance. An engine started up, and a transmission whined as a vehicle jockeyed back and forth in a road. We pursued the sound. They were easy to find, and when we made our discovery we sank into the ferns, watching.

Joe Timm folded a map, creasing it with great care between his fingers. He nodded, and one of the men, wearing an orange parka, spoke into a transmitter. A Jeep idled on a fire road, the beams from its headlights knifing the woods.

"You can't keep doing this," one of the men was saying.

Joe Timm shook a flask, examined it in his hand appraisingly, and then unscrewed the cap.

"It's not going to help her, Joe."

Joe didn't answer.

"We'll find them," said another one of the men. "If they're here they're ours."

Joe Timm nodded, smiling wearily.

"No question," said the man in the parka.

Joe Timm drank from the flask. He was the last one to climb into the Jeep, standing with one foot up on the chassis and the other one rooted while he gazed at the trees. I could see the intelligence, the need. He knew he was close.

"This isn't going to work," he said.

The man in the parka stiffened, about to disagree.

"They can be caught. There's no question about that. But we're making a fundamental mistake." He did not move like the Joe Timm I had met in the halls of power, a man who met friends with a hug not so much out of warmheartedness as out of his need to be possessive, commanding. He eased himself into the backseat of the Jeep, a man uncertain of his movements.

"He was a friend of mine," I said. "In a professional way. The husky man with the gray hair."

"I liked him. He had sad eyes," she said.

We stood in the road, in the fresh ruts torn by the four-wheel drive. "He's ambitious," I said. "But I know what you mean. He's more complicated than I used to think."

"They'll be back," said Rebecca.

An earwig struggled in Joe Timm's bootprint, pressed into the soil.

48

If the hunt continued it was silent and invisible. This made us more fearful. Were satellites searching for the infrared hue of spilled blood? Were listening devices aimed into the woods, keyed to the sound of a heartbeat, a drop of moisture falling to the forest floor?

I grew to believe that they had some new computer, each tree mapped out, each sapling with its own bar code. The old scripture about every hair being numbered, every sparrow's fall known, was a source of despair, not of hope.

Each daybreak we secreted ourselves a little farther into the woods.

"Maybe they changed their minds. They don't really want to catch us," Rebecca said one night as we followed a deer path.

"That's not the impression I have," I said. Old speech patterns sound reassuring. I could not help sounding like someone sitting at a polished teak table, signing a document with a fountain pen.

"They're following procedure, that's all," she said. "Maybe they don't really care. They're just going through the motions."

"It's possible."

She stopped and gave me a searching look. "That's what you told me about cops and banks. You said it was all the same—just a matter of procedure. Don't you remember?"

We left the trees, and crossed a clearing. "Of course I remember. It all seems too far away," I heard myself say. Rebecca took my hand, recognizing the disturbance in my voice.

Ahead was a group of trees grander than any others we had seen.

Two of them were hollow, lightning-charred, but still very much alive. The sight of these trees awed us, and it made us feel conspicuous, self-conscious. We had reached a bare crest in the mountains, much of the distant summit naked magnesium, inhospitable to grass. This stand of mammoth redwoods was a final colony, and beyond was the beginning of a more sun-punished land, rocky, oaks in the folds of canyons.

Everything will be fine as long as we don't think.

A bird twittered in a low shrub, a junco disturbed in its sleep. Rebecca made an answering trill. The bird squeaked, a query. She answered it, reassuringly.

"That's very good," I said. "If nothing else we'll be able to play Vegas."

"I think you were going to be a judge some day, on the Supreme Court."

"Some day my name was going to be in lights."

"We can stay like this, Richard. For as long as we want."

Few other trees neighbored these giants. They were not rust-dark like the younger, second-growth trees, but stone-gray. "We can live on the blood of chipmunks," I said, hoping the conversation would turn into verbal badminton, a game I could win. "And slugs. Is that what you're saying?"

But she persisted, "You know we don't have to hurt anyone. You know it, Richard. We have everything we need here."

I didn't want to say anything more.

"Don't you feel it, too?" she asked. "We belong right here."

A different variety of fern luxuriated under these tall trees, a larger, metallic fern, with serrated edges. "You miss your parents," I said.

"And the piano. Very much. And everything else. Ordinary things. I miss being a person."

I had trouble saying it, but I managed. "So do I." I was quick to add, "But maybe you're right."

It had been a long time since any people had made it this far into the woods. There was the deer path through the underbrush, the earth indented with the fine prongs of hoofprints.

"What is it you're not telling me?" she asked.

One night when I woke I could not remember my mother's face. The names of the people I had known were wooden beads, worn, colorless. Matilda, Connie. What did they sound like, these people, when they laughed, when they said good-bye? What sort of man had I been, one of those people who say good morning, or simply hello. Or had I been the type of person who never spoke at all, always in a hurry? Had I defended killers? Had I been an expert at maritime law, or perhaps sports law, when a football player can ask for a new contract? What sort of lawyer had I been?

This had been developing hour by hour. I had wanted to keep it secret. I had been out of touch with humanity too long. I could not remember. I had no judgment. My mind was dying.

It was early the next evening.

A deer crashed through the ferns, falling. We hurried to its side. The deer backed away and reared up, trembling. He could not command his forelegs. His eyes were wild, his breath hard, red mucus bubbling at his nose.

She embraced the creature, calming it with a whisper.

There was a hole in the deer's side. It was oddly bloodless, and I could smell the sulphur, the lead. The deer fell into a slumber, one leg kicking, its eyes unfocused.

Rebecca already knew what to do.

She sliced one of her fingers with a single bite, and let the blood flow onto the shivering tongue of the young buck. "Someone shot this deer with a pistol," she said, anger in her voice.

She shifted the deer so the blood streamed freely into his mouth. I had never heard her sound like this. "Who hunts with a hand-gun?" she said.

"It was a stupid thing to do," I said, suddenly afraid.

"Cruel," she said, her voice trembling. "It's vicious."

"This deer is going to be perfectly fine," I said. I didn't want to add what I thought, that the nine-millimeter had passed through both lungs.

She said, "Because of my blood."

I didn't like the way she sounded. "Things like this happen—"

"I can't let them get away with this."

I was afraid of what she was about to do. "They didn't mean any harm."

She gave me a look. I had never seen her like this. "They'll never do this again," she said.

I wanted to tell her to wait. I wanted to tell her that revenge was tempting but unwise. I wanted to urge her to forget. I wanted eloquence, but all I had was silence.

She was gone.

The buck woke, kicking, lifting his head. He scrambled to his knees. And when he looked up at me I felt the keen, wordless life at the center of him.

The deer jerked to his forefeet, and then at last stood on his four hooves. He stood like a marble deer, a statue, graceful, nose to the wind. He shook his head like a dog, his tail a quick blur.

He took a step. He trotted, and vanished.

As I hurried through a scrim of young redwoods I knew what Rebecca was about to do.

49

A shot, several shots, a string of them. The reports echoed un-evenly, the last shot louder than the others.

When I reached the scene it was peaceful. A hatchet lay on the ground, dark with old sap, and a few chunks of green firewood scattered where someone had dropped them. In a clearing a tumble of belongings spilled in all directions, sleeping bags and cooking implements, and a small stove with a shiny blue canister of butane. A yellow Bic lighter was half-tucked into a packet of Drum cigarette tobacco. A backpack with a two-liter bottle of Jose Cuervo leaned against a stump.

A man sprawled with his arms outstretched, watching for meteors, studying the constellations. He wore jeans and a thick sweater, the wool pilled and baggy. The cleats of his hiking boots were clogged with mud, his electronic wristwatch set to display a game, what looked like a tiny football field blinking off and on.

He was not breathing. He had no pulse. He was warm, and I touched the wounds in his neck with affection, even reverence. He clutched a packet of freeze-dried chicken in one hand, preserved meat the consistency of mixed nuts. The fire gave forth blue smoke, two or three slivers of flame struggling, snapping. In the backpack tossed onto a blue plastic ground cover was a box of bullets, torn open, the copper shells glittering.

I heard it out there in the darkness, a steely click, a ratcheting sound, the gun being reloaded.

I could smell the male sweat, hear the labored panting, the heavy step. He was watching. There was a gagging sound, retching, nothing coming up.

"Don't—" he said. His voice caught. *Don't move,* he meant to say.

"I swear to God don't move." His message and his actual choice of words did not quite match, but I understood him.

He was in deep darkness, but the firelight glittered off the gun. The weapon was pointed at me.

I'm not real.

He stayed where he was. I didn't blame him at all for surveying the fuming kindling, the wind snatching the edge of the ground cover and turning it, at one corner, like an invisible housekeeper. I took a position opposite him, at the edge of the clearing.

You can't see me.

We can tell by silence what a person will not do. This man was waiting for the next important event in his life. He kept still. He was telling himself he would stay like this all night, until daylight.

I am not here.

He approached the fire haltingly, the pistol in both hands, elbows locked, arms straight. The weapon aimed perfunctorily at one thing and then another, as though the barrel of the gun was his organ of vision. The gun pulled itself upward, aiming at the stars, aimed down at the backpack, back at the fire.

Only then did he kneel beside his companion, touching him on the arm, on the forehead, crouching beside his friend. He scrabbled on the ground for some dried spines of redwood needles, and tossed them onto a last, resurgent flame. The flame died, the flame returned. The smoke spun upward, and the man began to reason with his memory, telling himself a new version of what had happened, already becoming a bad witness.

Why did it continually surprise me, the warmth of living flesh?

When I was finished with him I felt it all return, all my memories. Of course I remembered my mother, the articles on child psychology she had picked out on the old Underwood, "How We Know that Infants Feel Pain and Joy," an article I had forgotten completely until then. And my father's pride in these articles. He would make photocopies of them from the *Contemporary Education Journal*, the words in white, the background black, my mother's name—Eleanor Campion Stirling—in letters of perfect porcelain.

I tasted the last moments of Richard Stirling, sunlight on the sidewalk, broken glass.

I did not find her that night. I called for her, but I believed I knew what she was experiencing.

When the next night began and there was still no sign of her I began to doubt.

If I had a child I would want him to learn this difficult truth: fear is what we have to accept. We will never be completely unafraid, and the best among us will learn to wear the fear like jewelry, fine points of color.

I knew Rebecca would come to me again. But I also knew that if I was not really Richard Stirling, then Rebecca was a stranger, too.

She came to me sometime after midnight. She stood across the warm pool from me, a woman wandering off from a soiree. Her posture was tentative, apologetic.

Then she hurried into my arms. "They're coming," she said.

Her step so close to the pond made it tremble. I was fully clothed, waiting there because I expected her to return to this place where we had been happy. It was the thing in the woods that most resembled a mirror, and I knew we were both drawn to it, the way a unicorn in the old tapestries is captured by a looking glass in the hand of a virgin.

"They aren't dressed like the other men," she continued breathlessly. "They're soldiers."

"What is that noise?" I said. There was a diesel racket in the distance.

"Richard, don't laugh. They have machines."

I was so delighted do be with her again, the news struck me as wonderful, a celebration about to begin. "Tanks?"

"And machine guns. It's been so wonderful, Richard. I've been so glad to have this."

I knew what she was about to say next. *But we have to end it.*

I picked my way across the water on the dark stones, leading her by the hand. Mist swirled on the surface of the pond, and a frog downstream splashed across the running water.

She tugged my arm, turning me to face her. Her gray eyes met mine. "We have to go back."

I sighed: that's impossible. But even as I made the sound I was aware how forced it sounded. I was trying to hide from both of us how angry her words were making me. *Back.* Back where the best moment a human being has all day is a hot shower and a carnal spasm of bliss just before falling asleep. Back to that?

She put her hand on my cheeks, my lips, as she had when greeting me in our first evenings together, seeing with her fingertips. "I can't do it again, Richard. I can't take a life like that ever again."

I surprised myself. I parted my lips to argue that of course she could. She could get used to it. She could learn what I had learned.

"You're telling me we should go back," I heard myself say, "to the mirror." It was another tactic that I had found effective. When all else fails pretend to be ignorant.

"Connie knows where it is."

"But I thought you said there was nothing inherently special about it. That what happened to me had to do with my own nature." I wanted to ask why, just once, she couldn't fail to get the point. Why couldn't she be mistaken? Why did she have to be so *right*.

Her eyes told me she knew something, a secret.

Then she shifted her gaze, a mannerism of sighted people. We can talk with our eyes, and we can hide. Was she learning to tell half-truths, the worst kind of lie? She smiled. "You forget—we may not be able to find the mirror at all."

It sounded uncomfortably like something *I* might say. "You're proving my point. It won't work."

She said, "I have something to show you."

"The cops have to react. They *will* react. It's a system—dutiful, joyless plodding. The whole world gets up in the morning. But we're more real than these people." Did I believe this?

She put her hand on my arm, a gesture I had always found lovely. But for a moment I felt she was telling me how wrong I was.

She said, "There's someone I want you to talk to."

50

"You told me he was a friend," said Rebecca.

A generator nearby fell silent. In the sudden absence of sound the chuff of the surf was clearly audible, and the electronic buzz of the Vacancy sign across the highway. Redwoods sheltered a strip of buildings, sweet alyssum flowing from a windowbox, the *Bud* sign dark. Adjoining the diner was a motel, a small office with a Coke machine and a row of cabins. Several military vehicles were parked among flowering acacias. The tires had cut tracks in the drifts of yellow pollen.

"Go see him," Rebecca urged.

A few low clouds drifted across the sky. Was it my imagination, or was Orion beginning to dim? I said, "Joe Timm is not going to be one of our benefactors."

She leaned against me, her breath at my ear. "What harm is there in trying?"

Even then one of my mental flashcards spoke for me. "Don't ask a question when you don't know the answer."

"You're afraid."

It sounded like a quip, a bit of mental tennis. "I'm afraid I'll kill him."

Something clattered among the military vehicles. A helmeted figure lay down, deliberately, yawning. The sound had been his gun, falling. The uniformed men in the shadows slumped, drowsing against the trees, lolling in the trucks.

I drifted, finding the crack in the door a passageway, folding between the door and its jamb with a surprising pleasure, straining my body through a slit.

The cabin had a pine desk, and a lamp with a green shade. The entire place was small, a small stone fireplace, and a bed with a firm, diminutive mattress. Joe Timm sat at a telephone. "I've been out with them most of the night. They've got the National Guard out of Camp Roberts," he was saying. "Tearing up the woods. The Sierra Club is furious because a helicopter startled a nest of red-tailed hawks."

You can't see me.

He turned, looking vaguely in my direction. The hand that held the receiver to his ear was pink, two or three hairs on each knuckle.

He turned back to the desk, idly fingering the beaded metal

chain of the lamp. The voice on the phone was faint, short of breath.

"I feel sorry for the birds, too. I feel sorry for all of us." His eyes darted from one point to another in the room, and then he gazed hard at the knotty pine wall, as though trying to visualize his wife so clearly she actually appeared before him. "I even feel sorry for the two of *them*."

The far-off voice spoke again, reassuring, soothing.

"No, I can't sleep," he replied. "I tried, but I just lie there thinking. How is that new night nurse working out?" He listened, the metal chain swinging when he released it. "Have her read you one of those E.F. Benson stories, Georgie and Lucia. Miss Mapp. I'll be home in another couple of days. It won't be long now." There was a silence, the mosquito voice of the phone the only sound in the room. Then he said, "I love you, too."

He hung up the phone but sat quietly, gazing at nothing with a gentle smile.

He heard my step and stiffened, his hand going to his hip. I expected a handgun, but he produced a radio, antenna wiggling.

"Put it away, Joe," I said.

He put the radio down. It stayed at his elbow. "This is just what I deserve. A personal visit."

"What happened to your wife?" I said.

"She's stable. Weak, but in no danger."

"Her heart?"

His eyes went hard. He didn't want to talk about her, not with me. "She's recovering from pneumonia."

"You shouldn't be here."

"I should have stopped you that first night, at the cemetery."

"You take on too much of a burden," I said. I liked the way I sounded.

"Do you have any idea what you have done to my career? I was on *This Week in Northern California* talking about how law enforcement isn't a matter of force, it's a matter of knowledge. I was great. It happens—you have a good day, all the words falling into place. I was casing office space for my campaign for state senator. Two days later I'm telling reporters I can't help them with their questions."

"I'm not going to hurt you."

"I know you're not." He reached into the desk drawer and withdrew a huge handgun, the biggest revolver I'd ever seen. When he put it on the desk the lamp shade trembled. "I understand that you're impervious to bullets. I'd like to see what you can do with your head blown off." It was only then I realized how scared he was.

"I'm impressed the way everyone keeps producing newer and bigger guns." All these Popeyes with their various cans of spinach. "All of this has really done wonders for your spirits."

Joe smiled like someone who'd just had facial surgery, not sure his mouth would stay in place. He had lost even more weight than I thought.

I straightened a framed reproduction on the wall, a Monet, a woman with a parasol. "Ever get those cracks in your patio fixed?"

He pinched the bridge of his nose for a moment and blinked. He shifted the radio to one corner of the desk, the pistol to the other. "I got some sealant," he said at last. "Rubber-based, used that on the cracks."

"It didn't work very well, did it?"

"No."

"I could ask Stella. A little legal coercion; we'll have a new slab poured by the end of the month."

Joe shook his head, laughing despite himself, putting one hand on his radio transmitter.

I said, "We don't want to hurt anyone."

"That's nice of you."

This mild sarcasm surprised me. I had considered Joe to be one of those people who didn't need irony, saying one thing and meaning quite another, to make a point. He had been so manly, hardhewn.

"They're going to finish the two of you," Joe was saying. He did not say *we*. He stood with a gasp. He fished in a pocket and brought out a roll of antacids.

He did not look at me when he said, "They have those dogs they use after plane crashes, hunting for bodies. The State Forestry people made an arrangement with the FAA. These hounds can find remains in trees, anywhere. I realized we were going about it all wrong, scanning for metabolic activity from the air. You'd be surprised how many big animals there are, bears, cougars. We took quite a census. But we forgot that you two aren't really alive."

I waited.

He chewed the antacids, and said, "I get these back spasms. Right here, right above my butt." He turned back to the desk, the bright circle of light. "One or two more nights, that's all you have."

"This is absurd." I said this with my best conference manner, flippant, disbelieving. You act this way when the opposition proves your expert witness got his geology degree from secretarial school.

He winced. "They shipped up a truck load of Ziegler coffins, those steel containers they use when bodies might be toxic. They brought up a dozen or so. They'll take you apart, put you in these metal boxes—"

I laughed.

He sat again. It was an effort. "You look great, Richard, except when you do that."

I recognized that new quality in his stare, that tremor in his hands.

"If I were you I wouldn't laugh. It destroys the illusion that you're human." He considered for a moment, his eyes cutting down to the gun on the desk. "They'll study you for years to come, little bits of you on microscope slides."

His tone disturbed me. He was afraid, but he was determined, or putting on a good act. "You sound so confident." I was suddenly weak. My mouth was dry.

"Maybe you can alter my mood, Richard. Is that what you're doing? Playing with my mind?"

These hands, these arms. While we sleep, the chain saws, men in protective suits, oxygen masks, visors. Cutting through my ribs. Gouging out this rhythmic champion, this heart.

"You have children," I said.

He hesitated before answering. "Two daughters, both married."

"You see the world as a place to protect. You want to keep it safe. For your children, your grandchildren. And other people's children. You're still paying off the mortgage on your house."

"If nothing else works we'll burn you. The army still stocks flame throwers, napalm."

"But you won't hurt Rebecca, will you?"

His fingers twitched, one of those unconscious gestures that show how unhappy a person is, *No, I'm not really saying this.* "Both of you," he said.

The air was maple sugar, dissolving on my tongue, painfully sweet.

Cars had streaked the yellow acacia pollen across the parking lot. Like chalk dust, there was so much of it, ordinary life in such abundant promise. A stepping-stone was stained with the criss-cross of leaves, leaf-dye remaining long after the twigs were swept away.

I waited for a car to pass, headlights and brakelights and a booming radio. I jogged across the highway, into the trees.

The generator started up. The machine rumbled, and I kept well away from the noise, bounding up a trail to the place where she waited, a pale smudge high above the road.

"They don't know about the mirror," I said. *We can go back and find it. And keep it for ourselves.*

She could look at me and tell. I shrugged and laughed, the *bon vivant* back from a party, that pleasant champagne glow down to my fingertips.

Her voice was low. "Tell me you didn't."

A plaster deer stood beside a birdbath, almost the exact size of a real doe. A stone fawn waited beneath a tree, a nick of paint missing from one of its eyes.

"Tell me you didn't touch him!"

I took her hand, ready to lie. Words don't have to reflect reality. Only the mirror, in its straightforward deception, is perpetually truthful. *No, of course I didn't.*

But I did not speak.

"Richard, you're frightening me."

Let me show you what we can do.

She wanted to hurry back to the motel. I took both of her hands. "I promise you I didn't touch him."

She put her head against my chest. "Why didn't you say so?"

"Let me show you," I said, "where we belong."

51

Perhaps when we keep a journal we are claiming a future, pretending it already exists, the smoggy summer day, the bright late winter morning, our children grown. We let the fiction carry us forward, *tomorrow*, a causeway across what we know is true, the floodplain of hope, the days that have not yet happened.

Early the next evening we reached Carmel, following the highway at times, and then following the coastline, the ragged margin of white sand. My mother had loved this town, and we had once owned a cottage here, a peak-roofed hideaway with a climbing rose and a huge blue-stone fireplace.

The sand was so fine it squeaked under our shoes. Rebecca hesitated on the beach, but I led her along, and we walked hand in hand up Ocean Avenue. The look of pleasure in her eyes warmed me. There was a quality of "let's pretend" about our stroll up the street. We acted like ordinary people, ordinary in the way love affairs are ordinary, life in flower, but normal, rooted life.

"We shouldn't do this," she said.

"This is where we should have come," I laughed, "all this time."

We could both smell them, taste them in the air, so many lives. She said, "But they can all look at us and tell."

Restaurant doors swung open, and inside were dozens of faces, the voices lifted in laughter, lowered in conversation. Even a gas station was a marvel, a man rubbing a spot on the windshield of a Jaguar, first with a squeegee, then with a paper towel, then with his forefinger and spit. In a candle shop a woman used a long brass implement to snuff out candles one by one, and the scent of bees' wax reached us between the glass, honey and paraffin.

"It's dangerous," she said, but there was no conviction in her voice.

We could not help window shopping, knowing all the while that the glass we gazed into did not reflect our images. We pretended it was otherwise, arm in arm, nodding mock-approval at the window displays, expensive leather suitcases, gold-edged china. A display of bridal accessories stopped us, the mannequin's face behind the stiff fireworks of lace.

It was true that a man walking a dog stopped in mid-crosswalk to watch us, ignoring the understated beeping of horns. And sometimes someone across the street took a long look, not sure what he was seeing. A newspaper vending machine caught my eye with its black headlines. A photograph was half lost beneath the fold, but I could make out the top of my head, my eyes.

I could imagine Connie. or even Matilda, complying happily, *sure I have a photo. Take your pick.* I had never liked the black-and-white glossy that had been selected, hating the close-cropped haircut, the *let's party!* grin on my face.

I drew her along, past floral displays and a real esate office. "I didn't know hats looked like that," she said. "Those floppy ones—"

"Berets," I suggested. "Cashmere."

The berets were displayed on Styrofoam heads, featureless, each egg-like head with a dainty prominence and a faint suggestion in place of nose and eyebrows. "I didn't know hats came in so many colors—"

She protested, but I tugged her arm. Once inside a clerk put his head around a curtain and said, "I'm sorry—"

We're closed he meant to say. The door had been locked, and I had forced it. I apologized for our mistake, but led Rebecca to a counter of scarfs, berets, gloves, so many colors. And purses, a scarlet patent leather clutch so vivid it hurt to look at it.

Drawers were pulled, and samples of silks and fine wool were poured out on the glass counter, the man eager now, delighted that we could stop in. "This one will look wonderful on you," said the clerk, the owner, I realized, hungry, tired, forgetting everything but the two of us. "Take a look," he said, tilting a mirror on the counter in Rebecca's direction.

I was surprised at Rebecca's presence of mind. She pretended, artfully, giving her empty reflection her best fashion model pout. The she turned the mirror aside. "Lovely," she said. I could hear how she felt, what a painful, pointless charade this suddenly was.

"We'll take it," I said with a smile.

"No," she said.

All of this is yours.

She gave me a steady look. "No, thank you," she said.

Outside again, we enjoyed this game, this opportunity to imagine what it would be like to be another couple, that man and women speaking German, or this man in the tweed jacket, leather patches on the elbows, waiting for his bride—surely they were on a honeymoon—to adjust the strap on one of her shoes.

Although Rebecca's gown looked strictly formal, there was nothing about her that looked dampened or faded by the punishment of the passing months. She had the highlights and coloring only the finest cinematography could offer, and anyone who saw her took in both the readily apparent, her eyes, her smile, and something else. The eye believed in her.

A man and a woman outside a restaurant paused to let us pass, and I could feel their mood change. The woman laughed, and the man looked up from the car he was unlocking.

Rebecca could not stop herself. "I want you to be careful," she said, taking the woman's hand.

"Whatever of," said the woman, surprised but not taking any offense at this caution from a stranger.

"He's not what you think," said Rebecca. "He's full of stories, but you know better."

"He's been lying to me," the woman said, her tone surprised but not shocked.

"About everything," said Rebecca.

"What's going on?" said the man, his smile fading. He looked at me as people did when they were not quite persuaded, when they sensed something wrong. For an instant it was a struggle to deceive him.

✿

"What was that about?" I said with a laugh.

"That man she was with. He's married, or cheating his business partners. Something. She should stay away from him." She put her hand out to a shop window. Behind the glass a marzipan alligator looked out at the passing street.

"You're tired," I said, not asking.

"No, I feel perfectly alright," she insisted, leaning against me.

"Too much excitement," I said.

We both pretended that was the problem.

We turned at last to enjoy the view. The main street sloped down to the Pacific, and the ocean loomed up, almost at an angle, an optical illusion that made the shops and the Monterey pines look festive and temporary, a town set out for a holiday, not made to last. Only the trees were permanent, fissured bark, roots buckling the sidewalk, bursting the stone planters.

A police car rolled down the other side of the street. Rebecca fell into a park bench. She said she was dizzy, and gave a little laugh of apology.

It would be dangerous to leave her here like this. Her hand was over her eyes, and I could see the heat fade from her. She shivered.

"It can happen suddenly," I said. "The sounds go dim. You can hardly feel your hands, or your feet. You have to drag in each breath, like towing something heavy through water."

"I'll be okay," she said. "Don't leave me, Richard. Please stay—"

"You'd expect us to be able to keep thinking," I said. "But that dies, too. You don't know who you are, or what you're doing. Forgetting is almost a pleasure, isn't it?"

"Please don't go anywhere," she said. I knew what she really meant.

But I had no choice.

52

I returned to the park bench, and broke open a vein between my ulna and my radius, and she drank. When we sat together on the park bench afterward we must have looked like two lovers, secluded by the shrubs of the park.

I was glad she did not ask. I could not have explained the scene I had just interrupted, a man and woman like objects in a still life, lovemaking just completed, a sheen of boredom already accumulating in each psyche. How their lust had apparently been stimulated by what played on the television screen, a woman in vocal but artificial throes, an orchestrated orgy I silenced with one touch of a button. Leaving the two blissful, each one a heartbeat away from never waking.

We found a house in the southern part of Carmel, not far from the Carmel Mission and the river, one light on in the den as proof that there was no one home, a desk light on a timer. I nearly turned the light off reflexively, but Rebecca stopped me. I recognized the dwelling as the product of architectural vision, a house all views and spacious, uncozy rooms.

"You think we can live here," she said in a guarded tone. "No one will notice." It was charming, the way she said *live*. Steve Fayette would like this house, I thought. Space and angles. I tugged a curtain shut, wondering vaguely why it had been left open, and how long.

An assortment of mail was fanned out on the dining room table. I touched my fingers to the table and came up with faint dust. "They've been gone awhile." Getting letters had always been a pleasure I had taken for granted. And magazines. Even the catalogs, slick pages of products, smiling men and women, all of it empty, promises no one really believed, some of the models hating what they wore, tired, one or two of them already dying, AIDS, drugs.

"Then they'll be coming back soon," Rebecca said.

For two nights it succeeded. We wanted to act out a miniseries, a honeymoon taking place entirely at night, but sexless, all normal desire having left both of us, but loving in a darkly fraternal way. Rebecca drinking from my wrist gave me a pleasure more bitter-sweet than sex, taking its place.

I lied to her. The lies were easy to utter, and afterward easy to forget, for a night or two. I told her I'd found a hospital in Monte-rey, drank my fill of whole blood, and returned. She liked this story —outsmarting an institution, making it a kind of hide-and-seek we were playing, a game we both could win.

We tried on clothes, the man's leather jackets and cowboy boots all too big and not a style I particularly liked. Rebecca had better luck, trying on skirts, pleated knee-lengths, plaid woolens, and one daring black leather miniskirt.

"I understand this marriage," said Rebecca. "It works because the man likes to pretend he's a cowboy, and the woman dresses like a librarian. He's a businessman, practical and calm—a horse would make him nervous. He bought her the miniskirt, and they both liked it, but somehow it doesn't work into any of her ensem-bles, only in the bedroom. She pretends to be sensible, he pretends to be strong."

"A perfect marriage," I said.

It was difficult to watch television. Something about my optic nerve made the stuttering images look fake and flat, the voices like the sound of antique telephones. Rebecca listened to the music she loved, but the sound of the music sounded labored in my ears. One or two of the musicians, I knew, were no longer living. The con-ductor himself had tottered into the early stages of senility. I could hear it in the silence between notes. I could hear the way the recording failed to keep anything alive but the dictates of a composer long ago decayed.

Rebecca kept the music quiet to spare me, and her ability to listen to such music proved something to me: that I was the more foreign, less human creature. Rebecca was still like a living woman in her quick pleasure in candlelight, her love of picture books, a child's atlas of the world, dinosaurs. I found any form of reproduced sound or image a bitter caricature, unmistakably counterfeit.

But we were joyful for two nights, believing that we could borrow other people's lives like this, from house to house, indefinitely. We had discovered a form of security, a future. We could play house like this forever, we found ourselves thinking. From town to town, city to city—there was no end.

And then, on the third night, a car pulled into the driveway. The engine switched off, and doors slammed and footsteps approached, all the signs of company arriving. The front door was unlocked, pushed open, and we had visitors.

"The owners?" asked Rebecca. She looked crestfallen. I wondered how much of this looked like home to her now, the unread, neatly folded *Wall Street Journals* beside a display of dried grasses, wheat and pussy willows.

Our intruders entered gossiping. "Someone so needful," said the young woman, "I get a bad feeling right here when I hear her voice on the phone."

Rebecca began to hurry from the room, but I caught her. I knew how to hide.

"Needful people are what you have to avoid," the young woman continued. "She tells me I won't cooperate. Cooperate in what?"

"*With* what," suggested the young man.

"Exactly," she said. The couple turned on all the lights in the living room. They turned on the television. They went from one room to another, snapping on pole lamps, desk lamps, ceiling lights. "I can't believe she's my sister," said the young woman. "It's not genetically possible."

The young man hooted, "Look at all the wine!"

"We can't touch it."

"You can't tell me they'll miss a bottle of—what's this, Montrachet," he said, pronouncing it with an over-fastidious roll of the r. "You can't tell me they counted every bottle."

"Wouldn't you?"

His voice came from the bathroom. "Okay, guess what's wrong with them."

"You aren't supposed to go through the medicine cabinet," she said.

"Evelyn," he said. "Guess the prescriptions."

Rebecca and I stayed just beyond, passing from one room to another to avoid them. "They took the pills they needed with them," said Evelyn without much interest. She buttoned her sweater. She went to the thermostat on the wall, turned the dial. Somewhere under our feet a furnace thundered softly.

"It's a game," he called, and I was starting to like him. "Guess."

"Okay, he likes to eat, he takes some kind of antacid. Maalox." She paused at the drapes, parted them, peered out. She looked back at the spider plants. She did not like this. She knew something was wrong.

"Correct" came the voice from the bathroom. "But too easy."

"Did you move these letters around? Bruce, did you touch these letters?"

"I steamed them all open," said Bruce.

"Bruce, stop fooling around," she called.

The heater was on, hot air forced through vents in the floor. "It is cold in here," he said. He flung himself into a chair, eyeing the liquor cabinet. "They have that tequila with a worm in it. Those guys are serious drinkers," he said.

"I don't like it here."

"Is the heater supposed to make that noise?" he asked.

She passed by him and he snagged her, pulling her down into his lap. "I don't feel right," she said.

He didn't either. "They don't mind. We aren't doing anything any normal person wouldn't do, looking around at stuff."

They both stopped, listening.

Then, to hear himself talk, Bruce continued, "It's like when you send a postcard. You don't mind if people read it, because that's what a postcard is—semi-private. When people pay you to housesit they expect you might have a friend come by and do normal stuff like watch television, maybe sit in the hot tub—"

"It's being repaired. It leaked or something."

"So here we are, and there's no problem."

"I don't feel good," she said.

She got up and walked away, tugging at her clothing.

No, don't hurt her, Rebecca warned me.

Just as the young woman reached the back door, put her hand out to try the lock, a pair of wings touched her, the wingbeats blowing her flowing sweater, dislodging her hair from its clasp. For a moment, her head back, she was a woman listening to delightful, distant music.

When I had finished taking as much as I could while still sparing her life, I stepped into the living room, confident that Rebecca would have embraced the young man. But Bruce was there alone, hunched forward, looking sideways at the television, its red *mute*, its scenes of distant carnage. I pushed the *off* button, and pleasured in the blank dark that filled the screen.

"You scared me," said Bruce, too heartily. "I thought you all were still on vacation." Then, after studying me for a moment, he called, "Evelyn?"

I stretched them both out in the master bedroom, fluffing up the pillows, unfolding a blanket. Each had a pulse, each had the expression of a person drowsing, not really deeply asleep, like someone stirred by a dream of homecoming or travel, life about to begin at last.

Only then did I hear Rebecca in a distant part of the house, weeping softly, so that I wouldn't hear.

I found her in a room full of toys, shelves of stuffed animals and plastic monsters. I thought for an instant that this was what troubled her, the sight of some child's innocent playthings.

"You lied to me," she said. "About Joe Timm."

If I didn't talk I would be safe. "I didn't kill him."

"But you did hurt him, didn't you?"

Was that how she thought of it—our touch, our kiss? I wanted to protest that it did not hurt anyone. But I kept quiet, rearranging the stuffed teddy bears, putting them on a shelf by themselves, away from the lions and naked plastic infants. I closed the vent in the floor, all that heat closed off to a faint whistle.

"You lied to me about the hospital in Monterey," she said.

I wanted to deny it, but she silenced me with a glance. "I know you did. I knew what was really happening. I lied, too. To myself. To you."

I felt too full of life to be having this conversation, tossing a beanbag shaped like a hippo in my hand. How could anyone give a grotesque toy like this to a child?

"What are we going to do, Richard? What's going to happen to us?"

It was a very simple question. "People travel, go to the hospital, die. They leave their homes empty." I flung the beanbag animal onto a top shelf, a perfect toss.

"I don't mean that," she said, with studied patience. "I mean— what will we turn into as time passes."

"Time won't pass," I said. Her question angered me. The willfullness of it. The deliberate attempt to be innocent. I was about to tell her that she wasn't innocent, that she was going to forget what it was like to feel guilt. She would have to mature, I was going to say. She was fortunate to be here, breathing. But even before I spoke I felt the falseness of my words.

I could not say such things, not to Rebecca. She left me without looking back, the door swinging silently behind her. When I heard the sound of wings I told myself to let her go. She was right. Richard Stirling was dead.

53

Silence, too, is a blank mirror. Winged, I strained after Rebecca, calling after her in that voice that was a color in the air, and there was no response. But I did not lose her. Even when she was a mote on the horizon, I followed.

I caught up with her at last in a garden, somewhere well north of Monterey. A concrete gnome stood guard beside a birdbath, a blush of moss across his shoulders. A purple china cardinal orna-mented a fountain. Rebecca wandered a garden, and I kept silent for fear of interrupting her mood.

I scented a sharp perfume, dark, earthy. I recognized it only after a moment. A muted muttering reached us from the house above the lawn. A clock radio, I wondered, or a jolt of CNN to go with the cup of hot chocolate, the beverage I could smell from so far away.

"I'm sorry," she said. "You've been doing all of this for me. If you lied it was to protect my feelings. All of this has been a wonderful gift, Richard."

I tried to silence her, but she turned away. I wanted to tell her she was right to be afraid of me. "I started studying the piano when I was six years old. There was no great epiphany, no discovery that I was playing Mozart with a teething ring in my mouth. My parents had a Wurlitzer spinet. I thought it was the most handsome thing in the world. I loved it when my mother used Lemon Pledge on the mahogany."

A ancient sound, ugly and heartening at once, made me look at the sky.

A rooster.

I said, "We can't stay here."

She heard the rooster, too, but she gazed upward with a smile. "I would play tunes that came into my head, but they were nothing special. Still, they must have impressed my parents. I studied under a woman who was herself partially deaf, with an old-fashioned hearing aid, one of those plastic boxes you pinned to the front of your sweater. I remember even as a little girl thinking surely I should have a piano teacher with good ears. That's how I thought of it—*good ears*."

"I want to hear this," I began. *Some other time—not now.*

"My father said she was very polite, and my mother said she had been written up in magazines, *world-renowned, gracing the Bay Area with her talent*. They drove me to her apartment on College Avenue in North Oakland twice a week. I never complained. I never said, *No don't take me to her, she can't hear*. I was good. *Good* in the way children use the word. Dutiful."

The rooster unbent another one of his cries.

She looked at me, put her hand over mine. "Isn't it strange all the meanings a word can have? I was a *good* girl. I was obedient, and I wanted to please. My teacher was Sylvia Richter. No, you wouldn't have heard of her. She had a framed letter from Arthur Rubinstein in her bedroom. I didn't see it until after her stroke, but there was that air about her of being on the edge of greatness. She had drinks with Horowitz once, at the Biltmore in Los Angeles. And she met Kurt Weill in Malibu, and Stravinsky when he was in Hollywood, but I didn't know any of this until later, when I met some of her old friends in Austria."

A hen began to cluck, or was it the rooster himself? How could people live around such noisy fowl? "We don't have time for this, Rebecca."

"She told me I had to practice the sequence C,E,G, over and over again. She told me to do it five thousand times. I did. She directed me to play the Minute Waltz sixty times a day, and make a mark on a sheet for every five times I played it. And I did. Day after day, during those smoggy afternoons. The smog was worse, then. Remember? You couldn't see across the bay some September afternoons."

"Please, Rebecca—"

"I think she was a person like Eric—someone who would never be a concert pianist, someone who knew she didn't quite have the focus and the talent. Or the good fortune. But she was a great teacher, Richard."

A robin fluttered in a nearby shrub, shaking itself awake, a *whirr* of plumage.

"She said I would need two things to develop my talents. The first was the gift, and that I already had. The second was to look neither to the right nor to the left. *Look neither to the right side, nor to the left side, but always straight ahead, on only your music.*" Rebecca spoke in the voice of an older woman with a German accent.

I remained silent. Maybe it was only right that we should fade out of existence encircled by this Stonehenge of fake animals. Each figurine spilled an elongated shadow across the grass. Shadows were everywhere, the birdbath casting a long, elegant shape like an inverted pawn.

"After the accident, the piano was all I had. When I realized I could still see the keys in my mind, that the black and whites had not changed position, it was like discovering that a promise had been kept."

The accident. What a way to refer to such a devastating event.

She said, "We have been distracted by all this." All this beauty, she meant.

Each yellow dandelion was a shard of light, painful, the glare off a mirror. I pulled Rebecca into the shadow of the fountain.

"I want to see my parents," said Rebecca.

"And you want the mirror."

"So do you," she said.

Of course I did. But now I wanted to find it to preserve it. "I want to destroy the mirror as much as you do," I lied, with a throb of insincerity in my voice. "This will never happen to anyone else."

My father felt that organization was not a masculine virtue, and he was a person who modeled himself after a general idea of what was manly and what was not. Most surgeons are meticulous in their records, trusting those bulging patient records to save lives. But my father cultivated a casualness that was, perhaps, a compensation for the exacting nature of his profession. He left his mail, with a studied absentmindedness, throughout the house. My mother was always straightening out magazines on the coffee table, balancing the checkbook. She alphabetized, indexed, filed.

There was one surviving photograph of my brother. I found it in my mother's papers after her death, in a folder that was not labeled. The snapshot was in an envelope, sealed.

He sat on a brick wall, his legs dangling. He wore short pants and a white T-shirt, and looked sideways at the camera, and at the sun behind the photographer, squinting. He looked like any boy out of another time, in some subtle way, the way boxers in fading publicity photos, stripped to shorts and bare fists, look old-fashioned in ways that are hard to define.

The shadow of the photographer barely crept within the white borders of the picture, just the top of a head on the lawn. Man or woman—it was impossible to tell. But I knew.

The mind is masterful. It can file away even a living human being. The practical approach adopted by my parents scheduled the visits months ahead, a hug and a kiss on days kept apart from the rest of existence. The will could determine that the light of day would not include this creature.

But my mother had never lived an hour without thinking of him. She snapped this picture, had it developed, and then never had to look at it. She carried him in her waking and in her sleeping, and in her last thoughts she took him up and held him in her arms.

54

If morning is such a treasure, dawn the noblest hour, why does it mature so quickly, ripening into common day? The brass-green nozzle of a garden hose gleamed. Chicken wire was a fine golden net, and a black rooster with red combs and golden talons stretched his neck and closed his eyes, pleasure in his own voice.

A woman in a yellow shirt, denims rolled up to her knees, carried a red gasoline can, looking up, sensing but not seeing us. What was for us scalding light was to her false dawn, and I could hear her shiver beside a pickup truck, trying to get the cap off the can.

Sometimes the observer alters the scene around him, the tourist descending from the bus, the videocamera entering the courtroom. We changed the woodland as we tumbled through it, snagged by branches, unsettling a brooding owl. A valley fell open below us, irrigation ditches bright with groundwater.

Police cars, side by side at truck weighing stations, turning up side roads. But their search was feverish, disorganized. They knew who they were looking for, and they didn't want to believe it.

Walnut trees were in bloom. The ash-white petals distributed themselves over flatbed trucks and the discount clothing parking lot. The land was a photograph taken in bad light, nothing visible but the points of polished furniture, glassed-over lithographs, a mahogany piano.

When we slept at last I had no sense of where we were, except that we were safe in that edgy, stupefied pride of crocodiles, stunned with sudden cold.

Water was somewhere below, stone or brick rough at my cheek. I whispered her name, and the echo mocked me.

The smell was wet sidewalk, concrete after a day of rain.

I inched, finding cracks in the masonry. The top of my head met a sheet of steel. I forced upward, and the steel complained, barely moving. I worked my fingers into a thin arc of gray light and then managed to lever an entire arm, my head, my shoulders, out of the well.

Plywood was in place over the windows of a farmhouse. The back door was open. Through the doorway, cracked linoleum reflected moonlight. My steps compressed bubbles and folds in the weathered flooring.

A telephone receiver was dangling, hanging all the way to the floor. I held the instrument to my ear. There was a dial tone, an abrasive, aural sandpaper. She had been here just minutes before—that electronic banshee sound phones make, left off the hook, had yet to start in.

A radio lay beside the sink, a transistor speckled with white enamel paint. I turned the dial and the radio chattered, an all-news station, a rush of words fading after a few moments, the batteries dying.

The ordinariness of the dwelling was a comfort. A bar of soap with the manufacturer's imprint still clear to the touch was stuck to the sinktop. Within easy reach of the back porch was a clothesline with a canvas bag of wooden pins dangling.

I could change her mind, I thought. Just a few more nights. That's all I wanted. But my desire lacked impetus now. The air tasted different to me.

Outside a horse flared its nostrils, nickering, tossing its mane. Rebecca stroked the beast, patting her. The beast chomped weeds from the ground, a low, pleasing sound, roots sundering. With a leap Rebecca was astride the horse.

"Imagine living like this," she said. "It would be so wonderful."

"You forgot to hang up the phone."

She ran her fingers through the horse's mane. "One of them died, Richard," she said.

Flowering mustard crowded a field of artichokes, a valley surrounded by redwoods. The artichoke plants bristled, all thistle and raspy leaves. Acacias bloomed, shedding pollen over wheel ruts and puddles. Our footsteps had tracked through the yellow dust, yellow chalk all over my shoes.

"One of the two housesitters," she said. "The young woman."

This could not possibly be true. I wanted to laugh.

"The young man is expected to live," she continued, "but he almost died, too."

Weak, I thought. They were weak, something wrong with their hearts.

"You make her nervous," she said, as the horse shied away from my touch. It was an artful way of changing the subject. Or reminding me of something.

An animal like this can be wrong, I thought, but she cannot lie. The horse flung her mane from side to side, lifting a hoof, avoiding my touch.

"We have to trust each other," I said. Was there something about Rebecca that made me uncertain?

Rebecca leaned forward and murmured something. The horse did a brief caracole, dancing through the deep grass, and then returned to me.

I tried to sense what Rebecca was thinking, and I couldn't. The horse stepped forward, and the twin gusts of air from her nostrils were hot. This mare had no belief, no questions. Rebecca's touch made her peaceful again. I stooped and pulled up a handful of green.

The horse accepted the grass from my hand, chewing with a sound like footsteps in gravel. "Who were you trying to call?" I asked.

"Listen," said Rebecca.

A tractor was plowing a nearby field, its headlights knifing the dark.

"They never rest," she said.

That's exactly what the living were. Insistent, restless, always waiting to begin, and, once begun, eager to stop. I remembered being like this, pacing, waiting for the football game, the basketball game, on television.

"Maybe they'll think we're farmers," I said.

"Here on our own little artichoke ranch."

"A quiet life," I said. "Herbicide and tomato worms."

"You can be called Tommy Billy, and my name can be—"

"Nobody has a name like that."

"Country people do. They have names like Joe Bob and Mike Pete—"

"Sure," I agreed. "But not Tommy Billy, that's goofy."

"Better take the cultivator to that mustard, Tommy Billy. It's too bright and wonderful. It's time to plow it up."

It was all over. Something had changed. "You'll go see your parents," I said. "And I'll find the mirror."

"And what will you do when you find it, Richard?"

She was giving me an opportunity to be honest. She knew what I was thinking. When we lie we are a mirror reflecting a face that is not there. Before this evening I had been stronger than Rebecca. Not more graceful, and not more loving—but more powerful.

The pollen all over the ground was a desert of trees that would not flower. The world squanders. We are not enough, says the thoughtless flicker of the leaves—make more, spend it on the air and on the water, a dune of life that will not happen. Not even death—a scattering of all that acacias know. We will be trees, says the silence, this dust, and there is nothing. And there are trees.

I asked, "Who were you trying to call?"

She was different now. "You'll tell yourself you don't know how to destroy the mirror. Will you break it? Smash it? You won't want to be so violent. It'll be too hard to make up your mind. I know how you think—that it might be best to let scientists do research on the mirror. You'll keep it nice and safe for a while. You'll lie to yourself."

"Who did you call?"

"You think you'll be able to see your reflection. That's where it is, that's what stole it. It's in that mirror, waiting for you. Isn't that what you think, Richard?"

Don't make me lie to you.

"You want to find the looking glass," she said. "And take it away. I wonder where you think you'll be able to keep it. Buried somewhere?"

"Tell me."

Her tone was affectionate, even then. "I wanted to call my

parents, but I couldn't. I wanted to hear their voices. I didn't want to suddenly be there with them. I wanted to warn them."

"You're lying."

My accusation kept her quiet for a moment. The she continued, as though I had not spoken. "But I realized what would happen. How the police would have the phone tapped. And how startled my parents would be. They must know. They must be afraid I'll suddenly be there, in their house. I love my parents so much, Richard. I don't want to hurt them."

I shook my head.

"You don't believe me." A tone of quiet amazement. "I was going to call them—but I couldn't bring myself to."

"Why would you tell me the truth," I said. "When it would be so easy to lie?"

"Do you *hear* yourself?"

"You called the sheriff's department. You told them where we were. There are a couple hundred men on the way right now."

"Why would I do that?"

I couldn't answer her.

"Tell me, Richard—why would I lie to you?"

"To get the mirror for yourself," I said, my voice hoarse.

She stroked the horse thoughtfully. "I love you because you aren't like me. You think life is a battle. You work hard, you win. You're willful."

I leaned against a fence post, barbed wire swaying in both directions.

"You know where it is," she said, "don't you?"

"I have a pretty good idea," I said.

"I trust you," she said. "You'll find it, and bring it to me."

I nodded.

"Richard—promise me that's what you'll do."

"Yes," I said. "I'll find the mirror. And I'll bring it to you." I was lying—promising her with a full heart, and meaning none of it. "But first, come with me to see Dr. Opal."

"Why?"

I was afraid to tell her what I was beginning to believe about my own family. "He can help us." Maybe we won't have to destroy the mirror. The mirror isn't what we want after all, I thought, convincing myself.

"Do you think he knows something?" she asked.

"I know he does."

A pair of headlights combed the bright mustard. A frog belly-flopped across the dirt road. Figures climbed out of a Jeep. It was difficult not to take pleasure in the sight, men enjoying each other's company, one of them cradling a shotgun, a smell of perspiration and the dark, licorice flavor of chewing tobacco.

My hair stirred, a brief, sudden wind. Wings, the tip of one brushing me, like a finger in a glove.

Let them come closer, I thought. I nearly called out to them.

The wings skimmed the top of my head, persisting, the fine, sharp claws at my ear, the sound like a cape shaken.

55

My call was answered after the first ring, a woman's voice. No, Dr. Opal was not available, she said. Then she paused. She did not want to ask, lowering her voice. "May I tell him who called?"

"Tell him it's Richard Stirling."

She muffled the phone. I could make out the words—Susan was not as subtle as she would need to be to keep Dr. Opal happy, I thought. But sincere. Sincere and afraid.

Dr. Opal's voice was hoarse. "You don't know how many questions I've had to answer, Richard."

"I need to see you."

"No you don't. You don't need me at all. Besides, I don't trust you."

"Have you been drinking?"

"No, I have not," he said, sounding bitter. "I am in a very bad mood."

"We can meet somewhere—"

"Richard, this call is being recorded and is going to be copied and translated into twenty languages by tomorrow morning. They'll do voice prints. They'll play it on CNN. They'll print transcripts of this call and put it on coffee mugs. This is not a private conversation."

"Do you remember Ten High?"

He inhaled, straining to understand what I was talking about. "My father hated it—"

"Yes," he said at last. "I remember."

"Meet me there."

"Nice try. But I can't go anywhere, Richard. I have too many companions."

We weren't there to hide. We knew they could see us.

He jogged toward me along the marina, past the sailboats moored in the dark harbor. A rope chimed against a mast, tapping musically, a light breeze, two on the Beaufort scale.

Bring them along I had said. Bring as many people as you want. *As long as they don't get too close—I want a private consultation with my physician.*

He embraced me, panting. "It's good to see you," he said. I introduced him to Rebecca, and he gave a little bow. She offered him her hand, and despite his lively good manners he hesitated for an instant before taking it.

"You're cold," he said, finding her pulse with his fingers.

She smiled, but did not speak.

"Richard has probably told you I'm a terrible grouch," he said. He still felt her pulse, and he could not restrain himself. He touched her cheek, feeling for a pulse in her neck.

"No, not at all," she was saying, her voice almost inaudible. "He speaks of you very fondly."

The shore was a mass of lights. From time to time someone stepped before a headlight causing the light to twinkle. "How many people are watching us?" I asked.

"Both of you need friends," he said. "It's cruel what they want to do to you."

A searchlight came on, the beam seeming to hiss as it fell across the water, and found the three of us.

He whirled. "Turn it off!" he called.

I could sense hurried consultation on the shore.

"Off!" he called again.

The light went black.

"A couple dozen police," he said with something like good cheer. "I saw a couple of high-powered rifles and some night scopes."

"Is Joe Timm here?" I asked.

"From what I hear Joe Timm isn't feeling well."

Ten High had been a yacht berthed beside my father's boat years ago. The owners of the yacht had held parties, riotous celebrations, bottles and bikini bottoms flung all over the adjacent craft. My father had hated the parties, the owners, the boat itself, heaving the champagne bottles back where they came from. As a boy I think I found the parties fascinating, a glimpse of adult debauchery.

"No, we can't talk here," Dr. Opal was saying. "I worked a trauma unit years ago. One of those rifles will take you off at the neck."

We followed him along the wooden walkway.

"It's a strange sort of manhunt, Richard. It's like they're afraid to really get close to you."

The nostalgia I felt just then was painful. I was glad when Dr. Opal led Rebecca by the hand, down a gangway, onto a vessel I had never seen before.

"Mine," he said. "Just bought it. Madness, of course. I never have time. But it's one of the joys your father and I shared."

He produced keys, and we went below, into a cabin with blue-cushioned chairs and the sort of decor shoreline cocktail lounges try to achieve, a sea-faring hideaway.

"You didn't tell anyone, did you?" I said. "Until the police paid you a visit. You weren't going to tell anyone about me, ever. Because you loved my mother. And because you swore to her that you would keep a family secret."

Dr. Opal was playing the host, offering us chairs while I seethed inwardly, wanting him to finish pouring himself a drink and sit down. "You are my patient," he said. "I used discretion."

"Until you knew I was dangerous."

He did not respond to that. He said, "Your mother was one of those people who are made of finer stuff than the rest of us." He sat, finally. "Your father was so fortunate." He took a sip of his scotch and winced, looking around for soda.

"I want you to tell me about my brother."

He fussed at the bar, bottles tinkling. "I don't think people grow more afraid of death as they age. I think it's rather the opposite. So much of your life has died by the time you see the inevitability of it. There are houses you can never visit again, valleys turned into lakes, orchards cut down, towns bloated beyond recognition. Not to mention people you'll never see, voices you'll never hear again. I love life, but I don't worry much about dying."

"My brother was mentally deficient—is that the right phrase?"

Dr. Opal gave up on finding soda, waved a pair of ice tongs at me, and dropped them into a drawer. "There was something wrong with your brother. But your mother loved him with all her heart. It was your father who was afraid."

"Don't you mean embarrassed?"

"He was afraid."

"It was on my father's side of the family, wasn't it? Something genetic."

He didn't answer at once. "Please forgive me for not discussing it with you before," said Dr. Opal. "I didn't really know very much."

"You knew enough. You were loyal, but not to me. And I don't blame you. My mother was a troubled person, and I'm glad she had a good friend."

"I admired your family," he said.

"My father's genes," I said.

"Genes reproduce. All the little adjectives and adverbs get reproduced by the great printing press of the chromosomes. That's all genes are—a way of making it happen one more time."

"Like a mirror." Rebecca spoke above a whisper for the first time. "Except the new image is the result of two people, not one. And the living image can step out of the glass, into the world."

"That's a good analogy," he said. "Pointless or not, meaningful or not, the genes bring it from the past into the future."

"What was wrong?" I asked.

"Your father's family," he said, "had a history."

"A history," I prompted, barely concealing my impatience.

"A tradition of mental illness," he said, "going back generations. It wasn't just insanity, or the sort of birth defect we see too often." He caught himself. *We*. "They died before puberty, the ones with a certain characteristic. You never had the trait—so you were safe from birth." He shrugged: at least, he meant, until now.

"What characteristic?" I heard myself ask.

"Medical people call it 'failure to thrive.' Many of the Stirling males died in infancy."

I felt dizzy, hating the ugly slop of the water around the hull of the boat.

"Your brother had to be hospitalized from within a few weeks of his birth. That he lived as long as he did was something of a miracle. There wasn't anything fantastic about it," he added. "It was a genetic flaw."

"You must have a theory."

"I'm wise enough, but my problem is I have to go around telling people how wise I am. Let me give you a big surprise, Richard. I don't have all the answers. Your brother needed constant transfusions. He didn't need to eat blood or drink it, and he wasn't dangerous. Some factor in his body dissipated blood, something in the spleen, or in the marrow. Something that ate blood up. It had to be constantly replaced."

"Why did he have to be hidden away?"

"Because it wasn't that simple."

"He was a child," I said. "He needed companionship—"

"Genes are very old, Richard. The way water is old, and air."

The vessel creaked. All three of us listened.

"They aren't going to leave us alone here much longer," said Dr. Opal. Steps hesitated on the planks of the walkway, and Dr. Opal stepped out onto the deck for a moment, made a show of being alive and well, calling, "I'm all right!"

When he returned he swallowed the remains of his drink, and said, "What are you going to do, Richard?"

"You haven't answered my questions."

"I could still arrange to take you into medical custody, someone who is a threat to themselves and others."

"How did this happen to me?"

He sat, leaning forward. "This can't continue."

"Explain to me," I said, "how I got up every morning and ate breakfast and lived my life, and then this relic from my past—"

"The mirror," he said.

"What is it?"

He shook his head. "The mirror wasn't stolen. Your father got rid of it."

"Why?"

He spoke reluctantly. "He began having nightmares about it. He dreamed a unicorn found its way into the house, looking for someone."

"Looking for my father?"

"Not necessarily," said Dr. Opal, avoiding my eyes. "Searching for someone who lived in the house. He asked me to arrange to sell the mirror."

"Did you?"

"I brought the mirror home, stored it in my cellar. And it vanished."

"Burglars?"

"There was no sign of forced entry," he said. "The mirror was simply gone one evening when I went with an expert to have it appraised."

"The unicorn in the old legend looks for a mirror, searching through the woods," said Rebecca. "He is seeking his own reflection."

"He found it," I said. "I am the reflection. My father dreamed the unicorn was after me, didn't he?"

Dr. Opal had not refilled his glass. He gazed into the empty tumbler thoughtfully. "I think when we study dreams, really examine them, what they mean doesn't amount to much."

"What is going to happen to us?"

"I cancelled my lecture series. 'The Function of Intuition in Diagnosis.' It's a pity—the lectures were pretty good. The point I keep discovering time and again is that we already know what the data indicates. Our senses already have the answer. You might say that this lapse between our true knowledge and our ability to act is a burden for most of us, a cross we all have to bear."

"You have done so much to help us," said Rebecca.

"The mirror doesn't matter," said Dr. Opal. "Your brother, all your ancestors—they are shadows, now. What happened to you, Richard, has something to do with you. With your own soul."

Part Five

Who would have thought my shrivel'd heart
Could have recover'd greennesse?

George Herbert, "The Flower"

56

Sometimes a recording preserves more than the concerto. When the first violin peels back a page of sheet music and the paper does not turn easily, that rustling sound, that absence of background silence, is recorded, too.

Sometimes the sound of the pianist's breathing is made permanent along with the nocturne. If one listens closely to the product of a fine recording studio, there is often the sound of inhalation, exhalation, and even more—the fabric of a sleeve, the tick of a fingernail, the etude interwoven with the quiet presence of the body.

It was easy to find our way across the water. Flight can be like inhaling the distant shore, breathing in until the destination is deep within the lungs.

We paused in the garden of my former dwelling, and as I surveyed the house from the darkness I was aware of Rebecca's breath. The sky was clear, and the wind was shifting; a warm, dry breeze came from inland. I had never loved the sky as I did now. The Big Dipper balanced on its handle in the Northeast.

Every light in the house was on. A tiny galleon, a snail made way across a stepping-stone. The handle of a trowel thrust upward from between the branches of the daphne. "This is where you lived?" Rebecca asked.

"We always had trouble with the back lawn. The poplar tree had these immense roots—see, that's where the power mower barked the roots every time I mowed the grass."

Rebecca touched the white navel of a holly bush where a

branch had been snipped. "Connie was always a firm believer in the pruning shear," I said.

"You said she was living with Steve."

"Connie's full of surprises."

"Don't be afraid, Richard."

I wanted to tell her that I was not afraid of anything. *I'll find the mirror, and bring it—*

Bring it where? We had not lied to each other any more than we had to. Without admitting it to myself, I knew what was about to happen. This was why I didn't want to leave her, in the place where, if there had been a sun, the shadow of the poplar would fall.

"I used to stroll from room to room at night," I said, "making sure windows were locked, enjoying the place. But I was anxious without being aware of it. I knew there were thieves, earthquakes."

She said, "I'll go see my parents."

I didn't say, *I'll meet you here, under this tree. I'll meet you at the cemetery. I'll find you wherever you are.*

Isn't this everyone's favorite time of night, early evening, rooms lit, curtains, the corner of a chair, the edge of a painting on the wall all anyone can see from the dark?

Rebecca had perfected the act of vanishing. She took a breath, and then I was alone. We both knew, and yet we both deliberately silenced our farewell, saying nothing.

How full of promise life seems when you stand like this, looking in.

Connie was always leaving her gardening sneakers by the back door, a jacket on the back of a kitchen chair, her purse on the breakfast table, right next to the basket of Balinese wooden apples.

I held her wallet in my hand, loving its familiarity. A folded piece of paper was thrust into the coin compartment, a receipt from a Shell station.

I enjoyed the sounds of the house I had lived in, the thrum of the refrigerator. It was one of the latest, energy-efficient models. After a week we wouldn't even notice the whirring, gurgling noises it makes, the salesclerk had assured us with a smile. If anything, the fridge had developed a new whine over the months, as though its interior was manufacturing food, not keeping it cold.

At first I couldn't see her. She was sitting in her wooden armchair, watching television with the sound off, an ad for *The Greatest Music of All Time*, ten compact disks.

I said her name, very softly.

She stood, putting out a hand to keep the chair from tumbling. A large bandage covered her right eye. "Jesus!"

She wavered, and I expected her to faint.

But she didn't. She turned her head slightly, side to side, trying to get a better look at me. She didn't speak for a very long moment, leaves pattering against the front window, a gust of wind.

"They told me you wouldn't come here," she said. "They swore it was out of the question."

"What happened to your eye?"

She touched the white adhesive, the pad of white gauze. "They told me they had you right where they wanted you. I used to wonder why women fainted. I thought it was a way of attracting attention to yourself. Jesus, I might throw up. I have to sit down."

"I wasn't even sure you'd be home." This was not the complete truth. I had sensed her presence as I entered the house, and even now I could feel the heat of her body, the new brand of perfume she had dabbed below each ear.

Connie did not sit down. She found the remote lying on a catalog of Turkish carpets, using it to keep the pages flat. She turned off the television after a few tries. The catalog stayed open, brilliant sheets of color. "Joe Timm swore this was the last place you'd show up."

"What happened to all your—" I tried to find the right word. "Wonderful artifacts?"

"My stuff." She shrugged. "Long story. I had too much money in wood and fiber. Nobody wanted it. People looked at a big balsawood head and they'd think—superstition. They'd think—bad magic. Metals are popular suddenly. Gold, and rocks. Gems."

"And glass," I said.

"Frankly, I'm not even dealing in stone statuettes right now. I'm keeping more money in cash. Staying liquid. You know what I'd like to do? I feel like calling Joe Timm on the phone and saying, here, there's somebody I want you to talk to."

"We both own this house," I said. "It's only right for me to drop by. What happened to Larkin?"

She didn't want to say. "The pet shop python ate him. I didn't stand around to watch."

I was troubled by this news.

"I have to do all the thinking myself. I have to decide to get out of Ivory Coast dyed cottons and into Navajo turquoise and nobody can advise me. I have to be smart all the time. Joe Timm should retire."

"You haven't sold the house or anything, have you?"

"Joe Timm said they'd—" She buttoned her dressing gown. "He said they'd catch you and—I think his phrase was 'render them both helpless.' He was so sure of himself."

"Are you in pain?"

"Richard, my life is in such ruins that it's a joke."

There was a whisper upstairs, someone crossing the floor. "You and Steve aren't getting along?" I asked.

"Steve?" As if he was someone she could barely remember. "Poor Steve."

"He isn't working out so well?"

"Steve is terrified."

"He's always been a little nervous," I offered, just to keep her talking. Steve might be listening to us, pacing the floor upstairs, although there was something about the tread that crossed and recrossed the floor that seemed careless, even happy, someone busy packing or taking an inventory. I tried to reach into the recesses of the house with my mind, but there was something impenetrable about the person upstairs.

"Maybe you could say he was a little nervous," Connie agreed. "Like a hamster in a snake's cage. He doesn't want to be associated with me because of you."

"But you're going to have a baby—"

"I have to look at my plans. I might have the baby, I might not. Don't look at me like that. *You* never wanted children."

I was wrong. "What happened to your eye?"

"I scratched it gardening," she said with a whimsical sulkiness I used to find appealing. "A daphne twig. Damaged my cornea. It'll heal in a week or so. Why are you here?"

This was my chance. I could be frank. I could tell the truth. "I want the mirror."

I could see her sort through the possible responses. She could play dumb, *what mirror?* She could keep her mouth shut.

"Language is always a little bit of a lie, Connie. When I say *man* you picture one thing—Steve, say—and I picture George Washington, Abraham Lincoln. Well, someone else. It's very imprecise, language. If you take a hard look at it you realize it doesn't mean very much at all."

"My other eye weeps sympathetically. I can't see very well."

"Even if you tell me it's up in the attic, where you always hide things you really want to keep, I might not quite understand what you mean. I might not remember that what you call an attic is just a crawl space with insulation stapled to the studs."

"It's Belgian," she said. "From Ghent."

"Really."

"It's the frame that makes it so valuable, that and the fact that it represents the best work of a firm that perfected the silvering technique. Actually, *silvering* is a misleading word. It was the cause of death for many of the craftsmen. They developed mercury poisoning and turned blue and had permanent nerve damage. They inhaled the paint they applied to the glass."

"How unpleasant."

"There isn't another mirror like it in North America. But if you think there's anything ghastly about the mirror, forget it. I had it examined at the lab that restored the Toulouse-Lautrec etchings, the one that bleached out all the mildew. I thought there might be a mummified face or some ancient blood behind the mirror, or mixed in with the amalgam. I was terrified of it, if you want to know the truth. And there's nothing. It's just a framed mirror and I wanted to keep it."

"You weren't afraid of cutting yourself?"

"Of course I was. But when I *did* and nothing happened I realized I could continue to own the mirror with impunity. Besides, Richard, maybe I gave the mirror to Rebecca Pennant's family. Maybe her brother has it in Crescent City, after all. I was always able to lie to you pretty well. What makes you think you can see through me now?"

"You cut your finger?"

"Yes, look."

There was a fine nick in one knuckle, a tiny smiling mouth. "I almost had a heart attack. I'm on tranquilizers, Richard. Stella Cameron told me about them. Better than Prozac, the new—"

"What makes the frame so valuable?"

"It's made of Mediterranean briar, the same root they make tobacco pipes out of. It's a very hard wood, fine grained, a very rare root."

"A root."

"Yes, like root beer. Please sit down."

"You're lying to me, Connie."

"I want to do the right thing," she said, pleadingly. "I can't stand here and be frank with you, Richard. My heart is pounding. I feel sick."

"I'm going upstairs to get it."

"All right, take it. That's what you want, you'll take it no matter what I do. I'm helpless. We're all helpless. What's it like, Richard, being right all the time, and unstoppable?" She said it sarcastically, as though it was not true.

I said, "I didn't want to upset you."

"Do you think people want to buy a Taiwanese tiki from somebody who used to be married to you?"

"We're *still* married, aren't we?"

"Jesus," she said, "it's a wonder I don't black out."

"Who's upstairs?"

"I used to do okay with Bedouin silver, but I wouldn't touch the obvious stuff, Richard. Everybody sells gold watches that haven't ticked in eighty years. Everybody sells those little coral cameos, Greek goddesses to keep your collar from hanging open. Anyone can make money selling Confederate battle flags. I was something different. I was *special*. I was a dealer in *exotica*, Richard, and you've ruined me."

"Is Steve upstairs?"

"There's no one upstairs."

"You didn't have a lab examine the mirror," I said. "You knew it was precious, worth more than all the other imports you ever owned put together. You never asked where it came from or tried to trace it. You stowed it in the roof and prayed nobody would ever ask for it."

"They did ask."

"And you lied. You told them you didn't know what happened to it. Why weren't you afraid?"

She held one hand over her bandaged eye. "I *deserved* it. It was rare and it came to my house and it was mine. You know it's true, Richard. If a package is delivered to a residence it belongs to the receiver, even if it's all a mistake."

"The *recipient*. It wasn't a mistake. Someone sent it to me."

"How was it labeled?"

It was addressed to me. But I couldn't say it. Because I was not certain.

She said, "Maybe I ordered the mirror from Paris."

"It wasn't like an international package. No foam rubber, no padding. It was just—"

"It's mine."

"You didn't cut yourself on the mirror," I said. "It's not from Ghent. You don't know anything about it."

"It belongs to me. Go ahead and steal it. Why not? You get everything else you want."

"It's dangerous." I wanted to say *evil*. "Why do you want such a thing?"

"You know why."

"No, Connie, forgive me, but I stand here completely mystified."

"Because I come from Turlock, California, something you used to remind me of every chance you could. When I was a girl I used to think the best part of the week was when we washed all our cars. We'd soap them up and hose them off, and I was in charge of wiping them down, getting all the drops of water off before they dried to little white zits. That's how I grew up. Looking forward to Sunday afternoon pickup truck washing, when we'd all join in, the whole family. I was a simple person, and I wanted to be special. And I was."

I knew what it was, the first sound, the first muffled crash. I knew what it was, and I knew exactly what would happen next. Connie looked up at the ceiling, one hand holding her bandaged eye, the other over her heart.

I spoke gently, even a little sadly. "Connie, get out of the house."

"I won't let you."

"Please, Connie. I don't want you to get hurt."

"Is this what you wanted, standing around asking about whether or not my eyeball was ever going to grow back? I'm not going to surrender to you like everybody else in the world, Richard."

She stumbled on the stairs. She hung on to the banister. I wrestled her out of the house, onto the dark lawn. She was noisy, kicking, scratching. I had to be careful to be quick and at the same time not hurt her. She struggled, and I felt her kicking and twisting in my arms. *A baby—there's a baby in her womb.*

When I turned back to the house the curtains were alight. There was a *huff*, a gentle explosion, and the scent of kerosene.

57

The wind was rising. Another breathy explosion blew out windows. I ducked involuntarily to avoid flying glass.

The explosions were hushed, the sound of splintering and fragmenting louder than the blasts. I had trouble pushing open the front door, the animal-pattern rug bunching, jamming the entrance. Already I could feel the heat.

Connie leaped onto my back. I shook her off, as gently as I knew how.

"Richard, don't go in there," Connie pleaded. "Please don't go in there, Richard—please stay out here with me."

She was clawing at me, and when I crossed the living room I dragged her with me. "I won't let you *do* this."

"I don't want to hurt you." I had to shout, fire thundering.

"I don't care about the mirror." Her one healthy eye reflected flames. "I don't care about the house. You *planned* this."

Fire oozed down the stairs. Connie was crying, stumbling after me into the smoke. "And I'm not going to lose you again, Richard." She was screaming to be heard. "What kind of a life do you think I'm going to have after this? What kind of life do you think I'm going to have for my baby?"

I swept Connie outside. Her bandage was smouldering, and her blouse twinkled, fine points of vermillion streaming smoke. I found the brass nozzle and pulled hard, straightening the garden hose. I drenched her while she sprawled, cursing me, telling me nothing that happened to her mattered anyway.

"I don't want it," she said. "I want to reach in there and tear it out." She was bawling now, and I knelt beside her.

"Please keep the baby," I said.

"It doesn't mean anything," she said. *It.*

"Have the baby," I said. I intended this as my farewell, my summation.

"You care! That's what you want—a baby! It's wonderful, Richard, to find this out after all these years. You wanted children. I could have had children, Richard. It wasn't my fault. It was *you.* This is Steve's baby, Richard. It isn't yours."

"It doesn't matter who the father—"

"No, it doesn't. It's a human baby, right, Richard? Is that what you think? If you stay out here with me I'll have the baby," she said, her fingers digging into my arm. "You go in there and it's all finished, Richard. It's not just you. You always thought you were the center of the world. But what about *me?*"

I was on my feet but she hung on, a sleeve ripping. I slapped her. I tried to be gentle. Even hurting Connie a little caused me pain, and I knew it was too late in the story of our lives to change anything.

Sleep, Connie. Rest.

I left Connie lying on the dark lawn, one arm outflung as she lay in a daze. Her position was almost that of a person holding out a telephone, *It's for you.* The hose was on full force, the brass nozzle lifting and tossing beside her.

The smoke was solid, filling the living room. I closed my eyes. I found the stairs and took three steps at a bound, and then the fire swallowed me. The heat was not what slowed me. I made myself not feel it.

My clothes writhed around my body, pant legs alive, jacket sleeves aflame. The smell of my seared flesh filled my lungs, and then my lungs were finished, each breath cauterizing the air sacs. I made my way into the room, wading against a tide, the floor waist-high with flames.

I called her name. The fire streamed around me, wind pouring through the broken windows. *Richard, stay away.* Did she say this, or did one of her thoughts reach me, like a cry from a shore?

I think I saw her once more, before my eyes were lashed by the fire and I lost all vision. She sat cross-legged, breaking the looking glass into fragments against the floor, at the bottom of a pool of light.

The ruptured spheres of hurricane lamps crunched underfoot. I could feel the satisfying grind of glass turning back into sand as I made my way, but the fire was deafening. Did she speak to me, once, parting her lips to utter flame? Or was I blind by then, imagining the scene, creating a mental image of the room so I could grope my way?

By the time I reached her she was gone. Her bones were a wooden cradle someone had cast into the bonfire, furniture no one would ever need again.

I told her I loved her. Or I tried to, with what was left of my organs of speech. I pressed my hands over the remains of the shattered mirror. She had done her work well.

Glass doesn't burn. It bubbles, and fuses. Fire transforms it, turning it into cysts of silica.

58

There must be a vocabulary in the body that we never have to learn. Even in a coma there must be a monument-lined avenue, a capital city—what we really are. The executive mansion, its empty windows. The obsolete automobiles are few, the cars of our child-hood, of all childhoods. Because when I was not a body anymore, was barely a skeleton, I still felt that there was something left, a trellis within the ivy, bones within the bones.

But of course I had always known this story, always known how it would end, even as I felt it not ending at all, a new chapter falling open, ancient—new only to me.

I had the dimmest sense of what was happening. Dr. Opal was consoling a weeping woman. He was telling her that the more you know the less you understand. I tried to take solace in this dream, my life leafing open before me, a collection of postcards.

Here was a street. Here was a sycamore, the patchy beige and green of its bark. How could I know this? I couldn't see, I could not walk. This was one of those last visions, what my life was like.

Water rose up around me. I lurched on tattered stilts, and fell. I lay at the bottom of a spill of running water. My bones disarticulated in the gentle flow. The sharp pebbles and the jagged minerals of my body intermingled.

Let me imagine that I remember sirens, fire trucks in the dis-tance. It may be true. But it was impossible for me to receive any sound clearly, there was too little of me left. Minnows probed me, finding some nourishment in residue, in char. They were hungry. Their mouths were like the ends of mechanical pencils, the lead drawn in, leaving the hard, round holes.

There must have been some reason the early recordings were man-ufactured in the form of black disks, plates fused by craftsmanship into circles. Recordings on cylinders could have been practical, but it was a general consensus that these black dishes of music were more appealing.

I think it was because you could see the entire piece of music at a glance, or feel it with your fingertips. Here was the groove where the song began, and here, at the label, was where it ended. And there was that circle around the label where the needle could spiral inward and bump and bump until the hand freed it, the circle of jittery silence that begins and ends all music.

How many nights passed? How many times did I seek and find what I needed from the living?

I always returned to the creek, the sandbag-lined bank, the horsetail reeds, the drainage pipes, all of it familiar to my touch even though I could not see.

This blindness was a familiar country. The sound of a 'possum's tail dragging as the animal crept through the reeds to its burrow was as clear to me as a spoken word. Each whisper named itself.

The sandbags had been filled with a mixture of sand and cement long ago. Now the canvas sacking was season by season wearing through, the inner core of concrete all that was left.

One evening I could see again.

I did not know what it was I was looking at, only that soon it would resolve itself, like a screen supervised by an absentminded projectionist. There were reeds. Reeds and a creek, and a family of marsupials, their pink snouts, their pink eyes, gazing back at me.

The 'possums were too hungry to be shy. The larger one crouched over a corn cob. But they were curious, and did not move. I found myself able to speak. First a whisper, "Don't worry. I won't hurt you."

They didn't even know enough to be afraid, these pink, snouty creatures. But perhaps they sensed something in me, some harm-lessness that was a part of their landscape, like the water and the reeds. They began to share the bare cob, gnawing it into chunks.

I wandered back to the site, the black scribbles that had been a house. A few scraps had been raked from the blackened geometry, a rind of carpet, electronic equipment fused and glittering. I whis-pered Rebecca's name over the last place I had seen her, where the poplar roots were exposed above the trampled, ashy lawn.

But I did not linger there beside the snaking branches of the daphne, the trowel still in place, thrust into the mossy ground. I had somewhere to go.

I did not remember these streets—but I knew where I was.

These thoroughfares were oddly familiar, short, steep driveways, houses with painted wooden shutters that would not close, orna-mental, and gardens of neatly clipped lawns and ferns. It was a street of ferns, fuchsias, rows of begonias.

I crossed a lawn, and found my way up the front steps to a door with a pleasing, tongue-and-handle door latch. The brass was warm, familiar. Closing my hand around it filled me with happi-ness.

This was a house I had never visited. But I knew exactly where to turn, where to find my way across a hall, my footsteps hushed by the firm nap of a carpet. Bookshelves, an African violet, the walls uncluttered, everything simple, spare, tidy.

I knew this place.

Only the piano surprised me. I had expected a spinnet, a com-pact, handsome piano of no great musical quality but the sort of instrument for which one develops affection. Instead, here was a baby grand, a Steinway.

I nearly laughed out loud. Of course, the spinnet had been sold years ago, and this Steinway had been here ever since. I could find my way here with my eyes closed.

It's easy to forget the beauty of a piano, the cream, the black. The hand almost does not want to interrupt the perfection. The pond is still. The fish sleep. The fingertips try to break the surface without flawing the peace.

Before I made a sound I warned myself that I could not do this.

I began to play, my hands finding the keys, my feet the pedals. I remembered the *Fantasie* only as I caused it to sound. It was like waking the music from a long sleep, from a coma, from a silence the music itself always resides in, a room beyond human habitation.

But I was in that room, playing the music I had been afraid I would never perform again, my hands knowing—a little stiff, but losing the stiffness with each heartbeat.

I played the music that would awaken my parents. I sensed them stir, sensing their disbelief, their love. They woke, and came through the house to the room where I sat playing Chopin in my sky blue gown.

59

"We knew you would come back," said my father, in a shaky whisper. He put his arms around me in the sudden lamplight.

How did you know? I wanted to ask. How could you have so much faith?

But I could only look at him, actually seeing him for the first time in years. The light was very bright. I ran my fingers over the folds in his face, his mustache, his eyebrows while my pupils adjusted to this new glare, the gleam from the black satin of the Steinway.

How weathered he looked! Not like the wiry, smooth-faced young man I recalled, drying while Mother washed, folding the towel afterward with strong, slender fingers. But he looked wonderful—keen and joyful.

He wore the bathrobe I had given him one Christmas. I knew its feel, soft cotton, but I was surprised at the plaid, black and yellow.

One pocket had been mended, the thread black, the stitches fine, my mother's work. My mother was in the doorway, not coming any closer, her hands clasped.

They had prayed for this. Not before dinner, one of the Presbyterian blessings over broken bread, but privately, after the service had ended and the church emptied, in the evening, the Bible closed. *If it be Thy will.*

But a visitation like this could never have His blessing. Why didn't I tell them that it wasn't really me? Why didn't I tell them that I was an image of their daughter, not Rebecca at all?

"I can't stay," I said, my voice soft, calm. My parents were quiet and exact, trusting the syncopation of events. I wanted to protect them from what was happening. Still, it sounded so harsh in my ears. *I'm here, but I'm gone.*

"Of course you can't stay," said my father, easily adjusting to this new reality, or trying to. Besides, the implications of my visit shook even my father. They loved me, but I should not be alive.

Home. These walls, this familiar rug I had not seen since childhood, my grandmother's prized Persian, the only florid object in the house. And even it was handsome rather than ornate, masculine, puritan grays, pale desert-browns. "But you know how much I've wanted to see you."

"We know exactly," he said. "And anything we can do to help you now we will do. We're your family, Rebecca. You know what that means."

It was like him to say the right things without quite knowing it. He had more common sense than feeling, but in his way he was rarely mistaken. I was so full of love for them that I could not say more. His ancestors had designed ships, and while he had made a living drawing up plans for cottages and two-car garages, he retained some of this forefathers' acceptance of any change in weather.

Still, his crispness surprised me. He had been sustained by uncanny faith. How could he have been so sure?

He read my thoughts. "I used to always want an explanation for things," he said. "Every effect had a cause. I had to understand what happened. But no more, Rebecca. No more, darling daughter." He took me in his arms again, and this time there were tears.

"I don't have to understand. I can only thank God that He's allowed me to see you once again on Earth."

My mother looked like a relative in an old scrapbook, a face I knew, a face I myself must resemble, but also the countenance of a stranger, unfamiliar kin. My mother stayed where she was, beside the African violet, her hand trembling, stretching toward me.

She knew, as my father did not, how wrong this was. "Rebecca," she said, her voice broken. "It can't be you."

Much later, in the vegetable garden, my father showed me where the basil was, and the crook-neck squash, the toad's-tongues of new green. His garden was tended thoroughly, to the point there were no weeds, no errant pebbles.

It was time to go. This time I could tell them I would return some night, and mean it, while the living say that they will see each other soon, and can only half believe their own promises.

It was still a discovery—how a step sinks into the lawn, damp welling faintly around the sole. "They'll ask us and we won't say a thing," my father was saying.

"You'll be our secret," my mother offered. I could hear her unanswered question—why couldn't I hide here, somewhere beyond daylight?

"You can tell them if you want," I said. "What can they do?"

We love houses. As children we can hardly wait to grow up and live in one, our own house from which we'll look out at the cars and the people passing by. Windows are what we love, I have come to believe. A way to possess the world, and to be apart from it at the same time, flowers in a box, the smell of morning through the barely opened glass. But to have windows we need walls, a roof—a house.

This was another place, another dwelling I could not remember, but as before, this sense of mystery was what carried me forward.

Each breath brought me something new that I recognized just a half-beat late.

A patio spread at my feet, cracked, the cracks sealed with rubber paste. Bonsai maples held new, green leaves and behind the rows of wooden planters, a view of Berkeley and Oakland spread outward, glittering lights. Far away, yellow words jittered and winked, a blimp drifting over the port of Oakland.

Our eyes touch the dark, the light, the corduroy of half-light, the high polish of the bare, empty sky. The eyes are our most sensitive sense, more subtle than the tongue, so fine mere wavelengths strike gold, strike fire.

This was like a dream of speaking a foreign tongue, sudden fluency, and more—poetry. I wafted into the house, folding through the crack in the sliding glass door. I passed down a hall. When I wore a human shape again I was at the bedside of a sleeping woman. She was gaunt, her gray hair spread across the pillow. A nurse drowsed in a corner chair, a magazine face down in her lap.

I looked down at my hands and started. I wore the dark suit, the broad, strong fingers, the body of Richard Stirling. I had to stifle a laugh. But of course it was Richard who wanted to do this, who felt he owed this debt.

I cut my lips with my teeth, biting hard. I bent down over the woman, and kissed her. Her lips had the bland warm flavor of Vaseline, and her breath was slow, constricted.

At the taste of my blood she stirred, and nearly woke.

"Joe?" she whispered.

He was asleep on the sofa but at the sound of my step, light and carpet-muffled, he was wide awake.

His hand fumbled at his hip. He was not armed, sitting in a bright yellow pool-robe. His hands searched further, pillow, sofa cushion. He was defenseless. "Why are you here?" said Joe Timm.

"I'm glad to see you well," I said, my best, closing-argument voice. "Quite honestly—I was worried about you."

He could not bring himself to speak for a moment. "You nearly killed me," he said. There was no anger, no bitterness, only a matter-of-fact disbelief.

"But we were both lucky. I managed to fail," I said. "Besides, I didn't really want your life, Joe. You must realize that." How strange and pleasurable it was to be Richard Stirling again, wanting more than anything to talk.

Joe looked drawn, new wrinkles in his forehead and cheeks. His handsomeness was half-erased, punished. There was a tremor in his hand, the kind that can be permanent, the mark of irreversible aging, or a shock from which one will never fully recover. "This isn't possible."

I was to blame for much of Joe's strain. I was aware of this—I knew the wrong I had committed, and was here to try to atone. "Your wife has been ill again."

He considered me, narrowing his eyes. "She suffered a relapse."

"Pneumonia in both lungs," I guessed, "leading to congestive heart failure."

"Don't do anything to her, Richard."

"The antibiotics don't work the way they used to," I continued. "The microbes don't die."

"It is absolutely impossible for you to be here."

"You fascinate me, Joe. I think I have never really figured you out. After all that has happened you become incredulous just because I drop by to say hello."

"They found your bones," said Joe after a long pause.

Joe's living room was big and tasteful, Danish leather chairs, bright colors. Someone had been reading Gibbon. There was a red leather bookmark in the middle of volume two of the history of Rome's decline, beside a cup of what smelled like lemon tea. "Surely not."

"In the fire in your house, all that was left of the upstairs was a few gnarls of melted glass and your jaw, a couple of vertebra—"

"The remains were not mine." I could not keep the sadness from my voice. "It was Rebecca's body."

"That was what puzzled the lab. There was no sign of Rebecca Pennant's skeleton in the ashes. Only yours. Your body burned, Richard."

I paced, not wanting to hear this.

"Much as I wanted you destroyed," he said, "I have to be honest. I found it impossible to celebrate. It was a great loss. Something about you—"

"*She* burned."

"No." His voice was clear, no sign of weariness there. "You did."

"Then—what am I? Who is this standing here?" I picked up the cup of herb tea, cold liquid splashing onto my cuff. "I'm real!"

"They found some other bones, too, but they weren't human. The mirror was framed in some kind of animal bone. Nobody can figure out what it is or where it came from. Connie has no idea—"

"She kept telling me a different story about the mirror—"

"She hasn't a clue what it was," said Joe. "Where it originated, what it was made of—she knows nothing."

"It found me," I said. "Like a unicorn, finding the mirror in a virgin's hand." Or like Judas, stepping forward with his betraying kiss.

"Joe." It was a voice from another room.

It was his wife's voice, from the bedroom. I did not follow him there, but I could sense what was happening. It took him a long moment to see the change in her, to realize what had happened. He went in and sat at her side, the two of them murmuring.

I put down the cup of cold tea. I could pick things up, I could put them down. Great moments in Newtonian physics. But beyond that I was beginning to know what I had lost.

Then he stood in the bedroom doorway, leaning against it, his eyes closed. "Sometimes," he said, "I wish I could forget everything, my whole life, and start all over again. Maybe this time I would really see life, really *feel* things," he said.

"You make it sound like it's too late, like your life is over," I said.

"I'm going to quit the police," he said. "Politics, too. I don't know what I'll do. But I can't keep on like this."

"You're a good cop," I said, surprised at my words, and at my sincerity. "We need people like you."

"You'll have the time you need to get away," he said. "I'll have to tell them what happened."

"What did happen, Joe? Who came to see you?"

He did not even consider the question. "But I can't wait forever," he said. "I promised I would call them right away if I saw or heard anything."

I understood then why Rebecca's father—my father—had been so sure I would pay them a visit. They all knew. Richard was gone. Only Rebecca survived. When had it happened? That evening with the yellow mustard, the artichoke fields, the horse growing calm at my touch? Or somewhere else, some nameless place?

One night, one day, Rebecca had taken on my shape, and I had taken on hers, along with her memories. I had parted from myself, and only realized it now. For some reason as the wonderment faded I felt the oddest sensation.

Along with a sense of loss I felt as though a terrible thing, a calamity, was over, finished, irrevocably past. Nothing so terrible could ever happen again.

"Who is it, Joe?" his wife was asking from inside the bedroom. There was the rustle of bedding, a dressing gown. Her voice was strong, her step quick. She peered over his shoulder, a graceful woman. "Who's there?"

Joe Timm met my eyes. He shook his head and gave me a tired smile. "A friend," he said.

60

Sometimes I heard Richard's voice.

Before I woke. He said my name, not calling me, speaking to me. He was here, beside me.

Look, he said. *Look and see.*

They keep the remains in a secret place. I stole into Dr. Opal's office, pored through his computer files, solving each password, each code with little effort. They have hidden what is left of him, those spindles of charred kindling, his bones. And what is left of the mirror is somewhere in hiding.

The tallest structures in San Francisco are the pronged black skeletons that lift television up into the sky. Points of red blink off and on. The hills mature to summer blond. The fog never actually flows. It is suddenly there, a high tide parting around the peaks, the city, bursting without moving through the Golden Gate.

What has been joined can be separated, I believed. I would see him again.

I always had to pause, to take in the sight of traffic, the flashing red warning pedestrians to stay, people hurrying, ignoring the scarlet hand. People are all that holds the sky in place. The answers we give to each other, when asked how we are, what our day was like. This is what the stars can never equal, this glittering minutia, the subtle accidents of lives.

I passed along the streets, crossing in the crosswalk, turning my face from shop windows. Tonight I was late, and I wore my human habiliments, flesh, garments, with a certain impatience.

There was a moon, three quarters, high above. A narrow sidewalk was overshadowed by hyperextended stalks of geraniums, the plants needing more sun. I stopped and listened, sensing heartbeats.

There was nervousness in the air. It was going to happen again.

I had never liked the place, but Matilda had insisted. It reminded her of old times, meetings to rearrange, folders to be filed. I humored her, although I knew the game could not last.

Perhaps I liked it, too, despite myself. I eased myself into the chair. For weeks now I had lived out of the tidy suitcase of my two selves, unpacking Richard because I loved him, wearing him, with his memories, his chatter, because I could not suppress the fear that I would never see him again.

I put my hand, Richard's hand, over the telephone. Matilda had insisted on a combination fax/answering machine. Matilda was loyal to certain products, Sony, Panasonic. She remained loyal to me the way I had once been, and I let her believe, thinking it harmless.

I called her number, her private line, and her Spanish accent answered. I can leave a message of any length, said her voice, and I enjoyed the sound, her voice turning a common English message into amber.

I left no message. I knew I could risk another phone call, because I had weeks ago learned how to steal past the computers that trace calls, slipping my voice like a thread through a needle's eye.

Stella Cameron was breathless, picking up the phone just as I was about to hang up. "The baby just squirted mustard all over my instructions to the judge."

"What case is that?" I heard Richard's voice inquire.

"That awful date rape thing."

I called her every now and then, and had come to think of her as a friend once again. It was one of my powers—I could transform shock and deep unease into their opposite. I wanted to ask Stella what was happening. What had she heard? What were the police about to do? Authorities were always raiding an elevator shaft in the Financial District at noon, storming a warehouse, digging up a vacant lot in Hunter's Point. "I thought you didn't do criminal stuff."

"The defendant's the obnoxious son of a college roommate," she said, "a horrible kid. He has a reputation as a junior cocksman. The girlfriend should have known better."

"That's a shabby case, Stella," I said. "I'm surprised at you."

"You're right. I'm not proud, Richard. I owed it to my friend."

"You made copies, though," I said. "Nothing is just one thing, unique. Everything is a photocopy of something else, hardcopy, a print-out."

"They have these huge mustard containers at Costco with pump lids. You barely touch it and a long yellow noodle leaps out, except when you want it to."

"You're trying to stall me, get the call traced," I said.

Stella sighed. "Christ, she's starting to eat it. It might be good for her. Extra fiber." She changed the subject, a habit of hers, quick switches, one of the many things I liked about her. "I don't think Connie has a case."

"Think of the publicity," I said. "I can see the headlines—*Wife Won't Share Insurance with Dead Husband*."

"You know Connie. She loves a struggle. She still argues that you aren't married because you're legally dead."

"Feeble argument, don't you think?"

"You know what Dr. Opal says, don't you?"

"Tell me."

"He was over here a few nights ago. They watch everyone who ever knew you. They're sick of it. I'm glad, in a way. I think the kind of person who wants to be a cop deserves to be punished."

"What does Dr. Opal—"

"He says you must be Rebecca, disguised as Richard. That's why they keep the bones hidden, top-secret. Maybe they'll use them as bait some day."

"What do you think?"

"I used to know you—Richard—pretty well, a long time ago. I think I loved you. I never told you that." She paused, perhaps self-conscious, thinking of all of this going on tape, technicians listening. "I think you're Richard Stirling."

"New and improved," I suggested.

She laughed. "You give me a headache, Richard. I hope they never find you."

My parents are perfect in their deception. One might suppose they had been trained as spies. They have never seen me, they told anyone who asked. That room my father rents, that carpeted cellar with a piano, is a secret to everyone but my small family. The key is simplicity. Keep only one secret, and build a plain box around it.

Now Matilda was half an hour late.

I knew what was happening. This was the night it would unravel. This cellar room was painted green halfway up, and gray the rest of the way, with an acoustical-tile ceiling, squares filled with round little holes. A calendar was pinned to the wall, Crater Lake the image for April. A former tax accountant's office, Matilda had said, comfortable and spartan at the same time.

Matilda thought of me as Richard Stirling, and as her old friend and employer she kept me supplied with gossip, and sometimes with a plastic tube of whole blood she had a relative misappropriate from the medical school. Some day, I had always known, they would follow Matilda here, or subvert her, convince her of the harm I was doing, persuade her that she owed too much to the living.

There was a step, the key, the background rush of sounds, traffic, far-off voices.

I knew at once, but I asked her a philosophical question, a legal quibble, and she was ready with an answer. "Of course you're a person," Matilda argued. "You can identify yourself, sign your name, bear witness. You can be sworn in under oath. You are of sound mind, and you can be fingerprinted. Legally, you are a human being."

I took flowers from her arms, yellow roses, seven of them. "And medically?"

"Medically," she said dismissively, as though the medical point of view was beneath notice. She was going to law school, and insisted some day Richard Stirling's name would be on the letterhead with hers. "You'd need to find a doctor who would testify that you can be defined as alive despite what Connie's expert might demonstrate. It would be very easy. There is nothing more compelling than an established fact, like a person standing up in person, *here I am*."

I lay the roses on the desk, on the green blotter. I had to ask, to give her an opportunity.

"There were two in tennis shorts tonight," she responded. "I lost them at Pier 39, by the clown selling helium balloons."

Again, I offered her another chance to be truthful. "Did they give you these flowers?"

She hated the words as she spoke them. "I thought you would like them."

"You don't have to lie to me, Matilda," I said. "Don't be upset. They courted you for days, bought you dinner, gave you things. One of them is a bit of a romantic."

"I am not lying," she said, turning to me, her hands against the chair behind her. She was plumper than ever, and there was a wheeze of asthma in her voice.

I smiled. "They told you it would be so much better if they took me in. It was Dr. Opal. He's very convincing. Maybe he fell a little bit in love with you. Yellow roses. It's touching."

"It isn't true."

I put my finger to my lips, telling her not to say another word. She tried to say *no*, but she was fighting tears.

"Because they are right," I said, "in their way. Don't think for a moment that you have betrayed me. You haven't. Whatever happens to me is an old story."

The silence was the balancing point. Truth is all we have. In that is our strength, our lives. As soon as we begin to keep our secrets, as soon as we knit our fictions, the color drains, the stars pale, the land weakens beneath our feet.

Among the many things I missed, I missed drinking water, standing at a sink and filling a tumbler, like this plastic container here in the corner, emblazoned with a football player making a difficult catch, his body horizontal, suspended in the air. "Where are they?"

She steadied herself. "Just outside."

"Can they hear us?"

Her eyes were bright. Anguish resembled some other emotion—wonderment, startled rapture. "They said it would hurt my career, my family—"

"I should not have put you in this position."

"What will they do to you, Richard?"

"They won't hurt you. They're too frightened of me."

She said, "They promised me they would protect you."

And I could not help myself—I laughed.

"Don't go out there, Richard," she said.

I turned back with a smile. "Don't you trust them?"

But I never knew what trap they would devise. I could never be certain. Each time I faced them there was danger. Even now I could smell gasoline, and the impatient sweat of men. It was the fire that made me want to stay where I was, behind walls. It was out there, explosive, waiting for me.

61

If there were nothing left of human kind but our books of law, a visitor from across the universe would reconstruct what sort of beings we were. Here were our failures, our crimes. Here were our contracts, our promises. I was to a living person what a law is to a day, its counterpart. I was an echo given flesh, the truth behind the ironist's mock. As though a footprint took on an existence of its own.

The crack in the door caressed me as I eased outward, luxuriating in the humidity, the warm evening.

I lingered, so much whiff from a quenched candle, before I stood in human form again.

The vigil was tense. The skepticism was evident in the way they waited, holding the tiny receivers in their ears with fingers, deaf to everything but the sound of Matilda, following my last, whispered advice, *make some phone calls. Act like everything is normal.* They frowned, a few thin-faced men. There used to be so many, so sure of themselves. These were figures out of World War Two, Guadalcanal, Okinawa, helmeted men with tanks of gasoline like aqualungs, flame throwers.

They turned to each other. When was I coming out? Why wasn't I saying anything in there, just the sound of Matilda arguing on the phone. *Call Connie—she always has something to say.*

I passed among them and they did not see me. Not until I took Dr. Opal's hand. "Don't harm Matilda," I said into his startled eyes.

"I don't want them to hurt you, Richard," he said. If he partly understood my nature, when he looked at me he saw his old friend. He had put on weight, and was glowing, robust, the search for me making him years younger.

"You know how important you are to us. I would give my own

life—my own personal, individual life—to keep you safe." He wanted to believe this. In the end he had been more doctor than friend. He wanted me for science, for his own career.

Men closed around us, hitching belts, adjusting valves. A pilot light flickered. One of the funnels spouted a preliminary gout.

Maybe to keep me safe, the old Richard Stirling would have said, but not to keep me free.

"Wait!" called Dr. Opal.

There was a shouted apology from one of the men as a geranium burst into flames. A wheezy blast from behind singed the back of my head. Another weapon blistered the paint from a parked car, the lion's-head of flame illuminating a gloved fist, a plastic visor.

"Wait a minute!" called Dr. Opal. "You're not supposed to be in such a hurry!" he barked, face to face with one of the military men. "You'll never see anything like this again! Never! And you're so afraid you can't wait!"

You might as well be quiet, I wanted to tell him. Words can only do some much.

"You can still come with me," said Dr. Opal. He reached out to me, his eyes bright. "There's no way you'll survive. You can help people, under my authority. Think of the discoveries we could—" He must have realized how he sounded, how false. He looked back at the tense faces. He wanted to vanquish them all with a look, send them all away. His voice was quiet with feeling when he said, "There could be just the two of us."

Fire made a sound like a crowd cheering, an ovation, victory at last. Men hurried for protection. Flame blasted a patch of lawn. A scrap of paper in the gutter vanished with a puff.

Fly, Dr. Opal was praying.

Fly away.

I ascended, wafted upward by the heat.

If I had a companion this was where he would rise up to meet me. My wings filled. Closing my eyes, I beheld all of this with my voice, carried it on my tongue. Spiraling higher, I was lost in the clouds, a leaf falling into the lake of sky.

Until the air was so thin my lungs ached, so cold I was frosty, each flutter of wings a beat weaker. The air dissipated, my spine iron with cold.

I banked, skimming downward, falling west. Something guided me, that promise in me I had been hearing for weeks. I dropped down, losing control of my flight, until I glided close to the water, salt seasoning each breath. It was warm here, and the fog broke up, stars and moon above.

Mercy, cruelty. Night, day. Even I have made this mistake, thinking there is silence, and then here on the facing page is music, as though the two were opposite. How could I have been so wrong? When I glided over the glass ocean I was surprised.

More than surprised—I was shocked. And for a moment I could not believe what I saw.

I thought he had returned, and he had never left me, this reflection that shrank and swelled below me, a black flame, wings in the mirror of the sea.

62

Stella was right.

I will never feel Rebecca's embrace again. I will never make love to her. And Rebecca will never take Richard in, whispering his name.

Some night I will take the warm arm extending from across the threshold, and cross into that foreign country that so resembles this. What is it reflecting now, that mirror in the next room? *We don't have all day, my father used to say. You can't look at yourself forever.*

Stella is on the phone in the dining room. It's a roomy apartment. One of Stella's clients, a man with complicated Las Vegas debts, has vanished. Until he returns I experiment with his clothes.

He tended toward size thirty-eight, and as Richard I am a forty-three. I can see why debts sucked the client dry, custom-made shirts, hand-lasted shoes. I lean against the desk in his dressing gown, a present, I surmise, from a woman who could not have known him well. It is a beautiful blue, shimmering, and it fits me.

"Connie, consider this. Maybe," Stella says, "he still has feelings for you, too. I know he feels happy you're going to go ahead with the baby."

Now and then Stella passes the archway and our eyes meet. She rolls hers, and I give her a Richard-Stirling smile, the accustomed role, another consecutive night, standing-room only. I owe this to Stella, letting her play lawyer, but I have no interest in the outcome. Or do I? Maybe it brings back pleasant associations.

Connie and Stella make complicated arrangements, pay phones, airport phone booths, cellular devices. "It's not the money," Stella is saying. In law, when they say it's not the money you can be sure it is. My fingers tingle. There is somewhere I have to be tonight. But I still have time.

"Don't talk to me about cash," says Stella. "He has no earthly use for it."

Connie's voice is so far away it makes me feel fond of her, urgent as she is, grasping.

Tonight Stella has brought pictures of her baby, pink and open-eyed on a white flannel pillowcase. I don't tell her that I remember her baby well.

I wait for full evening. I can look out the window and see someone come home from work this time every night. There is a narrow driveway, a manicured square of lawn on either side. Each night the young man stops the Toyota, sets the brake, steps before the headlights and stoops to unlock the garage.

"Maybe he likes to pretend," I hear Stella saying. "Maybe it lets him imagine he's a living man again. I mean, how can a dead man get a divorce?"

The car barely fits. The garage is small, and there are boxes, old clothes, piles of old magazines competing for space. He pulls the garage door down, and then locks it with a padlock. He gives it a tug. He tugs it more times than he needs to, testing it compulsively.

Tonight he skips back down the steps and I think at first that he is obsessed, as usual, with locking the garage. He unfastens the padlock, swings open the door, and vanishes into the interior.

I am on my feet, parting the curtains.

"Of course you still have strong feelings for him. *I* have strong feelings for him," Stella says. "He has that effect on people."

The young man hurries out with a large red squirt gun, the size of an actual assault weapon, two of them, one under each arm. He fires one up at the street light, an arcing stitch of water. He has brought home these toys as a surprise.

"Don't cry," says Stella. "No, I don't know where he is. I swear it. My absolute word."

She looks back at me, shaking her head, a friendly conspirator, but she frowns, puzzled. I am already leaving, already gone.

The young man runs up the steps, leaving the padlock dangling, and I am running with him, in his shadow, closing around him like a hand. Taking what I need.

"Tonight," says the heavy man with curly hair, a short-sleeved shirt, no tie. "If you're ready." He chews the cap of a pen, tapping a paper clip, the bright wire trapped under his forefinger. He wants to smoke; it isn't allowed.

"Of course I'm ready," I say. This is a voice I have never used before, and I try it out a little further. "And I must say I'm de-lighted." It's a nice voice, female, young, insipid enough to be pleasing.

He is pleased. "It's a little unusual for us to take on an unknown here at Arch Street. I mean, we're not EMI, but we're booked four months in advance. But I listened to the demos you sent over and I felt that I didn't have any choice."

I laugh, a pretty sound, and say, "Maybe you didn't."

He touches me, once, on the hand. He withdraws his hand and gives a little cough.

Down the corridor he stays one step behind me, and says, "Your work reminds me of someone else's."

"Really?"

"I don't even like to talk about her. It's a terrible thing."

White tile on the ceiling, carpet on the walls. A woman sits behind a pane of glass, drinking coffee from a white paper cup.

The coffee has seeped through the seam of the container, brown freckles. The voice comes from the speaker above the window, her lips moving silently, although I know only I can hear the delay, her voice looping through an amplifier before it reaches the room.

"We need a sound level," she says.

I say nothing.

"If you want to just play a little."

They are cool at first touch, but not cold. The black reflects my fingertips as they hesitate, barely touching the keys. I close my eyes, and follow the silence out to the limits of the room.

Just be there, I tell him. *I need you.*

One note and the piano would fill, as a moment fills, complete. I am afraid. I keep my eyes closed and I know I can't do it.

"Take your time," says the woman behind glass.

The day it happens we are happy, the station wagon air-conditioned, the air only half-cool, one of the vents releasing warm air, like the air outside. My father drives with both hands on the wheel listening to the radio, a baseball game, something I know he will never understand, but a tradition he honors anyway, saying approving things in his Scottish accent about the score, the players, trying to be American, and succeeding.

My mother sees it first, the car coming on sideways across the bridge, the tires not screaming, a sound like something deep in the ocean, a recording of whales. The note is so low my insides vibrate to it, lungs, private organs, all of me singing with this lowest A flat.

"Charles!" she says. She was wearing a hair clasp, a red barrette, like a girl.

Like that: as though we rehearsed it, as though this was our second time through, our second chance at living, not our first, not our only lives. And for years after that I cannot see, until that night on the boat.

I want to be there, he says. *I feel honored.*

You'll do wonderfully.

I open my eyes, look to my right, at the inquisitive face behind glass. I smile. I take a deep breath.

And play.